"*Present Danger* starts with a bang and never lets up. Goddard's fast-paced romantic suspense will have your pulse pounding as you turn the pages. Hold on to your seat and your heart as you enjoy this thrill ride!"

Rachel Dylan, bestselling author
of the Capital Intrigue series

"A plane crash, a dead body, and two people who decide that justice and love are worth fighting for all add up to a riveting read you won't want to put down. I highly recommend this book!"

Lynette Eason, bestselling, award-winning author
of the Danger Never Sleeps series

"A riveting beginning to the new Rocky Mountain Courage series, *Present Danger* takes readers on a wild ride filled with family tragedies, long-buried secrets, ancient relics, and broken hearts. Goddard has crafted a page-turner that takes off in the first nail-biting chapter, weaves through unexpected twists and shocking revelations, then culminates in a whirlwind of betrayal and redemption. I couldn't read the final chapters fast enough!"

Lynn H. Blackburn, award-winning author
of the Dive Team Investigations series

"I was captivated from the very first scene of *Present Danger* to the shocking conclusion. You can always count on Elizabeth Goddard to bring you dramatic action and adventure scenes that put you on the edge of your seat!"

Susan Sleeman, bestselling author
of the Homeland Heroes series

"Elizabeth Goddard starts her brand-new Rocky Mountain Courage series with an opening that sucks you in from page one and doesn't stop until the heart-pounding conclusion."

Lisa Harris, *USA Today* and CBA bestselling author
of the Nikki Boyd Files

"*Present Danger*—another edge-of-the-seat story by Elizabeth Goddard that will keep you turning pages to the end."

Patricia Bradley, author of *Standoff*,
Natchez Trace Park Rangers series

Books by Elizabeth Goddard

UNCOMMON JUSTICE

Never Let Go
Always Look Twice
Don't Keep Silent

ROCKY MOUNTAIN COURAGE

Present Danger

ROCKY MOUNTAIN COURAGE
· BOOK 1 ·

PRESENT DANGER

ELIZABETH GODDARD

Revell

a division of Baker Publishing Group
Grand Rapids, Michigan

© 2021 by Elizabeth Goddard

Published by Revell
a division of Baker Publishing Group
PO Box 6287, Grand Rapids, MI 49516-6287
www.revellbooks.com

Printed in the United States of America

Library of Congress Cataloging-in-Publication Data
Names: Goddard, Elizabeth, 1963– author
Title: Present danger / Elizabeth Goddard
Description: Grand Rapids, Michigan : Revell, a division of Baker Publishing
    Group, [2021] | Series: Rocky Mountain courage
Identifiers: LCCN 2020042209 | ISBN 9780800737986 (paperback) | ISBN
    9780800739676 (casebound)
Classification: LCC PS3607.O324 | DDC 813/.6—dc23
LC record available at https://lccn.loc.gov/2020042209

Scripture quotations are from the King James Version of the Bible.

This book is a work of fiction. Names, characters, places, and incidents are the
product of the author's imagination or are used fictitiously. Any resemblance to
actual events, locales, or persons, living or dead, is coincidental.

21 22 23 24 25 26 27   7 6 5 4 3 2 1

To my daughter, Rachel.
You're the light and joy of my life.

Greater love hath no man than this,
that a man lay down his life for his friends.
John 15:13

ONE

hance Carter should have known this last delivery wouldn't go down without a hitch.

A monstrous thunderhead had popped up in a clear morning sky and now loomed directly in his path as if forbidding, or at least challenging, his approach to his destination—a lone airstrip in Nowhere, Montana. As an experienced pilot and courier for an airfreight company, inclement weather didn't concern him as much as the troubled feeling in his chest, which he'd been trying to ignore since takeoff.

Given the cold, hard stone of unease that had settled in his gut, he'd failed miserably.

Earlier this morning, back at the FBO—fixed-based operator—the rhythm of his flight prep had seemed off. Excitement hadn't pumped through his every movement, and the usual bounce to his step hadn't accompanied him while he worked through his preflight checks. If that hadn't been enough, dread had replaced the anticipation that had always filled him as he readied to climb into the cockpit of his Piper Cherokee 235, which he affectionately called Ole Blue.

Now, as he neared the airstrip, he shook off the apprehension and grabbed on to the assurance earned from years of experience and hours spent piloting.

A good, strong headwind buffeted the plane, which was preferred for landing. He took comfort in the familiar deafening roar of the Piper breaking through his headset and droning in his ears. He wanted to focus on nothing but landing, delivering, and escaping. But this trip carried him back, and the evergreens of the forest, the winding rivers, the meadows, the crops, and the majestic mountains captivated him, reminding him of all he'd left behind.

Gripping the yoke, he sat taller and shoved beyond the melancholy.

At seven miles from his destination, he switched tanks.

The noisy engine sputtered and then stalled.

Nothing he didn't know how to handle. Chance would quickly remedy the situation. He trusted that forward movement and lift would propel Ole Blue along like an eagle riding in the wind long enough to give him ample time to restart the engine.

Only the engine refused its resurrection. The fuel gauge indicated a fourth of a tank of fuel remained. He switched to the other tank and confirmed it was empty.

As if emphasizing his earlier presentiment, Ole Blue's propeller slowed to a stop.

Utter silence filled the cockpit. Moments passed before the slow cadence of his heartbeat ramped up and roared to life in his ears.

The plane remained in the air, gliding on the current. But not for long. Creating a controlled descent was up to Chance and the tools at his disposal. Sweat beaded at his temples as his instincts took over, and he maneuvered the rudder, flaps, and ailerons, steering the plane through the air currents to maintain lift as long as possible.

Chance had to face the truth.

Ole Blue wasn't going to make it to the airstrip.

And those evergreens he'd admired moments before rushed

at him now as the ground rose toward him, much faster than was safe.

He was going down.

Chance pressed the button on the yoke and squawked to a local frequency. "*Mayday! Mayday! Mayday!*" He detailed what he knew of the expected crash location, which wasn't a lot.

He got no response. Nobody monitoring the frequency today in Nowhere, Montana. Just his luck.

Between evergreen-topped mountains, Ole Blue surfed along a ravine. Not a good place to land. He hoped for a clearing. Something.

Come on, come on, come on . . .

There. Between the trees, he caught sight of a forest road and aimed for it. It would be close. The trees were dense in places. Worst case, the wheels on his fixed-gear plane would catch the treetops and flip him forward. Dead or alive, he'd be stuck in the tops.

Come on, baby, you can do this.

Palms sweating, he squeezed the yoke. Continuing the mantra in his head, he willed Ole Blue to stay in the air just a little longer. When he'd proclaimed today was his last delivery, he hadn't meant that to be a literal prophecy.

He mentally shook his fist at God. *You hear that? I didn't mean I wanted to die today. I just meant I'm done doing what I do.*

A thousand thoughts blew through his mind at once, not the least of which was that if he made it, if he survived, he'd have to file a crash report with the NTSB. He was only supposed to take his flight bag from the crash site, but he'd have to make an exception this time and remove the package he was supposed to deliver.

The treetops reached up for Ole Blue, their lofty trunks and branches growing taller as if they would stretch to catch the plane's wheels. The Piper shuddered. Chance held his breath, working the yoke until, finally, he maneuvered above the narrow road.

Lower, lower, lower . . .

The wheels touched down, and the plane bounced hard.

Trees closed in on the narrowing road. Chance braced himself. The wingtips caught the trees. The sound of metal twisting and ripping vibrated through him as the tin can protecting him shook and rattled. The impact shattered the window and catapulted what was left of his plane, and Chance's body was flung like a rag doll despite the shoulder harness. Ole Blue slammed against a tree on the passenger side, crumpling the only door. Chance's head hit the yoke handle. Thunder ignited in his temples as pain throbbed across his chest.

But the plane had stopped. Finally . . .

Seconds ticked by. He drew in a few shuddering, painful breaths. Allowed his heart rate to slow.

Chance assessed his injuries. He could move his legs and arms. Maybe he had a few broken ribs. He touched his head and felt the warm, sticky fluid. Blood covered his fingertips. He stared at the tree branch protruding through the shattered window, caught a whiff of pine from the needles, and tried to grasp the near miss. He could have been skewered. That was only one of many possible fatal injuries that could occur in a plane crash. How . . . how had he survived?

He wouldn't waste time questioning Providence. For the moment, he was alive. But for how much longer?

And trusty Ole Blue was gone for good. Myriad emotions—anger, fear, grief—seized him all at once. His pulse raced again as dizziness swept over him.

He fought the darkness edging his vision.

Why had he harbored an ounce of hope that he would be able to walk away from this unscathed? He wished he hadn't broken his one rule and looked at the contents of that package.

If he wasn't able to deliver it, he was as good as dead anyway.

TWO

Grayback County Sheriff's Detective Jack Tanner dropped his forty-pound SAR—search and rescue—pack next to his boots.

He let his gaze slide down the five-hundred-foot cliff, a slab of granite left behind when this side of the mountain gave way a century ago. Evergreens—spruce, pine, and cedar—surrounded him and filled the landscape below as well.

Kylie, a volunteer with Grayback County Search and Rescue Dogs, stood next to her black lab. "George caught a scent and"—she gestured below, her frown deepening—"it ends here."

She didn't need to explain that George was a wilderness area search dog and that meant he would alert to *any* humans in the search area, not simply track a specific human's scent. Still, using the dogs to search covered much more terrain when minutes counted.

Please let it not be the twins.

Because the dog had caught a scent that ended here didn't mean the girls had taken a tumble. The Emmer twins— Tanya and Kendra—had gotten lost while hiking with their dad—Ross Emmer. Jack's gut clenched at the possibility that they had fallen. The county sheriff's department was responsible for search and rescue missions in all of Grayback County, and though Jack had been on the team only a few short months, he knew to pray for the best and prepare for the worst.

But he didn't want to prepare for the worst and accept that the twins could be gone.

He peered through his binoculars at the tops of evergreens below. This region of the national forest had seen more than its fair share of incidents—including the small plane crash only yesterday. Fortunately, the pilot had survived.

Through the treetops, Jack could make out the Grayback River in the distance, carving its way between mountains, through canyons and meadows, all the way to Yellowstone National Park, located seventy miles south in the northwest corner of Wyoming.

As he looked through the binoculars, he hoped he wouldn't find anything, but, of course, there may be something—or someone—to find. If there was someone to find, he prayed they were alive. He released his pent-up breath. "I don't see anything."

Except birds circling above. Never a good sign, but scavengers could circle for a number of reasons.

Adjusting his binoculars, he shifted to peer at the bottom of the ridge. Wait. Maybe. Oh no. "Yeah, I think I see something." Jack cleared his throat. "Someone."

Next to him, Kylie remained silent while George panted.

Jack's gut dropped with the falling sensation experienced on an amusement ride. Or . . . falling from a cliff.

"What are you going to do?"

"Gear up."

Kylie blew out a breath. "That's a big drop, Jack."

"I've got enough gear to rappel. Trust me, it's the *one* thing I'm good at."

"I'm sure that's not true, or you wouldn't be a detective with the county."

Jack couldn't think of a decent response.

Kylie crouched next to the Lab and gave him a treat. She rewarded him for finding someone, though that someone was likely dead.

After eight hours of searching the mountainous wilderness, the team of volunteers and various state and local agencies had become discouraged. Some worked well together and others not so much. Probably a good thing he hadn't had to work with Terra Connors.

He'd learned that she'd returned to the area and was working as a special agent for the forest service. He figured since she worked out of the forest service district office in Goode's Pass, and he worked out of the county seat of Big Rapids, he wouldn't run into her in his county detective job. Though she'd joined the SAR callout, he hadn't seen her yet.

Maybe his luck would hold out.

He shook off those thoughts. None of it mattered.

He had a job to do here, and though he wouldn't jump to conclusions, a knot twisted in his stomach. The search and rescue looked to be quickly shifting to a search and recovery.

With a heavy heart, he said, "We need to let the command center know we think we've found at least one body."

He reached for his radio as it squawked. "Tanner, go."

"We got 'em. We found the sisters alive and well. They got lost and were huddled together in a cave. Scared, but they kept their heads about them." Deputy Sarnes's smile could be heard through the radio.

Thank you, God.

Relief whooshed from the deepest part of Jack even as images from the past continued to torment him. He would concentrate on the here and now. He couldn't go back. He could only go forward.

He let the deputy's words hang in the air a few moments as he shared a look with Kylie, sure the woman had to be thinking the same thing.

"If they found the twins . . . ," she said.

His thought exactly.

Then whose body is down there?

THREE

The day had taken a turn for the worse. Dread filled US Forest Service Special Agent Terra Connors as she hiked through the thick woods with Officer Case Haymaker, a uniformed forest service law enforcement officer. Terra loved the outdoors, especially in the Gallatin National Forest, the geographic region for which she conducted investigations. But days like today reminded her that imminent danger waited around every corner, and even the most beautiful, captivating scenery could give way to a harsh, jagged-edged landscape. Other, more sinister hazards could wait in the shadows.

She'd joined the callout to search for missing twins. While the SAR team celebrated that the girls had been found safe and sound, tragedy had also struck.

Finding a body was a huge blow to them all.

She hopped over the pristine stream—the normally soothing rush of the water unable to compete with the unease in her gut—and caught up with Case. The incident commander, Deputy Sarnes, had asked for their assistance. As it turned out, she and Case had been searching for the twins near the same region in which someone believed they had seen a body. Volunteer SAR members had been dismissed because the twins—the reason for today's callout—had been discovered.

As she and Case neared where the forest met the five-hundred-foot granite cliff, she spotted movement. "Looks like someone's rappelling."

"Must be the deputy who spotted the body." Case stepped around the thick underbrush and swiped his arm across his forehead.

Like Terra, he was probably ready to drop his pack and pour water over his head. The record-high summer temperatures seemed to want to hang on as the season shifted to fall.

She hoped the report about a body being spotted from the clifftop was a mistake. How could someone get a good look from the top of that cliff, especially when looking down into the dense woods below?

"We should almost be on . . . um . . . the body, shouldn't we?" she asked.

Case paused and put his hands on his hips. "Maybe. I don't want to trip over it. And I don't want to walk all over a crime scene if there was foul play."

"Sarnes didn't say anything about foul play." She studied Case, detecting a hint of concern.

"He didn't." Case dipped his chin.

Good. "You're right to be cautious. We can tread slowly and carefully now." And hope this wasn't foul play, translated . . . murder.

She and Case each grabbed water bottles from their packs and drank, then began their search again.

A hawk screeched above them.

Case clapped his hands loudly to scare animals away from the area. Terra had received her training at FLETC, the Federal Law Enforcement Training Center, in Georgia, as all federal law enforcement agents did, but that didn't mean she had grown accustomed to the sight of death or, in the forest, what animals could do to a body.

Case signaled for her to stop, though he still crept forward.

"What is it, Case?"

"Up ahead, just past that white pine. I see jeans and a pair of boots."

Dread churned in her gut. "We'll skirt around until we can get a good look from a distance."

Sarnes had asked for their assistance to secure the area and body—protect it from animals if needed—but nothing more. As a special agent, Terra was responsible for complex investigations—crimes against natural or archaeological resources—but crimes against persons, such as homicide or property crimes, fell to local, state, or federal law enforcement agencies.

She and Case made their way through the trees to get a closer look.

"I assume the deputy who called this in had his reasons for relaying that we're looking for a body rather than someone who was simply injured or unconscious," Case said. "But how does he know the person is deceased?"

"You want us to check, is that it?" she asked.

Case suddenly stopped, and she nearly bumped into him.

From where they stood, she saw the bent form. "Okay, then."

"I could still check for a pulse." He eyed Terra. "Stranger things have happened."

Terra wasn't so sure. She removed her sunglasses and took in the broken form. She didn't want to think too hard about just how broken.

Case crept closer to the body.

Forcing down the rising bile, she kept her composure. "Only one of us needs to check. If this turns out to be part of a crime scene, we want this area protected."

Soft voices drew her eyes up. A few SAR volunteers approached and then, seeing Terra and Case, stopped as though imaginary crime scene tape blocked their path. Their soft murmurs were the only sounds in the forest. Terra could hardly consider herself fortunate to be one of the first on the scene.

The body of a man lay twisted. Terra was relieved that his face remained turned away from them, but the angle left no doubt that his neck was broken and he had likely fallen from the cliff. "I don't think we need to get a pulse, after all, Case."

Case crouched next to the body and angled his head. "His watch is broken too. Eight twenty-five. It probably broke with the fall, but we don't know if that was this morning or last night. My guess is . . . last night."

Nausea rippled through her stomach in waves again, but she would hold it together. "Since you're theorizing, what do you think happened? Did he jump to his death?"

"Or was he taking a selfie and fell? That happens far too often these days."

She bit back her words. The sheriff's department would theorize too—they all did—but they wouldn't say a word until they received the official report on the cause of death.

She spotted no footprints around the body, though pine needles could often hide the evidence. Still, as she observed the area, she couldn't see signs that the body had been carried or dragged.

She peered up at the cliff through the treetops. Could they find pieces of torn clothing in the trees?

"Here they come," Case said.

She glanced behind the volunteers and spotted deputies approaching.

A sound drew her attention back to Case and, beyond him, a man emerged from the woods, coming from the direction of the cliff.

Sunglasses sat on his sandy blond hair, and the angles of his face were sharp and jagged like the rock wall he'd descended. His navy-blue Grayback County Search and Rescue T-shirt stretched across his chest and left no doubt of his toned physique.

Familiarity crawled over her. Terra feared everyone could

hear her pounding heart. She wanted to turn away, but her gaze was drawn to his piercing forest-green eyes. Recognition slammed into her with full force.

Jack Tanner.

So, *he* was the deputy who'd spotted the body? He'd been the guy rappelling the ridge? Of course. That made total sense.

Except . . . well . . .

What was he doing here? He'd been FBI, working somewhere else. Gone from her life forever. Now he was a deputy?

Shock ricocheted through her. Calming her breaths, she slid her sunglasses back on. She kept her features straight when Jack stumbled but quickly righted himself as he hiked through brambles, stepping over fallen trees with ease. Was he shocked to see her too? Honestly, he didn't seem all that surprised.

At about ten yards out, he dropped his pack. Case rose from where he was crouched and waited by the body as Jack approached.

"Deputy Tanner." Terra kept her tone even.

Jack stared at the body, hands on hips. "It's *Detective* Tanner."

"*Detective* Tanner." She wished she'd kept her mouth shut.

He turned his attention to her. "It's been a long time, Special Agent Connors. It's good to see you."

Well, that told her a lot. He wasn't surprised to see her because he knew she was back in the area and also had a new title as a special agent. She'd changed over from NPS—National Park Service—after her undercover work on a task force investigating pothunters. The rest of it, nobody needed to know.

Jack returned his attention to the body.

He tromped around in a take-charge kind of manner, now in his deputy-detective mode. His deputy buddies started forward, and he held up his hand. "Wait."

He rubbed his chin, anguish twisting his features. "The deputy coroner's on the way?"

Deputy Sarnes pushed through the group and approached Jack and the body. "Yep. Emmett Hildebrand."

The grim set of Jack's mouth and the deepening furrow between his brows told her he was processing the scene. He peered at her then, and she removed her sunglasses so she could look closely at those dark-green eyes that she remembered so well.

He studied her and appeared to make a decision. Terra would love to know what he was thinking.

"We don't need an audience," Jack said. "Sarnes, can you get rid of the sightseers?"

Terra replaced her sunglasses and murmured to Case. "Our cue to head out too. Our assistance is no longer needed." To the larger group, she said, "Case and I will be happy to hike out with them."

"I'd like you to stay, Special Agent Connors." Those intense eyes pinned her again. "Terra . . ."

Oh? She glanced at Case. He shrugged.

"Okay then," Case said. "I guess I've been dismissed."

As SAR volunteers exited the area, the forest swallowed them up, and Terra turned her attention to Jack.

"I'm happy to assist, Jack." Since he'd used her first name, she would return the favor. "What do you need?"

"National forest is your jurisdiction," he said.

"Of course, but this, whatever it is, isn't something I would investigate. What are you getting at?"

Clearing her throat, she grabbed more water from her pack, giving her an excuse to look anywhere except at Jack.

"You know this forest like no one else. You spent your life in these woods." His professional county-detective tone had shifted to something more familiar and personal.

Chugging her water, she considered her response. When she finished, she capped the bottle and faced him. "You're talking millions of acres. I didn't spend my childhood in all of millions of acres."

"I'm asking for a little assistance, that's all." He offered the hint of a smile as he studied her, then his expression turned serious again as he shifted his attention to the body. "What do you think happened here?"

"Are you working a case now? As in, this could be murder?"

"I haven't been officially assigned, no. But we're here now. Sheriff Gibson wants me to assess things while we wait for the deputy coroner. I brought up the FBI. This is federal lands, after all."

"Are they coming?"

"He said they've deferred murder investigations to his department in the past, but of course will likely offer assistance if we need it, and he would keep them informed." Jack rubbed his neck. "They rarely investigate murders unless it involves a serial killer or crosses state lines."

"They just want to focus on politicians and terrorists?" She sent him a wry grin.

He barely nodded, his lips shifting into a grim line. Terra wondered if he would feel awkward working with the FBI, now as a county detective, if it came to that.

As for awkward, that feeling wrapped around her but for an entirely different reason. That, and well, this felt far too surreal. Why did it have to be Jack Tanner standing there asking her for help? Of all the places she could be right now and of all the people she could be with, why Jack?

And he looked good. Too good. She hadn't seen him in almost six years. Those years had been good to him in some ways—she hadn't thought he could be more attractive, but she was wrong on that point. In other ways, he seemed rougher. Like life hadn't been good to him, when she hadn't thought his life could get any harder. Terra realized she hadn't given him an answer.

She dusted off her pants and stared up at the trees. "Case

suggested maybe he was taking a selfie. You know how people are doing that and fall these days. Happens too often."

"I don't know. This guy was in his fifties, and he's up there on the cliff, out there alone?"

"Right. He doesn't seem to be dressed for the hike. No pack, unless it's up top. Worn cowboy boots, not the best for hiking, though people do often set out for a breath of fresh air, then end up hiking farther than they planned." And got lost sometimes.

Jack walked around the body. "Pine needles in his hair and clothes. A small black wire protruding from his hand."

She could almost imagine Jack was the deputy coroner. "A black wire? What do you think it is?"

Jack scratched his chin. "No idea. It'll be sent to the state lab to see what they make of it."

Terra approached the body too. She couldn't very well give Jack her opinion without getting closer, and she kept her features cool and calm.

Jack crouched much like Case had done but touched nothing.

"Terra." The way he said her name sent alarms through her head. He gestured for her to come to his side of the body.

Dread built in her belly, and she strove to keep it from spilling out and crawling over her. In all her imagining—and, unfortunately, she had spent too long doing just that—she never could have dreamed up meeting Jack again in this moment, under these circumstances.

She marched around the form and forced herself to crouch next to this man from her past, only to peer down at a familiar face.

FOUR

hance's eyelids seemed stuck together. He didn't bother trying to muster the strength to open them. Not yet. Instead, he would be safer if he pretended to sleep while he figured out what he was doing here, wherever *here* was. Location, location, location.

Was he in a good, safe place?

Or was he in the lair of a dragon?

Did he need to hightail it out of here?

His pounding heart settled enough so he could listen. Familiar sounds took him back to his mother's last days on earth in a hospital room. He must be in rough condition. Chance slowly opened his eyes and took in the room he shared with another guy—at least he thought it was a man that was snoring on the other side of the curtain.

His skull ached as though it were cracked. He lifted his arm and pressed his hand to his head. Good, he wasn't wrapped up like a mummy. He could feel his toes and move his legs. Move his arms. His chest ached. Bruised ribs?

Concussed skull.

Ole Blue. He'd crashed Blue, and now the events came rushing back.

Panic engulfed him.

His belongings. Chance ripped out the IV in his arm and threw off the covers. He ignored the fierce headache and his stiff, aching limbs as he searched under and behind the bed.

Where is it? Where is it? Where is it?

His pounding heart only increased the pain in his head.

He spotted a slim closet.

He took a step toward it, and dizziness swept over him. He steadied himself against the bed until it passed, then focused on the closet. *Please, please, please . . .*

He eased forward and took one slow step at a time. The fuzziness in his head seemed to clear with each step. Now if only the headache clawing at his skull would let go.

At the closet, he pressed his hand on the small knob, hope and fear lodging in his gut. He opened the door and found a bag with his tattered clothes.

Where was the package that could have meant his freedom?

His throat might just close up and he'd drop right there for lack of oxygen. That would be a better way to die than to face what came next—whoever requested he deliver the package would come looking for it. Come looking for him.

How did he find it and get it back?

Chance yanked the torn, bloody clothes out of the closet. He tossed his bomber jacket on the bed. He dug around in another bag and pulled out his wallet and flipped it open to see his ID. Chance Carter. Except that wasn't his birth name. He'd been forced to change it all and build a new life. He never should have left the armed forces of the United States of God Bless America. Crashing Ole Blue had caused all this garbage to resurface, and he pushed it back down to be dealt with another day.

He also found credit cards and some cash. Relieved, he exhaled. But no cell phone. Probably destroyed in the crash. He needed to disappear until he figured things out. He'd get a new cell and call the NTSB about the crash and put them off for a few days. In the meantime, he needed clothes.

Chance peeked around the curtain and found the nameless patient still snoring. He crept over to the other small closet and found a few belongings inside.

Sorry, buddy. Then he quickly changed into the man's newer, fresh clothes. He looked through his wallet to find his driver's license. Ron Howell. Chance hoped the sick guy had someone who cared and would bring him more clothes. Chance couldn't know if and when he'd be in a position to replace what he'd taken.

Despite a rip in the arm, Chance donned his beloved bomber jacket on the way out of the hospital.

FIVE

Jim Raymond had sold insurance, and his face was on billboards all over the county.

Stunned, Jack stared down at Jim's lifeless body. A few nuances caught his attention and spiked his suspicions. The man had taken a fatal fall. Had he been pushed or had he been murdered and then his body dumped here, of all places? In millions of acres of national forest, some designated wilderness regions, Jim's body might never have been found if a SAR team hadn't been dispersed to find those twins.

Jack hated the way his thoughts automatically went to the worst-case scenario, but his experience in law enforcement had paved the way for a thousand possible circumstances surrounding Jim's demise to rush through Jack's mind. He wanted the truth about what happened.

He moved back to his pack to grab water. Where was the deputy coroner anyway? While he drank, he reined in his chaotic thoughts. Seeing Terra for the first time in years had affected him in ways he hadn't expected. Even after a haggard day of searching, the woman could turn heads. Her dark hair was pinned up under a blue Grayback County SAR cap. Her blue eyes shone bright in her beautiful, tanned face. He'd seen in her gaze almost immediately that she'd lost her innocent, hopeful look and now instead held the sober air of experience. The harsh realities of life and time in law enforcement would do that.

Shoving aside the unbidden thoughts about Terra, Jack followed her when she joined the deputies who stood by the trees a few yards away from the body. At the same moment, Case Haymaker returned, emerging from the woods.

"What are you doing back?" Terra asked.

He shrugged. "The others took off at the trailhead. I figured you'd still be here. And besides, a body found in the national forest in my area, I want to know what's going on. The last thing we need in this county, in this national forest, is a murder."

Jack stiffened his back. "No one said anything about murder."

"We're all thinking it looks like foul play, though," Case said. "Be honest about it, at least."

"Falls can happen for any number of reasons. The deputy coroner will tell us the cause of death. In the meantime, we don't need more people stomping around the—"

"Crime scene." Haymaker again.

What's your problem? Jack bit back his retort and said nothing. The sheriff's department would investigate, but they also worked with other agencies. Let Haymaker think what he wanted for now. Jack wasn't in the mood to get into it with him.

"And in that case, you might need our help to search for a killer," Haymaker continued.

"Case, please." Terra's expression remained guarded. "We're all uptight right now. Let's not get ahead of ourselves."

Haymaker opened his mouth as if to protest her simple plea. Jack stared at the man, and fortunately, the officer appeared to think better of a retort in front of witnesses.

Jack needed space and would normally walk away, but no way was he leaving. Was that how Haymaker felt? The way the man kept close to Terra and frequently glanced her way, Jack got the feeling Haymaker's presence had more to do with her.

"There's no need for so many of us to wait here with the body," Jack said. "I'll stick around. You guys have been out all day searching for the twins. You probably ran out of water long ago. Head home. The coroner will be here soon with his own contingency to assist him."

"What about you?" Haymaker asked. "One of us could stay and you could go back."

"I want to get the coroner's initial reaction." Jack could be the detective assigned to investigate.

Haymaker shared a look with Terra. "Come on, let's go."

"I'm staying," she said. "But you should go."

"You sure?" he asked.

"Yes."

He frowned and shook his head as he turned to leave. The two other deputies were already heading out.

Though Jack had asked her to remain behind earlier, he'd simply wanted her assessment. And okay, maybe if he was being honest with himself, he'd wanted a few moments alone with Terra Connors, the woman he'd once loved. He shouldn't allow his personal thoughts and actions to overlap with his professional world. But he had a strong feeling that would be a struggle, and in that case, Jack should encourage Terra to go too. He wasn't entirely sure he wanted to face more time alone with her, considering their shared past. Still, that had been years ago, and he hoped she had moved on and let go. Maybe he was asking too much to think she hadn't held a grudge, because he certainly still held one against himself and his actions. Nor could he ever tell her the reasons for his actions—that would hurt her too much.

When the deputies and Haymaker were out of earshot, he said, "You didn't have to stay, you know."

"And leave you alone out here in these millions of acres

that I know so well?" A hint of a smile edged her lips to take the bite out of her sarcasm.

"The sheriff might come too. Maybe my sergeant." He wasn't sure who to expect next, or if he would be assigned to investigate if this turned out to be a crime. Whatever. Someone just get here, and soon.

Why did you really stay behind? "Are you okay?" he asked.

She lifted her face to the treetops and shuddered as if to shake off the emotion. "I'll be fine. How's his wife going to react when she hears the news?"

"I'm glad that's the sheriff's job."

"My grandfather knows Jim. Or *knew* him. I think Jim was his insurance broker too." Terra dropped her chin and stared at the ground. "I hope we can wrap this up quickly, since Jim wasn't a loner or a stranger by any stretch. He knew a lot of people."

"Which could make this more difficult," he said.

"We're talking like we know he was murdered. I find it hard to believe."

He'd spotted the bloody slash in the back of Jim's shirt. It was clean rather than jagged, as one would expect of an injury that had come from trees or rocks. Jack scratched his jaw. This guy wasn't dressed for a hike this far out. Jack wouldn't get ahead of himself on it. He could be jumping to conclusions that came far too naturally to him after too many undercover hours spent with murderers and traffickers.

"So, um, you *were* FBI." Terra crossed her arms.

Uh. Oh. He knew where this conversation would head if he didn't redirect it.

He couldn't read her eyes because she'd donned her sunglasses again. Jack got the feeling she was gazing off into the distance because she didn't want to look at him. They were alone for a few minutes. No need to act special-agent tough, but she'd suddenly put the cast-iron composure in place. A protective measure? If so, he could understand that she was sensitive about the topic, so why bring it up? Then again, Terra might want answers about what had happened before. Answers he couldn't give her.

"Yeah, I was FBI. Now, as you can see, I'm with the county sheriff's office. Congratulations, by the way, on your new job. I always knew you'd come back." Cringing inside, he wished he could take the words back. She could find a way to take them wrong.

Sure, he'd kept tabs on her like some stalking idiot. He'd walked away from what he could have had with her, for *her* sake.

"Thanks for the congrats. And you're back too. Now look at the two of us." She didn't bother to cover up the sarcasm with even a half smile this time. "What happened to you, anyway?"

Which happening did she refer to? "What do you mean?"

"You know what I mean. FBI was your dream."

Jack heard what she wasn't saying, loud and clear—she thought he'd given her up for that dream.

"Now you're here," she said. "Something must have happened."

Yep. Something had happened, all right, but he had other reasons for returning. "Aunt Nadine has dementia, so I came back to help her."

She removed the sunglasses, and now he could see the crystal-blue sincerity in her eyes. "I'm so sorry, Jack."

His aunt had raised him. She'd taken him in after his dad had failed him so completely. She was a much older sibling to his father, fifteen years his dad's senior.

"It's manageable. She's doing well. The medicine is helping."

Even if he'd been offered the sergeant or captain position, he would have remained an investigator so he could be more available to Aunt Nadine, though even this position was proving to take up too many hours.

"There was no one else." Aunt Nadine had lost her granddaughter, Sarah. That painful loss was the proverbial white elephant in the room.

"I understand." Compassion suffused her gaze. "I hope she knows what you've given up to stay here with her."

He shrugged, grateful to see the coroner and his crew heading their way. Jack had been ready to give up the undercover work, but more than that, he hadn't gotten over the fact that no matter how hard he tried he hadn't been there in time to save a trafficked young woman. And if that wasn't enough to eat him alive every day, the secret he kept would see to it.

SIX

"un fact for you," Terra said through gasps as she hiked.

"Oh yeah?" Jack trailed her. "What's that?"

He wasn't breathing nearly as hard as she was. Terra had thought she was in great shape until now.

She paused to look out over a vista, and maybe catch her breath—majestic mountains and welcoming valleys spread over miles, easily seen from this point on Stone Wolf Mountain. "Montana has at least three thousand named mountains."

"By mountains, you mean what?"

"Anything from a foothill to a peak."

He'd stopped next to her and leaned over his thighs. Catching his breath? Terra took some satisfaction from that. When he straightened, he stood a head taller than her.

"Fun fact for *you*," he said.

"Okay. I guess you can play too."

"There are eight towns in Grayback County."

Terra snorted a laugh. "How many towns are in the state?"

He hung his head. "Now that, I don't know."

When he lifted his face, his green eyes held shadows as he looked out at the magnificent view. "We should get going before it gets too dark. We still have a couple of miles, and I don't want to get lost." He winked. "That's why I wanted you along."

"So you wouldn't get lost?"

A tenuous grin lifted his cheeks, but the smile didn't reach his eyes. She had a feeling his comment had a deeper meaning, and one she wasn't willing to explore.

"Let's go then." She led him next to a rocky outcropping until they reached a meadow of short grass just before the evergreens grew thick and dark. Images of the deputy coroner and his assistants carrying Jim's body away flooded her mind. A county tech had arrived to collect possible evidence, most of which would be submitted to the Montana State Crime Lab.

The deputy coroner had been quick to identify what he believed was a knife wound to the back.

Deputies, rangers, and forest service law enforcement were now searching for a murder weapon.

Sergeant Aaron Brady had officially assigned Jack to the investigation. Then Terra and Jack had left what was now labeled the secondary crime scene and hiked to the top of the granite cliff to the primary crime scene, where they believed Jim was murdered then pushed or thrown off the cliff. The area had been cordoned off to protect the scene until evidence techs were done. They had kept their conversation to theorizing about the investigation rather than crossing over into anything personal, and for that, she was grateful.

This wasn't her investigation, and she wanted answers about Jim's death, so she was happy to be involved.

"Another fun fact," she offered, "which you probably already know. The Gallatin National Forest encompasses almost two million acres and several counties. It seems to me that whoever killed him, stabbed him, and then dropped him out here—"

"Because . . . given the terrain here several miles from the trail, we shouldn't have found the body so quickly. The killer had hoped by the time we found human remains, we wouldn't suspect or be able to confirm foul play."

"At the same time, he or she didn't go as far as they could have to dump the body."

"So they didn't have the time to spend dragging a body around," he said.

"Or packing on a horse." Terra picked up her pace. "We spotted the droppings a quarter mile away, remember."

"Jim also could have been riding, and was killed, then tossed. Or those droppings could have no relationship to this investigation. But we'll know more once we hear from the deputy coroner."

Talking about an investigation with Jack seemed completely foreign to her yet natural at the same time. Law enforcement agencies had to work together, especially when covering such a vast area. They continued on in silence until they reached the base of Stone Wolf Mountain's north face and . . . the Rocky Mountain Courage Memorial.

Terra waited for the dizziness to pass.

"You okay?"

"Yes." *Liar.* "I can't help but think this mountain is a death magnet."

"I'm sorry. Maybe I shouldn't have—"

"Don't." Terra stood tall and drew in a long breath. She'd been the one to lead them in this direction.

Stone columns pointed to the sky and stood like sentinels at the memorial. Each column featured a plaque with names.

Her mother, a forest ranger, had been forever memorialized here, along with the others who had died on the mountain. Some had died for various reasons and at other times, but her mother, along with two others, died while trying to save someone stranded after a plane crash. A SAR team was dispatched, and an avalanche killed three members of that team. The pilot survived the crash and the avalanche. Other plaques memorialized those who had died on the mountain to save thrill-seeking souls who had ventured out in the winter to climb or ski or snowboard in the backcountry. Terra's mother, Erin Larson's stepfather, and Alex Knight's father had given their lives to help others.

Terra strolled forward to look at the larger brass plaque, which provided general information about the memorial. The smaller plaques found on the pillars detailed each individual's act of heroism.

Their courage was commended as the ultimate sacrifice. Terra read the Scripture verse on the plaque.

Greater love hath no man than this, that a man lay down his life for his friends. John 15:13

She calmed the emotions that threatened to escape. She hadn't been back to this memorial since she'd left for her job with the National Park Service in southwest Colorado. Before that, she and Erin and Alex would visit the memorial every year on the anniversary of the incident that had killed their loved ones. At least they'd started out that way, but over time they'd begun coming once a year when they were able to get together. In fact, they were planning to visit the memorial together in a few days.

The pain and grief of losing her mother at fourteen—fifteen years ago—had never truly dissipated. Maybe that's because she'd lost her dad shortly after her mother died. He'd left Terra in her grandfather's care. Her older brother, Owen, had already enlisted in the Army by then.

As she remained frozen in place, the memorial served to remind her of her biggest fear—to lose someone else she loved. And, God forbid, on this mountain.

She could skirt the edges—much like she'd done today with Jack. Search for people on SAR missions. Do her job in the entire region, but she hoped she would never be required to go anywhere near where her mother died. Gramps took her and Owen one summer to see the place. She wasn't sure why—maybe that was more about him wanting to see where he'd lost his daughter, and he didn't want to do it alone.

Terra had fled down the mountain.

Jack, however, had climbed the summit of this mountain, and probably all ten peaks in this county, if not more. For a few moments, Jack had strolled around the memorial and given her space, but he approached now and remained by her side, silent but there all the same, as if he sensed she needed reassurance. If she needed that from someone, he wasn't the person she would want it from.

She hadn't expected to see him today, or frankly, ever again.

"You ready?" he asked.

"Yes. I know. It'll be dark before we make it the rest of the way."

She slung her pack over her shoulder. Together they found the path from the memorial that led back to the trailhead and where the incident command center had been located for today's search for the twins. When they made it to the bottom, they would get into their vehicles and go their separate ways.

"Do you still keep in touch with them?" Jack asked.

She knew instantly who he meant. Terra, Erin, and Alex had been teenagers at the time of the shared tragedy, though Erin and Alex were older than she was. They found support and encouragement in one another and had bonds deeper than many siblings. Owen wasn't around, so she needed Erin and Alex. Together they decided they could do no less than be willing to die for others if necessary and vowed to make the world a better place. Lofty dreams for those so young—but somehow those dreams had helped ease the pain of loss and given them a vision for the future.

"Sure."

"I have to admit I was a little jealous of your friendship with

Alex," he said, then sighed. "I'm sorry. Didn't mean to dredge up all that junk."

She shrugged. "If you don't mind, let's leave the past in the past."

"Of course."

At least when it came to her past where Jack was concerned. However, Terra would still like to know what had happened to Jack in the FBI, but she was absolutely certain he wouldn't be willing to share with the line she'd just drawn. Terra was still working through so much—would it take a lifetime to heal?

"Erin's in Seattle right now, but she comes to see her mom. She's coming up this weekend, in fact." Terra wouldn't bring up that one of Jack's coworkers, Detective Nathan Campbell, and Erin had experienced a heart-wrenching breakup. Terra believed that Nathan was the reason Erin moved. That and more opportunities in the city, but he was definitely the catalyst that sent her away.

"And Alex?"

Terra stopped.

His expression softened. "By your reaction, it would seem something's going on between you two."

Terra realized there'd been no jealousy in his tone.

"Not that it's any of your business, but no. There's nothing going on between us. He thinks of me like a sister." She hiked past him. "Don't you need to focus on finding Jim's killer?"

"You're right." Jack stayed behind her and said nothing more.

She'd shut him down, so why did she still want to know what he was thinking? He probably wouldn't ask for her help again.

Terra wanted to be involved in the investigation, and she'd just blown her best chance.

SEVEN

At the Outskirts Motel, where Chance had paid cash for a room, he counted out what was left of the few bills he always kept with him for emergencies. If this wasn't an emergency, he didn't know what was. He'd at least purchased a cheap burner phone. Depending on how long it took him to get out of this situation, he wasn't sure he could live on a hundred and fifty bucks. If he survived this, he would make sure to increase his emergency cash on hand.

If Chance didn't figure out who was behind the deliveries, he would be dead. But there were worse things than death.

Chance stared at the phone. What an idiot he'd been nearly twenty years ago. One simple mistake born of greed and stupidity had brought him to this point in his life—the ripple effect of one stone tossed on a pond.

He set the phone aside, piled the two shabby pillows behind his head on the bed, and rested his aching body while he surfed the television for a local news channel. Maybe he would learn more about his plane crash. He'd communicated with the NTSB that he'd been in the hospital and would call them soon.

Maybe his delivery contact had seen the news that the plane

had crashed, but Chance doubted that, even then, he would be given mercy if he didn't deliver the package. This one last delivery that was to secure his freedom forever might be the delivery that put the nails in his coffin.

Chance sat forward as a news story played about a body found in the forest, and the images revealed a vaguely familiar face.

Fuzzy memories came back.

He'd been twisted up in the cockpit for how long, he didn't know, when a concerned face appeared, the voice gruff as the man had spoken.

"Don't worry, buddy. Help is on the way. You hang in there. You're going to be all right." That man's face now appeared on the television.

A sick feeling engulfed Chance.

He had no doubt that saving Chance's life had cost Jim Raymond his own.

EIGHT

The next morning, Jack rose early and showered. He tried to get Terra out of his mind, but he couldn't shake images of the past that collided with yesterday's encounter. Distance and time had never completely removed her from his thoughts. Pulling on a T-shirt, he thought back to her words. She wanted to put the past behind them. Could they ever truly do that? Facing Terra and interacting with her had taken all his mental muscle. Emotional dexterity too.

Last night, he'd only been trying to make conversation to ease the pained look on her face at seeing the memorial again, nothing more, and she'd admonished him.

He forced his thoughts back to what mattered—finding Jim Raymond's killer. Was the killer still in the area? The county or state? Had Jim sold someone insurance that hadn't paid as promised and they had taken revenge?

Jack read a text from Deputy Sarnes—more information about Jim's activities that might or might not be related. His head was spinning in too many directions. He thought through his next steps. Sheriff Gibson had told Jim's wife, Pauline, the news last night and instructed Jack to hold off on talking to her until the morning. Said she was too upset to be coherent and that a doctor had given her a sedative. Jack was as compassionate as the next guy—or detective or special agent—but would have preferred to speak to her last night.

Regardless, news of a killer on the mountain would spread like a Montana wildfire through the county seat, Big Rapids, where Jim was known and loved, and eventually throughout Grayback County.

The pressure was on to find a killer.

Jack had grown up here, and had only been back in the area for about three months, working in his new capacity as a detective. While many of the same rules applied, the job was a lot different from his position as Special Agent Jack Tanner, or in his last assignment working undercover as a bodyguard to a high-profile criminal now behind bars.

He shaved his whiskers and took in the scar on his midsection where the bullet had almost killed him. At least he'd saved the journalist that night. He'd been too late for—

He gripped the edges of the sink and hung his head. Jack squeezed his eyes shut and steadied his nerves. He would be no good today if he didn't put what happened behind him.

He finished dressing, then rushed out of the bedroom and into the kitchen, where Aunt Nadine sat drinking coffee and playing with a dog he'd never seen. He chuckled to himself. Another stray.

"Morning." He kissed her on the cheek, then plated eggs, bacon, and toast that waited on the stove.

"Morning, Jack. You busy today?"

He paused. Uh-oh. The way she asked that . . . "Why? Did you need help with something?"

"I want to put some lost and found posters up for Freckles, here." She was looking to the new stray addition to the family, a copper-and-white cocker spaniel. "He has a boy out there somewhere. I just know it."

Aunt Nadine had a reputation for taking in strays—humans and animals alike. He couldn't fault her for her soft, caring heart. After all, she'd taken in her granddaughter when her own daughter was spending too much time partying and was too high to care for her own child. That seemed to be a family curse. Drugs and alcohol. Then Aunt Nadine had taken Jack in too. Some might have expected her to do that since she was his aunt, but he was a lot of trouble for her and Uncle Barry, before he died.

Jack downed black coffee. "I can help you with that, but I have something I need to do first, if that's okay."

"You mean on that murder."

"Yep. I need to stay on top of it. That's my job here, and you wouldn't want me to mess up. You want me to find who killed Jim, don't you?"

"Yes. I know you'll find that murderer. You were FBI before, after all. They can use your skills in the county. You're the best thing to happen to the sheriff's office in a long time."

"I wouldn't go that far." And that's why he kept his secret from her. If she knew one of the reasons he left his former job, it would break her heart. He rinsed his plate and hers. "You wait for me to get back. We'll put the posters up every-where, I promise."

In his vehicle, Jack headed straight for Jim and Pauline's home. Cars lined the driveway and the street. Relatives, fami-lies, and friends. Though Jack dreaded facing the bereaved widow, he needed to question her about Jim's day and his connections. His home could be part of the narrative, too, since evidence or clues might be found there.

Considering Jim knew everyone and was supposedly loved by everyone, this investigation could get complicated. But it was clear that at least one person didn't love Jim Raymond.

Jack received a text and looked at his phone. Terra. They'd ex-changed numbers yesterday just in case he required assistance.

I'm here with Pauline. Where are you?

Confusion rocked through him. She wasn't investigating the murder, so what was she doing there? Maybe she'd stopped in to give her condolences. He didn't waste time responding.

He hiked up the driveway, weaving between parked vehicles, then marched up the porch steps to stand at the door.

He dreaded causing Pauline more pain. Maybe Terra getting here and going in first was a good thing and would help his approach.

A stocky older man opened the door before Jack even knocked. Jack introduced himself and stated the purpose of his visit.

The man's face remained grim. "I'm JB, Pauline's brother. Follow me."

JB led him through the home, down a hallway, and past closed doors to one in particular. Jack hoped those gathered at the house would feel his compassion and understanding for Pauline's loss. JB opened the door to allow Jack inside. He stepped into a bedroom and found Pauline in tears and Terra at her side.

Terra shoved her shoulder-length brown hair out of her face. "Pauline was sharing about the argument she had with Jim the night before he died."

Jack glared at her. *What are you doing questioning his wife?*

Her brows pinched as she subtly shook her head.

Now wasn't the time to reprimand her, but he would make sure Pauline understood his role. "I'm sorry for your loss, Mrs. Raymond. My name is Jack Tanner, and I'm a detective with the county. I'll be investigating your husband's murder."

He drew out his pad to take notes.

Pauline wiped the tears away with more tissues, adding to the pile. A fist grabbed his heart and squeezed.

"I nagged him. I know I did. The washing machine had been causing problems for weeks now. And I was tired of it. I told him he could just wait for the repairman. I had to leave because my sister was having gallbladder surgery. I was going to stay with her overnight, but I got the call from the sheriff, so I came right home."

"Do you know if Jim had planned to meet someone that night?" Jack asked.

Pauline blew her nose. "You do realize that Jim was in insurance? That meant he was often gone in the evenings meeting people to sell them more insurance. He was old school. Loved the personal touch, and his clients appreciated that. We lived on commissions and not a salary, so he was always working."

"Did he have a home office?"

Pauline nodded. "He used to lease space downtown but recently decided to work from home."

"Could you show me?"

Pauline rose slowly, and Terra supported her when she appeared unsteady on her feet. "His office is down the hallway. I already told the sheriff you're free to look around and search wherever you need to. If you'll excuse me, I want to wash my face."

Good. That meant they wouldn't need a warrant. She stepped into the bathroom. Terra turned to Jack and spoke in hushed tones. "I'm sorry. I came by to drop off a sympathy card and gift basket from my grandfather. Pauline somehow thought I was official and started talking. Dragged me into the room. I told her to wait and that someone was coming." Terra rubbed her temple. "I should leave now."

She turned to walk away. Jack should let her go, but he touched her arm, stopping her. "Pauline seems to be comfortable talking to you. Let's not mess with the rhythm. Stay a little longer."

In Jim's office, Jack pulled on gloves. A calendar was spread on the desk with handwritten appointments. Jack took a picture. The laptop was closed. He would leave that for a forensic tech. He didn't see a physical filing cabinet.

Terra sighed. "I should go check on Pauline."

Jack followed her out. Terra turned right, and Jack took a

left to find himself in the last room down the hall—the laundry room. He stepped inside the space and spotted the washing machine. It appeared newfangled to him, but it could still be old. What did he know?

Pauline, appearing to have composed herself, stepped into the space. She had guests to attend to, he surmised, even though they had come to comfort her. Terra stood behind Pauline.

"Tell me about the day before when he called in about the Piper that crashed. Did he talk to you about that at all?" He remained focused on Pauline but didn't miss the subtle surprise in Terra's eyes. He'd only learned the news when Sarnes texted him with the information this morning.

"The Piper?"

"I mean the plane crash. He was the one who saved the pilot." Coincidence? Or was his death related?

Pauline's eyes almost brightened within her swollen, red features. "Yes. He came home breathless. Excited that he'd helped someone out."

"What was he doing up in those woods?" Terra asked.

Pauline stared at Terra. "I thought he was on a mountain road near the airstrip and saw the plane go down."

"Right, but do you know why he was in the area?" Jack asked.

Pauline frowned, and the tears came again. "I don't know."

Jack wasn't making much headway in getting answers from Pauline.

"He was a hero, Pauline. You remember that," Terra said.

Pauline leaned into her. "I know. He saved someone, but now he's dead."

The woman ran her hand over the top of the washing machine and released a heavy sigh. Jack stood back and took in the room where she'd had her last conversation with her husband. He glanced at the floor and spotted a small key.

With his hands still gloved, he picked it up. "What's this?"

"That's the key he kept in his wallet. It must have fallen out when he was looking for his credit card. He wanted to pay the man to make the repairs, and I wanted a new machine."

He kept a key in his *wallet*? "Do you know what it unlocks?"

Pauline slowly shook her head, then covered her eyes for a few heartbeats before dropping her hands to stare at the washing machine again. Jack wouldn't press her further, but she either knew something or ignored her husband's secrets. Jack would have guessed the dropped key was to a lawn mower or a backyard shed, except Jim had kept it in his wallet.

"Thank you for your time," Jack said. "If it's all right with you, I'll just hold on to this key. Do I have your permission to look inside whatever it opens if I can find it?"

She hugged herself and nodded.

"Also, I'd like to look around the house some more."

"Of course. Take your time." Pauline hobbled down the hallway, the grief weighing on her.

Terra watched Pauline go, sorrow reflected in her eyes. Pauline's responses, along with the uncertain key, left Jack with questions.

What were you up to, Jim? Jack tugged off the gloves for now and stuffed them away along with the plastic bag containing the small key.

Then he pulled out his cell and called Deputy Sarnes.

"Deputy Sarnes speaking."

"Sarnes, I'd like to question the pilot. What can you tell me about him?"

"Name is Chance Carter. I can tell you that he left the hospital."

"Where is he now?" Jack asked.

"We don't know. That's what I mean. I can tell you he left the hospital without being discharged, but I don't know where he went after that. The NTSB will need to investigate the crash. I have a call in to them to see if he's contacted them already. Maybe we could catch up with him that way."

"Let me know when you find him. I want to be the one to question him about the crash as well as what he knows about Jim."

"He couldn't have killed Jim, if that's what you're thinking. Carter was in the hospital when Jim was murdered. He was in bad shape after the crash."

"But not that bad if he left the hospital."

"Good point. We'll get on it."

"And Sarnes, get me a digital evidence tech out here. I need someone on Jim's computer."

"Say what?"

"You heard me."

"You got a warrant yet?"

"Pauline gave us permission." Jack ended the call.

Terra's brows arched. "Because?"

"There's more going on here. I'll look through the rest of the house to see if there's anything that needs closer examination."

Crossing her arms, Terra slowly nodded, approval in her eyes. "You know, if the pilot was injured in the crash, he might not remember much."

"I know what you're thinking. The plane crash could have nothing to do with Jim's murder, but I don't believe in coincidences."

"And you cover all your bases, Jack. I know you'll find the killer. As for me, I need to get back to work. Take care of yourself. You know we're here to help if needed."

Terra exited the laundry room. Would he ever see her again? Did he *want* to see her? He shoved those errant thoughts aside for another day.

Sighing, Jack scratched his jaw, dreading his next task. He didn't want possible evidence further contaminated. He needed to clear the house of all the guests, but Pauline wasn't going to like it.

His cell rang and he answered. "Tanner."

"You're not going to believe where we found Jim's vehicle."

NINE

After leaving Jack at Pauline's, deep in the thick of Jim's murder case, Terra had struggled to focus on her own investigations for the forest service. She'd gone into the national forest supervisor's office in Goode's Pass to get on top of the reports and paperwork that seemed to grow exponentially.

She didn't like to spend a lot of time in the office and preferred the outdoors. She hadn't imagined she would spend so much time at a desk, but that was the nature of the beast when working for the federal government in any capacity.

That's why, Jim's murder aside, Terra had enjoyed being outdoors yesterday even if it had to be with Jack.

Elbow on the desk, she rubbed her temple. He'd been serious and focused on the investigation, but at the end of the day, he'd started digging into personal matters. And for that reason, she should be relieved she wouldn't be working with him. But every part of her wanted to be included in the search for Jim's killer.

Who would have thought sitting at a desk would leave her so exhausted when the biggest muscle she had used was her brain? She could literally sleep for a week, but she'd only get further behind. She'd made no real headway on the timber theft case she was working.

But in all honesty, she wasn't truly focusing.

Her mind kept returning to Jim's body.

To Pauline's tears.

And to Jack's face when he'd first emerged from the forest after descending that cliff. His expressions throughout the rest of the day. And especially the look he'd given her when he found her talking to Pauline this morning as though she had taken on his investigation.

At five-thirty, Terra ended the tedious workday and stuffed paperwork back into drawers, giving her desk the appearance of belonging to a special agent on top of her game. Then she made the forty-five-minute drive to Gramps's ranch where she was staying for the time being.

She parked her forest service–issued vehicle along the circular drive in front of her grandfather's home. Robert Vandine's sprawling ranch house had been built in the middle of the almost ten thousand–acre ranch, though most of the acreage had been sold off over the years. Stone Wolf Ranch spread out in a small valley on the leeward side, or the eastern base, of Stone Wolf Mountain, which cast a rain shadow over the ranch that had been passed down through the family over the decades. The wealthy, especially movie stars, bought up the property in Montana and drove up real estate prices and taxes.

Terra climbed out of her vehicle and strolled to the house that had gone through several renovation projects when Nanna— her grandmother, Alvine Vandine—was alive. Now the home seemed much too big for one aging man.

His friends had been trying to talk him into running for office again. Terra wasn't sure that was a good idea, but she wouldn't interfere. Gramps had his finger in many pies—the local airport, grain storage, construction— and he still held on to a working farm, growing wheat and corn. He hired seasonal workers to drive the combines and take care of the harvest.

A horse's whinny drifted across the wind. Oh yeah, and Gramps had built a nice stable to house his horses.

When she'd exited the NPS and moved back home from Colorado, she'd rented an apartment in Goode's Pass near the office. She was close to family, but not too close. But she'd assured Gramps she would stay at the house since Owen had returned from the military hospital in Germany where he had spent months in rehab learning to use his prosthetic leg. He'd been through a lot, and it could take time for him to get settled.

Except getting accustomed to Owen being around again and knowing how to act around him left her unsettled.

As she approached her grandfather's home, she sucked in the fresh air and dragged herself up to the porch. She opened the door and the aroma of grilled steak wafted over her. Her stomach rumbled as she made her way to the kitchen.

"Terr!" Owen grabbed her in a side hug.

Okay, so he was in a better-than-usual mood.

She winced. "You don't know your own strength."

He released her. "I thought you weren't coming back today."

"Are you saying you didn't want to see me?"

"Of course not. I'm glad you're here."

"I'm staying for a while, you know that. Though I do need to check in on my cat once in a while." She hadn't realized she would be gone too much to care for a pet, even a cat, and was grateful for her neighbor Allie, who would probably end up keeping the cat. She couldn't bring Sudoku here because Owen was allergic. That's all he needed.

"You don't need to stay on account of me."

"Owen, please, I want to. It's been so long. I want to be here with you and Gramps."

Maybe she should move back in. There was plenty of room.

Gramps hadn't liked that she'd rented her own place when she'd come back to the area a few months ago.

Owen pulled out a head of lettuce.

She dropped her bag on the counter. "I'll let Gramps know I'm here. Are you making a salad?"

"Yeah, I'm not much for rabbit food, but Gramps insists he needs a good steak and fresh vegetables to keep up his health. He has big plans, you know."

"I'm happy to do it." She sidled next to him and stole the lettuce.

He handed over the knife.

She started chopping and immediately cut herself. Terra grimaced and peered at her sliced, bloody finger.

"Let me see." Owen grabbed her hand to look. "Good job, Terra."

She retrieved her hand. "I'll be fine. Could you get me a bandage?"

He nodded and disappeared.

She ran her finger under the faucet, turning the water hot, and her thoughts went to Jim's body again. Stabbed. By now the deputy coroner probably knew more about the weapon they should be searching for.

Gramps stomped in from outside with a plate of steaks. "Oh, honey, what happened?"

"Nothing. Just a nick. Owen's taking care of me."

Owen entered the kitchen, opened the bandage, and pressed it over the cut. His bright demeanor when she'd first arrived had now diminished. She focused on finishing the salad.

"Forget the salad. I'm ready to eat," Gramps said.

"No, there's plenty. I'll just toss it in a bowl." She finished up and gathered extra bowls, then sat at the small kitchen table with her grandfather and Owen. Just like old times. Sort of. Owen had been deployed most of the time she had lived with her grandfather.

Gramps gave her a sympathetic look. "Any news about the murder?"

"I'm not part of that investigation unless they ask for assistance. A few rangers and forest service law enforcement are helping look for a murder weapon."

"A needle in a haystack, that." Gramps cut into his steak.

She agreed and closed her eyes as she took a bite of steak, savoring the flavor and relishing the company.

Staying here gave her more time to spend with Owen, who was home now for good. He seemed to be doing well, but he was a different person from the brother she'd known growing up. And how could he not be changed after what he experienced.

But he and Gramps were here with her now, and she would enjoy every precious moment.

Gramps finished his steak but hadn't touched his salad.

Owen cleared his throat. "There's something I want to talk to you about."

His expression was somber, but she didn't miss the excitement edging his tone.

"Well, don't keep me in suspense." She sipped on iced tea.

"Now that I'm back, and we all know I didn't come back completely whole, I want to provide equestrian therapy for wounded warriors. Soldiers like me."

Terra glanced at Gramps, apprehension knotting her stomach.

Owen must have read her thoughts. "He's on board, Terra. I couldn't do it without his ranch and his horses. Unless I could get a grant together and investors, but I need somewhere to start."

"You have what you need right here." Gramps spoke to Owen but winked at her.

"Gramps and I are going to a therapeutic riding center in Idaho tomorrow. We'll be gone tomorrow night too."

"Really?" Terra glanced between the two. "You guys have been busy."

Owen rubbed the back of his neck. "I have a friend coming in a few days. Without him, I wouldn't have made it out of there." Owen hung his head. "I want to have my act together when Leif gets here."

Terra shared a concerned look with Gramps. When Owen lifted his face, she saw the fear, but he quickly shuttered it away and put on a smile.

She rubbed his arm. "I look forward to meeting him."

The doorbell rang and Gramps put his napkin on his plate, then scooted his chair out. "I'll get it."

Terra strained to hear who might be at the door, wishing she'd answered it herself. Gramps's tone sounded anything but warm and friendly. She left Owen sitting at the table and found Gramps still standing at the door. He turned to her.

"You know this fella?" he asked.

Jack filled the space, amusement dancing in his eyes.

Terra pushed her grandfather down the hallway. "You. Go. Back to your dinner. Jack is here on official business."

"I wouldn't be too sure. Watch your back with that one." Gramps stalked the rest of the way down the hall.

Terra stepped through the door and closed it behind her to stand on the porch with Jack. "I'd ask you inside, but—"

"It's okay."

Gramps would give him a hard time. Terra had been left in a puddle after Jack left. Gramps held on to grudges much too long.

"You could have called, you know." She crossed her arms.

"I did. Look at your phone lately?"

Oops. She'd left it muted in her bag. "What's up?"

"We found Jim's vehicle."

Terra absorbed the information. "And why are you telling me?"

He barely hitched a grin, as if he liked that she knew he had more. "I'm inviting you to the party, Terra."

Her heart pounded. She'd wanted that, hadn't she? "Why me? Why not Case Haymaker? He's law enforcement."

"Oh, he's invited. We're all working together to find a killer. But I'd especially like your help. Your specific skill sets."

"Right. I'm forest service, and I know these woods. So do a lot of people." Terra should stop talking because she did want to be involved in taking down Jim's killer. She'd also have to confirm with her superior, ASAC—Assistant Special Agent in Charge—Daniel Murphy. But she was searching for the truth. Terra wanted to know if Jack had ulterior motives for bringing her into his investigation.

"Yes, you know the woods, and you're experienced in complex investigations." He shoved his hands into his pockets and peered at Stone Wolf Mountain, part of the Gallatin Range. "Jim could have come across an illegal marijuana garden worth millions and run by a drug-trafficking organization."

That was something Terra would investigate. "But you don't think that's what happened."

"Do you?"

"We will certainly search the area for anything he might have stumbled on that could have gotten him killed, but where did you find his vehicle?"

Jack crossed his arms. "In Lake Perot."

"Wait. *In* the lake? Not near it?"

"Bottom of it, to be clear."

"That's twenty-five miles from where his body was found." Could be drug traffickers, but she doubted they would go to that much trouble. She frowned. "Okay. You've piqued my interest. But how did you find his car to begin with?"

"We obtained the GPS data from his vehicle, and that led us to the lake. His smartphone could possibly provide additional information. We're working on a warrant to get any data he backed up. The phone was at the bottom of the lake with his vehicle. I've since put someone on cross-referencing the homes of people Jim was actively targeting for sales against the data and activity on the days surrounding his murder."

Admiration swelled inside. But then she would expect a former FBI agent to think outside the box. Crossing her arms, she leaned against the door and hoped he didn't see that she was impressed. He was only doing his job, and he was good at it. "I have a feeling there's more."

"According to the data, he had parked at the Maverick Trailhead on the night of his murder."

"And you don't think he was meeting someone to sell them insurance."

"No."

"What exactly do you need from me?"

"I'd like you to accompany me up that trail and search for . . . anomalies." He shrugged. "I wouldn't ask, Terra, but evidence disappears quickly in the elements. And . . . frankly, I don't like Case, so I'm asking you."

His cheek hitched. Had he winked too? His dimpled grin and that wink still affected her, even now.

She couldn't help but return the smile. Jack had spent enough time in the woods, climbing mountains. He knew his way around too. But she wouldn't remind him. He'd invited her to the party, to join the investigation. She didn't care about the reasons, after all. "I'll meet you there at the trailhead at sunrise."

"Good." He lingered as if he had something else to say, but she knew he'd come to deliver the only news he had.

In person.

To be fair, she hadn't answered her phone. She held his gaze.

"Thanks for driving all the way out here, Jack." Big Rapids, the Grayback county seat, was about twenty-five minutes away, and Jack's aunt's house was just outside of town. But as a county deputy, he was accustomed to covering a large area.

Was it her imagination, or was he going out of his way to keep her close? So he could somehow make up for the past? *Oh, come on, Terra, you are reaching with that one.*

"I'm impressed that you learned this information so quickly." Maybe she shouldn't ask, but she couldn't stop herself. "Would you like to come in for some coffee before you head back?"

He seemed as surprised at her invitation as she was. "What about pie? Did you make a pie?"

A laugh burst from her. "Sorry, we're fresh out."

His shoulders sagged in exaggerated disappointment as he scraped his palm across the lower half of his face.

His warm smile brought back good memories. "Thanks, but I have to get home and check on my aunt, plus I really don't want to be the subject of your grandfather's interrogation. If you had pie, then I might risk it."

That elicited another smile from her. "Fair enough. Good night then."

He had worked some kind of magic to show up here and lift her spirits, make her feel warm inside.

She watched him head to his unmarked county SUV. Lingering as he drove off, she thought through their conversation while she attempted to ignore the way he made her heart pound.

Terra stayed to watch the bright pink sunset behind the mountain's silhouette.

And over by the stables near the corral, she caught Owen standing next to a horse, watching.

////////////////////////

Later that evening, Terra lay in bed in her old bedroom. Gramps had left it the same even after she'd officially moved out. She couldn't shut her mind down enough to sleep, so she stared at the ceiling. The day's events swirled in her thoughts. Too much information coalesced in her mind. She was the only agent for her region and was actively working twelve cases, including timber theft and assault on one of their ranger station volunteers. The job of forest service law enforcement included protecting the natural resources—water and soil—as well as the cultural aspects. Her investigations helped to enforce and prosecute those committing acts against the forest. And they could assist the county sheriff's department in searching for a suspect.

Finding a killer could unfortunately take months rather than days.

Would she and Jack be working together on this investigation in six months? Could she continue to work with him and not think about what they'd had before?

Both she and Jack had attended Montana State. She knew she would go into the forest service in some capacity to follow in her mother's footsteps, so she got her degree in natural resource management with an archaeology minor, her goal to somehow live up to her mother's legacy.

Strange to think that she hoped to live up to her mother's legacy when Jack strove to prove he was nothing like his father. He had nothing to prove, if you asked her, but he hadn't asked her.

Instead, he'd left town.

The week after they graduated college, Terra had sensed that Jack was anxious. She thought he was as in love with her as she was with him. She'd let herself hope for a proposal since they had often talked about a future together. But Jack had also dreamed of joining the FBI. Terra just didn't realize how their dreams could end up so diametrically opposed.

Jack had left a letter explaining that she deserved better than him.

His words scraped across her heart now.

"I love you enough to let you go."

The ceiling blurred as the memory took over—her heart crushing again at the news Nadine had delivered.

"I'm so sorry, Terra. He's gone. He packed up his things earlier today and left."

TEN

Jack parked at the curb at his aunt's house, barely registering that he'd arrived. He was relieved to finally be "home," though he still struggled to accept that he was truly back in Big Rapids, Montana, living with his aunt. This arrangement was the best one for her.

His mind kept flashing back to all the times he'd stood on that porch with Terra—before he'd left for Quantico.

He'd planned to propose. Bought a ring—weird that he still had that ring.

Jack carried some bad DNA in him. He had baggage and feared that, with his legacy, especially compared to Terra's family, he wasn't the best man for her. Still, he'd been in love. He would have proposed that night. And if he had, they could have gone to Quantico together, but he'd overheard Robert Vandine telling someone over the phone that Jack was from bad stock. He talked about Jack like he was nothing more than livestock. The man had bad-mouthed his father, and all Jack's doubts came crashing down on him. He definitely wasn't the man for Terra.

He actually thought he'd been doing the right thing by leaving her with only a letter instead of talking to her face-to-face. She deserved so much better than him, and it had been best to walk away cold turkey. He had never told her about the conversation he'd overheard. If she had known about her grandfather's words regarding Jack, it would have broken her heart. Considering that her father had left her, and then Jack too, Terra deserved at least one man whom she could count on.

Jack had broken both their hearts—the manner of his departure one of his biggest regrets.

He'd let her down. He'd let many people down. Now he was determined not to do that ever again.

Especially to his aunt.

Jack strode into the small ranch house he now shared with her and headed to the kitchen. A sensation swept over him.

Emptiness.

No one was home. He hoped he was wrong. "Aunt Nadine?"

Her car was still in the driveway. After searching the house, he rushed outside into the backyard. Two of the dogs, Dusty and Tux, also strays that had now found a home there with Nadine, met him and wagged their tails. But no Freckles or Aunt Nadine.

"Have you guys seen Aunt Nadine?" Jack crouched to rub the dogs behind their ears. "I know you tell us not to worry, Lord, but I can't help it."

Jack rushed around to the front of the house and looked down the county road. Aunt Nadine lived just outside the city limits, with a few neighboring houses nearby.

His gut clenched. He hoped he wouldn't find her out roaming around at this time of night. It was already ten o'clock. He should have come home earlier, as promised, but he'd wanted to give Terra the information and secure her help, then he'd stopped at the county offices.

Jack darted back into the house and looked at the list of Aunt Nadine's friends and phone numbers taped on the refrigerator. She hadn't driven anywhere, so a friend could have picked her up. He called the first person on the list—Francine

ELIZABETH GODDARD

Carmichael—even though it was probably past her bedtime, but he needed to find Aunt Nadine. He waited for someone to answer.

At sixty-nine, Aunt Nadine was young to struggle with dementia—at least what little he knew about it—though the risks increased with age. He'd read some information about the disease on the Internet, but he had better make the time to get thoroughly educated before she—or someone else— ended up hurt.

At least she was still well enough to be independent, but Jack had made his decision to stay close and live with her. Maybe his career move to county detective was the wrong one for this situation, and he should look for other employment.

"Hello?" A woman answered the call.

"Hello, Mrs. Carmichael?"

"This is she."

"This is Jack, Nadine's nephew. I'm wondering if she's there with you."

"Goodness, no." She coughed, then continued, "If you don't know where she is, that can't be good. Did you look to see if her car is in the garage?"

"It's in the drive, actually. I've already looked everywhere here at the house. I'm calling her friends before I call the sheriff."

A ruckus at the front door drew his attention, then Freckles dashed inside dragging his leash. The door shut and Aunt Nadine entered the kitchen from the hallway, wearing a purple hoodie and looking exhausted. Relief washed through him but was replaced with another concern as she paused to stare at him. Did she even recognize him?

"Mrs. Carmichael, she's here. No need to be worried. She just walked in." He ended the call and prepared himself for what came next.

"Jack, what on earth are you doing? Are you trying to make my friends think I'm crazy?"

"What? Of course not. I got home and couldn't find you." He hated seeing the disappointment in her eyes. "I'm sorry, okay? Let me get you a drink."

"I can take care of myself." She brushed past him to grab Freckles, then crouched to release the dog from his leash. She opened the sliding glass door to let Freckles into the backyard. "Go see Tux and Dusty."

Freckles dashed through the door, and the other two dogs barked and welcomed him like he'd been gone for a year. Aunt Nadine flipped on the lights in the backyard.

"Freckles wanted to take a walk, so I took him with me. We were out putting up posters, that's all. You were supposed to help."

Guilt surged. "I'm sorry. I got caught up with work. But it's after ten at night. You can't blame me for being worried about you. You shouldn't be out putting up posters late at night." Something could happen. But he'd scolded her enough.

Aunt Nadine glanced at the clock on the wall over the sink, a confused look in her eyes. "We left right after dinner. It was still light out."

That was hours ago, but saying so now wouldn't help her.

Time to lighten the atmosphere. "It sounds like you got caught up with work too, putting up those posters so Freckles can find his boy." Jack grinned. He hated that he wasn't nearly as hopeful as his aunt about reconnecting a dog and a boy who had lost each other.

Trembling, she pulled a chair out from the table and sat.

Jack opened the fridge and took out some orange juice. He poured his aunt a drink without asking if she wanted it and set the glass on the table in front of her. She drank it as though her mind were somewhere else.

He thought she had medication that she took at ten every night.

What am I going to do?

He joined her at the table and watched helplessly as her eyes filled with unshed tears. Was she thinking about Sarah, her granddaughter who had run away with her boyfriend and then disappeared? Jack wouldn't bring Sarah up if his aunt didn't.

Aunt Nadine suddenly shook her head and her face brightened. The tears disappeared.

"I never thought you'd come back here," she said. "That day you left to go learn how to work in the FBI, you were determined. You wanted to get out of here. I had hoped when I brought you here to give you a good home that you could forget what happened." She shook her head. "I was only fooling myself, yet here you are again. And look at you. I couldn't be prouder of what you've done with your life. What you've become. First FBI and now a detective for the county." She gasped and locked eyes with him. "The girl you left behind that day, what was her name?"

Of course, Aunt Nadine would have to remember. "Terra. Robert Vandine's granddaughter."

"Did you ever talk to her again? Make things right?"

ELEVEN

Chance dragged himself out of bed and shook off the strange dream. One more moment of fooling himself into believing the plane crash had only been a dream couldn't hurt, could it? His head still pounded. Before he'd gone to bed, he'd made it to the convenience store next door to grab junk food and sodas and pain relievers.

His ribs still ached, but he figured he would live, and his most serious injury had been to his head. Even that was slightly—only slightly—better this morning.

He thought through the last forty-eight hours.

The airstrip.

He'd never made it. He was supposed to have met someone there, though he had no idea whom. Really, it was a handoff and not a meeting. A package drop.

He should at least go to the airstrip and start there, but he no longer had a package to drop.

Chance counted his cash. He had one more night in this motel and then he would need cash. But maybe he would have answers and his package returned by then. Unless the authorities had the package.

He pressed his palms against his eyes. But no. Jim had found him, and Jim had been murdered. He'd bet his left arm Jim had been murdered for the package. Those who knew its value would commit murder.

And to that end, Chance had to find the person behind the delivery. The person who'd been blackmailing him all these years and who'd set up this particular delivery as if to get some sick retribution.

On the burner phone, he called for a cab to pick him up. He stuck his head under the faucet and shoved his wet hair back. Rinsed his mouth. One glance in the mirror, and he wished he hadn't. He looked like he'd climbed out of a hole that had been drilled straight from hell.

Fifteen minutes later, he asked the cabbie to take him to the airstrip in the woods.

"I'm not familiar with it."

Chance scratched his head. How did he explain? "Out by the old Blankenship place. That old flour mill that was turned into a restaurant that failed. It's out there somewhere. Can you just drive? I'll direct you."

Half an hour later, Chance got out of the cab near the smallest of the buildings at the end of the airstrip. Private or public, he wasn't even sure. There was no tower. He leaned in through the passenger side window of the cab. "Wait here. I won't be long. I'll pay you when I'm done."

The cabbie frowned but had no choice if he wanted his money.

Chance hadn't realized he had a limp. His leg started hurting. Maybe the drugs he received during his hospital stay had masked it before and now the pain was only beginning to ignite. Accident injuries could often appear hours or days later. What more could he expect?

He limped toward the building and found the door locked. Chance glanced back at the cabbie, who watched him. The man turned away as if he didn't want to be complicit in Chance's crimes or a witness to be dealt with later.

With his good leg, Chance kicked in the door. Worth it. A man had been murdered.

Had the authorities already been to this airstrip or searched the building? Were they watching now to see who showed up? He hadn't thought that far ahead. Difficult to think clearly with a pounding head and now an aching leg to add to his throbbing ribs.

The building had a counter and chairs like some sort of short-term waiting area or meeting place. Would he have met someone here in the building if he had landed? He hadn't been instructed to leave the package here, but maybe he would have received a call with those instructions.

Had someone been waiting here for him to land? He closed his eyes and waited like that would conjure up an image. Who was the person who was supposed to have received the hazardous package?

Had Jim been waiting here for the airplane? Heard the plane, then saw him go down? The crash site wasn't all that far. Jim had probably driven up the forest road to help Chance. But like Chance, Jim would have hidden the package from authorities, or he might have already delivered it.

Did Jim's contact kill him?

Too many thoughts fought for space in Chance's mind and confused him. He shook off the madness and focused.

He couldn't know if it had been Jim or someone else who had waited on him here. Chance moved around the ancient counter. On the floor behind the counter he found a tiny strip of paper with a phone number written in blue ink. The writing looked masculine, though he was no expert. He folded the slip of paper and stuck it in his pocket. The phone number could mean everything or nothing. Still, his heart pounded as if he'd hit the jackpot.

With a bounce in his good leg, he made his way out of the small building.

The cab was gone.

TWELVE

The next morning, Jack waited in his warm vehicle at the Maverick Trailhead. Terra should be here at any moment, and they would hike up the trail and see what was what. As he waited, he wished he could forget his aunt's question last night.

Had he made things right with Terra?

Too much time had passed already. They both had moved on. Then why did his aunt's words gnaw at him? In some ways, sure, he'd moved on. But in other ways, his heart and mind ushered him to the past as if he were still there. It was in the small nuances—the way he reacted to Terra's smile or her slightest frown. And he'd spent only a few hours with her for the first time in years. This investigation—and his insane desire to somehow "make it right," as Aunt Nadine had put it—could mean many more hours with her.

Terra's white SUV pulled in behind him and cut off his thoughts. *Thank you, God.*

He climbed out, tugged on his jacket, then headed for Terra. The morning was cold, but the day would warm up soon.

"Morning," he said.

Terra closed the distance, carrying two thermoses. She

handed one to him. "Gramps has a special blend. He roasts his own beans, you know."

He squinted at her. "I didn't know. I'm thinking that since he roasts his own coffee and you make the most incredible pies, you guys should open up a shop or something." He eyed the thermos with uncertainty. "Is it any good?"

"You tell me." Her conspiratorial grin could have meant anything.

He unscrewed the cap, sniffed the warm brew, then shrugged. He took a sip and nearly dropped the thermos. "Ouch!"

"What? Did you burn your tongue?"

"It must have been boiling when you left."

"I wanted to make sure it was still hot by the time I got here."

"Thanks." Since she'd been so thoughtful, he'd have to drink the coffee. He left the cap off so the air would cool it down a bit.

Terra sipped from hers while it was still way too hot and turned her face east to the mountains and the rising sun, the Maverick Trailhead behind them. They remained quiet as they sipped coffee and soaked in the fresh mountain air and picturesque view.

Jack had a beautiful view all his own. Terra's thick brown hair was clipped up. He couldn't help but think back to Aunt Nadine's question—one he hadn't been able to adequately answer without upsetting her.

Had he made things right?

No, and the opportunity to do so had long passed. But something inside him wanted to make it up to Terra. How, he had no idea.

If he had stayed in Montana with Terra back then rather than skipping town and accepting a job with the FBI, where would they be now? Terra had known about his dream, but neither of them had known how quickly that dream could happen. His major had been in information technology, and the feds snatched him right up.

He'd wanted her more than he'd wanted anything else in his life, but Terra came from a family of heroes. Jack had a dark family history. She probably thought he was a coward, but leaving her that day was one of the bravest things he'd ever done. She would never understand that he did it for her. He had to change his legacy. Prove that he wouldn't be anything like his father. He'd been driven to prove himself so he could finally measure up, but to whom, he wasn't sure he even knew anymore.

He blew out a breath. If he'd stayed here, he didn't think they would be together as a couple because Jack hadn't believed in himself enough.

"We should get going," she said.

He realized he'd been staring at her, caught up in his thoughts. "Looks like scattered thunderstorms today, and one seems to be developing right over us."

"That could wash away evidence, if there's any to find," she said.

"A county evidence tech already searched here at the trailhead."

"But you wanted me to go with you to search."

"Yes. We don't know if Jim did more than stand next to his vehicle here when he was murdered. We'll learn if any blood particles were found."

"Okay, then let's go." She held out her hand to take his thermos.

He held on to it. "I'm not done."

"You don't want to carry that, do you?"

"Good point."

He chugged the rest of the still painfully hot coffee, and she laughed at his efforts to conceal the pain and awful burnt taste, of which he was no fan. He handed over the thermos and she stuck it back in her vehicle, along with hers.

She secured a backpack. "Where's your pack?"

He scratched an itch under his eye. "I didn't think we'd be gone that long."

"Always take a pack with supplies with you into the forest." She started forward, and at the trailhead she gestured for him to lead.

He found it funny that he was spending an inordinate amount of time on trails with Terra, just like they had before. Nature loving was in her blood.

"So, tell me what you've learned so far," she said.

"We're still interviewing friends and family."

"And the pilot?" Her breathing remained steady even though they were hiking an incline.

"Haven't caught up with him yet."

"Why did he leave the hospital?" she asked.

"That's a good question. The attending physician explained that he had expected Mr. Carter to remain at least another night."

"He just woke up and realized . . . what? What would make a man leave without discharging?"

"He couldn't have killed Jim, so that's not it. As far as others, we're interviewing people Jim met with to sell insurance, his clients, and anyone else he worked with. The case is a priority, which brings me to this. Sheriff Gibson is deputizing you for the course of this investigation."

Terra stopped behind him. He stopped too and turned to look at her.

"We're pooling all the resources. If you come across a suspect during the hunt for a killer, you have the authority of the sheriff's offices to arrest them. You'll be read into all the information."

She angled her head. "My ASAC signed off on my participation, but this is even better. Is the sheriff also deputizing the forest service LEOs?"

"Yes. At least while we're searching for the murderer. Henry tells me it's not uncommon to cover all the bases in working with the forest service on an important investigation. Oh, and thanks for not sending Haymaker in your place this morning."

She laughed. "You're welcome. And . . . Henry?"

"Sheriff Gibson. I'm supposed to call him Sheriff Gibson, but it's hard when everyone else around here calls him Henry." Jack turned and continued hiking. Terra followed.

When she said nothing more, he continued. "We're still waiting to get a time of death, but we have a window. His vehicle was parked at the trailhead within that time frame. We're looking for evidence. Blood. Murder weapon."

"A cabin," she said.

"A cabin?"

"Yes. We've hiked about three quarters of a mile, according to my watch, but if we keep going for the full mile, the cabin should be just over a half mile off trail to the northwest."

He paused to look at her.

"What? You act as if you're surprised to learn that I actually do have something to contribute."

"No, it's not that." Sure. Maybe it was.

"Right. But we can't know if he hiked this trail or headed for that cabin."

"Was he having an affair? Was he blackmailing someone or being blackmailed? The list goes on."

"I think you were right when you said you had the feeling it's complicated. A plane crashes. Jim reports seeing the plane, and even makes his way to the downed plane—it was on a forest road, so he could have driven there. Within hours, Jim is murdered."

"And the pilot flees his hospital room."

"Wait." He thought he spotted a cabin through the trees, though it wasn't easy to see. If he took even one step, it was gone again. "There it is."

Jack stepped off the trail and over tree trunks and fallen branches into an area carpeted with pine needles.

"The cabin is part of the forest service's Recreation Residence Program," she said, "otherwise known as 'cabin in the woods.' In this case, the cabin is isolated."

"I'm not following you."

"The cabins are special use permit issued for twenty years at a time for personal use." Terra pushed on toward the cabin, and Jack kept pace.

At the door, she said, "Let's see if anyone is home."

He pressed his palm against his weapon and knocked on the door. "Detective Tanner and Special Agent Connors here. We'd like to ask some questions."

No one responded.

They hiked around the cabin. Curtains prevented them from seeing inside. At the back, a curtain hung at an angle, revealing a portion of the inside of the cabin.

Terra gasped. "Wait a minute."

She moved to the door and tried it, but it was locked.

"What is it?" he asked. "What do you see?"

"Shelves. Mostly empty. But I spotted a couple of Native American artifacts, pots actually, so contraband . . . probable cause."

"They could be completely legal," he said.

"Granted. They could be. But someone was murdered, and the artifacts are tucked away here in an isolated cabin, so I'm leaning toward illegal."

He produced the key he'd found on the floor at Jim's house. "We need to know what it's for."

He stuck it in and unlocked the door.

Terra gasped. "It worked. I can't believe it worked. This cabin is Jim's, after all."

"Or it belonged to someone else and he had a key he thought he kept hidden from his wife in his wallet."

Terra started to step inside. He stretched out his arm to block her.

"Pauline gave me permission to look, but since she claimed not to know what the key was for, I can't even be sure this cabin belongs to Jim and that she has the right to give that permission. I'm going to call about a warrant to cover my bases."

"But what about probable cause?"

"These aren't exigent circumstances. It isn't so urgent to justify a warrantless search. We have time to get the warrant, so let's make sure the evidence we find can't be challenged in court."

THIRTEEN

Terra followed Jack away from the cabin until he found a signal, then he made the call requesting a warrant. He eyed her the entire time he spoke into the cell.

He ended the call and tucked his cell away. "I need to stand here and wait for a call back. Or we could head back to our vehicles and wait there. You know, it could take ten minutes or hours."

"You stand there, and I'll look around to see if I come across any 'anomalies,' as you put it earlier." But she'd already come across one.

"Or you could stay here and talk to me. Tell me what you're thinking. You deal with this artifact business more often than I do. What can you tell me?"

She exhaled. The temps were starting to warm up, and she shrugged out of her pack and jacket. Terra grabbed water and tossed a bottle to Jack.

That storm had blown over without dumping rain on them. But thunder sounded in the distance.

"On my last assignment with the National Park Service, I worked undercover. We were working in the four corners—

where Utah, Colorado, New Mexico, and Arizona come together."

"Anasazi. Native American pueblo people." Jack flashed his dimpled grin.

Terra waited a few heartbeats, then said, "You know more than you let on, Jack Tanner."

"I should be honest with you. Aunt Nadine has a book on her coffee table."

Interesting. "People have taken arrowheads and more home for decades. We know that. Although depending on where and how the item was taken, it's probably still illegal. Our sting operation had to do with things taken and sold on the black market. They were pilfering from historic ruins, selling to collectors."

"And you think Jim could be involved in something similar?"

"I don't know. It's complicated."

"That, I already know." He swatted at an insect.

"Most pothunting, as we call it, is in the southwest. In Jim's cabin, I spotted a couple of items on that shelf through the window. Contemporary Native American art brings in millions, even billions of dollars. But a big problem exists in that people who buy the art might not understand if they are buying something old or something new. Something legal or something illegal—the new laws are curbing even the purchase of contemporary Native American art."

"And Native American artists depend on that for their livelihood," he said.

"The art they produce is contemporary and obviously completely legal to buy and sell, and there are even legal *artifacts* to be possessed too, but this is where it gets murky because of provenance."

"You mean, where did the items originate from?"

"Yes. And was it from public or private land? Was it taken from a gravesite? Or created from an endangered species?"

"Things have changed in the last two decades. Aunt Nadine used to take me out to collect arrowheads."

"And that's perfectly fine if the arrowheads are found on private land, and again, they aren't pilfered from a gravesite or a site of historic significance. But she would know that." Aunt Nadine probably wasn't breaking the law, Terra hoped, but many broke the laws without realizing they were doing so, especially since those laws had changed.

"There's even a law, NAGPRA—the Native American Graves Protection and Repatriation Act—that outlines how museums and federal agencies should return Native American objects to the original tribes. Again, complicated."

Jack chugged from his bottled water.

"There's also NHPA—the National Historic Preservation Act of 1966—but that's mostly to do with someone trying to bulldoze land or build a pipeline that comes across an archaeological site. As for my job as a forest service special agent, I'm more concerned about ARPA, the Archaeological Resources Protection Act."

"My head is spinning already. Dumb it down for me, okay? I'm only a meager county detective." He grinned.

"ARPA basically says you can't loot on historic sites or dig up graves, collect or deface historic sites. This is what the forest service special agents investigate. Forest service law enforcement officers protect the resources, and if there are violations and no one has been apprehended, those cases are then reported to criminal investigators—special agents like me so we can dig deeper. So far on my job here, I haven't had an archaeological case, but with my past experience, that's more my specialty."

Jack's eyes filled with appreciation when she'd expected them to glaze over like most people's did. Terra averted her eyes, hoping he didn't see her blush under his stare. The two of them had come a long way. They were both different people now, yet so much about her remained the same. It seemed that was true for Jack as well.

"All right," he said. "Let's say we get the warrant and get into the cabin. You're calling the items artifacts, but they could be made by contemporary Native Americans and not artifacts at all."

The pots still had dirt on them, as if someone had recently dug them up. "Maybe, but what I saw . . . I'm leaning artifact. The Montana tribes, the Crow tribe for instance, followed the bison. They were considered Plains tribes and didn't spend much time making pottery. These pots look more Hopi anyway." Even stranger.

"Hopi?"

"A nonmigratory tribe in the four corners. The Hopi are the descendants of the Anasazi." *What were you up to, Jim Raymond?*

"How do we find out what we're dealing with—stolen or illegal or perfectly fine?"

"A museum or a qualified appraiser could assess them. In our case, a forest service archaeologist could make the determination, and if the items are illegal, they would be held in a repository until they could be returned to the rightful tribe."

"If they are determined to be illegal items, they would be held as evidence." He crossed his arms.

"Or repatriated to the tribe they belong to. So, you see, it gets complicated."

He sighed. "First, we need to get into the cabin."

His cell rang. "Speak of the—" He answered, "Tanner here . . . Yep. We'll go in first. Send an evidence tech."

"You got it?"

He nodded. "We're good to go."

They each donned latex gloves. Jack held the door for Terra.

She remained at the entrance along with Jack, taking in the room.

Shelves lined the walls, most of them empty. Jim had furnished the two-room cabin with the basics for staying in the woods. The living space had two old plush sofas and a chair. A small kitchen in the corner. A double sleeping cot in another corner. But the shelves had drawn Terra's attention, and she peered at the two pots closely, noting the cracks.

"I don't see any obvious footprints, but let's limit our tracks and evidence contamination."

"Got it." She took pictures with her phone.

On closer examination, she noticed some staining, as though someone had tried to clean at least one of the pots with regular soap, and that confirmed her suspicions. "We'll leave these here for the evidence techs to see—maybe they can grab fingerprints, but I need them for the archaeologist."

"Fine. What else are you thinking?"

"All these shelves. What are they for?"

"I don't know. Books?"

She shook her head. "No. They've been wiped clean. But these two items were left behind, or they were added later. Recently. Maybe Jim brought them up here, and that's why he came to the cabin. Then he was killed."

"If that's true, was he killed because of what lined these shelves? And why keep what we're assuming is contraband here? It would be a chore to hike up here and stash the artifacts. And also risky if someone hiking in the woods decided to break in," Jack said.

Terra continued walking the cabin, looking for anything else that could give them more information.

"Honestly, I think if he was moving illegal artifacts, then this isolated cabin that only he had legitimate access to is a brilliant idea. And if someone were to break in, they would most likely do so to get out of the elements because they were lost. They probably wouldn't think twice about the Native American art on the shelves. Jim could have come often enough to check the cabin."

She held his gaze.

He nodded. "I'll have them look deeper into the tracking data to see how often he came here. We only looked at the week surrounding his death. We'll expand that. Still, Terra, I think this is a stretch. We need to find something more than conjecture."

"That he was killed for the items, you mean."

"Yes. It's a theory."

"Agreed."

She shined a small flashlight around the shelves, behind them, and on the floor while Jack perused the cabin. Then she moved to the wall without shelves and noticed hooks for hanging decorations. "The cabin has been cleared out of more than what was on the shelves. I'll be interested to learn what your techs come up with."

She found a keyed lock in the wall. "Hey, there's something here. A cabinet. But it's locked."

Jack approached. "Here, let me." He tried the small key he had used to open the main door. "Doesn't work."

"Let me try something." Terra retrieved her pocketknife and began picking at the lock. "I know . . . I'm messing with this. We should wait for evidence techs."

"And I'm going to let you do it. I really want to see what's inside."

The cabinet door swung open.

Terra gasped. "Looks like we hit pay dirt."

FOURTEEN

Terra stared at the headdress created from eagle feathers. The warbonnet was as long as Terra was tall. "Now, this is definitely Crow. And behind the headdress, deeper in the cabinet, I see more things. Some pottery shards, tools, and the like."

She reached to touch the beautiful features but held back. "This could potentially violate several acts, including the Bald and Golden Eagle Protection Act."

"Don't tell me, eagle feathers are illegal."

"You didn't know?" She couldn't take her eyes from the headdress. "Eagle feathers and body parts are illegal to sell. I think this is a stash of Native American relics. Regarding this headdress, unless Jim had certifiable American Indian ancestry, even having the feathers in his possession is a huge fine. And in this case, I don't think there's any doubt he knew what he was doing was illegal."

She tugged out her phone again and took more pictures.

"How huge is the fine?"

"Why do you ask? Got some eagle feathers?" She continued taking pictures. "A hundred grand or more. That's down from two hundred and fifty million a few years ago. Maybe jail time. That is, if this headdress is of cultural and religious significance."

"I get it. More violations. Where do you think he got the pots? Public or private lands?"

"The pots on the shelf and in the cabinet I believe were pilfered from an archaeological site, just not local. Some of the tools in the cabinet could be local. The archaeologist will have to identify the tribe. This headdress didn't come from a dig, but it's in good condition. If we find items actually taken from a gravesite, the penalties are much steeper. I *would* say that Jim has some explaining to do." Except Jim was dead.

"Maybe that's our answer—someone didn't want Jim explaining. He could have been a middleman. Fencing the items. I think that sounds more like Jim to me. He wasn't the type to literally get his hands dirty, but he was a businessman. Had a lot of connections."

"Or he kept secret this private collection that he came here to enjoy or share with other enthusiasts." She stepped back from the cabinet to catch her breath. "Someone could have killed him for his collection and plans to come back and get the rest. Or planned to."

"So, which is it then? Collector or fence?" Jack asked.

"In my previous investigation, no one was murdered. We have to consider that this might not be connected to his murder at all." Terra skimmed through the pictures she'd taken on her phone. "Between you and me—because, again, we're only theorizing here—I think he was fencing, buying and selling. But we're getting ahead of ourselves." And depending on which direction this investigation took, other agencies might want to weigh in. When she'd worked the sting before, the BLM—Bureau of Land Management—and FBI were also involved.

Terra finished taking pictures. As soon as the county evidence collection team finished here, she would transfer the artifacts to a secure room at the forest service supervisor's office in Goode's Pass.

She sighed. They could only be touching the surface of what was going on. Others, locals, friends even could be involved in a trafficking ring. She'd seen this before, and it could be devastating. *God, please don't let it be a repeat of the past.* The last sting she was involved in had devastated an entire community.

Terra wanted fresh air and fled the cabin, leaving Jack inside. Thoughts of her past job reminded her of so many things gone wrong. A man bent on going out in a blaze had driven into the national park and, using an assault weapon, had taken out a park ranger who was sitting in his vehicle minding his own business. As the man held off law enforcement, the ranger bled out before help could arrive. He was Terra's friend, who she'd gotten to know through a joint task force. Had a wife and a child. His death was a huge blow to them all and drove Terra into someone's arms and down the wrong road.

And now here she was, back in the same space with Jack. Another mistake?

Seriously. Sometimes she had to wonder about God's plans for her life.

So . . . yeah. She needed air, and she needed it now.

She walked a few paces away and soaked in the forest—the evergreens and rust-colored needles carpeting the ground. She drew in the scent of pine and clean mountain air. In mid-September, when summer shifted to autumn, the breeze held a hint of the cold winter to come. She listened to birdsong. A squirrel chattered in the trees and shook smaller branches as it jumped between them.

Had Jim been killed here at the cabin? Or in these woods? Or at the cliff?

Jack joined her outside. "We'll have company soon. I got a text that they're at the trailhead."

"Good." She needed to touch base with her ASAC and others in her district about possible looting at local sites, though she didn't think the pottery she'd seen was local. She wouldn't make that call. But she'd have to wait for a stronger cell signal. She would remain here until the evidence techs arrived so she could speak to them about the artifacts. They could collect evidence surrounding the pots, but she was taking the items.

She'd need assistance with that, especially the headdress.

"Bad enough he was murdered," Jack said, "but to find out he was involved in something illegal is a shock."

"At least we have a possible motive." Terra soaked in everything she had always loved about the outdoors, at the same time loathing the horrors of the crimes that were committed against nature and man alike in remote places such as this.

Would the forest give up its secret? Who had killed Jim?

Jack peered at the ground, the bushes and trees, like any good tracker looking for signs. Then he caught her watching him. "We should set up surveillance cameras near the road to see who drives by to watch, as well as cameras near this cabin to see if someone attempts to come back."

"Good idea." All of it required funding, resources, and time. She hated that feeling in her gut that told her they were already too late.

Through the trees, county deputies arrived with evidence techs. Jack instructed the crew to carefully look for evidence, including from around the cabin. In particular, the murder weapon. He then told them, after processing the cabin, to assist Terra in retrieving the artifact evidence.

As the day wore on, Terra and Jack waited while techs finished dusting the cabin for prints and searched for other evidence, including blood.

"With my experience in cases involving archaeological crimes," she said, "I have a few connections." Unfortunately, Dr. Jeremy Brand was the first to come to mind. "Maybe I can use those to see if I can get a lead on who Jim was working with. Where he was getting the artifacts."

"What else, Terra? What more is bugging you?"

"You can read me that well, can you?"

He shrugged. "My job description requires that I read people well. So what else is on your mind?"

"I was just thinking"—about how much she didn't want to contact Dr. Brand—"that these crimes come with a fine and prison time. Most of the time it isn't enough to deter the activities because there's significant money to be made."

He nodded. "Murder changes everything."

"Right. Was Jim's collection worth murder? Not what little I've seen. However, people have murdered for much less."

Thunder rumbled. So far, the scattered storms had passed them by. But this time, lightning struck dangerously close. This part of the mountain was a tinderbox, and lightning could ignite a fire, even though fire season was coming to a close.

"Let's go." Jack touched her arm. "The bottom is about to fall out."

"But I need to get the artifacts transferred. It's not like I've never been caught in the rain."

"I always miss the rain." He sent her a wry grin. "No point in ruining my reputation."

"There's always a first time."

"And that's not today. Don't worry. They'll retrieve everything for you. I promise we'll get the items transferred to the forest service since you insist."

"All right," she said. "We can arrange for transfer this evening or in the morning."

Terra hiked down with him. "About the murder weapon, Jack. If someone went to the trouble to throw Jim off that cliff so he might not ever be found, they probably didn't leave the murder weapon laying around."

"Well, we've searched the area where his body was found,

both the top and the bottom of the ridge, and still nothing. It can't hurt to look."

Dark clouds hung directly above them as the wind tossed the trees around. They picked up the pace, but Terra might just get to see Jack doused in a rainstorm despite his proclamation to the contrary. At the trailhead, county vehicles almost pinned their vehicles in.

"See you later." She waved and ran to safety before she, too, was doused. After climbing inside and buckling, she spotted Jack on his cell as he climbed into his SUV.

He made her smile.

Then a big raindrop plopped on her windshield. And another, until rain pounded against her car. She couldn't believe they'd made it before the rain started—maybe there was something to Jack's claim. Regardless, she hoped the rain got the whole mountain and not just this patch. The thunderstorms weren't called scattered for nothing.

Her cell chimed. ASAC Daniel Murphy.

"Connors here."

"I want a rundown."

She'd sent him an email yesterday and relayed the information regarding the cabin and artifacts. Dan blew out a low whistle.

"You've got the experience, Terra, so I trust you to work through this, though I'm happy to assist if needed."

Relieved to hear he had confidence in her, she allowed a slow exhale. She was in this now and wanted to find Jim's killer.

And work with Jack . . .

She ignored the errant thought.

"Got a report on a meth lab," Dan said.

"Can't the locals handle that?"

"Forest service officers have shut it down, but you need to look into it."

She bit her lower lip. "I think this murder and the apparent stash of artifacts is complicated, Dan. I'd like to stay focused on this." They were all spread far too thin.

"Because of the murder, the archaeological crime is a priority. I trust you know how to juggle your caseload. But let me know if that becomes an issue." He ended the call.

Terra slammed the steering wheel. One moment he complimented her, the next he challenged her abilities. She suspected that Dan hadn't liked that she'd gotten the job as a special agent. She'd heard that he had a friend he'd wanted for the position. She half-suspected that Gramps had put in a good word for her. If he had, she wasn't sure how she felt about that.

Her heart rate calmed, and she realized that Jack was still sitting in his vehicle. Was he waiting on her to leave? She steered away from the trailhead, and he followed her into Big Rapids. She wasn't sure where he was going. They hadn't discussed doing more today, but lunch and dinner had come and gone, and she was starving.

Jack turned left on Main Street, which meant he was probably heading for the county offices. She would have asked him to grab a bite with her, but she needed space from the investigation. Time to think about these new developments. And she needed distance from Jack.

She steered toward her grandfather's ranch, which required her to drive a curvy mountain road for about twenty miles. No one would be there to greet her tonight since Owen and Gramps were in Idaho to meet with an equestrian therapist. She was proud of her brother and hoped he would be able to secure the right connections to make this dream happen. With Gramps accompanying him, the chances were good.

She struggled to keep her mind focused on the road ahead of her. Gripping the steering wheel, she leaned forward, closer to the windshield, as though that would help her vision. Dusk, combined with the steady downpour, made navigating the curvy road troublesome.

A set of headlights had been following her since she left town. Someone else had the same treacherous drive tonight.

Or not.

Darkness seemed to grip her soul. Maybe it was Jim's murder—stabbed in the back, then tossed from a cliff—along with her discovery today that made her a little paranoid.

The forest she loved so much was no longer safe in this day and age, a morbid fact that was confirmed for her more each day on her job.

As the headlights behind her kept pace, her uneasiness grew. The car behind her was probably just a weary traveler like she was.

To test that theory, she turned down a road that led her away from the ranch. Sure enough, the car turned as well.

Next test.

She increased her speed. If the vehicle following also increased their speed, that would tell her something.

The vehicle not only kept pace—it sped up.

FIFTEEN

At the county sheriff's office, Jack tried Terra again on his cell as he made his way to his desk. He spotted the familiar poster. Someone had set it on top of the stack of paperwork waiting for him.

Cocker spaniel named Freckles looking for lost boy.

Once again, he'd failed to make it home in time to help Aunt Nadine with the posters. Shame anchored to his chest. Had she come to the county offices to put the posters up and left him one as a reminder? An admonishment? No. That couldn't be right. He knew her heart, and she wouldn't have left this here to make him feel guilty.

Terra's voice mail came up and drew his attention from the poster. He ended his fourth attempt to reach her, and this time he didn't leave a voice mail.

Plopping into the chair at his desk, he sent her a text.

She could still be on her way to her grandfather's ranch. And like last night, maybe she was eating dinner with her brother and grandfather and ignoring her phone.

Rubbing his eyes, Jack sighed. He could talk to her in the morning and let her know the team had completed retrieving the artifacts.

"Tough day?" Detective Nathan Campbell dropped into the chair at his own desk and rolled the chair closer to Jack, his nearly black hair a little scruffy for a detective, in Jack's opinion.

Jack didn't feel up to trading stories. He held up the poster to Nathan. "You're working late."

Nathan's dark eyes—nearly as black as his hair—warmed. "I saw your aunt. She was putting posters up everywhere today."

Jack let the poster drop and sighed. "I told her I would help her."

"Don't beat yourself up. She was with a couple of her friends. They're over at the diner right now. I think it's a knitting club or something."

Jack eyed his fellow detective and offered a half smile. "Thanks for letting me know."

"Sure thing. Everyone loves your aunt. We're all watching out for her."

A lot of people loved Nadine. She'd taken care of kids after school for decades, including Nathan at times. While Jack knew what Nathan said was true, others could only watch out for his aunt to a point. The county seat was big enough that not everyone knew one another.

"Look, I appreciate your attempt to reassure me, but you know as well as I do that this area can be a dangerous place."

Jim's murder emphasized that.

And you can't even make it home to hang a few posters. God, please let that boy find his dog. Or as Aunt Nadine had put it, let the dog find his lost boy.

Nathan rolled back to his desk and shuffled papers.

Jack turned his attention to his own stack. Then he noticed a picture printed off, along with scribbled notes from the deputy coroner. He peered at the notes. He'd asked for information as soon as possible. This wasn't an official report, but what he read piqued his interest.

Jack stood.

"You heading to the diner?" Nathan asked.

"Nope." Jack donned his jacket. "Do me a favor. If you're still here and you happen to see Aunt Nadine leave the diner, would you text me?"

"All right, but you owe me." The way Nathan's lips twisted up, Jack knew he was only kidding.

Jack got back into his vehicle and drove through town—the dark, rainy evening requiring all his focus. Lights reflected off the wet streets until he got to the Grayback County Museum, now located where the old county jailhouse had been before it was moved to a new location. Of course, the place was closed, but he spotted a light on inside.

No one answered when he knocked, so he tried again. "Detective Jack Tanner here."

The door creaked open and a man with spectacles and wispy silver hair frowned at him. Jack grinned. "Howdy. I'm Detective Jack Tanner."

"We're closed."

Jack flipped his credentials open. "As I said, I'm a detective. I have a few questions for you."

The man opened the door wider. "I'm Dr. Bellinger. Curator and manager. Come in and tell me what this is all about, Detective."

Jack entered and waited while Dr. Bellinger locked the door again. He gave Jack a shrug. "We're closed, and I don't want anyone wandering in."

"Understood. Thanks for opening up for me. After hours is probably the best time for me to be here though."

The man adjusted his spectacles as if waiting for Jack to go first.

Jack remained by the door and glanced around the museum featuring the history of the town and the state of Montana. Photos of settlers and farmers and Native American images covered the walls, and glass curio cases displayed artifacts.

Maybe Jack should have talked to Terra about meeting with Dr. Bellinger—this archaeological business was more her expertise.

Still, Jack had his own questions. "You're working late tonight."

"Yes. I'm working late. We're busiest this time of year when the tourists who are late to the party have their last big hooray before the school year begins."

Jack thought the school year had already started. "Mind if I have a look around?"

The man sighed heavily. "Detective, is there some reason you need to look around at this hour? I was just getting ready to head home. During the day, we have volunteers and college interns who could help."

"Good thing I caught you then. Why don't you give me the quick tour?"

"It would help if you could tell me what this is about."

"Let's make a deal. Give me the quick tour, and I'll tell you what it's about."

"Very well."

"Lead on."

Dr. Bellinger walked slowly through each room and gave a short review of the contents. Jack soaked in all this history, which he'd never much cared about before today. When they were done with the tour, Dr. Bellinger tried to usher Jack to the exit.

"What about in the back? Do you have artifacts stored there or in a secure location that you then move to the main displays when they're exhibited?"

Dr. Bellinger pursed his lips as if deciding if he would tell Jack he'd have to come back tomorrow, and maybe even with a warrant. Jack wasn't accusing Dr. Bellinger or the museum of anything. "Look, if you have any weaponry, let's say, knives, for example. I'd like to see those."

The curator cleared his throat. "Very well. Follow me."

Jack followed him through the museum and down a dark hallway, where he unlocked another set of doors. "These are climate-controlled rooms to better preserve our artifacts."

Dr. Bellinger ushered Jack through the door. "You'll find a display case of weapons over there. I still don't understand why you would want to see them."

"Could you turn on more light, please?"

Dr. Bellinger continued to dramatize his displeasure but flipped on all the lights, including the case lights.

Jack perused the display of old weapons—tomahawks and spearheads and knives—some not necessarily what he would consider ancient. But they were artifacts, the museum claimed.

"This one." Jack pointed at one of the knives.

Dr. Bellinger pursed his lips as he cleared his throat. Then he adjusted his spectacles and leaned in for a closer look. "What about it?"

Jack pulled out a folded piece of paper—the picture the deputy coroner had printed off for him. He lowered it closer to the knife. "Does this broken-off tip look like it would complete this knife?"

SIXTEEN

Chance stood under a dark canopy that protected him from the rain and watched the bar across the street.

After the cab left him, he'd limped along until he found one of the motels with individual cabins at the edge of the forest. His leg needed rest after that, but his mind needed rest too.

So he waited.

All the pain and hard work it had taken to start over and become a new person had brought him back to this one small county that he'd left behind. Had been forced to leave years ago—what seemed like a lifetime now.

Blevins strolled across the street and entered the bar.

Showtime.

Chance shoved from the wall, yanked his cap a little lower, and crossed the street for his impromptu meeting. Just a couple of guys having a few drinks in the dark corner of a western honky-tonk. No, wait. Not anymore. Now it featured Star Wars stuff. Maybe one of the old Star Wars actors had bought a ranch near town. Chance didn't know and didn't care, but he was surprised to see the bar was crowded. And glad too. Nobody would pay them any attention.

Today, he called the number on that strip of paper he'd found, and the guy answered. Didn't give his name. The instant the man said hello, Chance knew who he was. That face he'd wished for earlier in the day when he'd stood in the building at the small airstrip had finally popped into his head.

Chance had taken up residence under the awning two hours ago, mostly because it had taken him all day to walk back and rest his aching leg. And then he'd had to work up the fortitude to walk into town. No more cabs for him on this side of his nightmare.

Chance was taking a huge risk by showing his face, but on a dark and rainy night, along with the fact he was much older and stockier, and had a scraggly beard, he would wager that no one would recognize him.

Except for an old acquaintance who wasn't expecting him.

Blevins had been a creature of habit for far too many years. Chance could hardly believe the man was actually sitting in the same booth where he'd sat years before. Like church pews were often claimed by the same parishioners, Blevins had claimed his booth in the bar, and everyone knew not to take it.

Chance slid in across from Blevins and peered at him from under his cap.

"Buddy, you're taking a big risk. This is my booth. My private booth." The man's slurred words told Chance he'd already had plenty of beers before he even showed up to the bar.

Peering at his old connection, Chance said nothing. Would Blevins recognize him? Did he even want him to?

"You don't know me?"

"No. Now get out."

"I'm your delivery man. Name's Chance Carter."

Blevins's eyes grew wide, then he ducked his head. "We're not supposed to meet. What are you doing here?"

"My plane crashed."

"I know. And we're not supposed to ever meet."

"You could have at least come to the hospital and asked me about the package."

"Why would I do that?"

Not the response Chance had expected. Might as well get to the point. "Are you going to kill me like you killed Jim Raymond?"

Chance reasoned that Jim had been waiting at the airstrip. He'd dropped that slip of paper with his contact—the person he would call when he'd retrieved the package. Had he made the call before or after he retrieved the package? Or had he been intercepted?

"I'm going to get up and walk out of here and find another place to nurse a beer in peace. I didn't kill anyone. I'm only a go-between. I'm not supposed to know who gives and who takes. If you know what's good for you, you'll disappear."

"I already did. Hank, don't you remember me?"

Blevins lifted his gaze and peered at Chance long and hard. "I've been paid to forget."

SEVENTEEN

Terra sat in her vehicle on a hidden turnoff with the car's lights off. She'd called the county dispatch to ask for assistance. She was able to lose her pursuer when she topped a hill and immediately turned off on an old dirt road, then flipped off her lights. As a special agent who was also deputized to conduct investigations and make arrests on behalf of the county, she perhaps should turn the tables and face off with her pursuer, but backup would take too long to arrive. Her vehicle wasn't equipped with flashing lights and sirens either.

She couldn't even be certain she was actually being pursued.

No laws had been broken.

She had no idea of the driver's intentions. Follow her? Harm her?

Why would someone follow me?

Or had she misunderstood the driver's actions?

Terra calmed her breathing. Just because she wasn't going to confront the driver didn't mean she couldn't find out who was behind the wheel.

A car sped by on the street. It had to be the same car that had trailed her—she hadn't seen another vehicle on the road between them—and now she would be the one to follow.

She maneuvered the car from its hiding place and onto the

two-lane road, her only intention to get a look at the license plate. The vehicle was too far ahead for her to catch up without drawing attention, but it finally slowed. At the bottom of the hill, brake lights signaled the car had stopped, and then it turned left—the direction of Gramps's ranch.

Her heart pounded.

As she accelerated, she snatched her cell and returned Jack's call, but got no answer. She left him a voice mail to call her. Terra stopped and then turned left, but the vehicle had disappeared. She'd lost them. She banged the steering wheel.

What kind of special agent was she?

She'd been too scared to face off with her shadow. But a healthy dose of fear and wisdom kept people alive. Terra turned around and drove back the other way, looking for another road or turnoff. After a few minutes, she gave up and headed back toward the ranch. By the time she slowed to take the drive up to the house, she still hadn't seen another vehicle. She took the drive slowly as it wound between trees and around a foothill, all the while searching the shadows and any turnouts, remaining on alert to possible intruders.

Spotting no vehicles in hiding, she continued to the house and parked near the door. Motion-sensor lights came on.

Terra released a sigh and contacted the county dispatch, informing them there was no need to send a deputy, after all. The county was big, and the deputies were too few and far between.

Gathering her things, she quickly moved to the front door but still got soaked. Then she unlocked and disarmed the place, and then rearmed it. Now she wished she had opted to drive back to her apartment, which was much smaller and easier to guard.

After flipping on the lights, Terra changed out of her wet clothes and went to the kitchen to retrieve leftovers from the fridge. She was famished.

A knock came at the front door.

Terra's heart leapt to her throat, then she realized whoever the county had sent had probably decided to still make the drive to see if she was all right. She forced her shaking hands to steady.

Whoever had followed her wasn't going to knock on the front door. She gathered her composure, along with her weapon, and slipped quietly down the hall toward the door, where she hesitated.

She should look through the peephole. But what if—

"Come on, Terra," Jack said. "I know you're here. Please open up."

Relief swelled inside. Terra turned off the alarm and opened the door. Jack's outstretched arm held him up against the doorframe, and he was soaking wet.

"Hurry, get in here." She practically yanked him inside, then armed the security system.

Terra glanced at the floor. "You're dripping."

"Sorry. It started raining again as I got out of the truck."

"And you got out of the truck anyway? I'm impressed." *And so relieved to see you.*

"I heard you had some trouble tonight. I was already on my way."

"You were?" Her cheeks warmed. "Why?" He'd been on his way to see her about the investigation, of course. Why did she even have to ask?

"Well, one, you didn't answer my earlier calls."

"I was on my way home, and my cell was out of reach. I did call you back though."

She headed for the kitchen. He followed, dripping all the way. In the kitchen, she turned to face him. He filled her vision, all strength and determination. Her breath suddenly caught in her throat. Terra ignored her reaction. "Let's get you out of that jacket. I'll get you a towel to dry off and a blanket to warm up."

He snatched her wrist and pulled her back. "Tell me what happened."

Terra didn't want to reveal how scared she'd been, and that she felt like such an idiot on top of that. She didn't want to show any weakness in front of Jack.

"I'm getting a towel and a blanket, and when I get back, you can tell me why you were on your way to see me. It must be important." She shrugged free and headed for the bathroom, where she grabbed a towel and a wool blanket from a closet. Terra needed time to think through what had happened tonight and how to explain it. Repeating the words in her head—*someone followed me and I hid and let them get away*—almost made her wonder if any of it had really happened.

Mom would be so proud.

She forced an exhale. Dispatch had already recorded her message, and it was out there. No going back.

Terra returned and handed Jack the towel first. He'd hung his jacket over a chair.

"Thanks." He took it and dried his hair. "I don't need a blanket. I'm not cold."

"Too bad." With a soft smile, she wrapped the blanket around his broad shoulders for good measure, amused that he even allowed her to do so. When she was done, she looked into his face—his deep green eyes penetrating. She was much too close when she hadn't meant to be. At his nearness, her heart thrummed.

Move. Step away. Something.

Jack peered down at her, a wry grin twisting his lips.

Terra forced her feet to move. "Have you eaten?"

"I'm good, thanks."

"Coffee then?"

"Your grandfather's special roasted blend?"

The way he asked the question made her laugh. "I have the plain old store-bought variety too, if you prefer."

"Sure. I'll make the coffee while you finish eating."

"Deal." Terra could talk while she ate the leftover salad. "So, why are you here?"

"I was already over halfway here when I learned you'd made a call for assistance, and then another call that you didn't need assistance. So, I'm here. If you're not ready to talk about what happened, then I'll go first." He saw right through her. Knew her too well and knew that she would talk when she was ready.

"I'm listening."

"I think we might have discovered the murder weapon." Jack poured the coffee before it had finished brewing and explained about the deputy coroner's initial findings, along with his visit to the museum. He pulled out a chair, and she pushed her empty plate forward.

He reached across the table and took her hand. His action sent a familiar charge up her arm. She slipped her hand free, ignoring the realization of just how strong her lingering feelings for this man were. How much had remained. She didn't want those emotions and would do her best to ignore them. This was a man who had loved her, she was sure of it, and had been able to walk away with merely a note. That wasn't something anyone could easily forget, even though she thought she understood why he did it. They were Jack's reasons, and not necessarily good ones.

Okay. No going down melancholy lane. Terra straightened and downed a cup of coffee. She had to push away the exhaustion or else the day would get to her. And her emotional side, her heart, was already trying to take over.

"Now it's your turn. Tell me what's going on. You said someone followed you."

Terra gave a brief summary of the events, and just like how they played out in her head, she felt ridiculous. "I didn't feel comfortable facing off with whoever was pursuing me on a lonely mountain road without some sort of backup, so I got away from them. My plan was to follow them and get the license plate."

Jack crossed his arms.

"Now the whole thing seems ridiculous. Maybe I got it all wrong. They turned when I turned and accelerated when I accelerated, and it was all a coincidence."

"Where's Owen and Robert?"

She shrugged. "They're in Idaho meeting with horse people. Gramps is helping Owen get going with equestrian therapy for veterans."

Jack rubbed the back of his neck. "I don't like that you're here alone tonight."

"My grandfather has a state-of-the-art alarm system. I'll be fine. I have a weapon too, and I know how to use it." She fisted her hands, wishing she could have gotten them on the person who had trailed her tonight.

"Why do you think someone would follow you?"

"That's the billion-dollar question, isn't it? If I was even actually followed."

"You're trained, Terra. If you thought you were being followed, then you were. I suggest you stay at your apartment in town tonight."

"Thanks for your suggestion. If they know about the ranch, they know about my apartment."

"Maybe you're being followed because of one of the cases you're working on."

She shook her head. "Timber theft. A meth lab. That kind of stuff. I'm not close enough to any of it for someone to trail me."

"Past cases?"

Terra considered his question and shook her head.

"Why'd you come back?" Jack asked. "Did something happen in your previous job?"

"No. Nothing from my past job could be related to someone following me. What's with the interrogation?"

He chuckled. "Just doing my job, ma'am." That smile again. "But even if I weren't, I'm just trying to make sure an old friend is okay and going to stay that way."

Clutching her mug, she nodded, appreciating his concern. "Thanks for that. Now, let's talk more about the murder investigation. I'd like to talk to the curator at the museum too, but let's wait on any further communication with anyone there."

"This is a murder investigation."

"That's linked to an artifact cache. The curator or his staff might not be connected to either crime, but then again, someone might be. But I want to know more before we question them. I wish you hadn't gone to him about the knife without me. When I learn more about the things Jim kept, I can use that information while questioning the curator or those working for him. Working very closely on this is the best way to get what we want. To find Jim's killer."

Jack nodded. "The man's been informed he shouldn't leave town in case we have more questions."

"What about the interns and volunteers, other employees?"

"I have deputies working on questioning them in the morning. Relax, Terra. You can use the information we gather when you follow up. You can't be everywhere."

Terra avoided Jack's questioning look and scooted her chair back. She moved to the counter and got more coffee, which would probably keep her awake too late tonight. She calmed her frustration. Jack was right.

She slid back into the seat, wrapping her hands around the hot mug. "Why would Jim's murderer take a knife from a museum to use as a murder weapon and then return it?"

"Maybe he thought it was a way to forever hide the weapon. Who would ever look at the museum's artifacts?"

"Are you telling me he didn't notice the knife's missing tip?"

Jack angled his head. "He might not have noticed it because he was in a hurry or it was dark. Or he still didn't think the weapon would be discovered. But I see you're tracking a different way on this."

She nodded. "I think that if the museum is involved in illegal trafficking along with Jim, that would be the last place the killer would take a weapon from. It leads us right back there."

He crossed his arms. "Criminals make mistakes, Terra."

"Or leading us back to the museum wasn't a mistake at all and could be exactly what the killer wants. He wants to lead us the *wrong* way. Get us looking at the museum to pull our attention off the right path." Though that would be going to a lot of trouble. "How sure are you that the knife is the murder weapon?"

"Almost positive." He whipped out his cell and showed her the images he'd taken, along with the images of the knife tip from the deputy coroner.

"Okay, then. I would be surprised if this wasn't the knife. But this makes no sense to me. Jim's killer went to all that trouble to hide his body, then he put the knife back? He would have been better off throwing the knife into the Grayback River."

"I can't argue with you there." His deep green eyes bored into her.

She never imagined she would be in this position again. Looking into Jack Tanner's intense gaze. Emotions weaved with deep-seated memories rushed forward. Good ones up until that final devastating end.

She pushed herself away from the table. "Look, it's been a long day. I have a big caseload and need to follow up on a couple of them tomorrow."

"What about *this* investigation?"

She wanted to complain about her boss, but she offered a small smile instead. "It's my job, Jack. This case is my priority, but you know how it is. This isn't my only case. I'll see you in the morning to oversee the transfer of the artifacts. And if I don't see you then, I'll call you tomorrow afternoon and you can catch me up. For starters, send me the museum interviews you've gathered."

Jack scooted his chair back and stood, his gaze moving over her face before settling on her eyes. Her breaths quickened. Had she imagined his eyes had stopped at her lips before moving on?

"Call me, text me, email me with new information." She couldn't hold back her smile. "I'm absolutely sure I don't want you driving all the way out to the ranch to deliver the news, especially if it means you ruin your record of never getting caught in the rain."

"Oh, that's already gone. Obliterated." He sent her a crooked smile.

Terra wanted to touch the corner of his dimple. "Why'd you ruin it?" *Just for me?*

"You already know. I had to make sure you were okay. Now that I know you are, stay that way. Be safe tonight, Terra." Jack headed down the hallway. "I'll let myself out."

He didn't know that she'd followed him to turn off the alarm and stood at the door as he ran to his truck in the rain.

Terra closed and locked the door and armed the security system again. She pressed her back against the door and released the breath she'd been holding. Another disaster averted. She was safe for the moment. Safe from the likes of Jack Tanner.

Why had Providence suddenly thrown him back into her life in such a profound way?

EIGHTEEN

Terra plopped down on the sectional with her laptop. She'd made popcorn and hot chocolate and turned on the television so she wouldn't feel so alone in this big, dark ranch house. She considered several romantic comedies and decided she couldn't stomach those tonight. Her one and only serious romance so far had been anything but funny. *Tragic* was the word.

She wouldn't count the debacle during her time with the NPS as a romance.

Terra continued searching. Nope to crime shows and psychological thrillers. Especially with that old picture of her great-great-great—how many greats again?—grandparents hanging on the wall. Something about the photograph made it look as though the eyes followed her everywhere. She'd never liked it as a kid, and sometimes it had given her nightmares. She paid no attention to it as an adult, but alone in this big house on a stormy night, the same stormy night she thought someone had followed her, she suddenly felt those eyes were watching her again.

They were watching her now. She chuckled at the idea that she was definitely not alone if she counted her great-greats to keep her company. A shudder crawled over her and she rubbed her arms, then found a Disney movie that didn't involve a princess.

Except, she knew she wouldn't actually watch the movie. Instead, she opened her laptop. She would work on finding Jim's murderer by looking for possible connections through online auction houses.

She startled when her cell buzzed. Edginess was becoming a thing with her lately.

When she saw it was just Erin, Terra smiled and answered. "It's like you have a sixth sense or something."

"Why?" Erin crunched. Cheetos? "Did you need to talk?"

"Maybe. Lots going on in my head. It helps to have a sounding board. But this is about my investigation, so I shouldn't talk about it, even if you *are* a criminal psychologist and could help me figure this out."

"But that's not really why you could use a sounding board."

Her friend was too sharp. "Hey, before I forget to ask, are you going to make it to Owen's welcome-home party this coming weekend?"

"I'll be there. We have our memorial visit coming up too, remember?"

"I wouldn't forget," Terra said.

"How's Owen been doing since he got back?"

"Better than I expected." Except for those dark moments. "He has a new project now, but I don't want to steal his thunder. I'll let you hear about it at the party."

"Any news from Alex?" Erin crunched again.

"I emailed him. He usually answers quickly, but I haven't heard anything."

"And that disturbs you."

"It should disturb you too. Unless you've talked to him."

"No. I definitely need to be more deliberate."

"He's always been overprotective, like a brother even. Especially once Owen was gone." But then Alex left too. "So I'm worried about him."

Erin yawned. "Maybe he fell in love and that is taking up all his extra time. Wouldn't that be something?"

"He hasn't mentioned anyone."

"Honestly, Terra, I wouldn't worry too much about it. He'll be in touch."

"Says the psychologist." But Terra wouldn't be at ease until Alex contacted her.

The three of them had been so close before. She had the feeling that time and distance were working against them. Was that just life? Or could they be more deliberate about keeping their friendship, their bond, close? She worked hard to keep what she had left of her family—Gramps and Owen—close. Together. To that end, maybe she should move back in with Gramps permanently.

"So, what else is going on?" Erin asked. "Why do you need a sounding board?"

Should she share the news? Or did she need more time to process?

"Come on, I can tell something's eating at you. Something beyond an investigation. Oh, and by the way, I was sorry to hear about Jim's death. Mom told me that he was found in the wilderness. That he jumped off a cliff, but police think it's foul play."

"I can't talk about it."

"The thought gives me the creeps. Wait . . . you can't talk about it or you won't? Because you're a forest service special agent, so you're not investigating, which means you *can* tell me something."

"It's complicated. Can we talk about something else?"

"Okay then. Tell me what's bothering you."

"Jack is back."

Silence met her ears for a few heartbeats, then Erin said, "Wow. By back, you mean he's back in town?"

"He's a detective for the county. And what's more, the murder took place in the national forest and there are other anomalies, other pieces of the investigation that require my expertise. The sheriff deputized me as well."

"This means you're *working* with Jack?"

"Yep."

"Gosh, Terra. How are you handling that? Did you know he was back before you . . . um . . . ran into him? What did you think when you saw—"

"Erin. Stop with the questions." Terra laughed. "I was surprised. I had no idea he was back. I was even more surprised that he was working with the county instead of as an FBI special agent." Oops. She shouldn't have brought that up.

"Right, because he . . . um . . . he left for the job."

Terra wasn't ready to talk to Erin about all of it, just some of it. And sometimes Erin was too analytical. Terra almost missed the woman she'd known before she became a psychologist.

"Look, we're not kids anymore. I'm over the past and I've moved on. We've all grown up and have experience under our belt. Jack too."

Erin said nothing, for which Terra was grateful. Sometimes she knew how to be a true sounding board.

"And Jack, he looks . . ."

"I looked up his picture with the sheriff's department. He looks good, Terra. Really good."

"What are you trying to do?"

"Oh, sorry. I'm not trying to influence you."

"What he looks is hardened. I suspect something happened. Why would he leave the FBI? He claims it's because his aunt has dementia."

"And that could be the reason, but you're not buying it."

"I'm not sure. I think there's something more, but you know what? It's really none of my business."

"But you want it to be your business, don't you?"

Did she? No, she didn't. She couldn't. "Let's just leave it alone for now."

"You know you want to talk about it more."

"Erin, please."

"All right. Promise you'll call me when you're ready to talk more? I promise I won't analyze you."

"Are you sure about that?"

"Positive. I don't bring my job home with me. I don't bring it into my relationships."

"Well, whatever. There isn't anything more to talk about. We've both moved on. I needed to talk about it, and you listened, and I'm done." *Liar.*

"I'll refrain from further comment then." Erin chuckled. "I mainly called to let you know that I'll be there this weekend. Plus, I wanted to see how you're doing with all that's going on."

"Do you feel reassured now?"

"That you're doing all right? Not as much as I'd like, but I know you, Terra. You're made from steel."

Terra forced a laugh. "Good night, Erin. Sleep tight. I'll be in touch soon."

She ended the call.

"You're made from steel."

Like her mother. People had always said that Sheridan Connors had been made from steel. Right. Well, Superman, the "Man of Steel," wouldn't have been killed by an avalanche. But Terra knew people were referring to more than Sheridan's physical capabilities.

Before Mom had left for that fatal SAR mission, she and Terra had been arguing. Terra couldn't even remember what it was about now. But Mom had looked at her and said, "The direction your life takes can often come down to one decision, one moment in time."

Had she had a premonition that something was about to happen? Whatever. It happened. And on the other side of that, Terra feared she didn't have the same mettle her mother had.

But thinking about her fears wouldn't help her investigation, so she set her cell phone on the side table and concentrated on her laptop.

Time to research. Savvier computer techs could dive deeper than Terra was able to, including finding their way around the dark web, but in her last go-around with illegal archaeological digs and trafficking, the criminals had sold items online on the "legal" Internet. Given the current climate of crackdowns on artifact trafficking, one would think those seeking to sell illegal items online would be few and far between, but the reverse was true. Most pieces found online were either fake—not an artifact at all—or had been looted.

Terra started on eBay, but experienced traffickers would know better. The first items to pop up on her screen were labeled as Mayan artifacts, supposedly "ancient and authentic" with paperwork obtained legally by the original owner declaring a provenance through an estate sale. Terra scratched her head.

Could be true.

Probably wasn't.

The laws were decidedly complex, and the potential to sell illegal items online was dangerous but infinite. Terra had been told there had been an increase in this kind of activity on the web, with as many as, if not more than, a hundred thousand antiquities being sold online.

Snatching up her cell from the side table, she stared at her contacts. Besides Jeremy Brand, she had other connections. She could pay a visit to Joey DeMarco, who was still serving time in prison in Colorado. She doubted he would be willing to talk to her, much less give her additional information or names—but the guy was in deep. He'd been willing to negotiate, give up more names in return for a lighter sentence, even though the sentence was light to begin with. That was the downside of trafficking—the money was often worth the risk and a few months or years in jail.

But Terra had a plan. She'd befriended Joey's mother, who was heartbroken to learn what Joey had been doing right under her nose in her own home. The woman had been suffering with a debilitating disease, and Joey had cared for her. Mrs. DeMarco would want her son to cooperate.

She had thought her son was a simple collector of modern art. He attended antique shows and made his connections that way.

That was just it—Jim wasn't only a collector or he would have displayed items in his home. But she had seen no art in his home. Instead, he had wanted to keep this part of his life a secret.

And that secret had killed him.

Who were you working with, Jim?

The credits for the movie she hadn't watched scrolled across the TV. A couple of hours of searching online auction houses and the like hadn't led her to the Native American headdress she'd seen at the cabin. She was going about this all wrong—but she had to try. Terra's eyelids finally grew heavy, and she closed her laptop.

She stood, ignoring the sensation of being watched. It had to be because of the eyes belonging to her great-greats in that old photograph. Time to turn off the lights and TV and go to bed.

Terra reached for the remote. Before she touched it, the television screen turned black. Lights flickered off, shrouding her in darkness.

NINETEEN

Jack knew that Terra would never have agreed to this. Better to sit outside and watch over the house and Terra. He wouldn't be able to sleep anyway. Maybe he was overreacting. Watching over her wasn't his job. She was a trained law officer.

Jack had tried to ignore his gut, so he'd gone home to check on Aunt Nadine. She was safe and sound. Maybe Terra didn't need his help, but he couldn't sleep with the sense that something was wrong gnawing at the back of his mind.

So, he'd parked his vehicle off the beaten path to watch over her. He could see anyone coming and going, that is, if they used the remote drive into the small valley. And now he was glad he'd listened to his instincts.

The security light had gone off at the same time as the lights in the house.

Darkness engulfed him. Clouds hid the moon at the moment.

Jack shifted in his seat.

He texted Terra.

Are you okay? Saw the lights go out.

Then he grabbed a flashlight and his 9mm and climbed from his vehicle. He wouldn't wait for her response to take action.

God, please let her respond. Please let his gut be completely wrong. He'd prefer paranoia to actually being right.

He flipped on his flashlight so he could see where he was going as he continued toward the house. In the distance, horses whinnied from inside the stables. Outside the stables, the security lights were on. Unfortunately, Jack's cell didn't buzz with a reply from Terra. The muscles in his shoulders grew taut.

At the front door he rang the bell and pounded. "Terra, it's me! Are you okay in there?"

Sweat bloomed on his hands. How long should he wait for her to answer? She could be in real trouble. Instead of waiting, he opted to check the perimeter. Someone could have disabled the alarm and found a way in. He hoped she wouldn't think he was the intruder and shoot him.

He sloshed through mud along the bushes next to the house. That sixth sense that had warned him something was wrong grew stronger.

God, please let Terra be okay. Let her be aware and alert.

He couldn't handle something happening to her.

At the back of the house, he continued to check the windows and looked for irregularities. He needed to work quickly. After Terra had spent years trying to persuade him to do so, her grandfather installed a security camera. He grew up in a time when no one needed to lock their doors, especially living in the country in Montana, much less install security alarms.

Why had someone followed Terra tonight to begin with? Did it have to do with their investigation, or was it something entirely different?

He crept around where bushes were high against the window and the woods encroached—a good place to hide and come at the house.

Light flashed from a window.

Gunfire resounded.

"Terra!" he shouted.

A window shattered on the other side of the house. Gripping his weapon, Jack sprinted around the corner.

"Terra, hold on. I'm coming!"

Maybe he should have remained silent in case he was only alerting the intruder to his presence. But that could go either way. He could scare the danger away too—and give Terra hope.

As he rounded the corner, he spotted a figure running into the woods. He wanted to tackle the assailant, but Terra was his first concern. He dashed to the shattered window, avoiding chunks of glass.

She appeared in the window and pointed to the woods. "He's getting away. Let's go."

He wouldn't waste time arguing with her. She pushed the remaining shards of glass from the window using her arm wrapped in a blanket and began climbing out. He helped her through the rest of the way, and together they sprinted across the wet ground, flashlights lighting the way.

The clouds partially cleared, revealing a crescent moon. He flicked off his flashlight. "We can let the moon guide us without becoming a target."

She turned off her flashlight too.

Jack took off deeper into the woods, Terra on his heels. Neither of them spoke until he stopped to catch his breath.

He searched the shadows. "Heading into the woods like this could be dangerous."

"He could ambush us. But I don't think he wants to kill anyone. I think he wants to escape."

"He didn't fire his weapon?"

"No. I told him to stop. I fired a warning shot, but he escaped anyway."

Jack would learn more about what happened later. Right now, they had to focus on getting the intruder.

The moonlight dimmed, then faded completely.

Great. Now what? If he shined his flashlight, he could draw attention to them. And despite what Terra had said—that the intruder probably didn't want to kill anyone—Jack wouldn't risk their lives on it.

They stood back-to-back, weapons ready, and searched the dark woods as the trees dripped with rain. Coyotes howled.

And in the distance, an engine started up.

Jack sagged. "That has to be him."

"Agreed. The neighbors aren't close enough for us to hear their vehicles starting. Let's stay alert in case we're wrong as we make our way toward the road."

Jack started forward, turning his flashlight on. The clouds had covered the moon again. "I don't want to trip over a log. Did you get a good look at him? Tell me what happened."

Hiking next to him, she shined her flashlight around as they rushed in the direction from which they'd heard the vehicle starting. "I was about to turn off the TV when the lights went out. It's weird, because before that, I kept thinking . . . I had that sensation of being watched. You know? I attributed the feeling to that old photograph on the wall. It's always creeped me out."

"But you shook it off because you thought you were being childish."

"Yes. And now I'm even more creeped out to think it wasn't the photograph at all, but someone was in the house with me."

He stopped hiking when they approached the empty road. "Wait. He was in the house while you were there?"

"I'm not sure if he was already there when I got home or if he broke in while I was there, but when the lights went out, I grabbed my gun and searched the house. That's when I caught someone trying to escape through the window. He must have cut the power, hoping to guarantee he stayed in the dark as he made his escape, I don't know."

Or he'd hoped that would hamper the alarm system, depending on what kind was in place. Jack hadn't heard it go off. He would need to check into that. "So, tonight you think someone followed you, but you lost them. And maybe someone was already in the house when you got home."

"I know what you're thinking—if they wanted to harm me, they had ample opportunity."

"Let's get to the road. I don't know, maybe the license plate fell off the car. Maybe we can get techs out here to get the tracks. Something."

At the road they shined their flashlights around.

"Here." Terra's beam focused on a set of tracks.

Jack called and reported the break-in and asked for a casting kit for processing the tracks before more rain washed them away, as well as techs to process the house. Jack explained that the break-in wasn't typical and needed to be fully processed. A law enforcement officer had been targeted.

When he ended the call, she stared at him. "A law enforcement officer was targeted?"

"Yes. You. You were followed, and someone broke into the house where you were staying. Let's not downplay this."

"I have no intention of downplaying it, and I want the entire house processed for fingerprints."

"Of course. We're on it."

She rubbed her arms.

Clearly, tonight's events disturbed her more than she'd been willing to let on. Jack resisted the urge to draw her into his arms.

"I wish I knew what they were after inside the house. I didn't see anything obviously missing, like electronics."

"Does your grandfather keep any cash in the house? A safe, maybe?"

"If he does, I didn't know about it."

Jack and Terra waited in the cold drizzle until, finally, head-lights shone in the distance, along with red and blue flashing lights. Jack directed the vehicle's driver to avoid the tracks left behind so they wouldn't be destroyed.

Deputy Matt Whitmire stepped from his county vehicle, and Jack explained he needed the tracks marked off and protected from contamination while they waited on techs to arrive with the kit.

"Sure thing," Matt said. "It shouldn't take them long to get here."

Jack and Terra left Matt and hiked back to her grandfather's ranch house.

Questions fought for space in his head. Could someone have been waiting in the house, expecting her grandfather or Owen? Could be the intruder hadn't known Terra was tempo-rarily staying there.

"When will Owen and Robert be back?"

"Tomorrow."

"I won't leave you alone tonight." Because he couldn't be sure that she wasn't the target.

TWENTY

ramps stood with his back to Terra as he drank his coffee. He'd used store-bought grounds today instead of the beans he roasted himself. That should tell her something. She joined him in staring out the kitchen window at the mountains, and in the near distance, a couple of horses grazed in the meadow beyond the stables. A picture-perfect scene. Terra understood why he so often stood at this window—the scenery calmed his nerves and gave him peace.

He and Owen had arrived home late this morning to the news of the break-in. Investigators discovered the safe in his office had been broken into.

"What was in the safe, Gramps?"

"The usual. Insurance policies, personal and financial documents, some cash. Nothing special. Someone thought they'd check out the place and look for a safe. Maybe I give the impression I have money." A boisterous laugh erupted. "What was I thinking? A safe behind a picture is probably an easy target. I'll put Owen on moving it for me. Can't trust these yahoos out here. Someone at a bar probably blabbed about putting it in."

"So, you had the safe installed recently?"

"A few months back."

The safecracker had drilled into the locking mechanism

to open it, and with that information, authorities knew the intruder had been in the house and done his work before she got home. To think that someone had been in the house with her, biding his time for a chance to escape, left her unsettled. She rubbed the goosebumps that suddenly rose on her arms, then poured herself another cup of coffee. She would need it after the night she'd had.

"And why did you suddenly decide to install a safe after living here for decades?"

He set his mug in the sink and turned to study her. The skin around his eyes crinkled with his smile. "Well, you know, I added an alarm system. Figured I should go all the way."

He patted her shoulder as he moved away from her. Was he trying to avoid more questions? Gramps headed out of the kitchen.

"They'll find whoever was behind the theft, Gramps. They processed for fingerprints last night and got a cast on the tracks as well as the footprints in the woods and around the house."

He paused, then turned to face her. The lines in his face deepened, making him look ten years older. "You could have been killed because someone wanted in my safe." Gramps closed the distance and hugged her. "You and Owen mean everything to me."

"And you mean the same to us. Family is everything."

"One of these days, the two of you will get the ranch," he said. "You'll get it all."

She scrunched her face. "You'll probably outlive the both of us. You're as strong as those horses out there you love so much. You're not going anywhere anytime soon."

"I sure hope not. I have a campaign I need to focus on in the coming months."

He was really going to run for office. Terra wasn't sure how she felt about that, but it wasn't her life or decision to make, and she wouldn't get into it with Gramps now.

Owen stepped into the kitchen, smelling of horses and hay. He'd gone straight to the stables when they'd arrived this morning. Terra wasn't sure he'd even registered that an intruder had broken in last night.

A big grin spread across his face. "Hey." He eyed Terra. "I need to go wash up. You staying for a while?"

"No. I have to get to work."

"Come on then, I'll walk you out."

Terra rinsed out her mug and put it away, then grabbed her bag and jacket.

Owen strolled with her to her vehicle parked in the circular drive. "Are you okay?"

She opened the door but remained standing. "Sure. I'm wondering about Gramps. Has he been acting strange?"

He shrugged. "I've been away a while, you know. But not that I can tell. He was a huge help to me with the equestrian therapists. You know he has that way about him. Everyone likes him, and respects him. He can make anything happen, if he wants to."

"I'm glad the trip was good for you then. This is going to be great, Owen."

He grinned.

"Do me a favor," she added, "and keep a close eye on Gramps and the house."

"Because of the break-in?"

"Yes."

"I still have skills." Owen winked.

Owen put on a good show to hide his true misgivings, but he would be okay. She believed that. Now and then she saw a flicker of uncertainty in his eyes. He'd been a warrant officer and had planned to be a career helicopter pilot. Flying Apache attack helicopters in the Army was a dangerous career, and Terra was just glad to have him home alive.

Those thoughts she kept to herself.

A contemplative expression took away his smile as he glanced toward the house. Terra suspected he had more to say, but she knew that look. He wouldn't talk to her about it now, and she also knew better than to push him.

She gave Owen a quick peck on the cheek. "Don't forget to take that shower, but you should probably wait until you're done with the horses for the day."

Her cell rang. Jack. She flashed a smile at her brother. "Okay, I need to take this call. I'll see you later. Don't wait up for me."

When she answered her cell, either Jack had ended the call or the signal had dropped. She climbed into her vehicle and reached for the door.

"Terra, wait." Owen crossed his arms.

"What is it?"

"We haven't had a lot of time to talk, and I just wanted you to know that I do plan to get my own place. It's just Gramps. He asked me to stay and I agreed, at least for a while."

"You have to do what's right for you, Owen. If this therapy venture works out for you, then it makes the most sense for you to stay here. I'm sure Gramps welcomes the company. I think he feels lonely. Stay if you want. However, please don't be guilted into staying if things don't work out, but I'm sure they will!"

Terra kept to herself that she'd considered moving back in with Gramps too. She watched her brother walk back to the house. She was so proud of him. So grateful that he'd returned and seemed to be thriving and was throwing his heart into helping disabled veterans thrive as well.

Thank you, God.

Terra steered from the drive as she contacted Jack. "You called?"

"Where are you?"

She didn't like the tone in his voice. "What is it?"

"It's Pauline Raymond. She's had a medical incident."

"What do you mean?"

"A heart attack, maybe."

Terra squeezed the steering wheel. "Oh no." *Oh no, Lord. Please let her be okay.* "I'm heading to the hospital now."

"As of now, Terra, she's unresponsive."

"I can't believe this." Terra's heart seized. Poor Pauline. "Do you think Jim's death was just too much for her?"

"Maybe."

"She's just too fragile for all of this to be coming down on her." This was the part she hated about her job. She thought of Joey DeMarco's mom's reaction when she'd learned about her son's activities. Terra often thought one reason she and Owen never strayed from the straight and narrow path was because neither of them could bear to hurt Gramps and Nanna—or Mom, before she died. Forget Dad. And Pauline didn't know about her husband's collection yet.

"I'll see you at the hospital. Oh, and Terra, be careful." Jack ended the call.

When Terra arrived at the hospital, she made her way to Pauline's room. Family stood outside the door, and all eyes were on Terra as she approached.

Pauline's daughter, Abbie, swiped at tears. "When she woke up, she asked for you. Better get in there."

TWENTY-ONE

ack stood next to the hospital bed while Pauline's family waited in the hallway. He glanced at his watch, hoping Terra would arrive soon. Pauline had woken up and asked to speak to Terra. Apparently, she trusted her more than Jack. Finally, Terra eased through the door. Compassion flooded her wide eyes as she took in Pauline's form.

Slowly she approached the bed, and her lips parted as if she would say something, but no words escaped. At the moment, Pauline had her eyes closed. Jack believed she was conscious but simply resting.

Even though Pauline had asked Terra to come, Jack hoped that his and Terra's presence wouldn't upset her. That could result in medical staff sending them away. Pauline squeezed his hand, confirming his assumptions. "Mrs. Raymond, Terra is here to speak with you."

Pauline opened her eyes. Terra stood over her with a tenuous smile. "Pauline. I'm here." She leaned in. "You asked to see me?"

Pauline nodded. Terra's smile lifted. Jack suspected her brightened demeanor was merely for Pauline's sake. Seeing the woman looking this fragile—near death's door—when only two days before she'd been strong even in her grief had to be ripping Terra up inside. He knew, because his insides were in turmoil too.

Terra pulled up a chair to sit closer so she wasn't looking down on Pauline. The bed rails and tubes and machines prevented Terra from getting as close as she probably wanted. Jack had asked the woman's family to wait outside of the room while he questioned her. They had to be growing impatient.

"Pauline." Terra kept her voice low and gentle. "Please tell me why you wanted to see me. Is there something I should know?"

Jim's widow nodded as tears leaked from her eyes. "I'm one of those wives who ignored the truth."

"What do you mean?" Terra asked. Her tone was gentler than he could have spoken on his best day, and for that, he was glad she was involved.

"My husband was cheating on me." Pauline choked out the words. Terra's gaze flicked to Jack, then back to Pauline.

"Do you know the name of the woman he was cheating on you with?"

She shook her head, her eyes tearing up again. He wasn't sure if she knew the name and simply didn't want to speak it, or if she truly didn't know.

"Do you believe this has to do with his death?" Jack asked.

"That key." Pauline's voice hardened. She had gained control. "That key he kept in his wallet. The cabin. I followed him once and found the cabin. I knew he was meeting his lover there. I didn't wait around. I wasn't brave enough to see who she was. She could be anyone. Find her. If he was found dead in those woods, she had to have killed him."

Jack's heart sank. Pauline could be onto something, but Terra and Jack had theorized that Jim's death involved the artifacts they'd discovered. Surely it couldn't be as simple as an affair taking a turn for the worse.

He pursed his lips and held Terra's gaze. She'd wanted them to hold close the information about the items discovered in the cabin until she could question Pauline.

If Jim was having an affair, then perhaps the items in the cabin belonged to his mistress instead. Jack wanted to ask Pauline if she knew about the items or if she had ever seen them before, but he would hold off for now.

"Don't worry, we'll find your husband's killer," Terra said. "I have a few questions for you, though. Are you feeling up to answering them?"

Pauline closed her eyes for a few moments. Jack released her hand and almost backed away, giving up, but then Pauline's eyes popped open. "Okay."

"Was Jim interested in collecting Native American artifacts?"

Pauline frowned. "Not until he met her."

Interesting. Pauline knew something about the pieces, after all. Good. "We need a name. Anything you can tell us."

"Don't know her name. I took her picture. It's in my . . ." Pauline's eyes fluttered. She convulsed.

Jack's heart seized. Terra pressed the emergency button. "Help. Someone help!"

Nurses rushed into the room, and Jack pulled Terra out of the way and down the hallway. At his back, he felt the killing stares of Pauline's family.

TWENTY-TWO

At the window overlooking the parking lot, Terra held a cup of scalding coffee that Jack had purchased from a vending machine.

"I can't believe she's gone," she said. "I can't believe any of it."

Pauline's family could very well blame Terra and Jack for upsetting her. If Pauline had been allowed to rest, she possibly could have improved enough to survive. Still, Jim's wife had asked for Terra. Perhaps she suspected she might die and take the secret she held to the grave with her if she didn't speak up.

Jack tossed his cup into the garbage can. "Come on. Let's get out of here."

Terra allowed Jack to lead her to an elevator. Her defense mechanism had kicked in, leaving her feeling numb. At the moment, she didn't want to think or feel. The next thing Terra knew, she was sitting in his vehicle instead of hers and staring at her now-tepid cup of bad coffee.

"Try to pull yourself together," he said.

"I am. I need to grieve. To process." All this death. And for what?

Jack started his vehicle. "Pauline gave us something. We need to act on it."

Terra rubbed her temples. "She believed Jim was cheating on her. The thing is, I'm not so sure he was cheating in the way she thought. I hate that she died thinking he was having an affair. I should have said so. Maybe she wouldn't have gotten so upset that she—"

"You don't know that he wasn't. Maybe the woman Pauline saw him with is the person who got him involved in trafficking artifacts. Pauline hinted at that."

"We need to find the picture Pauline mentioned. Maybe it will turn up while we're searching Jim and Pauline's home for additional artifacts."

Jack nodded. "Or we could simply ask a family member about the picture, but I don't think they're too happy with us at the moment. Considering the circumstances, I got a warrant earlier to search the home. We need more than Pauline's permission now."

"Then let's head to the house and see what turns up."

He steered from the hospital parking lot and seemed to be caught up in his own thoughts. Just as well, since Terra needed to process all that had happened in the space of a few days. A half an hour later, Terra and Jack entered Pauline's home to join the evidence techs who were already there. Any discoveries could help lead them to his killer.

Terra stood in the master bedroom and took in the photographs on the wall.

Abbie entered the bedroom, startling Terra. "The detective told me I could find you in here." She let her bag slide from her shoulder onto the bed. Releasing a grief-filled sigh, she eased onto the edge and hung her head.

"I'm so sorry for your loss." Though inadequate, the words came from her heart.

"You're looking for a picture," Abbie said.

Terra assumed Jack had told her. "Yes."

"Mom kept important stuff in her jewelry box." Abbie lifted her red-rimmed eyes to the mahogany box on the dresser.

Terra wanted to somehow reach out and comfort the woman, because she understood how it felt to lose both parents within a short time. But she said nothing. Abbie needed comfort from someone else. "Thank you for your help. We'll do everything we can to find your father's killer."

"I know you will. I'll help you. Anything you need. In a way, I think whoever killed my father also killed my mother."

Abbie rose and moved to the box. She pressed her hands around the lid and hesitated. "Mom has a tall jewelry box in the closet where she keeps her long necklaces. This one contains social security cards and a few special things she held dear. I don't know why she didn't keep stuff like this in a safe or filing cabinet."

She opened the lid and revealed a felted drawer containing rings, bracelets, earrings, and a few collectible coins. Abbie lifted the top drawer completely out. Beneath it rested the social security cards and a few envelopes. Abbie seemed familiar with the items in the box. She searched until she pulled out a small manila envelope and eyed it.

"Everything else I know about. But I haven't seen this before. It must be new. Maybe this holds what you're looking for."

She offered it to Terra.

"Why don't you open it?" Terra asked.

"Mom is gone. She isn't going to care anymore. You go ahead."

"What about you? Are you sure you want to see this?"

Abbie shrugged. "I might as well know what got her so upset, but I'd prefer for you to open it."

She handed it over, and this time Terra took it. Abbie stepped back as if holding out hope that nothing incriminating was inside.

Terra opened the envelope and pulled out two photographs. Abbie gasped.

Jim stood with a blonde-haired woman in her forties. Terra wasn't sure the photograph revealed the two were together romantically. "Have you seen this woman before?"

Abbie stared intently at the image as if trying to comprehend that her father would actually have an affair. "Not only do I not know who she is, I don't think Mom took these pictures."

"Why do you say that?"

"They're too good, for one thing."

Terra eyed Abbie. "And she never said anything to you about this?"

"Before you arrived at the hospital, she'd been in and out of consciousness and mumbled that he'd been cheating on her. I don't think anyone else heard her. I can't fathom that my father would cheat on Mom. He loved her too much. Maybe she misunderstood what these pictures meant."

Exactly what Terra was thinking. "Can I hold on to the photos for now?"

"Sure."

"What about your father? What were his hobbies?"

Abbie moved to sit on the edge of her parents' bed again. "He worked in insurance. Was gone a lot. Mom was a secretary at the school. Occasionally they'd go out for dinner. It's not like he painted or crafted fishing flies or built model trains."

Terra blew out a breath. "I'd wanted to talk to your mother about what we discovered at the cabin, but that can't happen now."

Abbie rubbed her arms. "I'm here to help. I want whoever killed my father—if it's this woman in the picture—I want this person found and to get what they deserve."

Terra grabbed her cell and swiped over the screen a few times. She turned her phone so Abbie could see the images. "Ever seen any of this before?"

Abbie's pupils dilated, and she pulled the cell closer. She shook her head. "It just looks like pottery to me. Where did you find it? What does it have to do with what's happened?"

"The pots are artifacts."

Abbie shrugged. "So? What are you saying?"

"It looks like your father might have been trafficking these pieces."

"And you think this might have something to do with his murder?"

"It's too soon to know for sure, but I'm looking for his connections regarding the pottery he kept at the cabin."

Terra showed her the picture of the headdress. Abbie shook her head, clearly stunned.

"I can't believe this." Abbie pressed her face into her hands. "I didn't even know about that cabin. I didn't know he was keeping artifacts. It's like I didn't even know my father. Maybe he was having an affair too."

Anguish pinged Terra's heart. She hated being the one to deliver the painful news. She hoped she would learn that Jim wasn't having an affair. Terra left the room to give Abbie time alone and found Jack standing in the center of the living room on his phone.

He shook his head, staring at the floor as he listened. While she waited, Terra mentally listed everything she would need, including Jim's phone records. Maybe obtaining Pauline's phone records would be necessary too.

Terra moved to look out the window at the backyard.

Jack joined her at the window. "You look like you're a thousand miles from here."

She'd been about a thousand miles away in her mind, for sure, remembering something she'd learned in the sting operation with the NPS. "Did your guys bring shovels?"

Jack turned to her, a question in his eyes. She held his gaze.

She couldn't hold back her grin. "That's right, we might need to dig."

"Why would someone bury artifacts?"

"I knew someone who reburied items on his own property. Then over time, he could dig them up again and claim he'd found them on his private land."

"And you think that's a priority right now?"

"It won't take long. The yard is small. I'll give it a once-over, and if I see anything suspicious, then we can dig. If not, we'll revisit later—if necessary." Terra left Jack standing at the window and headed into the backyard. She lifted her face to soak up the sun, then gazed at patches of grass. She crouched to get a different perspective.

Footfalls behind her signaled Jack's approach. "Well, am I going to need a shovel?"

"I don't think we're going to find anything here."

He crouched next to her. "How can you say that? This yard's a mess. I think we should dig."

"If Jim had buried anything back here, he would have gone out of his way to make the yard look like someone cared."

"I'm sorry, but I'm not coming to the same conclusion." Jack stood. "My yard would look like this if I were the type to hide something."

Terra stood as well. "You're welcome to dig then. But I have a lead I want to follow, and then I'd like to visit the museum."

"Did you find the picture?"

"Yes." She removed the manila envelope from her jacket pocket and pulled out the photographs. "I don't know who the woman in the picture is, but I think a PI took these photographs."

TWENTY-THREE

Jack sat at his desk with Terra and copied the museum interview reports to give to her. Terra, meanwhile, looked up all the private investigators in the area. How many could there be? Pauline could have hired someone from another county for more privacy, especially since the general consensus was that everyone knew her husband. How could they not since his face was plastered on billboards around town and the county?

Nathan swiveled in his chair at his desk. "Hey, Terra. It's good to see you."

"You too." Terra didn't look up from her laptop.

Jack couldn't tell whether she was that absorbed in what she was reading or she held a grudge against Nathan because of his falling out with her best friend, Erin.

"What are you guys doing?" Nathan rolled his chair over to Jack's desk.

"We believe Pauline Raymond hired a PI to take these pictures." Jack laid out the two of Jim and the blonde. "We're trying to figure out who she hired. I'm working on getting Pauline's phone records."

Nathan scrunched up his face as he rolled back to his desk.

"Ah, man. A PI reported a break-in at her office yesterday. She called the police, but her business is just outside the city limits. Deputy Pendergrass—Linda—took the information."

Jack angled his face to Nathan. "And you're bringing this up because . . ."

"I should have told you sooner. The PI mentioned she had worked with Mrs. Raymond. Linda thought that could be important. She passed it on to me to pass on to you."

Nathan lifted a paper from his desk. "See? Now I'm passing it on." Then he handed it over to Jack, making that painful scrunched face again. "I'm sorry?"

"I wouldn't worry about it. The timing works out."

"The PI's name is Dallas Simpson." He briefly read the report as he stood and pulled on his jacket.

Terra stood as well. "Let's go."

Fifteen minutes later, they found the address—an old dilapidated building just outside of town. He parked at the curb and met Terra on the sidewalk. She glanced up at the three-story building with old fire escape stairs. She was probably thinking like he was that Dallas Simpson's private investigation business wasn't paying her enough.

He opened the door, and Terra stepped through with a smile. "Thanks."

She paused in the quiet hallway. "Should we have called to see if she's even here?"

"Oh, come on. You know you prefer the face-to-face surprise approach."

"Only she won't be that surprised to have a detective asking more questions."

"I'm sure she'll appreciate us looking into the break-in with more interest." He gestured for her to go ahead.

She led the way down the corridor and noted many of the offices were empty but not all. An insurance agency occupied one office, a bookkeeper and tax accountant another.

They headed up the stairs and, on the second floor, Jack knocked on the door with a window displaying the stenciled words *Dallas Simpson, Private Investigator.*

"Come in," a woman called.

Jack opened the door and held it for Terra again. A petite brunette woman was stuffing items into cardboard boxes. She paused as they made introductions, then Jack and Terra sat in the two chairs across from Dallas's desk.

"We're here to talk to you about a recent client—Pauline Raymond."

Dallas opened her mouth but hesitated, then said, "I thought you'd come to ask more questions about the break-in I reported yesterday."

Jack shared a look with Terra. "There could be a connection."

Dallas eased into the seat behind her desk and rubbed her head. "I don't know how much information I'm free to share."

"Did Pauline hire you for litigation purposes?" Terra asked. "If not, then there's no attorney-client privileges preventing you from sharing with us, if that's your concern."

"No, she didn't. But it's just not particularly good for business for me to share with the cops, though of course, we do like to work together."

Jack eased forward. "Mrs. Raymond passed away."

The investigator gasped. "I, oh no . . . I'm so sorry. I didn't know. Please, can you tell me what happened?"

"It appears she died of natural causes," Jack said. "But her husband was murdered. We'd like to know what you discovered when you followed him."

Dallas leaned back in her chair and closed her eyes for a few moments before opening them. "I heard that Jim had been murdered. But I still can't believe any of this."

"I know it's hard to fathom," Terra said. "Anything you can tell us could help. For starters, could you share what Pauline hired you to do and why, and what you learned."

Dallas gave a quick nod and shifted forward. "Most of my cases are cheating spouses. I do get some insurance fraud cases on occasion. Pauline, God rest her soul, came to me. She had a hard time talking without crying. She wasn't angry as much as shattered. She had hoped I would put all her fears away. She suspected Jim was cheating. I thought it was strange because he's an insurance agent. I mean, he's gone in the evenings and on weekends a lot. So that would be normal for their lives and had been for decades."

"Why do you think she suspected him?"

"She never told me. I suppose that her suspicions were in the nuances of daily living. The small things. She sensed they were growing apart. Maybe she thought he was thinking about another woman when he was with her. He was distracted. Who can know? I followed him around town. I was almost convinced that he wasn't cheating and I would have good news to deliver."

"Almost convinced? What happened?" Jack steepled his hands.

"It's not easy to follow someone out on a state highway and then out on a mountain road without them spotting a tail."

"But you managed."

"Yes. I wondered if Jim was onto me the way he was taking obscure county roads and seemed to be going in circles as if he was trying to shake me. So, I lost him on purpose. I turned off on a county road and waited."

Dallas frowned. "I came back around and headed in the direction I'd seen him, and then I spotted his vehicle parked at a trailhead. I hid my vehicle farther up the road and headed into the forest toward the trail with my camera."

"Were there other vehicles at the trailhead?" Jack asked.

"Two others. Not that surprising. I took pictures of the vehicles and got the license plate numbers. I followed Mr. Raymond off the trail by half a mile. I hung back a good distance so he didn't know I had trailed him, and I captured him talking to someone with my telephoto lens."

Terra retrieved the photographs and slid them across the desk. "This woman?"

"Yes." Dallas held Terra's gaze. "You knew this already."

"I only have these two photographs and no context. If you have more, please share them. This is all we could retrieve at Mrs. Raymond's home. Have you learned this woman's name?"

"I have her name, but Pauline didn't want to know that information. Honestly, these photographs don't prove he was having an affair. He could simply have stumbled on another hiker and had a conversation."

"But you don't think that's what happened."

"I don't. Jim . . . well, he didn't seem the type to hike. Though he could have been talking to a stranger, I got the sense that he was in a deep conversation with her."

"Can we see the rest of the photographs?"

"I can tell you her name, but as for the rest, my office was broken into and many of my files were stolen."

"Let me guess." Jack stood. "Everything on Jim Raymond is gone?"

"I didn't have that much, but yes, it's gone."

"What do you think is going on?" Jack asked. "Why would Jim Raymond's files be important?"

"I don't know. Jim never did anything suspicious other than meet with this woman. I only surveilled him for three weeks."

Interesting. "Why are you packing up your office?"

Dallas rose and walked around the small space, peering into opened boxes. "Business hasn't been so great. I'm in the bad part of town, and my office was ransacked. Files were stolen. Honestly, it's not worth the hassle to struggle so much. I had already been mulling the idea of switching careers when this happened. So, I'm moving to Georgia to work with my sister. She owns a catering business."

Terra smiled. "Can you cook?"

"I guess we'll find out." Dallas rubbed her arms and stared at the boxes.

Jack knew that look. "Do you feel like you're in danger? Is that the real reason you're leaving?"

She slowly looked to him and nodded.

He figured as much. Jim had been murdered. Dallas could be a target because she'd been following him. "I'll put a deputy on you until you're safely away, but please know that if any of this is connected to Jim's murder, you could be subpoenaed to testify later."

Gratitude emerged in her eyes. "Thank you."

"Is there anything you haven't told us?"

She reached into a box. "I had one file still in my car. Though it's not on Jim Raymond, it's related."

She tossed a manila folder onto the desk, and it slid across. Jack opened it and found a couple of photographs of the woman with someone else. "You followed her?"

Dallas nodded. "I was only hired to follow Jim, but I didn't feel like I had the complete picture. I wanted to somehow prove to Mrs. Raymond that Jim wasn't having an affair. I don't believe the pictures I took of them together would prove that either way. Two days ago, I decided to follow the woman he met. Her name is Neva Bolz, and she's a consultant with Star Oil Company. The next thing I knew, my office had been ransacked."

TWENTY-FOUR

Terra stepped into the hall and listened to the voice mail her superior had left. Dan had called to check up on her about the break-in last night and her 911 call to dispatch. Oh brother. She wished she hadn't made that call. But a dark and lonely mountain road wasn't the place to risk a confrontation alone.

While she listened to the message, she peered through the window in the door and watched Jack help Dallas tape up boxes. He'd insisted on waiting until a deputy arrived to protect Dallas. Sure, this was all part of Jack's job, but he truly seemed to care about Dallas's well-being, and right now he was going beyond the call of duty. He was listening to his instincts, and his gut told him she wasn't safe.

Something had changed him. Not that he didn't care about people before, but Terra wasn't sure *this* Jack could have left her without facing her like the old Jack had. Without looking her in the eyes and telling her one last goodbye. She had the feeling that he'd found whatever it was he'd been looking for. That he'd found himself.

Shrugging off the errant musings, she thought ahead to what came next. She was anxious to head to Neva Bolz's home.

In the meantime, she would listen to the rest of her voice mail messages, then she would search the Internet for anything she could find about Neva and the company she worked for.

The next message was from her neighbor, Allie. Uh-oh. Had something happened? She didn't take the time to listen to the message and instead returned the call.

Allie answered. "Hey, Terra. Did you get my voice mail?"

"I didn't listen, actually. Is everything okay?"

"Yeah, sure. I didn't mean to scare you. But I wanted to make sure you're still alive."

Terra snorted a laugh. "Yeah, about that. I meant to come home sooner. Sorry I haven't been back. What's up?"

"Sudoku has been rubbing up against the door. I can tell she really wants to get out. Probably wants to go home and see you."

"Aw, my cat actually misses me? I didn't think that was possible."

Allie laughed. "Of course it's possible. But don't worry. I don't mind watching out for her, but I thought you should know."

"Thanks, Allie. I owe you. I'm in the middle of an investigation right now. I'll see you and Su soon. Let her know I love her." When she'd taken this position six months ago and moved back to Montana, she hadn't wanted to be alone and had thought a cat would be the easiest pet. What had she been thinking?

Maybe staying with Gramps wasn't such a great idea, though she'd initially convinced herself that she needed to be there for Owen. It was only forty-five minutes away. But that was still forty-five minutes away. As long as Su was being cared for, she would wait until she had a decent break to return to her apartment.

Footfalls echoed in the hall behind her. As she turned, she reached for her weapon in her shoulder holster, then relaxed when she saw it was Deputy Linda Pendergrass. Linda, who was in her midthirties, greeted Terra in her no-nonsense manner, then entered Dallas's office. Terra waited in the hallway as Linda and Jack spoke about protecting Dallas.

The door opened and Jack exited, closing the door behind him, a serious expression on his face. He pursed his lips and turned to walk down the hall.

She kept pace with him. "You're that worried about her?"

He angled his head. "Aren't you?"

"Actually, I was holding out hope that you would come up with a valid reason she didn't need to be concerned about her safety."

"I think she's smart and leaving town is the right way to go. I don't know that her life is in danger, but Aunt Nadine always says an ounce of prevention is worth a pound of cure."

Terra chuckled. "I think Gramps has said the same a few times."

"That brings me to you. Everything okay? You haven't noticed anyone following you again, have you?"

"Not this morning when I headed to the hospital. I could have been mistaken about the tail last night."

He glanced at her. "Right. And then your grandfather's house was broken into, you inside."

"They were after his safe, not me."

He flashed her a concerned look.

They bounded down the last set of steps.

Outside, the sun shone in a bright blue, cloudless sky. The days seemed to start that way, but eventually scattered thunderstorms developed, leaving some places drenched with the potential for flash floods and other places bone dry.

They climbed into Jack's SUV.

"We're heading to question Neva Bolz now, right?"

"Yep. I have her address. But we'll drive through and grab burgers on the way. I'm famished."

Her stomach rumbled at his comment. "Sounds good." Terra was anxious to question the woman and didn't need her stomach growling in the process.

They purchased the fast food and ate as he headed toward Neva's, finishing up quickly.

Jack glanced her way, his features drawn. "I have to tell you I have a bad feeling about this."

She sighed. "I had hoped it was just me. I'm with Dallas in that I don't think Neva's relationship with Jim was romantic. Nor would he be meeting with an insurance client in those woods. Pauline made mention that Jim wasn't into the artifacts until he'd met 'that woman.'"

"Right, so Neva Bolz could be another connection to the things we found in his cabin."

"And to his murder," she added. "Except I can't picture her committing the crime, then transporting him to the cliff and dropping him over." Terra stared at her cell, hoping to bring up more information about Neva Bolz on the drive.

"If she killed him, she had help. Disposing of the vehicle also would have required help. The vehicle was driven to the lake. Whoever was driving would need a ride back, unless he or she hitchhiked back or stole a vehicle."

Jack slowed as he steered to the home address and then parked at the curb of the upper-middle-class neighborhood. Neva Bolz's home backed up to the forest.

"Her car is in the driveway. The same car that's in the photograph. She's home." Terra opened the vehicle door.

Jack met her at the sidewalk. "Let's not waste time. I'll get right to the point. If there's a door into questions about the artifacts, then I'll let you ask those. Depending on her reaction, we might invite her downtown for a thorough interrogation."

At the porch, he lifted his shoulders and rang the doorbell. He waited a few moments, then rang it again. Still, no one opened the door. "Maybe she isn't in a hospitable mood."

Terra knocked. "Ms. Bolz, I'm Special Agent Terra Connors, and County Detective Tanner is here with me. We just want to ask you a few questions."

Terra listened for signs of movement, trying to determine if the woman was inside. Someone could have picked her up, which would explain why her car was still in the driveway though Neva wasn't home.

A muffled sound came from inside—glass breaking? She and Jack drew their weapons at the same moment. He signaled that he would check the perimeter. She hopped from the porch and crept around the front of the home but couldn't see through the windows because of the mini blinds covering them.

"Stop. Police!" Jack's voice echoed off the neighbor's house.

Terra ran around the back.

A man in a gray hoodie sprinted into the woods at the back of the houses, and Jack ran after him. Terra called for backup. This was a repeat of last night, only at someone else's home. Terra wanted to follow, to be Jack's backup, but she needed to check to see if Neva was in the home, after all.

That bad feeling she and Jack had shared overwhelmed her.

TWENTY-FIVE

hasing a man through the woods was becoming too familiar. Jack sprinted, jumping over logs cutting through the
undergrowth. Small branches slapped him, but his laser
focus remained on the chase.

The man disappeared among the dense trees.

Jack stopped behind a thick trunk to hide. He leaned over
his thighs and caught his breath, then examined his surround-
ings to get his bearings.

Weapon at the ready, Jack crept forward, grateful for a quiet
carpet of pine needles in this section of the woods. The canopy here kept the forest in shadows. Movement fifteen yards
ahead drew his attention. The man's shadow told Jack what
he needed to know.

The man leaned against a tree, probably catching his breath
too.

Jack crept forward until he reached the tree, the criminal
leaning on the other side of it. He feared the man could hear
his pounding heart or even the sweat as it slipped down his
temples.

Here goes everything.

Weapon at the ready and his arms stretched in front of him,
he swept around the tree. "Police."

Gone.

The man had slipped away.

Jack suddenly felt exposed. He crouched and searched the area but saw no one. He maneuvered to stand behind another tree. He had to get a lead on this guy. He'd thought he had the advantage, but he'd made a mistake.

The muzzle of a gun pressed against the base of his head. "Toss your gun."

The man, who spoke in a low, whispering rasp, quickly took several steps back and, Jack was sure, out of his reach. The man remained behind Jack so he couldn't get a good look at his face.

Jack lifted his hands and let his 9mm dangle from his finger.

"I said *toss* the gun." Again, the rasping voice.

Frowning, Jack did as he was told. This wasn't going down the way he had imagined. He had to turn this around—and fast. He considered taking the action route—diving and rolling to grab his gun again. Could he disarm this man without getting shot in the head?

Or he could use the psychological method. "You shoot a cop, and they'll hunt you down. You'll be looking over your shoulder until the last day of your short life."

"I'm already looking over my shoulder."

"Who are you?" Jack wanted answers, and he needed to distract the man. "Come in, and we can help you. Whoever you're running from, we can help you."

"You can't help me."

In his peripheral vision, Jack saw movement.

Terra.

Blood roared in his ears. If Terra drew the man's attention, he would shoot Jack first and ask questions later. Or she might shoot and kill the man, and they would still need answers.

He would have to risk it. No other choice.

A twig snapped.

Jack threw himself to the ground and rolled as gunfire rang

out—the man had taken a shot at Terra and was now on the run. The guy dashed through the trees. Once again, the chase was on. Jack snatched up his gun and sprang to his feet as Terra rushed forward, gasping.

"Let's go." He took off after him.

After twenty minutes of running and searching the woods, he stopped to visually search the area as he caught his breath.

"I think we . . . lost . . . him." She spoke the words between gulps of air.

"He was running for his life." Jack still hadn't caught his breath yet.

"You want to keep searching?" she asked.

"Yes. Let me call in search helicopters and K-9s." Jack had a feeling it was probably already too late. He ground his molars. He had let the guy slip through his fingers.

"Good." Terra exhaled. "Because right now, it looks like he's a murderer."

His stomach clenched at her words. He shot her a look. "Neva Bolz?"

Terra gave him a grim nod. "When you ran after him, I had to check the house to make sure Neva didn't need assistance, and . . . I found her in the kitchen."

"I'm sorry."

"A police cruiser, responding quickly to my initial call for backup, appeared moments later, and then I left to find you. At first I thought I'd lost you, but I heard a lot of movement and followed that. Then I heard your voice." Lifting her hand, she shaded her eyes.

I'm sorry you had to be the one to find her.

Jim, and now Neva?

God, help us to catch him before someone else dies. Help us find him. Help us dig up the root of this whole mess.

TWENTY-SIX

The local police had locked down the crime scene and established the perimeter, as well as the path of contamination at Neva's house, before Jack and Terra returned. They'd needed to sign the crime-scene security log. The county sheriff's office would take the lead on the case since Neva's murder was likely connected to Jack's investigation.

Terra and Jack had donned sterile crime-scene garb, and she stared down at Neva Bolz's body on the wood parquet as they waited for the deputy coroner—Emmett Hildebrand—to arrive from the other side of the county.

This felt all too familiar—Terra waiting with Jack for the coroner.

Additional deputies and local police officers continued to search the woods and national forest on foot and by helicopter while the local police assisted in tracking down Neva's next of kin.

Squeezing her eyes shut, Terra released a slow breath. *Jim Raymond, what did you get yourself into?*

When two techs entered the space, she stepped away from Neva's body. Neva's murder could be connected to the stolen archaeological items, and it was time for Terra to conduct a search of her own.

Terra kept to the path of contamination marked by tape.

Jack spoke with the police detective, and they compared notes. Relieved to be away from yet another body, she drew in a few breaths but failed to calm her nerves. Grief and heartache for the loss of life throbbed in her chest.

She found herself standing in Neva's cream-colored living room. Cream carpet. Cream walls. Cream chairs. And nothing more. Jack approached and stood next to her but said nothing as he peered at his notebook. She hadn't seen him with it at Pauline's house. She had an investigations notebook in her bag but often entered information later.

Popping the notebook closed, he looked at her, catching her staring at him. He held her gaze a few moments longer than necessary.

"I can't help but notice this house is completely devoid of personality," she said. "I can't get a sense of who Neva was."

Jack stuck the notebook under his arm. "I thought Erin was the psychologist."

Terra shook her head. "You know as well as I do that getting to the bottom of any crime calls for understanding human nature. Who was Neva that someone would murder her? There are no pictures on these walls. No photographs of children or a husband."

He rubbed his chin. "Maybe she traveled for her job and wasn't home much."

"Maybe. But usually when someone travels that much, they live near a bigger airport."

"You're assuming she left the state. I was thinking she drove, sticking closer to home."

Terra shrugged. "I guess you need to find out what she did for Star Oil Company."

"She was a consultant," he said.

"What does that even mean?" Consultants could be hired for numerous reasons, including under-the-table kinds of reasons.

Jack sidled up to her. "If we're going to look around, we'd better get to it."

"Did the detective have any information for you?"

"Just preliminary pictures, to establish the scene, and main evidence areas, which include only the kitchen and her bedroom. I'll follow you through the house to look for clues, and then we'll get out of the way so the evidence techs can find the invisible-to-the-naked-eye kinds of things."

"Right. You're right." Terra had a feeling that at some point other agencies might want a piece of this investigation. This could quickly outgrow Jack's county and her national forest. But they weren't there yet.

She led the way down the hall and stopped at a coat closet. With a gloved hand, she opened the door and peered inside. Interestingly empty. Then into each bedroom. Only one room had an actual bed, and it was covered in a beautiful teal-colored duvet. The color instantly brought to mind the colorful Native American headdress they'd discovered in Jim's cabin. A suitcase lay opened on the bed, revealing a few of Neva's neatly folded clothes. Slacks and blouses suitable for a business trip.

"Well, either she was just getting home from a trip, or she was heading out," Terra said.

"Or maybe she was running scared."

Terra opened the closet door to find a few business clothes, along with pumps. "We have a picture of her in the woods near that cabin with Jim. We should find hiking boots in here, or at least something besides pumps. She didn't hike up that trail in heels." Terra turned to find Jack staring at her. "What do you think?"

"That we've only scratched the surface."

"If that." She shared a look with Jack, and together they finished walking through the home.

"What do you see?" Jack asked.

"I see an oddly empty place."

"I agree."

"No love for art or family." That in itself was a mystery that begged to be solved. "I don't think this was her real home. Just a stopping-off point."

"We'll be looking into everything we can learn about Neva Bolz, but I've seen all I need to see here for now," Jack said. "We need to talk to her family, friends, and work and business associates. Get her phone records and her computer. Unfortunately, I didn't see a cell, a laptop, or a desktop computer here, which is odd."

They exited the house and headed down the sidewalk, passing multiple deputies and police officers. The deputy coroner had arrived as well. This time, there was no doubt the woman had been stabbed to death. They didn't have to speculate like they had with Jim.

At the end of the sidewalk, they stood together at the grille of Jack's vehicle.

He hung his head. "Sheriff's going to love this. The county is already stretched. He'll need to call for assistance from other agencies. At the very least, the state."

"And that bothers you?"

"Too many hands in the pie. Maybe we can find answers sooner. I don't know. I just need to think. Give me a few minutes?"

"I'm not going anywhere since you're my ride."

He gave her a weak grin of appreciation. "I need to make a couple of calls."

She could do the same. Jack got on his cell. Terra guessed he was requesting the additional information on Neva Bolz. Terra called her boss and per usual got Dan's voice mail. She left a message like she always did, and considering the murder and her work with the county detective, she wouldn't make it into the office today, after all.

She was a lone special agent in a huge region with her own

forests to oversee. If she had to investigate this case alone—if she wasn't working with Jack—it could take her much longer to get to the truth. Leads would grow cold while she searched.

Jack stared at the house while he spoke on his cell. Terra heard parts of his conversation as he talked to his sergeant and then his sheriff, who were both on the way to the crime scene. Stubble had emerged on his cheeks. He'd rolled up his sleeves and thrust one hand into his pocket, while the notebook remained tucked tightly under his arm. She was so proud of Jack. She'd known he would go far in life. Terra was drawn to him before, and now, even after all this time, she remained drawn to him.

He looked from the house to her, as though he knew she was staring at him. He'd caught her watching too often. Heat flooded her cheeks, and amusement danced in his eyes. A small grin crept into his cheeks. Did he know she'd been admiring him?

She huffed and moved away from him. Walked around the vehicle and took in the silhouette of deep purple mountains against the darkening sky.

Though she'd dreaded the idea of working with Jack, they actually worked well together. That moment she found out he'd left for his dream job without even a goodbye seemed so distant now, but if she thought too long and hard, those memories could bring back the pain. She should let herself forget how he'd hurt her. Forgive him. They had been youngish. He'd always been damaged and hurt, and maybe Terra was like his aunt when it came to strays or the lonely and wounded. Maybe it was that same kind of compassion in Terra that first attracted her to him. But Jack wasn't some wounded forest creature that she could nurture back to health. And even thinking she could had been all on her.

She wouldn't be fooled again, except that Jack was different now.

"What are you thinking about?" His husky voice so near gave her a start and at the same time sent warm tingles over her.

She stepped away. "You startled me."

"Because you were a million miles away."

She brushed him off and moved to the passenger-side door, opened it, and got in. He climbed in on the driver's side, bringing with him the smell of woods and masculinity. Terra glanced at the house as he pulled from the curb. Had Neva ever walked in those woods behind her house? Enjoyed the view? Considering how sparse the house was, Terra wondered if Neva had ever even made the place her home.

"Will you please take me to my vehicle back at the hospital?" She needed time to decompress and think through everything.

He shifted in his seat as if her question made him uncomfortable. "Sure. Of course. I was going to invite you to help me work on a crime board, but I don't feel up to that. How about first we grab some coffee and talk through what we know?"

"I have a better idea. You made a comment earlier that made me think of it. You mentioned that Gramps and his coffee and me with my pie, we should open a shop or something. I don't know if I ever told you, but I actually do plan to open a pie shop when I'm too old to do this."

Jack jerked his gaze to her, astonishment and pleasure in his eyes.

A laugh burst from her, and she quickly subdued it. She was losing it, laughing at a time like this. Someone had been murdered. Two someones had been murdered.

"Don't look so surprised." Nanna had taught her to bake pies. At the time, Terra had wanted to please Jack. He loved pie. But who didn't? In the last few years, she hadn't had time to bake and missed the calm that came over her when she combined simple ingredients into an explosion of flavor. Early this morning, before Gramps and Owen had returned and while the chaos of the night still reigned over her, she'd baked one apple pie and one chocolate.

"Terra."

"Oh yeah," she said, realizing too late that bringing up pies probably wasn't appropriate given their history. "Sorry."

"Well, finish what you started. You're going to open a pie shop when you retire. Why bring that up now?"

"I made two pies early this morning. If Gramps and Owen haven't eaten them, we could have pie and coffee. That is, after you take me to my vehicle and if you don't mind following me out to the ranch."

"You had me at pie. Let's do it. While I hate to ruin a perfectly good pie with a conversation about crime, we should use the time to talk through what we have so far, while we're waiting on background information for Neva and her known associates."

"The guy who killed her." Terra touched Jack's shoulder. "He'll turn up. He won't get away. Do you think he's the guy we chased from Gramps's?"

"Why would you think he's the same guy who supposedly was only after your grandfather's safe? The two incidents aren't related. Barely in the same county."

"You're right. It's just that when we were chasing him, I just had the feeling of déjà vu, that's all. The incidents probably aren't connected. I shouldn't have said anything." Because if they were . . .

A chill crawled over her, and she rubbed her arms.

"We got impressions of footprints at the ranch. I'll make sure we get them in the woods behind Neva's home, even though deputies and dogs have tromped all over the place. Right now, I wouldn't worry about it."

"You're just saying that because you're waiting to talk about it over pie."

"So? You got a problem with that?"

TWENTY-SEVEN

Rubbing his neck, Jack turned onto the road back to the hospital to get Terra's vehicle. She'd chuckled at his remark, and he was glad that even during the harsh realities of working a murder investigation, they could find these humorous moments—and keep their sanity. That, and well, he hadn't liked the direction their conversation had taken.

Could the person who broke into Terra's grandfather's ranch be the same man who fled Neva Bolz's home, leaving her murdered body on the kitchen floor? He hated the cold sweats erupting from his body.

But maybe they would get the impressions, compare the footprints, and learn the two incidents were not related.

A guy could hope.

At least he would be following Terra back to the ranch. That would give him peace of mind, even if it was short-lived.

A half an hour later, he pulled up to Stone Wolf Ranch, right behind Terra, and followed her into the house. Jack was relieved that Terra's grandfather wasn't at home at the moment. The last time he'd seen the man, he appeared ready to give Jack a piece of his mind. The man hadn't gotten over the way Jack had left. He got that. Terra's family and friends were protective of her, and Jack had broken her heart.

He'd broken both their hearts. He'd also thrown every harsh word he could ever think of at himself, but it didn't change that he'd hurt Terra.

As for her—she appeared to have gotten over their breakup, if you could call it that. Either that, or she was the ultimate professional and had pushed those events out of the equation.

Still, if the right moment ever came, he should apologize for his behavior. Like Aunt Nadine had suggested when she'd asked if he had made things right.

Terra shrugged out of her light-tan jacket and hung it on a chair. "Owen's around here somewhere. Working with the horses probably, even this late. He loves them so much. He's a horse whisperer, I'm telling ya."

He did the same, suddenly feeling out of place and questioning his wisdom in joining her at the house. If her grandfather or Owen showed up, the awkwardness would only increase.

Or he could choose to act professional—the county detective—and compartmentalize this investigation, separating it from his shared past with Terra.

Could they forge something new between them? He shoved the errant thought away as he took in the large modernized country kitchen—granite counters and elaborate stained cabinets. Stainless steel appliances.

Terra squeezed his shoulder as she brushed past him to open the fridge. She pulled out a pie. "Surprise! They left us a pie."

Jack shoved his hands into his pockets. "Oh yeah, what kind?"

She glanced up at him as she cut a slice. "Apple. I'll warm it in the microwave. Do you want it à la mode? I have whipped cream or ice cream."

"No, thanks. Plain old apple pie is fine."

At the look she shot him, he raised his hands in surrender. "I'm not saying your pie is plain. The opposite, in fact. I want to taste it without any fillers. My mouth is watering already."

She smiled and popped a plated slice in the microwave. "That's better."

Terra started cutting the next slice. "I'm glad Owen found something he loves. And guess what?" She stuck the next plate into the microwave for fifteen seconds and handed Jack his pie.

"What?" Snatching a fork from the drawer, he set the pie on the kitchen table as he took a seat.

"Coffee's on, so grab a mug if you like." Terra explained about Owen's idea for equine therapy.

She grabbed her pie from the microwave and joined him at the table. She forked a piece of pie, then lifted her gaze to him. They shared a smile. The woman stirred feelings in him, and he found himself thinking of her much too often in unprofessional terms—even in the middle of a murder investigation. They couldn't possibly go forward, explore a relationship, with all the baggage. Could they?

Jack focused on eating the pie and let the warmth of the moment and the company relax him. Clear his mind.

"How's your aunt doing?" Terra took a sip from her mug.

He swallowed the last bite and hoped she wouldn't offer more, because he wouldn't be able to resist. "She asked about you the other day."

"Oh, she's so sweet." Terra smiled, but her eyes filled with concern. "I should stop by and see her sometime."

Jack didn't have the heart to tell her that Aunt Nadine hadn't remembered Terra's name. He was almost afraid she might not recognize Terra. "I think she's doing great one day and then the next day, she can't remember something. She's taking medication, and right now she remains independent. But if things get worse, I'm all she's got."

"You're a good man, Jack." Terra stared at him.

He struggled to believe those words coming from her, of all people. He wanted to be a good man. He tried to be, even as he constantly fought the fear that he had a weakness that would cause him to fail, to let someone down. Like his father had let him down in the worst possible way. Terra knew some of that struggle inside him. Did she know it played the biggest role in his leaving her behind and pursuing the FBI?

"I was sorry to hear about your cousin's death last year." Terra frowned at her empty plate, then glanced up at him. "I know it's hard to talk about. I just wanted you to know. You came back for your aunt to comfort her, didn't you?"

How much should he tell her? He nodded. "Yes. It was then that I learned about the dementia."

"And decided to stay." Terra reached over and pressed her hand over his.

Guilt suffused him. There was so much more to it. He wanted to tell her, but not yet. Maybe not ever.

"Like I said, you're a good man." Her cheeks colored, and she turned her attention to taking their plates to the sink.

I wish you'd stop saying that.

How could she say that—think that—after what he'd done, the way he'd left and hurt her? How did he even broach that topic or begin to apologize? He found it difficult to even thank her for the compliment, because there were things she didn't know that would probably change her mind about him if she found out. He had to turn this conversation far away from him.

"And not only do you make great pies, you're a great investigator. I always knew you would make something of yourself. Something worthy of the legacy from which you came."

There, he'd subtly let her know his thoughts. He hadn't been cut from that same kind of hero cloth, and the two of them sewn together just wouldn't work. That served as a great reminder to him. He had thought if he could make something of himself, things could be different. But he'd failed in the worst kind of way. He wasn't even man enough to own up to the truth with Aunt Nadine.

Except his compliment had earned him a frown. She hadn't

liked his reference to her mother's heroism? He opened his mouth to ask her more—

"We need to talk about the investigation," she said. "There's something I've been thinking I should do."

"Oh yeah? What's that?" Jack crossed his arms.

"I need to pay a visit to a friend in prison."

"You have a friend in prison?"

"*Friend* is a loose term. I put a man in prison when I testified six months ago about an illegal pothunting ring. It was part of a sting I was involved in with the NPS."

"You mentioned that before."

"I'm not sure if he'll have anything to share with us. I don't know that even if he does know something, he'll be *willing* to share. But it's worth a try."

"And if he won't share information?"

"I'll threaten him, of course."

Jack leaned back in his chair, almost amused. "With what?"

A crooked grin hitched half her face. "His mother."

"Excuse me?"

"I'll threaten to tell her a few things that he doesn't want her to know."

Jack scratched his head. "Okay, I look forward to hearing more about this."

His cell buzzed with a text. He read it out loud.

> Couldn't find Neva Bolz's computer or laptop. No cell either.

Jack looked at Terra. "Seems she must have kept important information on her devices."

Terra leaned against the counter. "Important enough to murder her and steal?"

"The guy we chased wasn't carrying a laptop."

"No, but he could have had her cell or even a tablet on him."

Jack replied to the text as he said, "I'm requesting that all her digital devices be tracked, if possible. We'll need to search her office at her place of employment too."

"If she actually has one. Maybe she's a freelance consultant."

"We're looking into all of it and should know something in the morning." They needed a good solid lead into the person behind the deaths. Jack was glad he'd tasked Linda with watching over the private investigator.

He hoped Neva's death would be the last. It was one thing to track a serial killer or a human trafficker while working in the FBI, but here in this county in a low-population state like Montana, it boggled his mind.

Owen stepped into the kitchen, and Jack put his cell away.

"You guys are going to eat all the pie!" He rushed to the counter.

Jack had only ever met Owen once. He was in the Middle East when Jack met Terra, and then he came home for a bit. It was later that Jack pulled his big disappearing act, and no doubt Owen heard from Terra and her grandfather that Jack had led her on and then abandoned her.

"I'll get you a big slice, Owen," Terra said. "You remember Jack, don't you?"

Owen's smile was genuine as he sat at the table, so Jack relaxed—if only a little. Owen thrust out his hand, and Jack shook it.

"I hope you're coming to the welcome home party this weekend."

"Well"—Jack looked to Terra—"I'd love to. That is, if I'm invited."

"You're invited." Owen's smile grew bigger as he stuffed his face with pie and eyed Terra.

When she finally slid her gaze to Jack, he hoped she would answer his silent question—*Do you want me there?*

But he was left with the awkward sense that she would not have invited him.

TWENTY-EIGHT

Sitting in the cabin near the forest's edge at the Gallatin Motel and Cabins where he was staying, Chance was officially out of funds, but he couldn't go back to his life until he resolved the missing package.

Blevins had been paid to forget.

But Chance had *chosen* to forget.

What had Blevins meant? He hadn't given him the opportunity to find out, because he left the bar when a deputy entered. Chance had remained in the booth until he could exit without being noticed. He had to find out who had been behind the package, behind the years of blackmail, before he was found and blocked from getting answers and preventing more loss of life.

Years of blackmail. Why didn't he put an end to it long ago?

Palms sweating, Chance repeatedly clenched his hands as he stood up and began to pace. He'd tried to avoid thinking about what had happened before. He'd pushed that far behind him and moved on. Carved out a new life.

Except his eyes were suddenly opened to the truth. He'd deceived himself for far too long. His past remained a constant knocking in the dark corners of his mind. But he'd already paid for his crimes. A higher price had been exacted than he ever could have imagined.

One mistake. One errant thought had led to a few misdeeds and cost him everything.

And he didn't want to think about any of it.

But if he could remember every detail of the past, that could help him solve what was happening now. He knew in his gut this was true.

He had to find whoever had blackmailed him all those years ago and coerced him into making a few shipments now and again, controlling his life and taking everything from him.

He'd been afraid to refuse to cooperate before. Afraid and stupid.

That was then. This was now.

He was older, maybe a little wiser.

Chance pulled the curtains open and let the greenery of the forest calm him. He was safe, and no one would find him here. Resting on the double bed, he stared at the log ceiling. He closed his eyes and thought back to his life-altering mistake almost twenty years ago.

The memory of the thrumming rotors on the AH-64 Apache he'd piloted for the Army's 11th Aviation Regiment filled his head. A city was sprawled beneath him when he'd been expecting desert. After the initial "shock and awe" of the campaign, the desert became his constant companion—one of the hottest places he'd ever had the displeasure of enduring.

Chance sat up on the edge of the creaking bed and rubbed his eyes.

His head still ached from the plane crash. He wasn't sure it would ever go away, but thinking back to those years increased the throbbing.

He inhaled deeply. He could do this. He had to do this.

"Oh, God, why was I so stupid?"

Chance forced his thoughts to that moment in time. That moment when he'd made the wrong choice. At the time, it had seemed innocent enough.

Even now, at the memory, he could taste the desert sand on his tongue.

TWENTY-NINE

erra had been able to charter a flight in a small plane owned and piloted by Ned Campbell, a retired forest service ranger related to Nathan and a friend of Gramps. There had been no question that Jack would join her—her archaeological investigation was intimately connected to his murder investigation.

Ned landed at a small airport near Denver, where Terra had rented a car. Jack finally ended the call that had taken up the short drive to the correctional facility.

"Well, that sounded informative," she said.

"Star Oil Company is based out of Tulsa. According to her sister, Jan, who lives in Bozeman, Neva owned the home in Big Rapids. But working for Star Oil as a consultant required so much travel that she finally decided to rent out the house. That's why it appeared empty of her personal effects. She had made a trip home this week to gather the rest of her things and settle some accounts. Jan and her husband had planned to move the bed and furniture out for their college-aged daughter next week."

Terra absorbed the news and let the moment of deep sorrow pass.

"I'm curious about those accounts she mentioned and what her dealings with Jim Raymond could be, though we have our suspicions. I'd like to know what she *really* did for the company."

"We're in process now."

"I know it takes time." Terra would do some digging of her own too. But they needed more information. Where and why did Neva travel? After flashing their credentials at the gate, Terra steered into the low-security federal prison, then entered the parking lot. She found a spot at the back.

Jack sighed. "This Joey DeMarco. Tell me about him before we get out of the vehicle."

Ned had done most of the talking on the flight, and Terra hadn't wanted to discuss their investigation in front of him. "He's the mastermind behind a big scheme to dig up the pots and sacred cultural items. He had a network of people and auction houses on the dark web through which he sold the items. A few ended up being resold on eBay. That's ultimately how he was taken down. I worked undercover for eight months on the case. Testified, as I mentioned, six months ago. Joey . . . he's not what you would expect."

"How so?"

She opened the car door. "You'll see."

They got out of the vehicle and walked toward the entrance to the sprawling complex surrounded by a double-fenced perimeter. Once again, they flashed their credentials and then signed the required paperwork.

A man stepped through a side door. "Special Agent Connors? Detective Tanner?"

"Yes." They spoke in unison.

"I'm Agent Bill Janssen, Bureau of Prisons Special Investigative Services."

Terra shook the man's hand. "Thanks so much for approving and coordinating this."

He gave a bland smile. "I'll take you to see Mr. DeMarco and will be supervising your visit today."

Terra wasn't sure if that meant he would listen to their conversation, but she would take what she could get. Part of her wondered if this would lead them nowhere.

Agent Janssen led Terra and Jack down a sterile hallway into the facility that housed almost two thousand criminals guilty of mostly white-collar crimes. Janssen opened a door and ushered them into a small room with a table and chairs.

Terra took a seat while Jack remained standing at the edge of the table.

Janssen remained next to the door. "Since his incarceration is largely due to your testimony and efforts, I'm going to give you privacy with the inmate."

He nodded and stepped through the door before closing it. Not that it should matter whether he stayed or gave them privacy, but Terra felt restrained in the man's company.

Jack crossed his arms. "No wall or window separating us here."

"Because Joey isn't a violent criminal. That's why he's in Club Fed." Another name for a white-collar, or a low- or medium-security, facility.

"Given the reasons we're here," Jack added, "I'm not so sure. I don't like this."

"We wouldn't be here if I didn't think there was a chance he could give us information—something he was able to hide from the task force. Something that will help us in this murder investigation."

Jack's response was to stand in the corner.

Terra's heart rate jumped. She worked to calm her breathing and appear relaxed so Joey would remain relaxed too. "Everyone involved in Joey's group was shut down. But his isn't the only artifact-trafficking organization out there. I just want to see if he can offer up anything else."

"He'll want a reduced sentence in exchange."

She pursed her lips, then said, "He only got eighteen months as it was. But as I said, I have some leverage."

"Right. The mother. I look forward to watching you work." Jack hitched a grin and, oddly, that reassured her.

It was taking too long for him to arrive. Was he refusing to see her? She might as well tell Jack what she'd wanted him to see firsthand.

Terra lowered her voice. "Joey is a twentysomething computer nerd who still has acne. He looks much too young to have been such a big player. But it was because of his tech-savvy skills and love of digging up artifacts from a young age that he was able to grow a far-reaching trafficking organization."

"Interesting. So, he's close to his mother."

"He lives with her, yes, well, not while he's incarcerated. She's sick, and he partly used his talents for illicit gain to care for her. She didn't know anything about his activities, and when she found out, it almost destroyed her." Terra hated that awful part of the investigation.

"And you're okay using that relationship as leverage?"

She heard the incredulity in his tone.

"I hope it doesn't go that far, but two people have been murdered. Pauline died indirectly. Relax, I'm not a monster."

The door opposite from where they had entered opened and in stepped Joey DeMarco, looking no worse for the wear. His eyes widened, then his brows shifted into a deep frown. He grudgingly plodded over to sit and stare at her.

"Hey, Joey. You look good."

"Prison life hasn't been so bad. Not what you wanted to hear, I bet. What are you doing here?"

"I've set you on the straight and narrow path, Joey. I hear you met Jesus."

"Yeah. So? I'm attending a Bible study." He suddenly stared at his hands, and his expression softened. "Okay, yeah. I'm doing okay. I guess maybe I do owe you for that."

"I'm glad I could help." Terra paced herself.

"You haven't explained what you're doing here."

Here goes nothing. Or everything. Her palms grew moist. "I've come to ask for your help."

"Help from me? You've already taken down my whole organization. I've got nothing to offer you."

How much should she share? If it meant preventing another murder, then she would be up-front. "Joey, two people have been murdered."

His eyes shot to hers, then to Jack, who shifted in the corner. "What? And you think I know something about that? Well, you're wrong. I don't know anything."

"And even if I did, I wouldn't tell you."

Terra saw that thought in his expression, but she pressed on. "Maybe not, but you know names. You know someone is still out there. Someone we didn't get."

Joey stood and the chair fell back. He moved to the exit and raised his fist to pound on the door.

"I'm going to see your mother next." Terra hadn't wanted to pull that card so soon, if at all.

He held his fist in the air but didn't knock on the door. Then he dropped it.

Joey returned to the table and sat. He hung his head, then lifted his pubescent-looking face and leaned closer as if he would whisper a secret.

"I'm out of here in a few months. I'm doing my time. I'm changing my ways. I don't need you messing up my home for me. I don't want to go home to find my mother still angry at me, or mad over whatever you think you're gonna tell her. Remember, she has a heart condition. This whole thing almost killed her. That's on me. I admit, that's on me, but it would have been fine if you hadn't interfered."

Shame washed through Terra. "I know. I understand. Please . . . I would not have come to you if I wasn't desperate. I don't want anyone else to die. Your crimes never amounted to murder, Joey, so if you know something, you need to share that information. You don't want to be an accessory to that."

"Is that a threat? Because I can't tell you anything yet. I need more, like why did you come to *me* with this?"

Terra leaned in too. She and Joey were close. Jack sat down in the chair next to her, a show of intimidation and protection.

"If two people have been murdered," she said, "then someone could be shutting down loose ends and moving shop. Or they're feeling threatened in some way. Who is it? Who is moving your kind of contraband through Montana?"

Joey's face paled, and his acne turned bright red. "I don't know anything about Montana. Even if I did, and I told you anything, then I could be threatened next. My mother's life threatened."

Terra leaned against the seat back and drew circles on the table. "You know something, Joey. I can see it in your eyes."

"Before you took me down, I was trying to expand my operations."

"Expand? What are you saying?"

"You have to think bigger."

Terra shook her head. "I need a name. Something."

He blew out a breath. "I'll see what I can find out and get back to you. Give me a week."

Joey pushed himself away from the table. He was done talking. He walked away, knocked on the door, and exited when a guard opened it.

Terra hung her head.

Jack took Terra's hand and squeezed. "You did your best. We knew it was a long shot."

"He said he was trying to expand his operation. I get the feeling he already has a name, and it's more that he's going to think about whether or not to hand that name over to me."

THIRTY

Jack made his way down the emergency room hallway until he found Aunt Nadine's room. He pushed through a curtain, realizing too late that he could very well have the wrong room.

Aunt Nadine's sweet face looked up at him, and her eyes brightened. Swift relief whooshed through him.

"Oh, Jack. I'm so sorry," she said, her expression shifting to one of sorrow and regret. "You didn't have to come up here to see me. Francine is here. She's out there somewhere searching for coffee."

No, she wasn't. Francine Carmichael had left Jack a voice mail that his aunt was in the hospital, and he rushed over once they landed at the airport in Big Rapids. Jack sent Francine on her way when he got to the hospital, but he wouldn't tell Aunt Nadine that news yet. He took in her broken wrist, stifling anything that would convey his frustration. He was glad she had nothing more than a fractured wrist.

He took Aunt Nadine's uninjured hand in his and squeezed. "She was right to think that I would want to know you had been hurt. I came as soon as I could." He released her hand and lifted his brows. "So, what *really* happened?"

Nadine's face scrunched up in a way that told him she didn't want to tell him. He suspected that she was taking her time responding so she could conjure up a more positive slant to the tale.

"Well, let's see. I took Freckles out for a walk and decided to take Tux and Dusty too. You know, they don't get to leave the backyard much, and they must think I've been playing favorites. I haven't meant to. It's just that Freckles is still missing his boy. So I took all the dogs. There's that wonderful neighborhood park a few blocks over."

"You took all three dogs? I hope they were on leashes."

She frowned at him. "Of course they were. At first." That scrunch again.

"Go on." He was starting to get an image in his head—and it might have been comical, except her condition took the humor out of it.

"I unleashed them at the park, and we played fetch. All four of us."

"Let me guess. One of them took off."

"Not one of them. All three of them. Freckles was the first to go squirrel hunting—or, rather, chasing. Then I found myself chasing three dogs on the loose. I'm sorry, Jack, I got a ticket. I didn't even know that was a law. Is it a new law? Anyway, a woman complained. She was playing with her three-year-old, and Freckles knocked the child over."

Jack tensed. This could be worse than he thought. "The kid is okay, though, right?"

"Yes. I'm the one who was injured. I was chasing Freckles and tripped at the edge of the playground area. It was the most ridiculous thing. I fell forward and stopped the fall with my hands. Like anyone would do. My wrist started throbbing."

"Can I ask what happened to the dogs?"

"I was in so much pain. Several people in the park helped

me up. I panicked. I couldn't see the dogs, and I didn't have my phone with me."

Aunt Nadine covered her eyes with her good hand as though she might cry.

Jack wrapped his arms around her and patted her back. "It's okay. It's going to be fine. Just relax."

When he sensed she was okay, he released her.

She looked up at him. "A young man releashed all three dogs. Someone called Francine for me, and she came right away. The young man was kind enough to walk the dogs home and put them in the yard for me."

Interesting. "Did you get his name so I can thank him?" And make sure he wasn't just taking advantage of Aunt Nadine and perhaps helping himself to goodies in the house.

"Andy Reamer, I think. Francine wrote it down for me somewhere."

"I'll check with her then. Aunt Nadine"—he grabbed her good hand again—"I'm so sorry this happened. I'm glad Mrs. Carmichael called me. She's a great friend."

Aunt Nadine sat up. "I called Francine so you wouldn't be called away from your work. I wouldn't want to do anything to mess up your job."

"You're more important, Aunt Nadine. You're a priority." But I was in Colorado this afternoon and wouldn't have been able to rush home. Again, he had that nagging sense that he was going about this all wrong. That Aunt Nadine was only getting worse, and he would fail her again in ways he couldn't yet imagine.

Doubt flitted across her expression. He knew where that came from, and regret squeezed his chest. "I'm sorry I haven't been around lately and I wasn't there to help you put up all those posters for Freckles."

"Because you're busy with your job. You don't need to apologize for that."

He pinched his nose. How did he explain? "Yes, I do have a job, and I'm in the middle of a murder investigation." Two murders now. "Putting up posters for a lost dog is one thing. But your health and your life are another."

His aunt seemed to stare right through him. Oh no. Was her mind going somewhere else? These episodes were getting worse. She suddenly focused in on him. "I understand. You don't need to talk to me like I'm a child. Remember that old adage, 'No one ever wished they had worked harder on their death bed.'"

He smiled. What else could he do? "I'm duly chastised."

Jack kissed her on the cheek. "When they set you free, I'll take you home."

He noticed the time on the wall clock. As much as he needed to stay focused on the investigation, he would take a couple of hours off to be with his aunt this evening and get her settled. He'd already spoken to Francine, who would come by and sit with her later.

Still, maybe he should call it a day to be with his aunt.

"Aunt Nadine. When do you go back to your primary doctor?"

"Not for a couple of months. Why?"

Jack wanted her doctor to run more tests. She seemed much too young to be suffering with dementia. He'd done some Internet research, but that could be both terrifying and dangerous and lead a person down an entirely wrong track.

He eased into the chair near the bed and hoped they would release her soon.

"Jack, why did you ask about my doctor?"

"Just wondering so I can make sure to be there with you for the appointment."

Maybe he should tell her the truth before it was too late for her to understand. He'd sent Francine on her way to run her own errands before she came by to hang out with his aunt. He crouched so he was eye level with her. "Listen, Aunt Nadine, there's something I need to tell you."

Her eyes teared up. "No, no. I'm the one. I . . . I have a confession to make. It's about your father—"

The doctor entered the room and cut her off. Jack introduced himself and learned the details about her fracture and when she would need to see her own doctor. Then he assisted her in getting up, and together they walked slowly down the hall to the exit, where he helped her into his vehicle.

Jack went around the car and got into the driver's seat, drawing in a few slow breaths. Curiosity gnawed at him. "Before the doctor came in, you said you had a confession to make. Something about my father."

"You're thinking of someone else, Jack. I didn't say anything about your father."

THIRTY-ONE

Standing at the trailhead, Terra breathed in the scent of pine and juniper and hoped peace would settle her tumultuous thoughts.

Terra had gone into the office this morning to make an appearance and fill out paperwork. She'd bumped fists with the likes of Case Haymaker and her other forest service coworkers for the area, and then with her duty there accomplished, she'd headed out to the national forest.

Yesterday might have been a colossal waste of time. The jury was still out.

Come on, Joey. Give me something.

But today she would make up for that. She determined to find something to connect Jim Raymond with Neva Bolz and the cache. The archaeologist should be reviewing the items soon, and she would know more about their origins and to where they should be returned.

Crouching, Terra pressed her hand against the hardened trail as though she could take the pulse of the earth. Here, the ground felt cool and damp from recent rains.

The thought of rain made her think of Jack the evening he stopped by the ranch and got drenched, when he'd proclaimed earlier that he never got caught in the rain. The image of him soaking wet just so he could talk to her warmed her insides.

She shook off the feelings flooding her.

Jack was supposed to meet her here.

But he was late, so she decided to hike up the trail a bit. Head to Jim's cabin. After a few minutes walking the path up Maverick Trail, Terra stood in the thickly wooded area and absorbed the nature around her.

This was unadulterated beauty at its finest. She soaked in the sounds and scents and gloried in the greenery, enjoying the peace she so often found while in the woods. Being out here close to God's creation—the air, the trees, the birds and animals—cleared her mind like nothing else.

She needed time alone to gather her thoughts, so maybe it was a good thing that Jack was late.

Terra continued up the trail, feeling more at home than she had in a long time. Because she was actually close to home, after all, unlike her time with the National Park Service when she lived in southwest Colorado, where she nabbed Joey.

What did Joey know about what was going on here, if anything? Or was she reaching too far—a long shot, as Jack had said about yesterday's venture to the federal prison.

This investigation was becoming complex in ways she hadn't anticipated.

And at the end of the day, when she couldn't shut down her mind to sleep, her thoughts always went to her mother. Her mother's heroism. And Terra never measured up.

To ever truly do that, she would need to die in the line of duty.

Sweat beaded on Terra's back as she hiked the incline, then finally turned off the trail toward the cabin.

What am I missing here?

"Think bigger," Joey had said. Or was he only trying to put her off?

Through the trees in the distance, Terra spotted Jim's cabin. The windows had been boarded up. Had Jack's deputies done that? For what purpose? Everything in the cabin had been removed and taken in as evidence.

Terra leaned against a tree and let nature calm her mind. Let God rein in her thoughts. The rain had poured down at Gramps's ranch and at the bottom of this mountain. But up here, it was dry and hadn't been cleared out—there simply weren't enough resources to clear the forest, and kindling rested everywhere just waiting to catch fire.

Jim had been sitting on a metaphorical tinderbox that had exploded and backfired on him.

Think bigger.

Bigger.

Bigger.

Terra pushed from the tree and approached the cabin. She found the door unlocked and stepped inside. The deputies had boarded the windows but left the door unlocked? Terra took a closer look at the knob but saw no sign of forced entry. Someone else with a key to the cabin had come back and didn't bother locking it? Jack had mentioned getting cameras up in these woods near the cabin, but she doubted that had been done yet.

She walked the perimeter on the inside, then stood in the middle and stared up at the ceiling.

Think bigger.

Terra moved back outside and walked around the cabin in ever widening circles.

Okay. Bigger.

A doe dashed away, startling her. She was entirely too edgy. She hadn't known the deer was watching.

"Foraging for berries in the bushes, were you? I didn't mean to—" A strange-shaped rock near a bush caught her attention. She stooped to look closer.

Was it stone? Wait, no. Clay. An artifact they'd missed? Terra pulled on gloves to scrape away the earth, except the corner wasn't buried, after all, but rested on pine needles beneath the bush, as if it had broken off from a larger piece and fallen to the ground. She assumed this was related to the cache they'd found. She took a few photographs of the object and the area surrounding it, then took a wider image showing where the object rested in relation to the cabin.

Then she carefully lifted it. Roughly the size of her palm, it appeared to be the corner of a clay tablet. Turning it over, she noticed etchings unlike anything she'd ever seen—except in photographs.

Her heart rate kicked up.

Terra hadn't heard anything back from the forest service archaeologist about the artifacts they'd secured from the cabin. This broken corner was something different altogether. Hands shaking, she carefully wrapped the piece in the gloves to protect it and placed it in a zippered pocket of her jacket.

Terra would give the cabin another look before she left. If this was missed, maybe something else had been missed too. She had the feeling that the investigation had just gotten . . . bigger. But she wouldn't jump to conclusions until she had an expert examine the object.

And, unfortunately, she knew just the expert.

Inside the cabin again, she flipped on the flashlight and shined it around. Though she didn't believe she and Jack had missed anything, or the county evidence techs either, stranger things had happened. After all, she'd found the unusual fragment near the cabin.

She gave up the hunt, stashed her flashlight, and opened the door. Or tried to.

It was locked.

What? Terra pulled and yanked and kicked. She shined her flashlight on the knob. Was it the kind of knob that could be locked and unlocked from the outside only? No. Twisting from the inside should release the locking mechanism.

Okay. She could unscrew the entire thing. Except she didn't have a screwdriver. She'd climb out the windows then. Oh, right. They were boarded up.

Terra moved to one of the windows. Maybe she could remove enough boards to climb out. A pungent odor tickled her nose. Alerted her senses.

Smoke.

Panic grabbed her.

Peering through the crack in the boards to see outside, Terra had the eerie sense she was trapped behind prison bars. A pop resounded. Sparks drifted across her line of sight. She shifted to peer at the woods behind the cabin and saw nothing. Then . . . fire.

And a hooded figure running away.

Terra stepped back from the window, her breath catching in her throat. She turned around.

Flames licked at the far corner of the cabin. Soon it would be engulfed.

Fear ignited her whole body. She reached for her cell, her slippery fingers hindering her efforts to grab on. Come on! Of course she had no signal here.

She texted Jack, hoping at least that would go through. But she wouldn't wait for someone to save her. She had to find a way out of this cabin before toxic fumes overcame her.

THIRTY-TWO

Jack had received news that the preliminary comparison of shoe prints from the woods behind Neva's home didn't match prints near Terra's home the night of the break-in. He'd been hoping for that answer.

Regardless, he was late to meet Terra when he parked his vehicle next to hers on the Maverick Trailhead.

Of course she had already hiked up the trail without him. He wouldn't have waited on him either. Before he got out of his vehicle, he thought to text her to let her know he was on his way, though she might not receive it up the mountain.

He noticed that she'd beat him to it with a text of her own.

The words jumped out at him and grabbed him by throat. Alarm ignited.

Oh no.

Jack called 911 while he still had a signal and reported the information Terra had relayed—the woods were on fire and she was trapped in the cabin—then ended the call.

He hopped from his vehicle and instantly smelled the smoke. Heart pounding, he rushed up the trail, hoping he hadn't just wasted seconds making that emergency call. Seconds that could make the difference in saving her life.

"Terra!" Jack's leg muscles screamed as he pushed himself faster up the trail, then he slowed before his heart burst. He picked up the pace again. If he survived this, he would take up trail jogging.

His lungs burned as he sucked in oxygen and smoke. The acrid stench thickened as he drew closer. He stopped in his tracks to catch his breath.

He kept going as far as he could go, but it wasn't nearly far enough. The forest burned, creating a wall of flames and heat so he couldn't push deeper into the woods.

Terra.

The blaze crackled and hissed, its fiery fingers hungrily reaching for more as sparks swirled into a sky already darkening with toxic smoke.

No . . . Terra . . .

His heart spasmed.

He hadn't realized he'd fallen to his knees. Shock. Grief. He didn't know. He couldn't let that cripple him now. He wouldn't give up. Because if he knew anything about Terra—she was a fighter. She would find her own way out. *Please, God, let it be so.*

Jack got to his feet and moved around the edge of the fire, heading northwest from the trail, to find a way to get closer to the cabin if he could. The smoke and heat caused his eyes to water, his lungs to convulse. Still, he searched for a possible way closer, belying the obvious hopelessness building in his heart. Denying what he knew to be true. And finally, through the burning trees, he saw what he feared.

The cabin was gone.

If Terra was still inside, she was gone too.

THIRTY-THREE

Groaning with the effort, Terra launched up and onto a massive boulder, finding a foothold before she slipped. Then another. Climbing wasn't her thing—it was Jack's thing—but she knew enough, and her survival depended on getting to safety. She scaled higher and higher until she made it to the top of the boulder. From there she could find the safest route out of the forest, and the likely route taken by the arsonist.

Someone who also wanted her dead. He'd purposefully locked her inside that cabin by somehow jamming the locking mechanism. She didn't know how or why, and might never get the chance to find out now.

To escape the cabin, she had removed the log shelf from inside the cabinet where the artifacts had been stored. Then she'd used the shelf to pound out the nails in the boards covering a window and climbed through, barely escaping the flames that were now consuming the forest she loved. Terra focused on surviving and refused to give in to sheer terror. She had to remain single-minded.

A whimper fought to escape her dry mouth. Jack. She hoped he didn't get caught in the wildfire.

With one last grunt, she pulled herself off the boulder and onto the higher ground of the mountain slope. From here, she could see the fire raging below and the smoke rising. Wildland firefighters should be on their way if they weren't there already. Even if her text hadn't gone through, Jack would have seen the fire. Terra swiped her arm across her sweaty brow and eyes. A bitter taste filled her mouth.

All the times she'd advised others to take a pack with supplies, especially water, and she'd left her pack in her vehicle. She needed water. The forest needed water.

Apprehension gripped her and could paralyze her if she didn't push through. She couldn't imagine any sane person would intentionally set a forest fire.

Whatever the reason, a fire raged. Anger flared inside her.

From her perch, Terra searched the areas the fire hadn't touched. The flames traveled east with the wind. She peered at her cell, which had lost its charge, and she doubted she could have gotten a signal anyway.

God, oh, God, oh, God . . . please let them put this out before it grows even bigger.

Though fire played a natural role in forest management, it was a destructive force to be reckoned with.

Especially when you were in the middle of it!

Terra was on the side of the blaze opposite of where Jack would have approached on the trail. She hadn't been able to text him again.

Terra rubbed her temples.

If only she could let him know she'd made it out of the cabin alive. The only way to do that was to make her way to safety and tell him herself. Even though the fire was heading east, the direction could change at a moment's notice, putting her in danger. Depending on how hot the fire burned, it could rage through previously soaked areas, which could slow it down but sometimes not enough.

As it was, trapped on this side of the fire line was bad enough without the fact that the arsonist was out there somewhere too. He could still be a threat. Terra did a 360. Her breath caught when she spotted more flames coming in from the west. The arsonist?

Whatever the reason, her escape route options were diminishing fast.

A wave of heat hit her. She turned back to the closer fire racing this direction. Trees crackled and burst into flames much too close for comfort. A small swath of evergreens still remained between her and the Grayback River to the north of her no more than two miles away.

Terra scrambled down and over the rocky outcropping, heading for the thick woods that would soon be engulfed. Making it to the river before the flames caught up would be a race against time. She would have to run even though she was already dehydrated. Terra paced herself as she dashed between trees, over dry pine needles, and around shrubs and undergrowth. Here most of it was dry and would feed the fire.

Terra gasped for breath. Sweat beaded on her face, her back, every inch of her body. She couldn't afford to lose more fluid, but what could she do?

What's more, her limbs cramped and threatened to give out.

Hot flames bore down on her from behind as she made her way to the river. Hundreds of glowing sparks floated and swirled in the air.

Chuff, chuff, chuff.

A helicopter.

She glanced up and spotted the chopper swooping over the forest. Terra was in the trees. They would never see her. She had another half mile or more to get to the river. Leaning over her knees, she caught her breath. Sucked in the dry, hot air. Pushed through a coughing spasm before she pressed on.

As she neared the river, the terrain grew rocky. A wide band of large boulders lined the river all the way to the bank. At least it wasn't a canyon or a ravine that could trap her in the forest. She could climb down.

Terra clambered over the boulders, making her way toward the river, which she hoped would stop the blaze. But fires could jump water when trees exploded and sparks drifted.

God, please . . .

The air was hazy with smoke, and she struggled to breathe. If the flames didn't get to her, the smoke would take her out. She continued making her way toward the rocky bank of the Grayback River. Where the boulders extended across the river, they caused whitewater rapids. She would have to make her way farther down if she was going to cross.

Terra breathed in too much smoke and a fit of hacking spasms hit her.

Don't panic. Don't panic.

Panic could get her killed.

Calm down.

You're the daughter of a forest ranger. You're a forest service special agent.

Across the river in the shadows between the trees, a man in a gray hoodie stood watching. Terra almost shouted for help. He turned his back to her and disappeared.

THIRTY-FOUR

There!" Jack shouted. "I see her."

His heart might have exploded with overwhelming relief, except Terra was by no means out of danger. Firefighters still fought to gain control of the flames.

Jack had "hijacked" one of the state's Huey helicopters to search for Terra. Other Hueys were carting three hundred-gallon buckets of water to dump on the fire.

The chopper swooped closer to the Grayback River and hovered over the whitewater rapids, the din joining the rotors in intensity.

Hands on hips, Terra stood on a boulder near the rapids. Dirt and ash smudged her face and body, and despite the dry heat, her hair fell limp with sweat. His heart jumped to his throat at the sight of her. Alive. She was still alive. Jack had to keep her that way.

"Obviously, it's not going to be a ground landing." The pilot's voice resounded through Jack's helmet. "We'll use the hoist. I'll keep a good distance to avoid the rotors hitting the trees."

"Good to know. I'll go down and get her." Jack secured himself on the cable and motioned for a state guy who went by the name Elk who had joined him on this search operation. Elk worked the winch that lowered Jack's cable.

The smoke grew thick. A gust of wind caught the chopper, and Jack swung wildly over the rapids. His pulse spiked even though he was secured to the cable. Squeezing his eyes shut, he focused on calm, controlled breaths.

Please, don't let me spin.

The cable began to lower him again, and he opened his eyes. Once again, the helicopter hovered above Terra, the pilot attempting a dynamic hoist—maneuvering the bird so the cable wouldn't spin—which Jack appreciated.

Terra shifted back and forth. Fire and smoke crept dangerously closer, but she didn't seem to care. She kept looking across the river, then up to Jack. Finally, he was on the rock. He almost stumbled, but she dragged him onto the boulder until his footing was sure.

Even though the rotors above them should have drowned out most every other sound, the rapids roared in his ears.

Hope, and something else he couldn't read, poured from Terra's wide eyes.

She yanked him forward into a hug, her voice thick with relief and emotion as she said, "Jack. Thank God!"

He wanted to keep her there against him. To look at her face and contemplate that she was standing in front of him alive and well. Jack had so much to say, but he had to keep her alive—and they were out of time. He assisted in securing her in the airlift rescue vest, making sure it remained attached to the hoist equipment. Then he glanced up at Elk, who managed their lifeline, and signaled they were ready.

Terra held on to Jack while the winch pulled the cable back to the helicopter as it lifted higher. Jack took in the terrifying view below. The violent rapids beneath threatened to reach up and grab them while the blistering fire raced toward them, a furious monster intent on thwarting their escape. When the thick smoke cleared in spots, he could see the bright orange flames that devoured the forest below them—a heart-stopping sight.

When the cable had been winched all the way to the helicopter, Elk assisted in hauling Terra and Jack inside. They disengaged from the hoisting equipment and shrugged from their harnesses.

Jack looked into her bright blue eyes, relieved to see the fear subsiding. Again, he considered that he had so much he wanted to say to her. But now wasn't that moment. Would he ever find the right time?

Terra's mouth hung open as if she, too, would speak words she'd been holding back. He could have lost her today, and in a way, he was getting a second chance with her, but he couldn't know if she even wanted that. His emotions were getting the best of him, and Elk was giving him a funny look.

He followed Terra's lead and strapped into his seat, and Terra donned the helmet Elk had handed her. She glanced at Jack but then focused her attention on the woods below.

Elk offered them both bottles of water. Terra guzzled it. As soon as she came up for air, she said, "Go back. Go back closer to the river where you picked me up."

"What? Why?"

She'd been focused on those woods even as he rescued her. "He's down there, Jack. He's in the woods."

"Who?"

"The guy who started the fire! He locked me in the cabin. I saw him running away while I was trapped inside. Before you arrived, I saw him watching me from across the river. He was wearing a gray hoodie."

Jack instructed the pilot to return and swoop as low as possible so they could search as long as it remained safe.

He hesitated before radioing the sheriff. "But you didn't actually see him start the fire, though."

"No. But who else could it have been? No one else was out there. He could have been the guy we chased. The man who killed Neva. I don't know, but he jammed the lock somehow, then started a fire to destroy the cabin. I don't know if I was a bonus for him or his target."

Jack radioed the sheriff what Terra had seen, and that she was safe, but to be on the lookout for anyone fleeing the forest wearing a gray hoodie. He squeezed her shoulder, but like Terra had done, Jack now concentrated on the dense woods below them and searched for the man who could be behind everything, including the murders.

Finding anyone in the thickly forested area was like finding the proverbial needle in a haystack, but there were clearings now and then. And the arsonist was sure to hide while the chopper was above him. After a half an hour, the smoke grew even thicker, and visibility decreased to near zero. They couldn't see a thing. Jack called the search.

Terra closed her eyes and rested her head against the seat back. She shoved her still-damp hair behind her ears. "I can't stand that he's out there. That he's free to commit more crimes."

Jack took in her appearance. Her hair a tangled mess, smudges along her temple and cheeks. Her clothes, dirty and torn. That she was sitting here with him now seemed nothing short of a miracle.

He thought he'd lost her.

Jack wanted to do so much more than sit next to her. He wanted to hold her tight and never let her go, as if that could take all their troubles away. Maybe human touch would comfort them both and help them power through. Jack could use the reassurance.

Terra opened her eyes and held his gaze. She must have sensed him watching. Sorrow, regret, and anger twisted her features.

He couldn't stand to see her this way, so he lifted a hand to wipe the smudges from her face but thought better of it and quickly dropped his hand.

Terra propped her elbows on her knees and buried her face in her palms.

"What do Jim and Neva and this guy who killed them have in common?" She pushed up to sit straight again. "Jim and Neva potentially have the artifacts in common."

"Then what's your role in this?" Jack asked. "If this is the same guy, then why did he try to kill you today? That reminds me. I learned that the tracks in the woods behind Neva's don't match those found near your grandfather's home."

"So the two incidents are not related." She rubbed her arms.

"Regardless, you're somehow too close to it all. Why would he try to kill you?"

"I could have just been in the wrong place at the wrong time. He locked me in so I wouldn't get in the way of his plans."

Or the man wanted her dead because he feared she was getting too close to the truth.

"Jack, it could be a distraction. Start a fire, and we all scramble. Our focus is divided."

He nodded. "That's something to consider."

Whatever his reasons, this guy didn't act like someone who had anything to lose. Jack remained concerned that someone had followed her to her grandfather's that night. Had someone monitored her activity, working with the safecracker to warn him to get out before she arrived home, and that effort had failed?

"Good news. The eastern side of the fire has been contained," the pilot said.

"Oh, thank God." A relieved sigh whooshed from Terra. It seemed like a week since she'd gone to the cabin, but it had only been a few hours.

"Can you take us back to our vehicles near the Maverick Trailhead?" Jack asked.

"Sure thing."

Terra closed her eyes for a moment and silently prayed. When she opened them, she unzipped her jacket pocket and pulled a coin-sized object wrapped in latex gloves. "I found it."

She unwrapped it so he could peer at the jagged corner of a stone.

"Looks like a square piece of stone or clay. Another artifact? Where did you find it?" he asked.

"A few yards from the cabin. It was in the dirt under a bush. I took pictures, don't worry. I would have marked it with an evidence marker, but I didn't have that with me."

"You don't think it's part of another archaeological site that needs to be protected, do you?"

Frowning, she shook her head. "No. This was clearly dropped there."

"What do you make of it?"

"I'm not sure yet."

He scratched his chin. "What if Jim fought with someone there. Somehow it got broken during the altercation, and that's also when Jim was stabbed. There could be more evidence. Blood. Something. Somehow this was missed when we searched. And now the fire has destroyed anything else we might have found. That could be the sole reason he started the fire. We're getting too close to the truth."

She nodded. "You could be right. Yeah, that makes sense."

She turned the piece over to look closer, studying the broken piece a few moments. "I've made the decision to show it to a friend in the field. An expert."

"Wait. This is evidence."

"And I'm securing it as such and will take it to a safe place."

"A friend in the field. You mean you're not giving it over to your forest service archaeologist?"

"Let's just say when there's artifact trafficking going on, one can never know how far and wide it goes. I'd like to put some distance between this and the locals, and I know I can trust my guy."

The helicopter landed in the middle of the mountain road. Jack climbed out first, and Terra ignored his assistance and hopped down on her own. They ducked and rushed away as the Huey lifted.

Terra turned to head to her SUV but stumbled. Jack caught her before she tumbled to the ground. He held her against him, admittedly right where he wanted. Again, he thought about those moments when he'd feared the worst—that she was gone. That he'd lost her forever. He . . . he wanted her back. How did he say what he was really feeling? Terra wouldn't accept those words from him. Not yet. If ever.

Terra pressed her hands against his chest, and his arms encircled her. "That was a close call," he whispered.

She eased away slightly and peered up at him, a soft smile on her lips. "Thanks for catching me. I'm more exhausted than I thought."

Jack had been referring to the fire, but he didn't correct her.

He released her but kept his arm around her waist for added support as he ushered her to her vehicle. "You've been through an awful trauma today. Give yourself a break."

Though he didn't want to, he relinquished her. Terra opened the vehicle door and fished her cell from her pocket. Jack lingered—he wasn't sure she was okay. Or maybe he was the one who wasn't okay.

She found the charger and plugged it in, then turned her attention back to him.

"I need a favor from you," she said.

"Anything."

"Anything? Wait until you hear what I have to say." She stood taller now. No stumbling for her.

"I don't think I was actually targeted today. Just in the wrong place at the wrong time. I don't know about being followed the other night. That could have been my imagination. Or, again, I was in the wrong place at the wrong time. Someone wanted in the safe, and I came to the ranch house too soon. The point is that if you report that someone is trying to kill me, then I could be taken off this investigation. We don't know that's what's happening. And I have to see this through."

"Why is it so important?"

"Come on. Forest service special agent. Those jobs are few and far between. Not easy to get."

"Don't tell me you feel like you need to prove yourself."

"Of course I do. Didn't you feel the same way when you headed to Quantico? I want to prove that I can do this job." Her searching stare wouldn't let go. Her eyes pleaded with him to understand.

He understood far better than she knew. This was about her living up to her mother's legacy. Funny that he was trying to change his father's.

"Only if I can get something from you in return. Wait. That didn't sound right."

Terra sent him a wry grin. "What is it?"

"Don't take chances like you did today going up the trail without me. Don't put yourself at risk. Do we have a deal?" He wanted to say more. *If it turns out that someone really is out to kill you, then you need to consider dropping this investigation. Let's report and get protection too.* He wouldn't say more because she could end up keeping any attempts on her life from him, and he couldn't have that.

She was a professional. A good agent. But she was also human.

Everyone had their weaknesses.

And their failures.

"Okay. Sure."

"That means I want to stick close. That's my part of the deal."

"Within reason. We have a job to do, and sometimes that will mean you go one way and I go another. I promise to let you know my every move." Terra's lips twisted into a full-on smile that did crazy things to his heart. "The bottom line is that the sooner we solve this, the better for everyone—including the next potential victim."

Terra's cell buzzed, and she snatched it up. Her eyes grew wide.

"What is it?" he asked.

"It's a text from Joey's lawyer. He has a message from Joey."

THIRTY-FIVE

Terra contemplated what the text could mean.

"Well, what is it?" Jack sounded impatient.

She didn't blame him. "One word. *Janus*."

"Who's Janice?"

"No. J-a-n-u-s."

"What difference does the spelling make. Who is this person?"

"Janus is an ancient Roman god. It's said he has two faces, and he looks into the future and the past."

"What does it mean?" he asked.

"It means Joey sent me a cryptic message, and I'm not sure what he's telling me."

She climbed all the way into her vehicle to sit and started the engine. She wasn't sure she was up for driving after today's events. Her legs were still shaking.

Jack was watching her much too closely. She didn't want his scrutiny.

"Meeting with Joey didn't help us to find out why two people are dead," she said. "At least not yet. I need to dig deeper to understand the significance behind Joey's cryptic text. In the meantime, I have a fragmented piece that could shed some light. If Jim was killed for it, that is. I need to get that into, um . . . my friend's hands."

"A friend? An expert? Come on, Terra. I need more information than that. Potentially both the victim and the suspect touched this. It's evidence."

"It needs to be analyzed, and I'll maintain all the proper documentation. Don't worry. His name is Dr. Jeremy Brand. He's currently an archaeology professor at the University of Wyoming. I think he's still in Jackson Hole leading a dig."

"He's someone you keep up with then?"

"I met him during an earlier investigation with the NPS."

Jack searched her eyes, like he often did, trying to get a read on her. "I'm going with you."

"Fine. But I'm not going anywhere until I wash the grime away. I'll call first. Maybe I can Skype with him or send him a picture."

"You don't think he'll need to get his hands on it to make an assessment?"

"One step at a time. I'm heading to the ranch to get cleaned up. I'll see you later. Don't forget Owen's party."

Jack looked beat. But at the same time, he looked good. How did he do that?

"I'll be there," he said. "You'll see me tonight too. I'm following you to your grandfather's to make sure you get there okay."

"I can take care of myself." With those words, she remembered that desperate moment when she thought she had to choose between the river and the fire, and then Jack showed up in the Huey to pull her out of death's reach. She had so much more she wanted to say to him, to confide, and she sensed he was holding back as well. "Listen, Jack . . . I . . ."

He angled his head. "Yeah?"

She couldn't hide the emotion that surged inside. And she also couldn't tear her gaze from his. Instead, she soaked in his forest-green eyes. "How . . . how did you know?"

His brows crinkled, and he edged a little closer. "Know what?"

Her heart rate inched up at his nearness.

Standing inside the door, Jack looked at her with such longing, Terra had the strongest urge to get out of her vehicle and get closer to him again. She struggled to remain seated and, for the first time, to remember why she shouldn't be in his arms.

Terra hoped her voice sounded steady. "My text said I was locked inside that burning cabin. How did you know I had survived? How did you know to even search for me? I . . . don't even know *how* to thank you." *Thank you* should have been the first words out of her mouth, but her thoughts had been on getting the man behind the fire.

"I didn't know you had survived." Jack looked away, but she hadn't missed the emotion welling in his eyes, and he almost sucked her into that wave with him. He cleared his throat as he looked at her again. She saw in his eyes that he still cared deeply for her, and it took her breath away.

He reached across the short distance to cup her cheek. "But I couldn't live with the thought of losing you, Terra. I kept telling myself that you were still alive. I listened to my instincts, my heart . . ."

Oh. My.

That was it then. She couldn't hold back. Terra slid from the seat and into his arms. With her head against his chest, she heard the steady beat of his strong heart. If he hadn't listened to his instincts and followed through, she could have died in the fire or in an attempt to cross the river. She could still be out there in those woods.

Jack had come for her.

Was Terra losing her grip? She'd been in his arms already today—and that had felt good and right, despite the reasons she'd ended up there.

If Terra could forget the past, forget the pain he'd caused

her, then maybe . . . maybe she could get comfortable snug against him.

"Thank you," she whispered, the emotional connection with him tugging at the deep places of her heart. But not deep enough. A wall still remained. She could forgive him, and she had, but she wasn't able to fully trust him not to utterly devastate her again. Terra couldn't seem to get beyond that scar over her heart.

She should move away from him, but . . .

Jack was the one to step back.

He left her feeling cold and empty by comparison.

His features had grown stern. "It's getting late, and you should get home. We need to give our statements about today's events."

She rubbed her eyes. "Tomorrow."

Jack's expression softened. "Remember, I'm going to follow you home."

Terra was too exhausted to argue with him. She steered from the trailhead and headed back to Gramps's ranch. She glanced in the rearview mirror to see Jack still following her when she finally turned into the circular drive. A smile broke through her exhaustion. Former FBI Special Agent Jack Tanner turned county detective had a way of making her want a relationship even in the midst of a nightmarish day.

At the front door, she waved and he took off.

She could smell the smoke, but the fire was far from Stone Wolf Mountain and the ranch, and she prayed it would be contained soon.

The day had been long and exhausting, and she was relieved when she didn't run into Gramps or Owen, each of them caught up in doing their own thing, which was just as well. Terra grabbed leftover tuna from the fridge, along with a fork, and headed to her room to finish it off. After showering and changing into comfy clothes, Terra carefully set the artifact on a ziplock bag and took a better picture in brighter light.

She pursed her lips. She needed answers from someone she could trust, so she sent a quick text.

> Dr. Brand, we need to talk.

While she waited for his response, she rested on her bed and closed her eyes. Images of the raging fire filled her mind. Terra jolted awake. She hadn't meant to fall asleep.

She eyed her phone. Still no text.

She tried again.

> Jeremy, I need your help.

Terra chewed on her lip, then sent the photo. She explained briefly where it was found and that it was linked to a murder investigation. Then she sent another text.

> What is this?

While she waited for his response, she knew she would fall asleep unless she kept busy. So she checked her email and wrote a report of the events of the day. Her cell buzzed with a text.

> Not Native American.

The text became a call. Terra frowned. She wasn't sure she wanted to hear his voice. "Hey."

"All right. My interest is sufficiently piqued."

"If it's not Native American, then what is it?"

"I can't tell you much from a picture."

"Of course you can. You have all you need."

"I'm going to have to get a close look at it. That is, if you want my help."

Did she want his help that much?

"I could have the local forest service archaeologist assess it."

"But you contacted me. Why?" His brusque tone didn't give her the warm fuzzies.

Something's going on, that's why. But how did she tell him she was getting some weird vibes? "Listen, two people have been murdered, and I think their deaths could be related to this. I can't be sure, but I just didn't want to turn this over to the wrong person."

"I'm surprised to hear you think I'm not the wrong person."

Touché.

"Wait, you're not turning it over to me either." He huffed a laugh.

How long could a person hold a grudge? But Terra was one to talk. She weaved her fingers through her damp hair.

"Does the word *Janus* mean anything to you?"

Silence filled the connection. Before she could ask if he was still there, he spoke.

"In what context, Terra?"

She didn't miss the hesitation in his tone. Good. That meant she should push it. "In the context of stolen artifacts, what else?"

He heaved a sigh. "The term isn't used often, but the Janus is a person who facilitates the movement of an illegally trafficked item to the licit world market. Think of the Janus as a portal, the laundering point."

"Any thoughts on the profile of such a person?"

"Wait, are you suggesting that there's a Janus connection through Montana?" His voice sounded incredulous.

"You know as much as I do. Maybe the person is here right now. Has a ranch but another home elsewhere. What kind of person am I looking for, Jeremy? A scientist like you? Someone who's wealthy and is a collector? Or a museum curator? Someone who travels?"

"My answer will depend on the item. I need to see it, Terra. I could drive up to you."

Wow, he wasn't kidding. "No, that's okay."

"The Janus has many connections, political and social, and probably travels a lot. More than that, this could mean a world market. It could mean . . . international collectors. Bigger money."

There was that word *bigger* again.

Just as she was thinking, but she didn't want to believe it. Jeremy had been the right person to ask. "Okay. You have a deal. But I'm coming to you."

THIRTY-SIX

Chance sat in the dark corner and waited. This wasn't his preferred method, but he had no choice.

Blevins flicked the lamp on at his bed and spotted Chance in the chair aiming a gun at him.

Fear flickered across his face. "What are you doing here?"

"It's time for you to remember something."

The man lifted his palms. "You don't want to do anything stupid."

"I already did that a long time ago. You're the one who doesn't want to do anything stupid."

"You're not going to shoot me."

"I have nothing to lose."

"What do you want from me? Why are you doing this, man? This isn't like you. Not at all."

"Oh, so you do remember me."

Blevins stared at Chance but said nothing.

"Who's behind the deliveries?" Chance asked.

"I don't know anything."

Chance fingered the trigger, hoping Blevins believed the bluff.

"Okay, okay. I remember you. But maybe you shouldn't be

so anxious for me to remember. Maybe it's better that I forget I saw you."

"Yes, please forget. But only after you give me something I can use. I need to face off with him. This was supposed to be my last run, and then I was free."

Blevins laughed. "Did you ever stop to think that your freedom simply meant your death?"

Chance paused at that. "No, actually, I hadn't. But since it sounds like my life is threatened, you'd better start talking."

Blevins wiped the sweat from his brow. "Friends stop by the bar and have a beer with me. Sometimes it's a stranger who hands off information for a drop point or pickup point. Or we walk out together, and I take the package. It all happens in plain sight. When you sat down, I knew that something had gone very wrong."

"How did you know I wasn't supposed to be there?"

"I was told to expect the delivery. Then I saw on the news that the plane had crashed. Then you—the pilot from the crash—showed up, and I knew you were going to be trouble."

"So once the package is handed off to you, what do you do with it?"

"I hand it off to a woman. She meets me at the bar. We have a beer and a few laughs. We sometimes leave together like there's something going on, and I hand off the item. I'd say she could tell you what you want to know, but she was murdered."

"She was murdered. Jim was murdered."

"Tonight I was packing up to get out of town for a while."

"Because you could be next?"

The man barely nodded. "If you know what's good for you, you'll disappear too."

"I already disappeared once. Biggest mistake of my life. I intend to end this once and for all. But if you don't have the package, then who does?"

"I have no idea." Blevins sat on the edge of the bed. "Do you know what you were delivering?"

Chance pursed his lips. Unfortunately, he did know. In fact, he'd looked inside the box. Just this once, on his one last trip, he wanted to know what all the fuss was about.

He'd been shocked to see what was inside.

And . . . the one person who Chance would suspect to be behind that particular delivery had died a long time ago.

Chance eyed Blevins. "I'll help you pack."

THIRTY-SEVEN

The next day started early. After giving statements regarding the previous day's events, Terra and Jack piled into her vehicle to drive to an archaeological dig near Jackson Hole—a three-hour drive one way.

She'd suggested that they could accomplish more by going their separate ways, but Jack insisted he wanted to ride along. She hadn't wasted time arguing with him, though she knew he'd shifted to protective mode. They'd both been left shaken by what happened yesterday. In the end, Terra was glad for his company.

The day would be a long one, most of which would be spent traveling. But they could use the time to discuss what they'd learned so far.

The first couple of hours, they rehashed everything that had happened. Terra hoped she would remember something more about the man she'd seen. Some small clue that would give them insight into who he was, but he was good at creeping around and keeping his face in the shadows. Neva, Jim, and the cabin were entangled, and Terra strongly suspected the man she'd seen running from the cabin was the same man she'd seen running from Neva's home.

"We're driving three hours so you can show the artifact to your expert friend. You know, you could have let the Billings Curation Center look at it. That's sort of out of the circle of locals."

"That's Bureau of Land Management's repository. Not forest service."

"So? Think of artifacts discovered when an oil company is drilling, and the BCC holds stuff for all kinds of agencies. They could have kept it for you, and their archaeologists could have looked at it. No need to spend six hours driving."

"Are you trying to tell me you don't like being in the car with me this long, after all? I mean, you insisted on riding along."

He chuckled. "Not what I mean. You know what I'm saying."

Terra passed a car on the curvy two-lane road leading into Jackson Hole—the valley between the Wind River and Teton ranges. Home to Grand Teton National Park and gateway to Yellowstone National Park. Gorgeous place.

"Look, that's still local as far as I'm concerned. And as I mentioned, I trust this guy, at least where artifacts are concerned." Oh, great. Terra hadn't meant to say that last part out loud.

"Sounds like there's more to the story."

"There's no story."

"If you say so."

Terra hadn't wanted to drift into personal territory during this drive, but she and Jack shared a volatile past. One they'd never talked through or worked out. In a way, it was just left there hanging with no true closure, and here they were together again in a completely different capacity.

She opened her mouth to give at least a heads-up about her expert friend. Her openness would head off any knee-jerk reactions on his part, though she couldn't know he would have any reaction at all.

She sucked in a breath to speak—

"That's it." Jack snapped his fingers. "That must be it."

"What are you talking about?

"Neva Bolz's connection. We were talking about the curation center."

"What does she have to do with the curation center?"

"Not the center, but the oil and gas. Think about it. Artifacts can be discovered when oil and gas wells are being drilled. Federal or private, aren't archaeologists called in at that point? Maybe Neva was somehow involved with the looting of a drill site turned archaeological site."

"I don't know why I didn't think of that." Admiration swelled in her heart. "Seriously, I should have made that connection already."

Jack stared at his cell. "I'll see what more we've come up with on her company and her background, and look into any archaeological sites her company has run into."

"She traveled, Jack, so that search has to be broad and wide."

"She was murdered in Montana. Jim was murdered in Montana. We'll start in the county seat of Big Rapids and work our way out from there."

Terra turned onto a winding road leading into the Gros Ventre Wilderness area.

Jack groaned. "I think my call is going to have to wait."

"No signal?"

"No. Oh, wait, there it is. No. Gone again."

A burst of laughter escaped. She hadn't laughed so hard in far too long. But no more laughing for her as she turned onto a challenging, rocky, and twisted drive up the mountain.

"Just where are you taking us?" he asked.

"I put this address in the GPS, but I was warned it was kind of tough to get to. A guest ranch. Owned by somebody McKade out in the boonies near the town of Grayback. Apparently they were dozing to install a new structure when they came across human remains and artifacts, so the construction has stopped.

Dr. Brand is leading the team of archaeologists, interns, and volunteers."

"Dr. Brand. He's the guy you don't have a story with?"

She steered slowly under an archway with "Emerald M Ranch" carved into the pine arch.

Terra angled a look at Jack. "That'd be the one."

THIRTY-EIGHT

Jack hiked with Terra across the meadow where several white, tented domes had been set up. A few people worked in excavated grids dug several feet down. Some crouched or squatted. Whatever their position, their focus remained in the dirt. He glanced back at the sprawling log cabin in the distance and presumed that to be the main house.

He'd run into Liam McKade when he was an FBI special agent working in the Jackson Hole area. And he owed the guy his life. Would he see Liam today?

"You seem distracted, Jack. You okay?"

Terra's voice drew him back to the moment. "Yep."

They approached the back of two tented domes situated close together. She slowed.

Jack stopped walking. "You're hesitating. Why?"

"Someone's talking."

"Yeah? So?"

A man stepped from between the two tents, followed by a woman. At the sight of the familiar face, shock coursed through Jack.

She shook hands with the man. "Thanks for the interview, Dr. Brand."

He smiled as if immensely pleased with himself, then his eyes landed on Terra, who instantly stiffened.

"Rae?" Jack stepped forward. "Rae Burke? I can't believe it."

Rae's eyes grew wide. "Jack. Oh my gosh, Jack." She rushed forward and gave him a hug. Then just as quickly stepped back. They hadn't known each other all that well but had been in a life-threatening situation together, and that alone had connected them in ways that couldn't be put into words.

He looked her up and down and smiled. "You look well. What are you doing here?"

Rae turned and smiled at Dr. Brand. "Liam asked me to write up a few articles about the archaeological site discovered here on the ranch, or part of the ranch. Some of it extends into the wilderness area."

"Liam. How is he?"

"You can ask him yourself." She gestured behind Jack.

Wearing a Stetson, Liam McKade hiked toward them from across the meadow. Last Jack knew, Liam owned a security business that covered private security for high-profile clients as well as area ski resorts.

"So, you guys are close?"

She held up her left hand and flashed a big diamond ring. "We're engaged!"

"Oh, Rae, that's wonderful."

Liam stepped up and wrapped his arm around Rae's shoulder and pulled her close. He thrust his hand out to Jack. "It's good to see you, Jack. Who's your friend?"

"Forest Service Special Agent Terra Connors, meet Liam McKade and Rae Burke."

Introductions were made all around.

"Jack, everyone's up at the big house for a get-together," Liam said. "You and Agent Connors are welcome to join us for dinner. You too, Dr. Brand."

"You've been too good to us already"—Dr. Brand pressed a hand to his midsection—"considering how much food you've catered out here completely free of charge. We have a lot of work to do if we want to close up the site before the first snow hits. We're behind schedule as it is, so I'm going to pass, but thank you for your generosity." Brand eyed Terra. "Terra and I have some business to attend to. You ready?"

She nodded. "Sure."

She followed Dr. Brand between the two tents without a backward glance.

Jack needed to be part of that meeting. "I tell you what," he said to Liam. "Depending on how long it takes us to finish our business here, I'll pop by the house before we leave." Liam McKade's family—brothers Heath and Austin and their wives— had been grateful for Jack's work last year and had kept Jack company while he recovered in the hospital. "Maybe I should have kept in better touch than I have, but I've been busy."

Liam squeezed his shoulder. "No worries. Looks like God is keeping us connected." Liam tilted his head toward the site. "Which brings me to my question. Why are you here?"

Without giving away too much information about their active investigation, Jack gave the succinct version. "I should catch up to them."

"Hope to see you later then." Liam walked away with Rae, his voice drifting back to Jack. Liam asked Rae how her interview with Dr. Brand had gone.

Jack could see those two were meant for each other. He'd heard a quick summary of their story from Rae. They'd overcome a huge struggle and found their way back to each other.

Their story resonated with him, but he struggled to hold out hope for him and Terra—they were too far gone, and it had been too long. Who was he kidding? Terra probably wasn't even on the same page as Jack was, or even interested in opening up that book with Jack. In fact, what was he even doing thinking along those lines?

Either way, he didn't like the idea of her spending time alone with Dr. Brand, a man with whom she had no story. Right.

THIRTY-NINE

erra had followed Jeremy into what he'd clearly designated as his private yurt. But before she and Jeremy could talk, a lovely young woman peeked inside to ask for his help. Jeremy stepped out with her, leaving Terra inside. She waited at a table where dirt-covered artifacts were laid out next to a box. Jeremy's crew was obviously packing up the site, preparing for the winter, and then would probably come back next summer.

She stared at the items on the table, the stacked papers and tools, but her thoughts were on Jack and his reaction when he'd first seen Rae Burke. His eyes had lit up, and Terra's gut reaction had been jealousy.

Jealousy. She needed to come to terms with the fact that she might still have strong feelings for the man or that whatever she'd laid to rest before had not completely died, and his sudden appearance back in her life served to reignite their past. Whatever. She detested the confused feelings wrestling inside her.

"Terra?" Jack called from outside.

"I'm in here." She lifted the tarp attached to the domed tent, and he spotted her. "Over here."

He picked up his pace and stepped inside. "Where is he?"

Jeremy entered behind Jack and smiled. "Were you looking for me? I'm here. I apologize. One of my students had a question."

Terra couldn't help but wonder if Jeremy was in a romantic relationship with the beautiful woman. She shoved the thought far from her. Not her business. She didn't care. And interestingly enough, her relationship with Dr. Brand had been more recent than her romance with Jack, and no jealousy had surged when Jeremy spoke with the woman who appeared slightly enamored with her professor.

"Did you bring it?" Jeremy asked.

Terra realized both men were staring at her. *Special Agent Terra Connors to Earth.* She opened her bag and pulled out the box containing the artifact.

Jeremy donned gloves and carefully lifted the corner stone out of the box and placed it on his worktable. He switched on a magnifying light and stared through the lens.

"Terra tells me you might have some special knowledge to assist us," Jack said.

"I hope I can be of some help." Jeremy focused his attention on the piece. To her, it seemed he had already made a decision but for some reason was holding back.

"Dr. Brand, Jeremy, worked as an archaeologist for the Army." She held Jack's gaze, hoping he would understand her deeper meaning. Jeremy's archaeological experience spanned the globe. "Plus, as we discussed, I know I can trust him."

Did she imagine the slightest reaction from Jeremy?

He exhaled slowly as he pulled his gaze from the magnifying lens. "I'm going to need some time to confirm my initial thoughts and provide a general assessment about when and where this originated, but I can say with significant confidence that it's from the Middle East. If you'll look closer."

Terra and Jack gathered in and peered through the wide

magnifying lens. Jeremy pointed with a small tool. "These marks are cuneiform inscriptions, or what's left of them. The ancient Sumerians created this style of writing, so this object—my guess it's part of a tablet—could have originated in ancient Mesopotamia."

Jack backed away from the lamp and locked gazes with Terra, a question in his eyes she could easily read. *What is an ancient Middle Eastern artifact doing in Montana?*

//////////////////////////

Back in the vehicle as they headed north to Montana, Terra tried to calm her swirling thoughts. Jack had insisted they stop at the main house of the guest ranch for a few moments to meet the rest of the McKade clan. If she was ever going to learn from him what had happened on his last FBI assignment that brought him home to work as a detective, now was that moment. She'd at least gathered that it involved Liam and Rae.

Jack must have been caught up in his own thoughts too. The silence wasn't comfortable like she had hoped or expected. She reached for the radio, but Jack pressed his hand over hers.

"Don't."

"Okay, then. Um . . . I enjoyed meeting your friends, the McKades. And Rae Burke. Want to tell me what happened? How it all went down?" *Why it ended in you giving up the job you left me for?*

Because that's what it had been about, hadn't it? It couldn't have really been about Jack loving her enough to let her go because he didn't believe he was good enough for her.

He leaned his seat back an inch. "You first."

"Excuse me?"

"I want to know the story of what happened between you and Dr. Brand. Oh, pardon me, I mean Jeremy."

She huffed a laugh. "You know how juvenile you sound right now?"

Jack crossed his arms. "You don't have to tell me."

"What, about how juvenile you sound?"

"That's not what I mean. I meant if you want my story, I'm getting yours. I don't care if you think it's juvenile."

Okay. Well, then. They were getting personal, after all. And she thought she could make the drive without diving into those waters. But she hadn't wanted to admit that somewhere along the way—maybe when she nearly died in that fire and Jack came to the rescue—she and Jack had crossed into personal territory. Even now, sitting next to him in the vehicle, a satisfying warmth filled her heart and a thrum had started deep in her belly.

How did she escape it? Did she even want to?

Jack cleared his throat. Oh yeah, he was waiting for an answer.

"Look, it's no big deal. I was on a task force with several agencies when I was working undercover for the National Park Service. Jeremy was our archaeologist. He was the specialist on the team and could assist identifying some unique pieces. We worked closely together on one particular sting operation." How did she explain without sounding weak? "I . . . something terrible happened."

Tears surged. She wouldn't speak until she knew her voice was steady.

"Terra, I'm sorry. I shouldn't—"

"No, it's okay. I want your story, so I'm going to tell you mine. One of the park rangers got killed. Just some crazy person out to end his own life and take others with him. He was speeding through the park when he pulled out an assault rifle and blasted his way through the ranger parked by the road. He bled to death before help could arrive."

She blew out a breath. "I know you're wondering what this has to do with Jeremy. I was upset, and so . . . I needed a someone. Jeremy and I turned to each other for comfort. It grew into something more than simple friendship." She'd let her emotions get the best of her. "Obviously we're no longer together."

"I'm so sorry."

"Don't be. That relationship never should have happened."

It was a full five years after Jack had left her utterly broken before she'd gotten romantically involved again. From Jeremy she learned that she didn't have it in her to fully trust or love. She remained too guarded.

"Why shouldn't it have happened, Terra?"

He wasn't going to let it die, was he? "Because we were working together. We were a distraction to each other." Terra briefly glanced at Jack to gauge his reaction.

Talking about Jeremy reminded her that she and Jack couldn't have a thing going. Thinking about their past would help rein her in. But there was still . . . something. It wasn't interfering with this investigation, was it?

"And?"

"And I broke it off, and it got ugly to the point it was difficult to work together and remain professional. That didn't go unnoticed." Terra blew out a painful breath. "I was reprimanded, okay?"

"I'm sure Dr. Brand escaped unscathed."

"He didn't have anyone to answer to like I did. I . . . I feel like I . . ."

"It's okay, Terra. Believe it or not, I understand. You feel like you disappointed your mother. As long as I've known you, it's always been about you trying to be as good as your mother. To be a hero." He sucked in a small breath. "I'm sorry. I hope that doesn't upset you."

Relief washed over her. "No. I'm not exactly upset, but you got it wrong." Should she reveal so much of herself to this man who had broken her heart so profoundly? He was different now. They both were. "I guess it's no secret that a part of me would love to be a hero too. But Mom gave her life that day. She gave up everything—including me and Owen and Dad." And a part of Terra resented her for it.

"And you're not sure you can be so self-sacrificing."

"Let's just say that she wasn't the only one to make a sacrifice." Terra worked to steady her voice. After all, Mom had died years ago. But Terra hadn't talked about this in so long. Not even with Alex and Erin—her closest friends.

"So, yes, I work hard so I won't let myself down, and I can live up to her reputation that way. But as far as what I'm truly afraid of—" She swerved when another car cut her off passing her and laid on the horn. "You want me to pull that driver over?"

"No. I want to hear what you were going to say. We're not in my county anyway."

"Okay. Yeah. You're right."

"What are you afraid of, Terra?"

"Losing someone else." *In death . . . or in love.* Either way, she'd lost enough already. "I . . . I hate the mountain where she died. Mom had gone up to save that guy from the plane crash, and the avalanche killed her instead. I blamed Stone Wolf Mountain for her death. I try to ignore the fact that Gramps named his ranch after it. Now, fast-forward fifteen years, and Jim died on that mountain too. Or at least his body was thrown off a cliff on the mountain. Ever since the day she died, I've had dreams about that mountain killing someone else." Terra grimaced and swiped a hair out of her eyes. "Sorry, I didn't mean to go off."

Jack touched her arm, sending a gentle, comforting current through her. Jack said nothing, of course, because he couldn't guarantee that no one else would die up there. All she had left now were Owen and Gramps, and she was so grateful Owen had returned to them alive. Now that she had a semblance of family again, she would work hard to keep them close together. She would move out of her apartment and stay with Gramps permanently. That was it then. She'd made the decision. And she would be more deliberate about keeping Alex and Erin close.

But talk of the mountain and Mom's death ignited the pain again. And the memory of overhearing Gramps and Dad arguing that night, two weeks after Mom died.

"You can't just leave her here. She's your daughter. I can't raise her for you. I don't need that kind of responsibility."

"You're the best person to raise her. The truth is, Sheridan and I were planning to divorce. Terra would have ended up here with you anyway. Do this for your daughter and your granddaughter."

"You leave, and you'll break her heart. She doesn't need it broken over and over again. If you leave now, don't ever come back."

Pain and anger edged his voice.

Terra rushed in and hugged her father, sobbing, hanging on to him. In the end, she wasn't able to stop him from leaving, and he crushed her.

Alex and Erin were her lifelines not only because of the bond they shared after losing a loved one in that avalanche, but also because Terra had lost so much more. She felt unwanted by her father and her grandfather. But she knew Gramps loved her.

Then she made the mistake of falling for Jack, who left her too.

She'd lost people she loved—by their own choices or by the hand of the mountain.

Either way, why did people keep leaving her?

FORTY

Jack felt like a jerk for asking Terra to share about Mr. Archaeologist. He wished he could somehow make it up to her. He wished he could take his question back. She didn't owe him an explanation.

He was definitely a jerk.

She nudged a few tears away and sat taller, composing herself.

He never should have crossed the line into a personal discussion or allowed unfounded jealousy to direct his mood and conversation.

His cell alerted him to several texts. Good. He needed to focus on their investigation.

"Anything important?" she asked.

"I don't know. Maybe. Let me read. The Montana State Lab says the small wire in Jim's hand was a nose ring."

"Huh. That's one I haven't heard before," she said.

"I've heard stranger, honestly."

"You think he fought his killer? Pulled the nose ring out, was stabbed and pushed? That messes with my theory that Jim was killed at the cabin and then carted to the cliff."

"Well, at least we have more information, unless Jim wore a nose ring."

He read the next text out loud. "Star Oil Company had to halt drilling plans three years ago due to an archaeological discovery."

"Could Neva have taken something then and found her way into trafficking?"

"It would make sense," he said.

Terra said nothing more, and Jack was fine with that. He'd dodged her questions about his job at the FBI, and in the meantime, they'd learned a bit more about the investigation.

"Your turn," she said. "You insisted I talk first. Now, I want to know why you left the FBI."

"You know some of it."

"Only that you worked undercover and somehow that involved the guest ranch family."

"There's not a lot to tell, actually. I worked my way up in an organization until I was like the right-hand man to a guy at the top. Things went sour. Someone died." Jack stared out at the passing trees. *I couldn't save her.*

He wasn't sure how he was even living with himself now.

"Jack?" Terra's voice was soft. She'd been so good to share so much, and yet he knew she'd kept some of her deeper thoughts close. And he would do the same. Now wasn't the time to open up that festering wound and bleed out on her. If he did, he would become much too exposed.

"Yeah," he said.

"I heard mention of you getting wounded."

"I got shot, yes."

She grabbed his hand and squeezed. He almost brought her hand to his lips to kiss it.

"I'm glad you're okay." She released his hand. "So, you really did come back because of Aunt Nadine."

"Yes." And because of the guilt that plagued him. The secret that burdened him.

She didn't press him further, and they spent the rest of the drive in silence, lost in their own thoughts. And for that, he was grateful.

When Terra dropped him at the county sheriff's office, he couldn't have been more relieved. He opened the door to get out, feeling like he was escaping the somber mood in the vehicle. Though, at the same time, he hated leaving Terra for even a moment.

"Jack."

He leaned toward her, his gaze landing on her lips. The desire to kiss them hit him at the worst possible moment, but he reined it in, forcing his eyes to meet her crystal-blue gaze. "Yes?"

"Owen will be disappointed if you don't show up to the party tomorrow."

Jack doubted Owen would even notice. Maybe Terra was the one who would be disappointed.

"I'll be there."

///////////////////////

The next afternoon, Jack steered along the drive, passing a long line of vehicles at Stone Wolf Ranch. Aunt Nadine rode next to him.

His gut clenched.

"Oh my." Aunt Nadine pressed a hand to her chest.

His sentiments exactly.

"I should have expected a big crowd here." She stared down at the splint on her wrist and adjusted her shirt sleeve as if hoping that would hide it. "Lots of people know the family."

Owen definitely wouldn't have missed him, but Jack came for Terra. Plus, this was a great opportunity to get out of the house with Aunt Nadine.

"I'm going to pull around so you can get out at the door, and then I'll park."

"I don't want to have to wait there alone."

"Aunt Nadine, you know most everyone there. You won't be alone."

"I'd prefer to walk with you."

Jack found a recently vacated spot between two cars. As soon as they got out, the aroma of grilled food made his mouth water. Food instead of smoke. He was glad the recent wildfire had been contained and the air wasn't filled with the stench and haze or the threat of fire so they could enjoy the day. He escorted Aunt Nadine to the house, careful not to bump her injured wrist, and the door swung open as if automatically.

A young brunette girl and who appeared to be her younger brother held the doors. "Welcome to the party. Head through the kitchen to the patio out back."

Aunt Nadine chuckled. "Why, thank you. You're doing a great job welcoming the guests."

The boy giggled, and the girl frowned at him. Jack left them to their jobs and ushered Aunt Nadine through the house to the backyard. About two hundred people mingled in the back. He spotted a small gathering near the corral, and someone was sitting on a horse.

"Wow, this is quite the gathering," she said.

"Nadine, over here!" A woman drew his aunt's attention. Jack followed her while he glanced around the get-together in search of Terra.

And then he spotted her. She stood in a circle of friends. Jack recognized Erin and Alex. The guy drew close to Terra and whispered something that made her smile. No reason to be jealous. She didn't belong to Jack, and he reminded himself that he might not ever measure up, in his own mind, to someone like Terra.

He forced himself to look away so he wouldn't appear obsessed with her. He should join her and say hello to Owen as well. Then he and Aunt Nadine could get out of there.

Hands in his pockets, he tried to relax as he took in the crowd gathered to celebrate Owen's return. These were Terra's friends and family. A good mix of locals, including farmers and ranchers. The town mayor and the police chief. The county sheriff would probably show up as well.

He hoped Terra's grandfather, the previous land commissioner, wasn't planning to use this party for political gain as he started raising funds to campaign for higher political aspirations, but Jack couldn't help that it felt political to him. The raising up or fortifying of a political base, at least. Certainly, nothing was wrong with that—it was just the way of things.

That didn't mean Jack had to like it.

He hadn't been watching Terra, but when his gaze slid over her way again, he caught her watching *him*. Maybe their gazes collided at the right moment. Her smile brightened, and she waved him over. He excused himself and left Aunt Nadine with her friend Josey and headed for Terra's small group.

Her closest friends.

"Guys, you remember Jack, don't you?" she asked. "He's a detective for the sheriff's department now."

Jack shook Alex's hand, and then Erin's.

"It's good to see you were able to make it to the party," Jack said.

He'd never been good in a crowd, but he would make this work.

"Oh, I wouldn't miss it for the world," Erin said. "Mom still lives in town. In fact, she's at the party too. This gave me a great excuse to get away for the weekend, and, well, we're going to see the memorial early next week too." Erin smiled at Alex and then Terra.

Terra quirked a grin. "As if you need an excuse to come see your mom."

Alex crossed his arms. The guy seemed to have completely

clammed up since Jack arrived. Owen approached the group and, tilting his cup, shook ice into his mouth and chewed.

A man marched forward as if on a collision course—and Jack's reflexes kicked in. He mentally braced himself as the guy almost knocked Owen over when he grabbed him in a bear hug.

Owen's smile brightened as he turned. "Guys, here's somebody I want you to meet. My longtime Army buddy, Leif Morrisey. We've been through a lot together. Leif saved my life."

Jack studied Leif, who was a little older than Owen and also a little taller at about six foot. Everyone appeared mesmerized by Owen's life-saving friend.

"As soon as I learned about Owen's big welcome, I made sure to head this direction during my furlough."

Jack rubbed his chin. "What did you do in the Army?"

Leif disarmed him with his smile. "Warrant officer. Helicopter pilot and Owen's gunner."

He elbowed Owen, and they laughed like they shared a private joke.

Leif and Owen told stories from their experiences. Owen shared about his helicopter going down, caught in a spin, and how he and a few others had jumped out and landed in a lake before the crash. "Not usually advised, but in that particular situation, it saved our lives."

Jack spotted Aunt Nadine standing alone and looking lost. Oh no.

He inched around to Terra and leaned closer. "Going to check on my aunt."

She appeared mesmerized with Leif's and Owen's stories and probably wouldn't have even noticed he'd left.

He approached his aunt and offered his arm. "Hey, where's Josey?"

"Oh, she left already." Aunt Nadine pulled a slip of paper from her purse—a poster about Freckles—and handed it to

Jack. "Will you help me put up posters here for Owen's friends to see?"

Taking the slip from her, he smiled for her sake, though his heart ached. "Why don't we wait for now? I'll be sure to give this to Terra and Owen, and they can share with their friends. In the meantime, let's get you something to eat and drink."

He ushered her over to where burgers were being served. They got plates and grabbed all the fixings, including drinks. Jack found a table where he could sit with his aunt and hoped there would be a good moment to simply slip away unnoticed. He felt out of place.

Then Terra took the seat next to him. She smiled at his aunt. "I hope you don't mind if I join you."

"Oh, Terra." Aunt Nadine's face lit up. "It's been so long."

His aunt reached across him to touch Terra's hand.

Jack feared sitting together was a bad idea. Aunt Nadine might say the wrong thing since her mind sometimes went back a few years. She might refer to Jack and Terra like they were still together or remind him he needed to make things right with Terra.

He produced the paper with Freckles's picture and placed it on the table.

"Oh," Aunt Nadine said. "Where did you get that? I didn't realize you had brought a poster." She squeezed his arm and then looked at Terra. "My nephew is such a thoughtful person."

"What's this?" Terra lifted the poster. "Another stray? He's a cutie. I hope you find his owner soon."

"You mean, his boy."

"Pardon?"

"Freckles has a boy, and we're searching for his boy."

Terra briefly glanced at Jack, compassion in her eyes. "Well, of course Freckles has a boy. I can't wait to meet Freckles so I can know him better and help search for his boy."

Aunt Nadine ate some of her burger.

"See that man talking to Gramps?" She glanced at Jack.

"Yeah. Who is he?"

"His name is Marcus Briggs. Gramps hired him to be his campaign manager."

Jack almost choked on his drink. "So he *is* running. I kind of figured." He caught himself before he said more. "What office?"

"State representative," she said.

He wanted to ask more, but Aunt Nadine asked Terra about the rosebushes out front, and the conversation shifted to landscaping. Jack moved so they could speak directly instead of around him. He quickly finished off his burger, then chugged his drink. Over the rim of his cup, he caught two figures stepping into the house. Terra's grandfather, Robert, and Owen's Army friend, Leif.

Jack excused himself and entered the home as if he belonged there. After placing Aunt Nadine's poster on the counter, he headed down the hallway for the bathroom, but his instincts kicked in and he just kept walking until he heard voices outside Robert's office.

Robert and Leif were behind closed doors. Jack couldn't make out what they were saying, and though it certainly wasn't his business, he found it interesting they would choose this time to have a private conversation.

A sound drew his attention. Terra stood at the end of the hallway, a question in her eyes.

What are you doing here?

FORTY-ONE

Relieved the party was finally over, Terra eased onto the comfy sofa in the living room. She was also thankful that Gramps had hired caterers and a cleanup crew. At first she'd wanted to be involved in pulling the party together for her brother, but with her caseload, it just wasn't practical.

She'd said goodbye to her best friends and agreed to meet them for dinner Monday evening. Erin wasn't heading home until Tuesday. Tomorrow Terra would attend church with Gramps and hoped Owen would join them for a change.

Owen had already crashed. She'd worried that today might wear him out, but she shouldn't be so concerned for him. He seemed in better condition than she'd ever seen him—even after boot camp. She knew that was because he had a vision to help others.

Terra yawned and put the cup containing her last sip of herbal tea in the kitchen sink.

Gramps came up behind and gave her a quick hug.

"I'm surprised to see you so energetic," she said. "This was a big day."

He chuckled. "I might as well get used to it. Once I start officially campaigning, today will be nothing by comparison."

Terra slid into the chair at the table, hoping he might linger. "I was away last year when you made the decision to even consider putting your name in the hat for state representative, Gramps. We've never really talked about it." She lifted her hands as if in surrender. "Not that it's my business. It's totally your decision, but I guess—"

"You want to understand why." He eased into a chair, his hands around a warm mug of milk. "I'm too tired to sleep. I'm hoping the milk will help. Need to be bright-eyed and bushy-tailed for church tomorrow."

For the public eye? That wasn't fair, and she shoved the judgmental thought away. "Yeah. I want to know why."

"Because I'm not done yet. I want to give back. Owen served his country. You're protecting natural resources and fighting crime. I don't want to feel like I'm not contributing. I don't want to feel old. People like me, we have life experience. It's good for something. The thought of running for office, of working as an elected official, makes me feel alive again."

Terra thought maybe he was still searching, trying to fill that emptiness after losing his daughter. "That all makes sense, Gramps. I'm proud of you."

"At least you got to meet Marcus."

"Tell me more about him."

"He's a political consultant."

"When you were transportation commissioner for this region, you were appointed by the governor, so you didn't need a campaign manager. Is that right?"

"This is a whole new ball game, Terra. I need someone who can handle the pressure."

"Okay. I can see that. So, who is this guy, really? Where did you meet him?" Terra sure hoped Gramps knew what he was doing. Sure, he'd had his fingers in every industry pie in Montana, but he could be getting in over his head. But who was she to make that call?

"He's someone I've known for a while. He knew your mother."

"So . . . you just called him up and asked him to work for you?"

"No, nothing like that. As Providence would have it, he called me to catch up. We got to talking, and he agreed to come up and chat. Or consult. He mentioned he wanted to meet with you and Owen. Get to know you. All part of building a strategy."

"Well, I'll be around. Speaking of meeting people, what did you think of Owen's friend, Leif? You met with him in your office today."

Gramps's breath hitched, but he kept his smile in place—the smile he'd always had for her. Still, she didn't miss that he was surprised she knew about that meeting.

"Everything okay?" she asked.

"Of course. I invited Leif to chat in private. I wanted to know how he thought Owen was *really* doing. Leif went through everything with him but came out with all his limbs." Gramps's face twisted with pain at the words. "I love you and Owen. You're all I've got."

Terra smiled and rose. She moved to stand behind and hug him. "We love you too. Now, you'd better go get your beauty rest."

He laughed and pushed from the table. "Are you calling me an old man?"

"I would never. You can hold your own. And right about now, I think you could outlast me tonight. I'm beat."

Terra left her grandfather to finish his warm milk and sauntered down the hallway. She noticed a light on in Owen's room.

She knocked on the door. "Owen, you still awake?"

He opened it for her. "Sure. Come on in."

He left her to sit at his desk and stare at his open laptop.

She eased into a corner chair. "I figured you'd be three sheets to the wind by now. Today was a great day, seeing all those people here to welcome you home."

Preoccupied, he nodded but said nothing.

"Don't worry, Owen. Your idea is a good one, and before you know it, this will be *the* place to go for therapy."

He glanced up from his laptop and smiled. "You're right. I am beat. I think I'll go to bed now, so I'll shut this thing down."

She sensed he was trying to get rid of her. "Suit yourself. I hope you get some sleep so you can join me and Gramps for church tomorrow."

As she headed for the door, she noticed some print photographs on the side table and stopped for a moment. She lifted the pile to thumb through them. "This is you and Leif."

"Yep." Owen hovered near as if he would snatch the photographs from her.

"Who's the girl?"

"His sister." Owen gently relieved her of the photographs. "She was killed."

"I'm so sorry to hear that." Terra watched Owen. Maybe the party today had exhausted him and he wasn't able to put on a good show for her, but he appeared troubled. She would give anything if she could help him through this.

"I'm glad he was here for you today. He looked different tonight than in those pictures."

"Of course he did. In the pictures, his sister was still alive."

That wasn't what she'd meant. Terra couldn't quite put her finger on it, then . . . yes . . . she saw it now.

FORTY-TWO

Early Monday morning, Jack nursed a hot coffee and waited for Terra in a booth at a local diner. He spotted her vehicle parked down the road and focused on his coffee. He looked up as she entered the diner. His heart rate always spiked when she stepped into view, especially with that smile and those bright blue eyes.

How had he ever walked away from this woman? How many times would he think about what a fool he'd been?

She scooted into the booth across from him. "Did you order for me? I'm starved."

He kept his tone even. "Um . . . I did."

The waitress approached the table and set several dishes in front of Terra. Pancakes, bacon and eggs, hash browns, a colorful display of donuts.

Terra rewarded him with a smile that he felt to his toes. Appreciation flashed in her luminous eyes. Yeah. That was the reaction he'd been going for. And it tethered his heart to her.

"Now, can I get you anything else?" the waitress asked.

"No, I think I'm good," Terra said.

"I'll be back to check on you." The waitress left.

Terra's big blues held him captive. "You want to explain this?"

He hid his smile while he salted and peppered his eggs. "I wasn't sure what you wanted. I could have waited."

She threw her head back and laughed. A twinge of longing coursed through him. This moment triggered good memories from their past together. The past he'd ruined—or rather, the future he'd ruined.

"Well, thank you. I needed a good laugh today." She peered at her plate but lifted her eyes to look at him through her long lashes.

His breath caught.

Jack cleared his throat, testing his ability to speak. "In the meantime, tell me what's new."

"Since I saw you on Saturday? Not much. I talked to Gramps about meeting with Leif. He just wanted to talk to him about Owen to find out how he's really doing. He's worried about his grandson, that's all."

And you believe him? But Jack would be overstepping to say the words. She acted like something was bothering her, but then again, so did he. They hadn't made much progress in solving two murders.

"Anything else?"

"Gramps and I talked about his running for office. I'm just worried about him. He's excited about the challenge, and I wouldn't take his happiness away for the world, but I get the feeling he's trying to fill a hole. Like he never filled the emptiness after losing my mom. And then there's Owen. He needs Gramps to help him with this new equestrian therapy thing. If Gramps is off campaigning, he won't have time to help. I guess I'd just like to understand where this is coming from and where it's going."

"I get it. Families have their stuff."

She laughed. "Right. I know you've got your hands full with your aunt. How's she doing?"

"Her wrist is on the mend but still hurts. Fortunately, she has an appointment next week to see her doctor. I'm going with her. I want to talk to him about the dementia. She's scared. I'm scared for her."

Terra reached across the table and grabbed his hand. Compassion filled her gaze, but she said nothing. He appreciated that she didn't offer platitudes. The concern in her eyes was enough.

He cleared his throat. "Let's get back to the investigation now that we've taken some time and stepped back. So, what's a Middle Eastern artifact doing here in Montana?"

"Well, I'd say we could ask Jim, but someone didn't want him talking about it." Terra lifted a chocolate donut and took a bite. She was going for the bad stuff first.

Jack ate a few bites of his omelet. "And since the forest and cabin are ash now, we're not going to find more answers there."

He poured more coffee from the carafe the waitress had left.

"That could be why he set it on fire." Terra set the donut aside after only a couple of bites, then started in on the eggs and bacon. "I still need to pay a visit to the museum. I read through the interview reports your people gathered. Have you learned anything else?"

"I think there's a possible connection here that we're overlooking," he said.

"What's that?"

He hesitated. Should he bring it up? Or wait for her to think of it on her own? He saw in her eyes that she had already thought of it, but she wasn't willing to put that on the table. Should he just bide his time and only bring it up if it came to that? "Never mind."

Terra's hand shot across the table to grab his again, and he savored the softness of her skin. "Don't do that. I want to know what you're thinking. Don't hold out on me."

He sensed the desperation in her. The fear of losing the connection they'd found. "I'm not holding out, Terra." He squeezed her hand. "You are."

"What . . . what are you talking about?" She eased her hand from his grip.

He wanted to snatch it back. Instead, he toyed with his napkin and blew out a breath. They'd been walking a fine line—growing closer, maybe reaching across the distance their tumultuous past had created—and crossing that professional line in the midst of what was becoming a high-profile investigation.

Jack couldn't deny he had feelings for this woman.

But this conversation could serve as the detonator to a possible future with her. Still, he wouldn't hold back. "We both know what I'm talking about. I'm trying to catch a murderer here. Those murders are somehow linked to artifact trafficking. Unless we're off track. I'm willing to look at all the possibilities. Are you?"

Terra closed her eyes for a few breaths, then opened them. "You're talking about my brother who served in the Army in a Middle Eastern country. And his friend Leif. There are a lot of soldiers from Montana, a lot of veterans who make their home here, Jack. But I . . ."

"Yes?"

"Well, Saturday night I browsed through a few photographs. Not digital. Actual photographs that Owen had left out. Leif was in the photos with him."

Terra shut her eyes again. When she opened them, she stared right through him. "Leif was wearing a nose ring in the picture."

"You mean like the small black wire in Jim's hand?"

"Exactly like it," she said.

Jack dropped his napkin onto his plate. "Then we're onto something. I'll get people to dig into his background. See what we can come up with."

Terra shoved her hair behind her ears, then hung her head. "I don't want it to be Leif."

Jack understood why Terra didn't want to bring the investigation close to her brother. Her family was everything.

"Yet he suddenly shows up," she added as she glanced up. "We need to know when he got to town."

She took a bite of bacon.

"We'll look into that. In the meantime, Montana State Lab will work on DNA from the nose ring. But we both know that could take months," he said. "There's something else. I found out more about Neva Bolz. You were right to suggest we search far and wide. She was a world traveler in her job as an oil consultant."

Terra stopped chewing and stared at him. She swallowed. "Are you going to make me pull it out of you? Where exactly?"

"Algiers."

"That could be the connection we're looking for." Terra sounded relieved to shift the conversation away from Leif and her brother. "Star Oil Company stumbles across an archaeological site during exploratory drilling. Neva somehow gets her hands on something of value and sells it on the black market. She gets connected, and since she travels to Algiers, her reach and her clients and connections grow."

"It's one theory," he said.

"Jack, she was murdered. She's definitely part of this."

"We know she's connected, and now we have an idea why," he said. "Still, the only thing we know about her murderer is that he's about six feet tall and sometimes wears a gray hoodie."

Terra stared into her coffee. She had to be thinking what he was thinking.

Leif was also about six feet tall.

FORTY-THREE

Terra wished she wasn't following Jack's thinking, but how could she not?

If Leif was involved, then it logically followed that Owen could be as well. But she refused to believe that her brother could be part of this. And she held on to hope that Leif wasn't their murderer. Because if he was, that would be too destabilizing for Owen. Terra rubbed her eyes as nausea rippled through her stomach. Time to move on to the next topic. "I'm going to talk to the curator myself today about the murder weapon found at his museum. I feel like there are some inconsistencies after reading the reports."

"We can go together. But I think it's a priority that we should shadow Leif. See where he goes while he's here."

"You mean in addition to meeting with my grandfather in his office." Looked like the day and her teamwork with Jack were getting off to a bad start. Terra resented the shards of offense jabbing through her. "I already explained that. I'm glad Gramps asked Leif about how Owen was really doing." As if Leif would know better than she and Gramps, who'd been with Owen since he got home.

Maybe they were only seeing what Owen wanted them to see. She thought of his late night on the laptop and how he tried to get rid of her.

Nausea again.

Oh, Owen. He couldn't be trying to raise funds for his equestrian project by selling artifacts, could he? No. He wasn't involved. She knew Owen. Or at least she had known him before he left when she was a teenager, and he'd spent his life on the other side of the world, experiencing God knew what.

"Yes, I do mean in addition to your grandfather's office." Jack arched an eyebrow, a questioning look in his eyes.

What kind of investigator would she be if she tried to steer them away from Leif because of her brother?

Her throat constricted. "I agree we should shadow Leif."

Terra pushed down the rising bile. *God, please let Owen be innocent here.*

She admitted to herself—but not to Jack—that the Owen who had come home to them was not the same Owen who had left. But everyone changed. She certainly wasn't the same person she was when she'd moved to Colorado.

"Hey, where'd you go?" Jack's voice broke through her thoughts.

"I'm here. Sorry."

"Any idea how much money can be made trafficking artifacts? Native American or otherwise?"

Terra sipped her water before answering. "I wouldn't think it would be worth murder. Especially not two murders. But this Middle Eastern item, I have no idea. I'll look into it, but I suppose it's about what collectors are willing to pay. Collectors and auction houses." Terra had a lot more work to do.

"And the money paid goes to individuals? Or . . . certain nefarious organizations?"

She nodded. "I know where you're going with this. Like guns and drugs, anything that can make money can fund the cause of terrorism."

And her brother was definitely not involved in funding a cause he'd lost his leg fighting against.

FORTY-FOUR

Jack finished his coffee while he watched Terra head out the door and get into her vehicle. A call had come through, and she'd used it as her excuse to end their breakfast together.

He would sit there until he worked off his mounting irritation. She'd been angry, though not necessarily at him. More like frustrated with the path their investigation was taking. The possibility of Leif being a murderer was drawing them much too close to home—Terra's home, specifically. And that had been enough to douse the spark of growing affection between them. Terra was unwilling to even consider her brother's involvement. She could be too close to this investigation. But there wasn't enough information to say one way or another. Not yet.

So much for working with her today. And where would the two of them be on the other side of this? He sure hoped Owen wasn't involved, for Terra's sake.

He reached over to grab a slice of the bacon she'd left on the spread he'd ordered for her and grinned as he thought about that look on her beautiful face.

That had been priceless.

His cell rang. "Tanner here."

"Hey, Jack. Deputy Sarnes. I've got something for you."

Jack sat up. "I'm listening."

"I have a friend who overheard a conversation at a bar."

The waitress approached again and started clearing Terra's plates. Jack eyed her. "I'm still working on it."

She smiled and refilled his coffee cup.

"You're still working on it? How do you even know what I'm going to say?"

"Not talking to you. I was . . . Just tell me."

"Bartender down at the bar called Bar Wars mentioned he hadn't seen a guy in a few days. Comes in every night and takes up a whole booth for a couple of hours. Keeps it all to himself. The regulars know not to sit there 'cause Blevins is coming. You know, like a church pew."

Um, okay. "Go on."

"Bartender says Blevins hasn't been in. Says another guy took his place."

"Yeah? So?"

"He thinks it's strange. Something's going on. I was going to go by and ask around myself."

"And why don't you? I have my hands full with the murder investigation." And Terra Connors.

"Well, see, that's the thing. There could be a connection."

"So far I don't see it."

"Neva Bolz was in there. She met with Blevins once or twice. But if you want me to—"

"No. I got it. You did the right thing to bring this to me."

Jack pulled bills from his wallet and laid enough on the table to cover the bill and a good tip. "What bar did you say it was?"

"Bar Wars."

Jack knew the place. An odd establishment for this part of the world, if you asked him.

"And the bartender's name?"

"Now, to be clear, my friend won't want his name brought up. And if you start asking questions, the bartender will get suspicious."

"Sarnes, two people have been murdered. I'm trying to stop the madness before someone else is killed."

Sarnes sighed. "You're right. I thought you could stake it out instead of asking questions. But if you need to know, the bartender is called Billy Dee. You know, like that Star Wars actor."

Jack scratched his head. "No, which one?" Shoot, why had he asked that? He didn't care.

"Lando. *The Empire Strikes Back*." The deputy snorted. "The bar is like a tribute to Star Wars. Posters and memorabilia. Makes it interesting. The bartenders and waitresses have Star Wars names. One of the movie actors has a ranch in the county. Didn't you know that?"

"No." Jack had been away for too long and still clearly had some catching up to do. "Listen, thanks for the tip. So, I go ask for Lando. No, wait. Billy Dee, like the actor instead of the character."

"Right. Billy Dee."

"Anything else?"

"No."

"In the meantime, let's start looking for Blevins. See if he's home but hasn't gone to the bar as usual. Find out everything you can about him. I'll be the one to question him, though." This Blevins guy could be a witness, suspect, or . . . a victim.

If Terra had waited a few more moments, she could have learned about his conversation too. He'd check up on this lead, and if it went anywhere, he would let her know. Part of him wished she wasn't involved and they weren't collaborating, but the artifacts and murders were tied together.

Since Bar Wars was a couple of blocks down the street, he took the opportunity to get some fresh air and exercise. Would the place even be open at ten-thirty in the morning?

At the door, he pushed and pulled, but it was locked.

A bulky man—midfifties, graying yellow hair—slowly walked toward him and stopped at the door. "Can I help you?"

"I don't know. Can you get inside the bar?"

He produced a key. "That, I can do. But we don't open until eleven o'clock. You'll have to wait."

Jack hadn't wanted to throw around his weight, but he didn't have time for this. He flashed his credentials.

The man quickly covered his frown with a smile.

"What?" Jack asked.

"Talking to the cops is bad for business." He opened the door.

Jack stepped into the dark, waiting a few seconds for his eyes to adjust. "I don't see why it's bad for business. You're not doing anything illegal, are you?"

The man moved to stand behind the bar and crossed his arms. "No, I'm not. But the way I see it, people come here to talk and let off steam. They won't feel so comfortable talking to me if they see me talking to you."

Jack slid onto a stool. "Like anyone could tell I'm a cop. I'm not wearing a uniform."

The man laughed. "I pegged you as soon as I saw you standing at my door." He grabbed a couple of small bottles of club soda and handed one to Jack. "It's on the house."

Jack produced a five-dollar bill. "Thanks, but I'm more than happy to pay. If we get this over with before you officially open, then you don't need to worry that anyone will see you talking to me."

The guy nodded. "Fine. Mind going out the back when we're done? I usually come in that way but stopped in at the pharmacy across the street."

"I don't mind at all." *Thanks for the invitation.* That would give him a chance to look the place over on his way out. "So, what's your name?"

The man started wiping down the bar, a predictable work habit, and right now, an obviously nervous habit. "You mean my real name?"

"That, and I'd also like your Bar Wars name." Jack took the moment to take in the memorabilia. Huh. Interesting a place like this would be popular in Montana.

"My name's Chet Reeves. But here, it's Jabba the Hutt."

Jack chuckled. "You're kidding."

Chet burst out laughing, and Jack joined him. The guy seemed friendly enough, and Jack hoped he could get some good intel.

"Yeah, I'm kidding. I'm Boba Fett." Chet placed a replica of a Star Wars laser kind of gun on the counter.

Jack hated to admit he wasn't a Star Wars geek, but he still knew a few things. He snapped his fingers repeatedly. "He's . . . he's . . . no, wait, let me get this one. He's the bounty hunter."

"And a Mandalorian."

Whatever you say. "Should I call you Boba or Chet?"

"Take your pick."

"Okay, um . . . Boba." No, wait. He couldn't have a serious conversation like this. "I mean, Chet. Who is Mark Hamill or Luke Skywalker?"

"The owner. The owner and his wife founded this place probably thirty years ago. It started out western-styled, and eventually they added more pop culture, then shifted to the Star Wars theme."

"After that actor moved here, I'm guessing."

"Yep."

"And where are they now?"

"They come in now and again."

"They own it, but they aren't hands on when running it?"

"She is. Oh, she's here to make sure the stuff is arranged just so. They collect all this Stars Wars stuff at shows they attend."

"Who is she?"

"Princess Leia?"

"Um . . . yeah, who is she really?" Jack could discover that information himself, but he found this conversation fascinating and it got Chet talking.

"Mabel Porcella. Dirk is her husband."

"Dirk, who goes by Luke here at the bar. So, is there a Darth Vader?"

Chet laughed again. "We could go on and on, ya know? But I have a feeling you didn't come here to talk about the Star Wars collections or names."

"I came here to talk about Blevins."

Chet stilled. His face might have paled a few shades, but it was too dark inside for Jack to be sure.

"Just tell me about the guy who took his place."

"I don't know what you're talking about."

"Well, I could just wait around until Billy Dee gets here and find out then."

Someone pushed through the door and entered the bar.

Chet leaned forward and relayed the information in such low tones, Jack almost didn't hear him. "Tonight at ten-thirty, the guy who took Blevins's place will be here. You can ask him yourself when you see him. Why so interested?"

I'm following up on all information connected to two murders. Jack suspected Chet had probably figured that out, but he kept it to himself. He shrugged.

"There's something more, and this might be the best part," Chet said.

"I'm listening."

The news Chet shared definitely intrigued him.

"Thanks for the information." Jack left a big tip as he bid his new friend goodbye and headed through the back, amazed at just how many collectibles could be displayed on one wall.

He pushed through the exit door and found himself in a back alley facing the back entrance to the museum.

FORTY-FIVE

Tension corded her neck. Terra needed to rein in her focus if she was going to get caught up before her early dinner with Alex and Erin so they could head out to the memorial together.

After leaving Jack at the diner, Terra had stopped by the museum, but it was closed on Mondays. She'd then driven into the district office and spent the rest of the day catching up on paperwork on her various investigations.

Case Haymaker approached and leaned against the edge of her desk. "Terra, how's it going? Haven't seen you in too many days."

"Hey." She glanced away from the computer to smile at him and saw the deep concern in his eyes.

"What?"

"I'm glad you made it out of the Maverick fire alive," he said. "That had to have been terrifying."

So that's what they'd named it. She exhaled slowly. "It was, at that. I'm relieved they contained it before it reached Stone Wolf Mountain." Though so much forest had been lost. "Listen, it's good to see you, but I have a lot to get on top of here." She couldn't afford to fall behind.

"I understand, so I'll leave you to it." Case made to leave, then hesitated, turning back to her. "Watch your back, Terra. It seems like you're caught in the crosshairs a lot lately."

Case disappeared through the door and left her to think on his words. Wait. What had he heard? How much did he know?

Case . . . Case was about six feet tall, wasn't he? Terra rubbed her temples. Every six-foot-tall man couldn't be a suspect. She was grasping at proverbial straws. Anything to keep the investigation from turning toward Leif, and by default, her brother.

She stared at the cell on her desk and itched to call Jack to find out if he'd learned anything more. Also, to hear his voice. She hadn't meant to rush out of the diner—especially after that breakfast he'd ordered for her—leaving him in the wake of her frustration.

And she was still distressed, struggling to focus on her other cases while this investigation looked to potentially expand around the globe. She was waiting to hear from Jeremy about the Middle Eastern piece. He'd offered to try to identify it. No sense in notifying other agencies—like the FBI Art Crime Division or Homeland Security—until she had solid information to share.

Terra made a list of more people to talk to. She wanted to speak with Jim's daughter, Abbie, again, and Neva's family as well. She tucked the list away for later before heading to Gramps's to quickly change and then to the restaurant to meet her longtime friends.

Heart pounding, Terra rushed into Fazzori's Italian Restaurant, where the hostess greeted her. The aroma of garlic and basil and cheese made her mouth water. "I'm here to meet—" Erin waved at her from across the crowded restaurant. "Oh, there they are."

Terra left the hostess and weaved through the tables, finally plopping down next to Alex and across from Erin, who smiled.

With silver hoops dangling from her ears and her long blonde hair stacked on top of her head, her friend looked elegant as always. And Alex flashed his roguish grin. Terra had always thought Alex could model for *GQ*, and that hadn't changed. He wore a crisp white button-down shirt, and his thick brown hair was neatly trimmed and his gray eyes serious.

"I'm glad you could make it," Erin said.

"I'm sorry I'm late."

"I was afraid you got caught up in something work-related. No such pressure on me." Erin angled her head at Alex.

Alex quirked a grin but said nothing as he picked up his menu and seemed to bury his head in it.

Terra took a calming breath and a sip of water from the glass placed before her. "It feels good to finally be here. We don't get to do this that often anymore, since you guys have both moved away." And even if they lived closer, would their busy lives prevent them from getting together?

Erin laughed. "You're one to talk."

Her friend referred to Terra's time living in Colorado.

"Well, I'm back now." Terra grabbed a menu and stared at it.

Would they share their secrets like they used to, or hide behind menus and Italian food?

"And since I'm back, I'll say that I hope you both will move back too," she added. "That would make things so much easier to keep in touch." They'd been her lifeline for so long, after all.

Well, shoot. She shouldn't put pressure on them like this.

"I admit that I miss living here," Erin said. "I would be closer to Mom. But I'm not sure I could find a job with the locals as a criminal psychologist. Nor would I want to, considering Nathan's a detective here. I don't think I could work with him."

Erin gave Terra a look over her menu. Terra knew exactly where Erin's mind had gone—straight to Terra and Jack's current joint investigation. "That stinks, Erin. I'm sorry."

"Instead, I've been trying to get Mom to move out to Seattle to live with me." Erin closed her menu and placed it next to her plate.

Oh? Terra hadn't known about that. Disappointment crept in. Alex still perused the offerings.

"What about you, Alex?" Erin asked. "What are you up to? I don't even know who you're working for these days."

Alex set down his menu. "I've decided what I want."

"Oh, I get it," Erin said. "Your job is classified. Secretive. You always said you—"

He lifted a hand. "I don't need you psychoanalyzing me, thank you very much."

"I'm not psychoanalyzing, but I get it. You can't talk about it."

He leaned on folded arms. "I'd prefer not to talk about work tonight, all right, ladies? Now, what I'm really wondering is why you two gorgeous women aren't married yet."

Great. Terra hadn't wanted to get into those issues, because that could lead to talking about working with Jack. But leave it to Alex to cut right to the more sensitive topics. And she'd wanted them to share their secrets, hadn't she?

Terra gave Alex a friendly arm punch. "I beg your pardon. Why is it that we're supposed to be married already? What about you? You're a real catch, Alex. Bad attitude and all. You've got so much more going for you than that six-pack underneath your button-down shirt."

He eyed her. "And how would you know about that?"

"It's just a guess. You're in great condition, and it's easy to see you work out. You have to stay in top form for your job. Am I right? Or am I right?"

The waiter brought a basket of bread and seasoned olive oil for dipping, took their orders, then left. Alex cut a slice of bread, dipped, and chewed. Terra figured he had no intention of answering her.

But he finished chewing, then surprised her. "I'm no catch. The truth is, after what happened to us, seeing families torn apart in one swift tragedy, seeing the brutal world out there, I'm not sure I want to suffer through the pain. You guys, you're my best friends. You're all I need."

Terra wanted to scoff a laugh. "And as your friends, we know that we are certainly not all you need."

She considered Erin and Alex the closest people to her, but the truth was that life had torn them apart. Alex especially was becoming a stranger to her. Kind of like Owen had when he left. She felt helpless to do anything about it.

The waiter reappeared and set steaming plates of lasagna, spaghetti Bolognese, and chicken parmigiana before them. The aroma was heavenly.

"Can I get you anything else?"

"No, thank you. I think we're all good," Erin said as everyone nodded in agreement.

Terra cut into her lasagna to let it cool while Alex didn't seem to be bothered by a hot dish and started right in on his chicken.

"You know what," Erin said. "I feel like we're not as close as we once were. As close as we could be."

"It doesn't take a psychologist to see that." Alex frowned. "Look, you two are the sisters I never had and my best friends. Let's say you're my *only* friends. The only two people I can completely trust. I look out for you the best I can. Call when I can. And like this weekend, I took off to come out here for Owen's welcome-home party and for a visit to the memorial." He hung his head. "I'm sorry if I've been a little preoccupied and somewhat disconnected. Maybe I can talk about the reasons some other time. And who knows, maybe life will bring me back to live closer to my two favorite people."

Terra's heart warmed, then it turned stone-cold when she spotted the man who approached the table.

She knew that look in Jack's eyes, and he brought no good news.

FORTY-SIX

'm sorry." Jack approached the table where Terra sat with Alex and Erin.

He should have waited. Why didn't he wait? Three sets of confused eyes stared up at him. "But I thought you'd want to know."

"Know what?" Terra's chair scraped the floor as she stood. "Is it Gramps?"

He shook his head. He'd caused unnecessary concerns with his approach. Jack took a seat next to Erin, and Terra sat down too.

Jack leaned in so only they would hear. "The memorial to your family members has been vandalized."

"What?" The three shared glances.

"I knew you had planned to head that way this evening, and I wanted you to know before you got there."

"Thanks for giving us a heads-up," Erin said.

"Well, ladies," Alex said, "looks like our dinner plans have been waylaid. Unless you want to finish eating."

Terra stared at half-eaten lasagna. "I've lost my appetite." She lifted her gaze to Jack. "Can we look at the damage?"

"Yes."

"Will you take us there?" Terra asked.

Terra knew the way, of course, but Jack wouldn't refuse. "Sure."

"Well, what do you say, guys?" Terra glanced at her friends.

Erin nodded as the waiter approached. "Can we please get the check and this food to go? Something has come up."

"Give me a few moments." He turned around with the tray and disappeared into the kitchen. Erin pulled out a few bills, as did Terra and Alex.

Erin shrugged. "I figure, why waste the money? At some point tonight we'll be hungry again. Or we can eat the leftovers for breakfast tomorrow. You guys head on over with Jack. I can wait for the food."

Terra squeezed Erin's shoulder. "We're in this together, so we'll wait."

A few moments later, the waiter returned with each dish stored in a separate delivery bag, and the friends handed him enough cash to cover the check, plus tip.

Jack had assumed when Terra requested that he take them, he would be driving them, but they each climbed into their own vehicles and followed him out of town and all the way to the memorial near the base of Stone Wolf Mountain.

When Jack had received the news and went to investigate, he hadn't known how best to break the news to Terra or Owen. He'd made the drive to the ranch and explained the situation. Robert had suggested that Jack deliver the news to the three friends who were having dinner. According to Robert, Owen had been invited out to dinner with them but had chosen to meet with Leif.

Awkward didn't begin to describe how Jack felt walking into the restaurant to find Erin, Alex, and Terra staring at him. When he and Terra were together as a couple, he'd always felt like an outsider when it came to her friendship with Alex and Erin. Still, their bond had been created when their hero parents died on that mountain. That wasn't a friendship circle Jack would ever fit into, considering his own unheroic ancestry.

At the trailhead parking near the memorial, he waited for Alex to park. Terra and Erin got out and headed over to meet Jack. Good thing they were both wearing slacks and comfortable shoes.

Jack turned and headed up the trail.

Terra caught up to him and grabbed his arm. "Wait, Jack." She looked at her friends, then back at him. "Can you at least prepare us? I should have asked about the damage. How bad is it?"

How did he word it? The weight of it pulled his heart down to his gut. "Bad enough that I wanted to tell you in person."

Shadows chased away the light in her eyes, darkening her already somber demeanor.

The memorial was only a quarter of a mile in, and they slowed as they neared it. Crime scene tape marked off the area. No visitors were allowed. A couple of deputies, a ranger, and a forest service LEO remained.

Jack crossed his arms and stood back to watch the trio. Terra started to walk under the tape.

"Terra, no. We're still hoping to find even a small piece of evidence." Crimes against persons and property fell within the county sheriff's jurisdiction, otherwise Terra might investigate. Except in this case, the vandalism was linked to her.

And that's what worried him.

Was it deliberately linked to her?

Terra, Erin, and Alex walked around the edges of the tape. Grief carved into her features, Terra made a full circle, leaving Erin and Alex standing on the other side, while Terra joined Jack.

"Who and why, Jack? I don't understand. Random vandalism? Is someone sending a message? If so, what's the message? I just don't get why someone would do this. Why now?"

Why now, indeed. Jack's chest constricted. Terra's mother's plaque had been obliterated as if someone had taken some kind of vengeance against it. He had no answers. This could be a distraction to pull her focus from her current investigation.

"We'll find whoever was behind this," he said. "In the meantime, stay focused on *your* investigation."

Her eyes held his. "You think this is about our investigation?"

He leaned closer and caught the scent of vanilla in her hair. "I didn't say that. But all possibilities are on the table." He peered at her beautiful face, saw the hurt mixed with anger, and Jack wanted to hold her. Tell her it was all going to be okay. Since he'd given up his undercover work, he was done with lying or putting on a facade. "I'm concerned about you."

Her lips revealed the smallest of smiles. And something in her eyes—trust. Something he'd longed to earn again from her, though he hadn't realized it until this moment.

"Then I have nothing to worry about if you're concerned," she said. "That means I can trust you to find who did this."

She didn't understand that he'd failed in the worst kind of way before. How did he tell her? He couldn't bring himself to open up about it any more than he could tell Aunt Nadine. So he admitted the truth to himself.

He'd been wrong.

He was still a liar.

FORTY-SEVEN

Back at Stone Wolf Ranch, Terra, Erin, and Alex finished off the reheated leftovers, then moved to the sectional in the living room.

After visiting the vandalized memorial site, the three had been mostly silent. The atmosphere somber. When Mom was killed, Terra was fourteen going on twenty-five, so she, Alex, and Erin spent a lot of time there at the ranch. On the horses. Hiking trails. Anything to move beyond their despondency.

"Okay, look. We're all dancing around the elephant in the room," Alex said.

"Dancing?" Erin sank deeper into the sofa and crossed her arms. "I don't see any dancing, Alex. But if you'd like to entertain us, go ahead."

"Funny." Alex frowned.

Yep. They were like siblings. Family. Terra would have soaked up the warmth of the moment if they weren't all so miserable. "Okay, kids. Now isn't the time. I hear you, Alex. The memorial got vandalized on the very evening we were going to hike out to see it. Coincidence? Intentional?"

"What do you think, Erin?" Alex asked. "You're the criminal psychologist."

Erin sat forward and rubbed her eyes. "I'd like to know more. Like were any other memorials destroyed? That would tell me something, like if there is some sort of political ideology behind it. What I saw—that damage was no child's game. That was malicious. Violent." She shuddered, then rubbed her arms.

"What about revenge?" Alex asked.

"Revenge?" Erin studied him. "What makes you suggest that?"

He shrugged. "I don't know. This year is the fifteenth anniversary. Maybe there's something about what happened that we don't know."

Terra found herself staring at Alex, along with Erin. "It was an avalanche, Alex. An accident."

"I would think if it were some sort of message or revenge," Erin said, "whoever was behind it wouldn't have waited fifteen years."

"It just seems like a weird coincidence." Alex steepled his hands against his lips.

Unfortunately, Terra agreed.

His gray eyes bored into her. "What cases are you working on now?"

She bolted from the sofa. "Okay, enough. Jack is going to handle it. Let's let him do it. Frankly, I can't add one more thing to my plate."

"And you trust him to figure it out?" Alex asked.

"Yes. Of course I do."

He leaned back, a smirk on his face. "I want to hear that story. Since when do you trust Jack Tanner? You haven't said much at all about him. In fact, I knew nothing about his being back." Alex glanced at Erin. "By that look on your face, I can see that you knew."

"There's nothing to tell," Terra said. "I'm working an archaeological crimes case that's connected to Jack's murder investigation. Oh, and the sheriff deputized some of us for the foreseeable future. We're pooling our resources, that's all." Time to redirect. "I just hate that this happened. It'll be all over the news tomorrow."

Alex sighed. "Will it? I'm not sure anyone cares anymore."

"Of course they care." Erin stared at Alex. "And if they don't, we need to make them care. We need to make sure it's rebuilt." She rose from the sofa. "I need to head home to Mom. I told her I'd be a little late, but I'm leaving tomorrow, and I need to pack but also visit with her."

"What? No game of Parcheesi?" Alex genuinely sounded disappointed.

Terra tossed a pillow at him. "You're welcome to stay and play. Owen should be home soon."

Alex stood and moved closer to Terra. "I should get going too."

Regret flooded her. This evening certainly hadn't gone as expected. Terra hugged Erin. She got to see her much more often than Alex, but she still missed her. Erin headed to her vehicle while Alex lingered.

Terra was glad for a few more moments with him. "I'm worried about you."

Hands in his pockets, he shrugged. "There's no need to be. Honestly. I'm good."

"Would you tell us if you weren't?"

He grinned. "Probably not. That's only because I want to protect you like an older brother."

"I have an older brother."

His grin dropped. "Yeah, well, he wasn't really around for you when you needed him."

Terra fought the retort as hurt and anger flashed through her.

"I'm sorry. I shouldn't have said that." He shifted closer. "Look, Terra, I'm worried about *you*. You're involved in a big investigation. You're close to the memorial geographically, and your mother's plaque suffered the most. What if it's somehow related?"

"Is that all?" She braced herself.

"You know it's not. Jack Tanner is back in your life. It tore me up the way he hurt you." He swiped his hand over his face. "I mean, do I need to quit my job and move back here to make sure he doesn't hurt you again?"

That brought a chuckle, despite his serious tone. "You don't need to worry about me and Jack. There's nothing going on between us."

He studied her long and hard. "I'm not convinced."

"He's different. Something happened to him, and it changed him somehow. I'm still trying to figure things out. Don't worry about me. But as for you, young man, I want to hear from you in a few days. Call me and tell me what's really going on in your life."

He sighed. "I might just take you up on that."

Alex leaned in to kiss her on the cheek, and she gave him a big hug. At least the evening had ended on a good note. Terra felt like she'd reconnected with Alex, who had seemed somehow distant the whole evening until the last few moments.

After he left, she cleaned up the mess and washed out the few dishes in the sink as she considered Alex's words about the vandalized memorial. Her mind shifted to Jim and Neva, and the devastated forest around the cabin.

A creak startled her. She whirled and caught Owen standing in the kitchen, watching her.

She exhaled with relief. Terra smiled and folded the dish towel. "When did you get back?"

"A long time ago. Gramps told me about the memorial."

Terra dropped her gaze and shook her head. "It's just crazy, the things people do these days. They'll just have to rebuild it and set up some cameras or something. I don't know anymore."

Arms crossed, Owen continued to watch her but said nothing more.

"You got home a long time ago?" Terra asked. "I thought you were going out with Leif."

"He canceled on me."

"That's too bad. You could have come to dinner with us, though it wasn't much of a dinner since Jack showed up to give us the news."

"So I heard."

"Uh . . . Owen, why didn't you just come out and visit?"

"That's your circle, Terra. Your best friends. I wasn't around for you back then. I'm sorry I wasn't, since it turned out that Dad wasn't either."

Owen seemed in a dark mood tonight. She wasn't that familiar with this side of him, and it could be that he developed this mood while he was in a foreign land. She didn't know. But she did know that she didn't like it and wasn't sure what to do with it.

"It's okay, Owen. We're all grown up now. It's all good, especially now that you're here." She approached and gave him a quick hug. "I'm heading to bed. I have a lot to get done tomorrow."

She paused in the hall and turned back. "About Leif. How well do you know him anyway?" She instantly regretted the question. This wasn't the time to ask.

"You could say that he's *my* best friend, since he saved my life. On a mission, our Apache got shot up, along with my leg. I lost consciousness. He used the autorotation maneuver to land the helo and got us both out. I owe him everything."

Owen turned from her then, as if talking about what happened dredged up an unwanted memory.

"I'm glad he was there when you needed him."

"Yeah." Owen left her in the kitchen.

After she heard his bedroom door shut, Terra headed for her own room. She shut the door behind her. Closed her eyes and forced back the nausea. She was jumping to conclusions. But . . .

God, Owen can't be involved in the artifacts trafficking. He just can't.

Her cell rang, and she grabbed it. Jack. Her heart jumped and moisture bloomed on her palms. What was she? Sixteen? She blew out a breath to steady her reaction. Terra hoped he didn't have more bad news.

"What's up?" she answered.

"You want to go with me to Bar Wars?"

She couldn't help the smile that erupted. "Have you lost your mind?"

"It's a stakeout. I got a lead. We're going to watch the bar and see who stops in."

"Tonight? You want me to meet you tonight?"

"No. I want you to open your door. I'm outside. If you want to go, you can ride with me. Come on, Terra, it will help get your mind off what happened. And we need a break in this."

"Where'd you get the lead?"

"Boba Fett."

"Excuse me?" Terra almost barked a laugh.

"Bartender named Boba Fett said he spotted a guy who looked a lot like the pilot who disappeared from the hospital."

FORTY-EIGHT

Jack steered around the corner a little too fast.

Terra reached for the handgrip above the passenger window. "If you were worried about missing this guy, maybe you should have just called me to meet you there."

"The truth is that I didn't decide to invite you along until after what happened tonight. I thought you could use the distraction."

"You didn't think I'd want to be part of it?"

"I figured you were with your friends, and I didn't want to interrupt."

"But you ended up interrupting anyway."

"Did I? Looked like they were gone to me. Oh, you mean the dinner. I thought you would want to know about the memorial. Terra, I hated tracking you down. I just didn't know how to tell you. I—"

Terra touched his arm, sending a warm current through him. "You handled it the right way, Jack. And thank you for inviting me along tonight as well. But can I ask you, from now on, to please not make decisions for me? If a lead turns up that is important to my investigation as well, then please inform me. Let me make the decision whether I will be part of the stakeout, okay?"

"I'm duly lectured."

Downtown Big Rapids was still hopping thanks to the local casinos, pizza joints, and ice cream parlors. But farther into the shadows, the section that included the bars, otherwise called dives, began. Bar Wars was at a halfway point—not quite in the limelight, not quite in the darkness.

He parked a block down and across the street from the bar, grateful that he drove an unmarked vehicle. Now that he was here with Terra, he thought maybe he'd made a mistake. She was a huge distraction. As he stared out the window, taking in the area, a strand of hair fell from the clip and curled across her cheek. Jack gently lifted it and tucked it behind her ear.

A small gasp escaped from her as she turned to look at him, her eyes shining.

And her lips . . .

The stakeout, Jack. Remember why you're here.

"So, I'm told this guy comes in every night. Sits in the booth and drinks a few beers."

"Oh, that's a new one," Terra said.

"The thing is, someone took the regular guy's place a few nights ago. Nobody sits in that booth, right? Because they know the regular guy, Blevins, likes to drink his beer alone. And he's a bully. Nobody gets in his way. And every Monday night at ten-thirty, someone comes in to sit across from Blevins. Like a meeting."

"The same person every time? Or someone different?"

"I haven't confirmed anything yet, except I was told that Neva Bolz had been in to meet with Blevins. Since a new guy took Blevins's place and the bar employees think that's unusual, I've put a deputy on finding Blevins. We still don't know where he is, and it looks like he might have skipped town."

"You mean he disappeared?"

"I mean . . . we're looking for him."

"You don't think he's the killer, do you?"

"I hope he's not our next victim. I hope there won't be one. Now, if we can question this new guy who took Blevins's place, whether he's the pilot or not, we could find out more."

Terra sighed.

"What's the matter?"

"Everything. Investigations just take too long."

"I'm getting impatient too, Terra." The evening had started to cool down, so Jack turned his vehicle back on and cranked the heat. "Were you able to talk to the museum curator?"

"They were closed."

"When I left the bar today, I went out the back into the alley and I saw the back of the museum."

"What are you thinking?"

"It's just something to note. The Bar Wars owners are collectors."

"Of Star Wars memorabilia. But you think there could be more going on behind the scenes?"

"Something else to look into."

"Again, it seems too obvious. Too easy. No one would be so bold to operate like that."

"In plain sight? Sure they would."

"I'd like to talk to the Bar Wars owner, then—about their collections. But we're staking out the bar tonight, sitting in your vehicle. You haven't explained how we'll know this guy when we see him."

"The bartender said ten-thirty. It's ten twenty-five. Let's see if our guy walks in soon."

"Then what will we do?"

"We'll see who goes in after him."

"But we won't know which persons coming and going are there to meet with him. I think we should go in."

Jack rubbed his jaw. "Earlier today the bartender said he had me pegged as a cop from a long way off. I don't want to disrupt the flow of things. Let's wait." He didn't add that he was counting on that gut feeling that was an important part of any investigation.

"That's it. I'm going in. I don't look like a cop." She flipped the mirror in the car open and let her hair down from the clip, then mussed it.

"What. Are. You. Doing?"

"I'm going in to see who he meets with."

"You're not going in alone," he said.

"Name one reason why not? I can handle this. I'm law enforcement. This is my investigation too."

"When I brought you into this, I hadn't meant for you to step in the middle—" A guy moseyed toward the bar wearing a baseball cap. He glanced over his shoulder, wary. "I think that's him. It's hard to see in this lighting."

Terra opened the door and stepped out. She leaned in and smiled. "I'll text you a blow-by-blow account."

He started to open his door.

"Don't you dare," she said. "You'll ruin this for us. We need to find out who is behind the trafficking and the murders. I'll text you when the guy he met with leaves, and you can snag him for questioning."

"Uh . . . Terra . . . the booth to watch is the one at the very back far right."

She ducked her chin, acknowledging that she appreciated the tip.

"And I want a blow-by-blow," he said. "If I don't get one, I'll think you're in trouble and then I'm coming in."

He watched her walk away and head across the street. She opened the door and entered the bar just as a couple spilled out, leaning on each other and laughing. They strolled down the sidewalk weaving back and forth. He hoped they had called a cab.

Then a familiar face walked into the bar.

Not good.

FORTY-NINE

At least Bar Wars wasn't the seedy kind of bar she'd imagined. With all the Star Wars memorabilia, it could even rank as family friendly. Unfortunately, too many heads had turned her way when she walked in. She would not walk through to check out all the decorations and draw more attention. Instead, she found a corner from which she could watch the entire place and quickly took in the far back booth in the shadows, a man already sitting there. The pilot?

A waitress approached. "What'll it be?"

"I'll have a club soda with lime."

The woman arched a brow. "Suit yourself."

Terra dropped her cell and picked it up from under the table. Then she sat up and started a text to Jack like she told him she would. A man pulled out a chair and sat at her table.

"Excuse me, but I'm waiting on a friend," she said.

The guy winked. "I can be your friend."

Oh brother.

"I have a boyfriend."

"I can work around that."

Really. "Look, I'm not interested."

The waitress approached with Terra's club soda. "This guy bothering you?"

Terra did not want to make a scene. She wanted to blend in. Maybe this had been a bad idea, after all. "I can handle him."

The waitress laughed. "Bobby, go find another lady to hit on. This one's too classy for you."

"Look, I—"

Another man approached the table wearing a leather bomber jacket and a cap. She did a double take and realized it was Jack. He pressed his index finger on the table in front of Bobby. "This one's taken, buddy."

Bobby glanced up as if he would argue, then thought better of it. He lifted his hands in surrender. "Sorry, dude. You can't blame me for trying. You're a lucky guy."

He exited the seat.

And Jack slid into it, his back to the booth where their person of interest was sitting in the shadows.

"What are you doing here?"

"Saving you." He leaned forward. He looked too good. With the jacket, the cap, and the more arrogant demeanor, she had to admit that he didn't look at all like a cop or a local detective.

Her mouth went dry, and she'd never been so grateful for a club soda. She took a few sips, then said, "I had it under control, thank you very much."

"I'm sure you did. I'm here because there's been a change in our plans."

Terra glanced at the booth at the back, and someone was now sitting across from the man already seated. She'd missed his entrance. His back was to her, so she couldn't see who it was. Terra inwardly groaned.

"Who's sitting with him?"

Jack's lips flattened. "Owen's friend Leif. I spotted him walking in not long after you did."

Leif? Terra's pulse jumped. *Oh, please, God, don't let him be involved in this.* "Do you think he saw me?"

"My guess is that he missed you since he's now in the meeting with the man who took Blevins's place."

"Or he isn't committing a crime so he has nothing to hide by sitting with our subject."

"I think he would have said something to you, had he seen you."

"I agree. He seems like the kind of guy to be aware of everything going on in a room. I bent over to pick up my cell phone when I dropped it. He could have come in the bar at that moment and missed me."

Jack shrugged. "What are they doing now?"

"Just talking."

"How are we going to handle this?" Jack asked.

"Maybe we should just head back there and slide into the booth and join them." She grinned.

"We'd get more out of them by simply questioning them each on their own. I called for backup, just so you know. No one is coming in or interfering. Just a couple of deputies to wait outside in case things turn ugly."

"Backup? Our point in being here tonight was to watch. Even if we're only going to ask questions, we're not charging anyone. They haven't committed a crime."

"That we know about. If it *is* the pilot who took Blevins's place, we have questions for him. My deputies should be in place now. One at the entrance and one at the back door, just in case."

The same waitress approached, and Jack ordered a soda. She smiled, but Terra didn't miss her frustration. She probably figured her tip wouldn't be worth the effort. But Terra would be sure to leave a good one.

In fact, before things started moving, she pulled out a twenty and laid it on the table. "If this guy in the booth is our pilot,

Chance Carter, and he's trying to keep a low profile, then hanging out at the local bar doesn't seem wise."

"Unless it's worth the risk." Jack ducked his head, hiding under his cap as more patrons entered.

"I might not have connected the two events." Terra leaned forward on her folded arms. "The plane crash and then Jim's murder on the heels of that, except that Carter disappeared. Why?"

"He's got something to hide. Or he's afraid for his life." Jack thanked the waitress, who set the drink in front of him. He took a sip. "But that's what I intend to find out tonight."

Terra finished her drink and swirled the ice in her glass. "We know he's a courier for an airfreight company, so his job is to deliver packages. It's possible he was delivering contraband related to Jim's and Neva's murders."

"Agreed. Given the chain of events, I'd say highly probable. We know Jim helped Carter and was murdered while the pilot was in the hospital, so Carter didn't commit the murder. But did Jim lift the package Carter was delivering? Because it wasn't on the plane or with Carter when he was taken to the hospital. Was Jim murdered for Carter's package?"

Terra blew out a breath. "So, it stands to reason that Carter came here tonight to look for the package so he can deliver it and get paid. Or deliver and not die like Jim and Neva."

"You could be right." Jack held her gaze. "What's happening now? Still talking?"

"A waitress delivered beers. Maybe they haven't gotten down to business yet."

Terra looked into Jack's eyes and saw the questions swirling. They had more questions than answers.

A ruckus at the back drew her attention. Adrenaline shoved through her veins, and she palmed her weapon in her shoulder holster. "Carter stood up. He's reaching across the table now. He's grabbing Leif by the collar like he's threatening him."

"Another change of plans." Jack stood. "We need to leave now."

"What? Why?"

"You don't want to be sitting there when Leif walks out."

FIFTY

Chance had taken more risks than usual tonight. Anger boiled through him, and he sucked down another cold beer before he trusted his legs not to follow that murderer through the door. If he hadn't known to watch his back before, he knew to watch it now.

He thought back to the moment he'd watched the man enter the bar, nod and wink at the waitress, take in everyone in the room without being obvious, and stroll to the back. Recognition slammed into Chance, and he almost choked on the microbrew he'd been trying thanks to the waitress's recommendation and some extra cash, compliments of Blevins.

He'd gotten control over his emotions. Regained his composure mere moments before the guy slid into the booth across from him.

Then the guy had the nerve to smirk. "So, you survived."

Chance gained control over his anger, but he still ground out the words. "*You.* You were responsible for the crash. You sabotaged my plane."

Chance had seen him back at the hangar right before he'd left for Montana. After Chance had finished his preflight check, he made sure his tanks werc full of fuel and then he ran quickly to use the facilities. This guy had been talking to another pilot across the hangar.

The guy lifted his hands. "Nothing personal."

"Just business?" Chance gripped his beer mug much too tightly. That was to keep from slamming it into this guy's head. He didn't need to draw attention to himself, especially since he'd spotted a plainclothes cop enter the bar.

"Yes. My business. I had planned to meet someone else here tonight. But it looks like you've taken his place."

Blevins. "I'm here to deal in his place." *And get my hands around your throat if given the opportunity.* "What's your name?"

"No names."

"You already know mine. Since you're uncooperative, I'll call you Darth Maul, in keeping with our Bar Wars meeting and the mask above your head. So, Darth Maul, where's the package you were supposed to bring tonight? Did you sabotage my plane just so you could get your hands on it to make the delivery, and that somehow got messed up? Do you realize you could have destroyed the package completely? You killed Ole Blue."

"I don't care about the condition of the package. I only care about who wants it and where to find them."

Darth Maul only knew that Chance was delivering a high-priced item, but he didn't know to whom. "That isn't how it works. You said no names, remember. Besides, I courier packages and drop them off where I'm told. I don't know the what or the who."

"Then why are you here?"

"The same as you, I suppose. I had hoped to get the package and finish my delivery so that I would know who's behind it."

"And no one has contacted you to make new arrangements?" Darth Maul's eyes were sinister. Chance could imagine his face painted with red and black like the character.

With the murders, Blevins was scared and only too happy to

let Chance take his place while he disappeared until it was safe to return. Chance hoped to meet the murderer, the person who had intercepted the package and taken it from Jim. This guy had sabotaged Chance's plane—why? So he could pick up the pieces? What was left of the artifact? Destroy the delivery? Chance believed he had to have murdered Jim. But they were at a standoff if Darth Maul was also asking who was behind trafficking this item. Chance was after the same information. He wanted to know the man behind the blackmail, and then he would personally deliver the artifact to make sure that he was free forever. Except he didn't have it.

However, if he got his hands on the item in question, then he should turn it over to the police and connect the dots for them. But if he did that, he had no doubt he would be the next murder victim. Other lives were at risk too.

Without the name behind the blackmail and this delivery, he couldn't face off and end this once and for all. In the meantime, Darth Maul needed to be locked up for his crimes. In addition to Jim and Neva, this man had killed Ole Blue.

Chance was no murderer, and he didn't like that he had any part in this. He wouldn't be working with this guy. Instead, they were competitors.

Darth Maul narrowed his eyes. "I know who you are."

Chance's pulse spiked. "I thought we had already established that."

"No. Your real name and identity before. Chief Warrant Officer . . ." He trailed off. True to his words. No names.

Chance couldn't believe it.

"I know how you're connected now, and thanks to you, I also know who's behind it. Thanks for the intel."

"What intel? I haven't told you anything. What are you talking about?"

Darth Maul pulled a photograph from his pocket and slid it forward to Chance. Chance reached across the booth and grabbed him by the collar. This guy knew more than he was sharing, and Chance wanted answers.

Darth Maul gave him a name. That information confused Chance, and he released the man, who slipped out of the booth and walked away.

Chance had watched the cops head out the front door ahead of Darth Maul. Myriad emotions had spiked through his head. This had gone on too long and too far.

Chance could probably expect to greet a few cops himself on the way out the front door. Maybe even the back. He didn't have time for the cops. He had to end this before it was too late and someone else ended up dead. Chance had seen it in the man's eyes—he was a killer. Darth Maul didn't care about the package. He only cared about who was behind the deliveries. Just like Chance. And Darth Maul had figured it all out by simply sitting here looking at Chance.

He stared down at what Darth Maul had left behind. How had the man gotten his hands on this picture? Chance and his crew—maintenance guys and his copilot/gunner—in front of an Apache helicopter.

FIFTY-ONE

Jack and Terra kept to the shadows as they made it to Jack's vehicle and jumped in. He instructed the two deputies to back off and wait for further instructions.

"I don't think Leif saw us." Jack started the vehicle. "He's getting into his truck."

"Good thing we left first," she said. "But you had wanted to question the guy who we presume is the pilot. I didn't get a good look at him."

"And I still intend to question him." Jack got on his cell and instructed the deputies to enter the bar and bring the pilot in for questioning about the plane crash and Jim's death. He also requested someone remain at the back in case Carter tried to slip through their hands.

Glancing at her, Jack ended the call. Leif pulled from the curb. Jack waited for another vehicle to get behind Leif, then Jack steered onto the street. The car in front of Jack turned, so he kept pace several car-lengths back from Leif as he drove them out of town toward farmland—fields of wheat, soy, and corn.

"I almost think we should have stayed behind to question Chance Carter, and that's not because I don't want to follow Owen's friend. But you know the saying, a bird in the hand—"

"Is worth two in the bush. Let's see if we have a bird." Jack got back on his cell and called Sarnes. "Well? Did you get him?"

"No, sir. Sorry. He went out the back."

"I told you to station a guy back there."

"We did. That was me. He walked out the back and cold-cocked me before I had time to react."

Jack gritted his molars.

"Find him and arrest him for assaulting an officer." He glanced at Terra and ended the call. "Now he has definitely committed a crime."

Jack focused on following Leif on the two-lane highway. Just where was Leif taking them anyway? Was he onto them and leading them on a wild goose chase?

His cell rang. "Tanner."

"Nathan here."

Jack put the cell on speaker. "Detective Campbell. What's up?"

"Sarge pulled me in to assist. I hope you don't mind. I mean, we have the forest service deputized, so why not—"

Jack cleared his throat loudly. "Nathan. Terra's in the car with me. We're following a lead. Sarge pulled you in. What have you got?"

"Did some more digging on Chance Carter. He doesn't show up until about thirteen years ago."

"What do you mean?"

"He didn't exist until then."

"How can someone suddenly exist?"

"Good question. It could be a synthetic ID."

"Keep talking," Jack said. The car in front of them suddenly turned off onto a county road. Jack slowed. He needed to keep his distance so Leif wouldn't know he had a tail. It might already be too late.

"Cut to the chase, Campbell."

"A person could spend a couple of years building an ID. Get

a social security number from a child or a homeless person. Or the deceased. Then accumulate fake information associated with the ID. Bottom line, Chance Carter isn't really Chance Carter."

"Then who is he?"

"That's what we're trying to find out."

"Thanks for letting me know. I'd prefer to know his true identity." Jack explained what had happened in Bar Wars and that he and Terra were following Leif. "We're closing in."

"Careful out there." Campbell ended the call.

Jack glanced at Terra and caught her frown.

Up ahead, Leif finally turned onto another farm road. Jack sighed. "I wish we had a drone to do this work for us."

"What? No funding?"

"No funding."

"We can't lose him," she said.

"Oh, so *now* you want to follow him." Jack chuckled.

"I never said I didn't. I want to find out why he was meeting with the pilot as much as you do."

"We won't lose him." Jack slowed as he approached the county road Leif had taken. "We'll follow him all the way to his destination."

"I have a gut feeling he's going to disappear because he knows we're onto him," she said.

He grinned at that and glanced her way, then back to the road.

"I call it my forest service special agent instinct."

"I like it."

Jack turned onto the road lined by cornfields on both sides and drove slowly. No car lights ahead. "Unfortunately, I think you were right. He's gone dark on us."

"I'm sure he's parked in the cornfield somewhere or we'd see his lights up the road."

Stopping the vehicle, Jack opened the windows. Terra said

nothing. He listened for a few moments, then finally urged the vehicle forward again—slow and steady as if they were just out for a late evening drive through the cornfields on a beautiful star-filled night. The silhouette of a grain silo stood tall in the distance.

"Um, Jack. What are we doing?" Terra whispered.

"Looking for signs that someone drove into the crops." He kept his voice low.

"Crop circles." Her quiet laugh sounded lyrical. Warmth curled inside. He shook off the nonsense. They had to remain on guard. If Leif was involved, he could be the man who killed Jim and Neva. He could be the man who tried to kill Terra. "No, seriously. The corn mazes. We're close to one. Don't know if it's opened for business this late. I hope not."

Terra's small intake of breath clued him in. He slowed the vehicle.

"Keep driving," she whispered.

He did as she directed.

"We don't want him to know we saw his turnout," she said. "I don't know if he's waiting for us to give up and then he'll take off or what."

"He can't sit there all night." Jack hated to keep moving. He wanted to turn around.

"He could," she said. "Or he could simply leave his truck and just walk out."

"Nah. That's too far."

"No, it's not, Jack. First, he's been military trained to survive under impossible conditions. Not that he has to here. There's a farmhouse out there. He could steal their car."

"Or harm the farmer and his family." That was it. Jack shut off his lights and maneuvered his vehicle until he'd turned around. "We'll wait here for a few minutes and see if he comes out. I had only meant to follow the guy tonight and not engage him. But I have a bad feeling about this."

Jack closed the windows and used his radio to call for backup. The man was evading them for a reason. "We can't let him slip through our fingers."

"Especially since you lost the pilot."

"Come on. The first time we didn't even know he was a flight risk. No lame pun intended." Jack looked at Terra. "You're not wearing a vest, are you?"

"Neither are you."

"I have one in the back that I'll grab. Sheriff only requires detectives to have them with us and use them in enforcement situations. This has turned into something different than I thought." But it wouldn't fit her well enough to be efficient.

Though he hated to bring more deputies into it, the last thing Jack wanted was to go into that cornfield after Leif. "I don't want to lose him, but we'll wait here until backup arrives."

Bullets pinged his vehicle.

"Get down!"

FIFTY-TWO

Terra shoved down the screams and covered her head as she ducked.

"Go, go, go, go! Get out on your side." Jack shielded her.

She opened the door and slid out.

Jack crawled over the seat and joined her on the far side of his vehicle.

"An assault rifle," she said. "He's using an assault rifle."

"Battlefield firepower." He grunted. "The guy has lost it. PTSD or something."

Terra's heart pounded. The night sky. The tall plants. The gunfire. All of it seemed surreal. The fear could paralyze her.

"Terra." Jack gripped her shoulders. "Breathe, Terra. We have to get out of here. But I need to warn the other deputies on their way, if it's not already too late. I need to tell them before my radio is toast."

Crouching, he reached across the seat to grab the mic and radioed again for backup. "Officers in danger. We're being fired upon with an assault rifle!"

Jack relayed numerous codes to warn the deputies and also ask for additional backup. Then his radio squawked its last.

The gunfire continued to demolish Jack's vehicle. No chance they were getting in a shot. Not here.

"Go . . . go into the cornfield." He shoved her away from the vehicle and covered her as she plowed into the six-foot-tall cornstalks.

He urged her forward as if the tall plants could somehow protect them against bullets. "Let's go. I can't let anything happen to you. I won't."

"Then we'll protect each other." She gasped for breath. She'd seen something similar happen before, and that ended in tragedy.

God, please don't let it end that way this time!

She and Jack pushed deeper into the cornfield, running down rows. The tall plants and thick green leaves slapped her face as she ran.

"I'm not sure the corn will protect us from the onslaught," she said. "If we have to face off with him, I'm not carrying an assault rifle. You?"

He swiped the sweat from his face. "It doesn't matter. All we need is to be strategic."

"Strategic. You mean like make our way around behind him? Ambush him?"

"No, *I'll* be the one to make my way around behind him. You're getting somewhere safe."

"What about waiting for backup?"

"I'm not sure if he's going to give us a chance to wait. It'll take a few minutes for others to get here."

Terra knew what could happen while waiting for backup. People could die.

"You're not leaving me, Jack. I'm your backup. We're in this together. Let's hide in the cornstalks and wait for him to come find us. If he comes, we'll be ready for him."

She crouched down, then lay flat on her belly.

Jack dropped next to her. "I don't like to cut and run."

"I don't either. But staying next to your vehicle would have been suicide."

"Listen," he said.

Silence filled the night. No sound of gunfire. Nor sirens. Nothing.

"He must be checking the vehicle to confirm we're dead," Jack whispered.

"He'll be coming for us."

"Or if he's smart, he'll get into that truck of his and get out of town. He has to know that law enforcement is going to rain down on him from all corners of the state. Why would he do something like this?"

The truth was, they knew next to nothing about Leif Morrisey.

Jack's face was close to hers. He held his weapon at the ready and eyed her. He pressed a finger to his lips. A breeze blew through the cornstalks.

Time to listen.

Someone made their way through the corn. More like marched without fear.

Leif was coming for them. Indignation settled in her gut. If Owen knew what his friend was up to, he would stop him. If anything, Leif should be running from them. Terra squeezed her weapon, wanting to shift her position, but that would make too much noise. Even in the cool of the evening, sweat crawled over her back and dripped down her temples.

Jack motioned for her to get up. She scrambled to her feet, quickly and quietly, and backed away from her hiding spot, this time careful not to disturb the plants. If Leif decided to fire his weapon into the field, they would be at risk.

Sirens resounded in the distance. Finally. But would they arrive in time?

Jack tucked her behind him. She stepped into a wider row of mowed stalks.

The corn maze.

The footfalls sounded closer. Terra ran with Jack, following the corners and curves of the maze. She gasped for breath.

They were making entirely too much noise.

"The more distance, the better," Jack whispered. "But we'll follow the maze, and then head back toward the road. Backup has to get here soon."

"I have no idea which way the road is. Do you?"

Jack slowed to a stop and stepped into the cover of the cornstalks, pulling her with him. Weapons drawn, they stood perfectly still and quiet.

Sirens sounded louder.

The movement in the cornstalks sounded distant. Leif was now the one on the run. Jack pushed back out into the maze and she followed, though still wary of more assault-grade gunfire.

"We can't let him get away, Jack. He has to be behind the murders."

"The roads will be blocked, and he'll know that. My bet is he's going to try to get back to his vehicle and go through the cornfield. Or to that farmhouse. He could take hostages."

"We need to make our way there to warn them."

Jack once again slowed and held his hand up. Through the cornstalks she could see the road, and Jack slowly approached. They should have at least heard Leif's truck. And if not, then he was on foot.

An engine roared to life.

Jack stepped out of the cornfield and onto the road. He aimed his weapon.

Terra stood by his side, her weapon ready.

Leif swerved out of the field and onto the road. Jack aimed for the man himself while Terra aimed for the tires, but neither of them fired since the truck disappeared down the county road, heading in the opposite direction. Jack limped around as if he would climb into his own destroyed vehicle and opened the door. It fell away and clanked to the ground.

Jack collapsed to his knees and hung his head.

Terra raced to his side. "Jack, it's okay. We did all we could."

He slumped to the road.

"Jack?"

Terra lifted the bomber jacket and saw the blood.

FIFTY-THREE

Jack!" Terra's voice sounded as if it were coming from down a long tunnel.

"I'm okay," he said. "It's just a flesh wound. A graze."

"You are not okay!"

"Maybe I'm a little dizzy." He felt like a complete wimp. He'd let that guy get the best of him. He'd really messed this up.

"Because you're bleeding. Where exactly are you shot? I need to stop the bleeding."

Must have happened when the guy surprised them by firing on their vehicle. He had only noticed a pinched feeling, and not the pain. Adrenaline had probably kept him going and alive.

"I think it went all the way through." He'd been shot before and should have recognized the signs. "I'm going to live, Terra. Don't look so stricken."

She kneeled beside him. Opened up his shirt. "Where is it?"

"My arm. We can stop the bleeding. Make a tourniquet. But they're already here. Help is here."

Pain and terror filled her wide eyes. He hated putting that look on her face. Jack wanted to squeeze her hand, but the strength had run out of him.

Vehicle lights filled the edges of his vision, along with flashing colored lights of county vehicles. Terra put pressure on the wound and pain ignited. He gritted his teeth to keep from groaning. He didn't want to scare her. With his free hand, he pushed the hair out of her face, then ran his hand over her cheek. Trailed his thumb down her jaw. He wanted a second chance with her.

He didn't deserve it, but . . . if he survived . . . *God, please, give me another chance with Terra. I need to make it right like Aunt Nadine said.*

Her eyes flashed to him, the whites bright in the shadows. "What are you doing?" Her voice shook.

She tried to pretend he had no effect on her, but he saw in her eyes that his touch sent a current through her. The same current that ran through him when she was near.

Or was it the loss of blood and adrenaline crash that was getting to him? Maybe his condition acted like a truth serum, and he was being honest with himself.

He tried to push up. Some hero he was.

But she was alive. They'd made it out alive. Unlike . . .

Unlike . . . "Sarah."

"What? I'm not Sarah." Her face was now filled with full-blown panic.

"Sarah, you're alive."

"Jack. It's me." Terra drew close enough he could kiss her. "It's me."

"Terra." He tried to reach up and touch her lips. Pull her closer, but his body wasn't cooperating.

"Here, here! Help, we need help . . ." Her words trailed away, and when she stepped out of view to let the EMTs take over, he saw her trembling, blood-covered hands. She leaned in. "I'll let them know to keep searching. And just how dangerous he is."

"Stay with me, Terra." *Stay with me . . .*

Had he said that out loud?

"I'm here, Jack. I'm not going anywhere." She weaved her fingers with his.

Jack closed his eyes. Blood loss. That's all this was. Too much blood loss.

Images accosted him. The girls. So many girls being trafficked. One in particular. The shock of her familiar face. The anger and panic that engulfed him. But he'd worked to get her out. To save her before they took her out of his reach.

His cousin, Sarah.

Her body dumped in the snow in Wyoming.

Because of him? Someone knew he'd tried to save her?

Terra was here with him. Her words floated through him, close and yet far. Trained officers died all the time. He couldn't lose Terra too.

Jerking, he opened his eyes. She was there. But she'd released his hand. He kept her in his line of sight as she walked with the two men who had now placed him on a gurney.

Jack didn't want her to leave, because if she remained by his side, then she wouldn't be facing that madman.

Or her brother. He could see her facing off with her brother. Putting herself in danger.

Jack gasped for breath. He had more to say. He had to warn her.

An EMT pressed an oxygen mask over his face. What was the matter with him? He had no power to move. To speak.

The thought of Owen being connected to Leif and the possibility that he could be involved made Jack more nauseous.

Terra!

He closed his eyes and wished he hadn't, because now he wasn't sure if he could open them again.

"I'll meet you at the hospital, Jack," she said as if she heard his silent screams.

"I'll be right behind you," she called again.

He found the strength. He pushed his arm up. Shoved the mask away. "Terra. Ride with me!" He eyed the EMT. "She has to ride with me." He grabbed the paramedic's arm and squeezed. "Special Agent Connors is going to ride in this ambulance with—"

FIFTY-FOUR

Jack had lost consciousness.

Terra's knees shook. She wanted to climb into the ambulance with him like he requested. The EMTs were shutting the door on her, ignoring Jack's request.

"Wait a minute!" She tried to force her way in.

A hand touched her arm from behind. "Agent Connors. I'll get you there."

Terra turned to see Detective Nathan Campbell.

"Terra." Compassion filled his tone. "My vehicle's right there. We'll follow the ambulance. In fact, I'll lead it into town."

"Let's go!" She ran with him, and they jumped into his vehicle. He placed the flashing lights on top of the unmarked vehicle and ran the sirens. Sped around the ambulance and paved the way on the lonely county road.

"What happened out there?" he asked.

Terra clutched the handgrip. Nathan would make sure the ambulance didn't waste time. She just hoped he got them there alive.

"Leif pulled out the big guns. We were caught off guard. How could we have known that he would pull this?"

"You couldn't have. Sarnes had pulled up information for Jack, but only prepared the report tonight."

"What does it tell us?"

"He was a warrant officer. Piloted helicopters for the Army. And yes, he served with your brother. He was a hero and saved lives. The other information paints a sad picture. His sister was killed. Leif kind of went off the deep end after that. He was discharged, though we don't know the exact reasons."

"Well, he went off the deep end tonight too. He's armed and dangerous, and I need to talk to my brother, to warn him. He needs to know what Leif is doing. Can I use your cell? I lost mine out there in the cornfields."

Nathan handed it over. "I know you don't think Owen is involved in illegal activity, and I can't see it either. So, for now we'll give him the benefit of the doubt. And don't worry, Terra. We'll get Morrisey tonight. Every agency has been called in. Anyone who would engage law enforcement in this way has lost all control, if you ask me."

Terra used the cell and called Owen. Gramps would be asleep by this time, and she didn't want to disturb him. There wasn't anything he could do. But she left a message for Owen, keeping it vague. She didn't want to scare him, but he needed to be warned in case Leif showed up there. Terra sent Owen a text too. That's all she could do for now.

She squeezed her eyes shut, trying to block out the constant sound of rapid-fire bullets slamming into Jack's vehicle. She covered her mouth to stifle the sobs. Jack had been shot. The whole time he was trying to protect her and he'd been shot.

Nathan squeezed her shoulder. "He's going to be all right."

Terra wiped her eyes and glanced at him. Despite his words, he was worried too. Nathan was a good guy, and she felt sorry that he and Erin hadn't made things work.

Nathan slowed his vehicle at a four-way intersection, lights flashing, to assist the ambulance through.

"I get the feeling you *like* charging through town, sirens blaring."

"This isn't one of those times. I don't like it when a cop is in trouble."

"Jack told me the bullet went all the way through and that he would be okay."

"Let's hope he was telling you the truth."

He steered through the emergency room entrance and parked. Leaving his vehicle running, he rushed around to open the door, but Terra was already out. She and Nathan watched the EMTs roll the gurney carrying Jack down the hallway. Terra made to follow, but Nathan blocked her. "Let them work without distraction. You say your prayers. The doctors will tell us the good news when they're done. In the meantime, let me get you some coffee."

She hugged herself. "Yeah, sure, okay. You're right."

Nathan led her to the cafeteria. Bought them coffees and sat with her at a small table. Terra didn't want to be here. Not like this. Anguish flooded her.

"All I can think about . . . I keep seeing him reaching for me. Begging me not to leave him. And I left him. I'm out here."

"You know you can't be in there with him while they treat his injury."

"Thanks for being here, Nathan. But you don't need to hold my hand. Don't you need to get out there and help find Leif before he kills someone else?" She hadn't meant to sound so harsh.

The tears welled again but didn't overflow. She was a special agent. A professional. But first responders and special agents could get emotional too.

Nathan touched her arm. "I'm right where I need to be. Take a deep breath. Jack wouldn't want you to go into shock over this. As I mentioned earlier, the sheriff called in for assists from the state. Two additional counties. I think they can spare me. He's my friend too, Terra. We go rock climbing now and then."

A chuckle escaped. "I'm glad he has a friend like you then."

His eyes met hers. "He's going to make it. He was shot before, you know, back with the FBI."

"I heard about that. But not much. What happened to him?" Her question was barely a whisper.

"I don't know the whole story. Maybe he'll tell you. I think he nearly died, but he saved a woman and took down a big human-trafficking ring."

Her heart pounded. "Jack did?" She thought she knew the woman—if it was Rae Burke.

He leaned closer. "Maybe I wasn't supposed to tell you any of that. I asked him about it, and he didn't say much. But since he came from the FBI, some of what happened got out. Word got around. He's private about it."

Nathan frowned as he stared at his cup.

"What aren't you telling me?" she asked.

"Jack will tell you what he wants you to know."

Did that mean Nathan knew something he wasn't free to share?

"Back there, he called me Sarah," she said. "He didn't recognize me. He was seeing Sarah. That nearly broke my heart that he would see his dead cousin."

Nathan cleared his throat, clearly uncomfortable. "I just . . . I thought you'd want to know that he's a hero. And more than that, he's a survivor."

Terra stared across the room at an elderly couple getting coffee. A survivor. Yes. She'd known that, given his background. And now she thought she better understood why he'd left her. That day she had thought he would propose but instead disappeared and walked out on their possible future together.

That day, Jack had been doing what he needed to do.

Jack had been surviving.

FIFTY-FIVE

Jack opened his eyes. Light from the hallway spilled through the half-opened door. He'd drifted to sleep after the surgery and blood transfusion and was told he would be kept overnight.

He needed to get out of this prison.

Jack forced his eyes to stay open. He vaguely remembered the doctor explaining something about a vein being lacerated. His humerus needing to be set. The bullet had barely missed an artery. He'd lost a lot of blood—enough that he lost consciousness but fortunately not enough to kill him before he got help.

A soft sigh drew his attention to the corner. He shifted his head and spotted Terra slouched in a chair, sleeping. Her brown mane was tousled and hung over her left shoulder. Her dark eyelashes fluttered. Was she dreaming?

Would she wake up and catch him watching her?

The thought brought on a half smile.

What was I thinking to give you up?

He had thought he was doing the right thing for the both of them. Aunt Nadine always said hindsight was twenty-twenty. Easy enough for him to look back now and see his mistake.

The echo of bullets ricocheted through his mind, yanking him from his thoughts.

Terra could have been killed.

Beautiful, amazing Terra.

He'd been an idiot to leave her. How strange they found themselves together again under this dangerous, high-pressure situation. Her lashes fluttered again, then her eyes opened and she stared right into his as if she'd sensed someone watching and that alone had stirred her awake.

Her lips parted with a small gasp.

She stood and moved to his side. "You're awake."

Unable to find his voice, he nodded.

She grabbed his hand. He appreciated the warmth and strength in her grip, and her soft skin. And that she was here in the room with him.

"What . . . what are you doing here?"

A confused frown twisted her beautiful features.

An idiot's question. "I mean . . . thank you for being here."

A soft smile replaced the frown, and her bright blue eyes shimmered. "Of course I'm here. I had to make sure you were all right."

Terra released his hand.

"Wait. Where are you going?"

"I'm getting the chair." She moved the chair she had been sleeping in closer to the bed and sat down, but it still wasn't close enough for Jack.

"Your aunt will be here to relieve me in the morning. She wanted to be here tonight, but I convinced her to get some rest."

"I hope to get out of this place before she gets here. What time is it?"

"It's four a.m."

"And they let you stay? You're not family."

"Aren't I?" Her beautiful eyes held so many promises.

Or was he imagining she felt more for him than she really did?

He forced his thoughts to the immediate threat and danger to her and others. "Did we get him?"

A shadow crossed her gaze. "Not yet."

Anger boiled through him. "How could he get away?"

"It takes a while for the forces to gather out there. You know that. He was probably long gone."

He thought about her brother. If she was here with him, he assumed that meant she hadn't gone to face Owen. Jack hoped that the sheriff or someone within his department had already approached her brother with a few questions. If Owen was involved, the last place Terra needed to be was at the ranch.

Nor should she continue her investigation. He hoped her superior would put her on desk duty while the shooting was being investigated, but he wasn't sure how the forest service did things, considering they had so few investigators. She had to have thought of all this already. But he wouldn't bring it up now because he didn't have the energy to argue. He couldn't stop her if she walked out that door.

How could he keep her here until it was over?

"Can you hand me my cell?" he asked.

She frowned again. "You don't have a cell, Jack. Let's just say you survived the bullets, but your cell didn't."

He started to sit up. "I'm getting out of here. There's too much to do."

She pressed a hand on his shoulder. "The doctor hasn't released you yet. Even if he does, you know you'll be on desk duty for a couple of days."

He groused. "I don't care. I can't stay here. There's something I can do."

Jack's left arm screamed when he tried to move it. Dizziness swept over him, and he gripped the bed until it passed. Then he eased his bare feet onto the floor and sat on the edge of the bed. Realization dawned that he was in a hospital gown.

"See, Jack. You're pushing it."

"I've been through worse. A graze isn't that bad. I lost some blood, that's all. The doctor patched me up." He reached for the landline phone next to the bed.

"Who are you going to call at this hour? Nobody is expecting you to check in."

He slammed the phone down. "I don't know his number off the top of my head."

"Whose number?"

"Detective Campbell's." Nathan could share details about what was going on.

"Nathan? Fine." She stood and handed over a cell. "I lost my phone out in the cornstalks. But this is a burner. Nathan wanted me to text him."

Jack grabbed the phone. "So, you guys are friends now?" That sounded entirely too possessive. But at the moment, he didn't care if she thought he sounded jealous.

"He's worried about you," she said. "I was supposed to text him with any news."

Jack hit Nathan's name next to Owen's in the contact list. Nausea threatened. Had she talked to Owen? The call buzzed a few times.

"Terra, what is it?" Nathan answered with the question.

"This is Jack. What's going on out there?"

Terra crossed her arms.

"I was going to call Terra in the morning with the news," Nathan said. "Or maybe deliver it to you in person."

"Well? Did you find him?"

"Yeah." Campbell blew out a breath. "In a grain silo. He's dead."

"He fell in trying to hide?"

"He fell in, all right. Right after someone put a bullet in his head."

FIFTY-SIX

"**N**o idea who?" A stunned expression on his face, Jack kept her pinned with his gaze as he listened to Nathan. "This just gets better and better. Keep me updated. I'm getting out of here soon."

He ended the call and handed the cell over to Terra.

She moved closer and wrapped her fingers around it. "What is it, Jack? What did he say?"

"Someone shot and killed Leif."

What? She let the shock of that news roll over her. She hated to think it, but that almost seemed a fitting end. Still, she gasped and tried to step back, but Jack stood and gently grabbed her wrist, then reeled her in. He urged her even closer until their foreheads touched.

Being so near, especially when she wasn't sure she had control over her emotions, scared her. She tried to back away, but he held her in place. He was much stronger than she imagined he would be after his injury.

"What . . . what are you doing?" Her voice came out breathy and revealed far too much emotion. She didn't know if she could hide it anymore. Hide behind the facade of professionalism that had been required to work this case with him.

Did he know how he affected her? Did he understand how

deeply she cared for him, despite her efforts to move on? Jack had been her world back then. And if she wasn't careful, he might become her world again. She could see it happening so easily, feel it happening when he held her like this.

"I'm holding you close, that's what. I'm holding this moment close. I almost lost you out there. I can't let that happen ever again."

"Me? You were the one who was shot. If anything, you almost lost yourself. What happened to you? I mean, before you came back to Montana. Don't hide it from me. I saw how haunted you were that first day we met again."

A few breaths passed, then he said, "I lost someone close to me. Someone important. I failed them."

"Who did you lose?"

"I can't talk about it yet. Not until . . . just trust me, I'll tell you someday. Maybe soon. But in the meantime, I want you to know that I don't want to lose you again."

He spoke in the language of hearts, and deep inside, she understood all too well that he was still emotionally connected to her. Jack gently touched the back of her neck and drew her closer . . . closer. She lingered near his lips, waiting for him.

But Jack waited on her, his way of asking permission.

With her heart calling the shots, her mind had no control to stop what came next as she closed the distance. Tenderness surged between them while a whirlwind of past and present emotions swirled in her mind. Their hearts connected, touched, entwined. Jack deepened the kiss until he left her breathless. Terra broke away to catch her breath but lingered near, her heart beating erratically.

"We have unfinished business, you and I," Jack said.

Did they?

The tenderness, longing, and desire pouring from him could draw her deeper, if she wasn't careful. Putting up the wall required to walk away would take every ounce of her strength.

She eased away, her heart cracking, breaking all over again as the whirlwind of their past died down, leaving her with the memories of brokenness. "I've lost people too, Jack. Whether by an avalanche or by choice, people I love have left me, and I don't have it in me to set myself up to feel that pain again. I'm sorry." Owen, Gramps, Alex, and Erin made up the small circle of people she could trust. But as far as giving over her heart like she once had to Jack? No.

I can do this. I have to do this.

She took a full step back and stiffened her backbone. "Now that I know you're going to be okay, I should go. Our business, Jack, our personal business, is finished. It's over. You left me, walked out on us before, and I won't let you do that again."

Terra gathered her bag and headed for the door.

"You don't understand. Terra, wait—"

//////////////////////////

In the predawn hours, Terra sat in her vehicle, Jack's last words to her as she walked out of his hospital room still echoing through her mind and heart. What had she done? Had she just wanted to be the one to walk away this time?

She swiped at the tears. She had plenty to distract her from the pain. Staring at her grandfather's ranch house, she tried to work up the nerve to go inside. Worry had kept her company through the night while staying in Jack's room. She had also wanted to head to Gramps's house to speak with Owen. To warn them both. Terra believed that Owen had nothing to do with his friend's crimes. What's more, he had to be devastated at the news.

Owen . . . was a hero.

She was half surprised no law enforcement vehicles were at the house now. She'd known the sheriff's department would want to talk to Owen because of his association with Leif. Maybe he had opted to answer their questions at the county offices rather than upset Gramps. Or bring potential issues into a political campaign that was only beginning.

So, she sat in her vehicle, helpless to fight the uncertainty that had settled in her gut. Her superior could very well remove her from this investigation completely now.

Regardless of what happened, how did she approach Owen? He would feel betrayed if she didn't talk to him about Leif, yet how did she tell him those sordid details? Did he even know that Leif had been killed? This incident could crush him when he was beginning to build a new life here.

Her throat tightened. She had the distinct impression the world was closing in around her.

No lights were on in the house yet.

Oh, Owen. She wanted to reach out to him.

But she couldn't face him. Not yet. Now was as good a time as any to head back to her apartment for a few days, if not giving up her temporary stay at Gramps's entirely. To think she'd only recently decided to move into the ranch house permanently. Life kept changing the rules on her.

She started the vehicle. *God, help me. What do I do?*

Someone pounded on the passenger-side window, and she yelped.

"Owen?" She unlocked the door.

He got in. "Can we just drive?"

"Why? What's going on?" Dread flooded her.

"I need to get out of here." His eyes were pleading, his tone desperate.

"I don't know if we should."

"Terra, I'm your brother. Please . . . just drive."

His own vehicle was parked there—why didn't he take that?

"Okay, then." She steered from the house, down the long drive, and stopped where the drive intersected with the county road.

"Drive away from town, please," he said.

You're scaring me. "What's going on?"

"Two deputies came by the house last night really late. I was up, so I stepped outside. I didn't want to wake Gramps."

"And?"

"Don't act like you don't know. They were looking for Leif and wanted to know if I knew where he was. Why don't you tell me what's going on?"

Okay, that was it. Terra swerved to the side of the road and shifted into park. She drew in a few calming breaths. "Leif shot at us, Owen. He used an assault weapon and . . ." Her voice closed up. She swallowed, breathed, and found it again. "I barely escaped with my life, Owen. Jack . . . he's in the hospital. He was shot."

Owen gasped. "Is he—"

"He's going to be okay. But we both could have died."

"Terra, I had no idea." Anguish filled his words. "The deputies didn't mention any of this, only that Leif had evaded officers and was considered armed and dangerous. I was worried about you when you didn't come home. You texted that you were all right and nothing more."

Owen leaned over and hugged her hard and tight. "I'm glad you're alive. I can't believe any of this."

"It's okay. I'm okay." She eased away from him. How did she tell him the rest? "Owen . . . Leif didn't make it. He's dead. I don't . . . I don't know the details."

Owen hung his head. She gave him a few moments to absorb the news. He blew out a few breaths.

"In the message you left," he finally said, "you warned me that Leif could be dangerous, but you told me none of this. You didn't share those details about what happened because"—Owen's eyes narrowed—"because you're not sure that I'm not involved." Hurt and anger edged his tone.

"No, Owen. That's not it. I *know* you are not involved. I know that. But I had to be careful what I said to you because I'm part of this investigation. Or . . . I was."

He released a heavy sigh and leaned back against the seat, deflated.

"Tell me something," she said. "After the deputies left, what did you do?"

His eyes clouded with disappointment. "I texted you to find out if you were okay. They didn't tell me that you were involved, but you hadn't come to the ranch."

"Then did you try to contact Leif?"

"Of course."

"Did you get ahold of him?"

"No."

"And what would you have said had he answered?"

"Terra, you can't—"

"And I don't. I don't believe you're involved. But you guys were together for so long, this has to be hard on you. Did you have any idea something like this would happen?"

Owen nodded. "I didn't want to believe it. I heard that he'd done things before. But he's . . . he *was* . . . like a brother to me, and I guess . . . I guess I ignored that he was close to the edge." Owen pressed a hand against his eyes for a few moments, then dropped it. "I think he was out for revenge. He never got over his sister's death."

"How did she die?"

"She was murdered."

"By who? Is that who he wanted to take out his revenge on? What aren't you telling me?"

"I'd tell you if I knew anything. Leif was here in Montana for me, but he was here for another reason too. He wouldn't tell me more because he didn't want me involved. See? He . . . was like a brother."

"Who tried to kill your sister tonight."

Owen hung his head and squeezed the bridge of his nose. "If I'd had any idea he was that dangerous . . ."

"Tell me what you would've said to him if you had gotten ahold of him."

"If he had answered, I would've asked where he was and what was going on. But I figured he wouldn't answer me because he knew I would give him away. I would give him up. He knew I would do the right thing, and he didn't want to put me in such a tough position."

"Would you have given him up? You once said he saved your life. So that means you owed him."

Another car steered along the road, and Terra watched as it passed. She pulled back onto the road and kept driving—to where, she wasn't sure.

"Of course I would have done the right thing, Terra. How can you even ask me that? And, yes, he saved my life. And he'd come to see me here. Not only that, but he said he could help with my new venture. He wanted to be part of it. To invest in it. Said he had come into some money."

"This is what you should be telling the other investigators. I shouldn't have come to the ranch. I don't want to jeopardize the investigation or—"

He held up his hand to stop her. "You're going to want to hear this. He wanted to invest in Gramps's campaign."

The discussion in Gramps's office during the party.

"And you know this because he told you? Or Gramps told you?"

"Because I overheard the conversation. And I overheard another conversation but thought I had misunderstood. Now I'm not so sure."

"Tell me."

"I think Gramps wanted someone to break into that safe. That he planned for us to be gone."

Terra kept driving, but she wanted to park again. "How can

that be, Owen? This is all . . . I don't believe it's what it looks like."

"You don't *want* to believe it."

"You're right. I don't." She tightened her grip on the steering wheel. "Just what do you think was in the safe?"

Owen stared at his hands. "I don't know. All I know was that I was at the stables this morning, early. I couldn't sleep last night. When I saw your vehicle, I made my way over. I knew we needed to talk away from the house. What do you make of it?"

"I need time to figure it out." She needed time and access. Knowledge she couldn't get if she was no longer in on at least her part of the investigation.

"What are we going to do?"

"You're going to keep doing what you do, Owen. There's no reason why this has to ruin your plans for the future. You aren't involved in anything criminal. You keep working with the horses and your connections to build your team. I believe in your project, and I believe in you."

"And you? What are *you* going to do?"

I'm going to face Gramps. "Me? I'm going to get answers."

FIFTY-SEVEN

Head pounding, Chance woke up in his motel room. Cabin. Whatever. He had no idea how he'd made it back. He didn't remember anything except those moments with Darth Maul. The man had left him with that photograph—only God knew how he'd gotten his hands on it—and that name. Chance had exited the bar out the back. Escaped the deputy and hobbled to his temporary dwelling.

He had to get out today. His time was up here. But maybe not his luck.

He had a name now. He still wasn't sure how Darth Maul had figured it out.

An incredulous laugh escaped. His laugh grew larger. Louder. He was sure he would wake the neighbors in the nearby cabin.

Chance turned his thoughts to Baghdad.

The name? *Anthony Gray.*

Anthony "Tony" Gray had been Chance's copilot and gunner. Before that, they'd grown up in the same county in Montana. Then they ended up serving in the same platoon in basic. They attended flight school together and were stationed together. Brothers-in-arms forever, it would seem.

After the initial shock and awe of the campaign, they were stationed near Baghdad. Chance couldn't remember how he ended up following Tony that night. They moved stealthily through the smoldering courtyard, expended RPGs and Iraqi soldier uniforms scattered everywhere. The Iraq Museum had been used by the soldiers as a fighting position, then when they scattered, the looting began. An inside job. Professionals. Then everyone else.

Tony led him beneath a hand-scrawled warning, "Death to all Americans and Zionist pigs," and down the halls. Others were working. Flashlights shining. Mumbles and shouting. The sense of urgency. They passed hundreds of display cases. Hundreds that were nearly empty.

Tony slowed and sidled next to Chance. "We need to help them."

"How do we stop this?"

"No, I mean help them. I'm thinking of my wife, my parents back home. They could use a few nice things."

"You're not saying . . ."

"I am saying. What's the harm in a few items being put on display to be seen rather than stolen and lost forever?" Tony's justification sounded reasonable.

Chance followed him down a set of stairs. He should have stopped following the guy, but Tony was larger than life. Charismatic, and sure, Chance would blame Tony for drawing him in to his reasonable cause of not letting the looters get it all.

"Where are we going?" The way Tony led him, Chance knew the guy had already been there and checked it out.

Tony shined his flashlight along a dark stairwell.

Chance felt like he was going into a dungeon from which he would never return. "I think we should go back."

Tony grabbed him and shoved him through the huge metal doors that were open for anyone to enter. Stuff—Chance didn't have a name for all the items—lay sprawled all over the floor.

"See?" Tony said. "The good stuff is probably gone. But this is worth something. Grab a box and start picking it up. If you don't, someone else will. We're the heroes here."

"I can't. I won't."

"Then hold the flashlights while I do," Tony growled.

Chance couldn't leave his friend. He could end up killed in here. And staying would only mean he was complicit in the crime. Tony made it sound like it wasn't, but Chance knew deep down it was a war crime. "If it'll get us out of here faster, I'll help."

Tony grinned. "That's the spirit."

As the days changed to weeks, their efforts shifted to looting from the many unprotected archaeological sites. Looters crawled over them like thousands of ants, digging, pilfering, plundering. And Tony and Chance were among them. Tony had developed a system for moving the items out through a complicated network of handlers rewarded for their efforts. Chance had never wanted in, and he couldn't figure out how to extricate himself from the trafficking or from his gunner. Until the last item.

Tony opened the box for Chance. "This is our last job. The last one we'll ever need to do."

Chance stared down at the item—a gold diadem, a crown of sorts. Mesh with a lot of jewels. Chance didn't know what the jewels were, but Tony did. He had been studying. Doing his homework. Chance dropped onto the edge of his bunk. All their years together and this, this was the straw to break the brotherhood. "No. I'm done. I can't do this. Tony . . . I have a bad feeling. Please don't do this."

"I can't do this alone. I can't move this piece without your help. Without you covering me. You said you had my back."

Chance scraped both hands through his sweaty, dirty hair. "I never wanted to be part of this. You have to return this. Give it back. Hand it over."

"Are you nuts?"

He had no choice but to get up and walk out on Tony. The pain of what Tony was doing, of what Chance had let his friend do and been complicit in, knifed through him. A thousand stabs to his heart.

That night, Tony tried to move the object on his own, without Chance accompanying him, covering for him. He recruited someone else, and that person ratted Tony out. Chance heard Tony was supposed to be court-martialed, but the helicopter delivering him crashed and he was killed.

Chance returned home to his family in the US, but the shame and guilt followed him. Mere months later, someone sent images of him smuggling artifacts, along with a message: *I know what you did. Your secret is safe with me. Your family is safe too, as long as you cooperate.*

His family had been threatened, so Chance agreed to deliver a few packages here and there to add to his load, no questions asked, if his family would be left out.

Eventually, he realized his life as he knew it would need to end—for his family's sake. He disappeared and created a whole new identity.

FIFTY-EIGHT

Aunt Nadine sat in a chair in the corner, her arm in a sling. She stayed with Jack as he paced the hospital room waiting for the official discharge papers. His sergeant, Aaron Brady, and Sheriff Gibson had both come to see him and give him stern instructions about doing everything by the book, including signing discharge papers.

They'd taken his statement about last night. The incident would need to be investigated, and like Jack had feared, he had to turn over his department-issued weapon and was put on desk duty, but mostly for his injury. The doctor would look at his wound again in a couple of days.

It was just a graze, people! Okay, maybe my bone got grazed too. Whatever.

Still, Henry needed all the resources he could get on this and asked that Jack continue to work the case from the conference room, which he'd been told had been transformed into a command center for the multi-homicide case.

If only he could have found a lead, something that could have helped him resolve this sooner so it wouldn't have to come to this. He almost thought he'd done a better job as a special agent in the FBI working undercover for that dirt-bag.

Then again, that wasn't true either. He eased onto the bed.

He should tell Aunt Nadine the truth. Tell her now. He could have been killed last night. He would have died and gone to his grave without telling her. He should do it now before he lost his nerve.

Oh, God, how do I tell her?

Jack hung his head. "Aunt Nadine, there's something we need to talk about."

"What is it?"

He could feel her eyes on him, so he lifted his gaze to meet hers. Loving, trusting, take-in-the strays Nadine. How was this woman even the sister of a man like Jack's father? Jack felt the first burn of tears, but he swallowed the emotions. Pushed them back. He had to talk this out.

"Oh, son, whatever it is, it can't be that bad." She rushed over to sit on the edge of the bed next to him.

Aunt Nadine took his hand.

She couldn't know what she was saying and would change her tune soon enough.

"You took me in and raised me. I can't ever thank you enough."

"There's no need."

"I didn't want to be anything like my dad. An addict. He tried, I know, but he didn't care enough about me to stay away from drugs. Even after Mom died. He was weak. I've always been so afraid that I'd be weak too, when it mattered most. I was so afraid I would end up being a loser just like him. That's why I wanted to be in the FBI. I could prove myself that way. Prove myself to you, if not to myself." *Prove I was good enough for Terra. Except in the proving, I lost her.*

"There's something I should have told you a long time ago," she said.

"No, wait, I need to get this off my chest. I've kept a horrible secret from you."

"I'm listening, but nothing you tell me can be that bad."

"I wanted to prove to you that I wasn't like him. I wasn't like your brother. And that I was a hero. I was so afraid I would disappoint you. Let you down. And as it turns out, I let you down, after all."

"Jack, please calm down. Whatever it is—"

"Sarah."

His aunt's features twisted.

"What about Sarah?"

Sarah was Aunt Nadine's granddaughter and Jack's second cousin, but she'd been more like a sister to him. "I was like the older brother she was supposed to look up to. I should have protected her."

"Jack, you weren't around when she ran away with the love of her life. Or at least the man she thought she loved. There was nothing you could have done."

The breath rushed from him. "I saw her. I was working undercover, and I saw her come through with a group of trafficked girls. I tried to get to her to save her, but I was too late, Aunt Nadine. Don't you see? Sarah died on my watch. She died because of me."

Aunt Nadine let go of his hand. She clasped her hands over her mouth.

Jack hung his head. There. He'd told her everything. And with the words, the deep ache of loss and failure racked through his body.

"I should have told you, but I didn't know how." And he struggled to live with himself—all his efforts seemed like they were for nothing.

Aunt Nadine composed herself. "You can't carry that burden. You did your best. Sarah made the choice to leave with her no-good boyfriend. Her subsequent disappearance isn't on you. It never was. I've come to terms with her death, and you need to do the same."

She remained silent a few breaths, then said, "Now that we're confessing, there's something I've been meaning to tell you too. You worked hard to be different from your dad, but you're just like him, Jack. You're a hero."

What? Jack stared at his aunt. Was she losing a grip on reality again?

A nurse stepped into the room. "Are you ready to get out of here?"

He nodded but hated the interruption. The nurse set papers to be signed on the small table.

Nathan rushed into the room. "Am I late?"

Jack signed the discharge papers. "I don't know. That depends on why you're here."

"Your aunt asked me to pick you guys up."

"Why? I can drive." Then Jack remembered his obliterated vehicle and his aunt's injured wrist. Neither of them was driving today.

///////////////////////

Jack stood in the conference room staring at the crime board. He needed to make quite a few corrections. Someone had tried to tie everything together.

He spotted another clue, a connection he hadn't known about. In high school, Neva Bolz had been best friends with Jocelyn Porcella, the daughter of Princess Leia/Luke Skywalker, or Mabel and Dirk Porcella.

This association raised questions. Were the memorabilia collectors showing the world their interest in more contemporary pop culture while secretly trafficking artifacts?

Someone had written that question on the crime board. Jack guessed Nathan.

Nathan had dropped Aunt Nadine off at home. She was

worried that Freckles's lost boy might stop by the house, and she needed to be there for him. But her poster only included her cell number, not the house address. Reuniting a dog and his boy was a worthy cause for someone as conscientious and compassionate as his aunt.

He'd come back to be here for her and never could have imagined what had transpired in the last few days. Somehow, he'd have to do better—for her sake. But today, Jack needed to be at the county offices to work. He needed to see this through.

He could have stayed home to listen to what Aunt Nadine wanted to tell him about his father, but he couldn't take it right now, because she wasn't making any sense. Had she even understood what he'd told her about Sarah?

Nathan shoved through the door to join him in the conference room, carrying a drink holder with extra creamers and cups of coffee—the good stuff from the café down the street. "How are you feeling?"

"How am I feeling?" Jack repeated the question because he didn't know how to answer it. He slumped at the table. "I need coffee."

"Here you go." Nathan set the drink holder down.

Jack grabbed a cup and dumped in the creamer. "Thanks, man."

Nathan fixed his own coffee, then stared at the board. "You didn't answer my question. How are you feeling?"

"Concerned about Terra."

"Yeah, I get that. She can take care of herself, but she's more than a special agent. She's special to you, isn't she?"

Again, Jack wasn't sure how to answer.

Nathan chuckled. "It's okay. She cares about you too. You should have seen her last night. Man, she was ripped up."

"I figured she would be here by now, that's all. She didn't return my call, but I texted to invite her to join us. She responded that she had a few things to do but would try to stop by." She was definitely avoiding him, and what did he expect, given their kiss and the way she'd walked out on him?

He'd deserved that and needed to accept her decision and move on. Leave her alone.

"Are you sure you shouldn't stay home and rest today?" Nathan asked. "I can question whoever you think needs questioning. Just bring me up to speed."

"We thought if we found who killed Jim, we'd find the man responsible for Neva's death too. And the man behind an artifact trafficking ring that could include pieces from the Middle East. Or at least one." Jack scratched his jaw. "After Leif fired on us, I thought we had our man."

"But he's dead now. Someone cleaning up loose ends and moving out?"

"All the more reason we need to figure this out today." Jack chugged his coffee, finishing it, then tossed the cup in the corner trash can.

His arm throbbed, but he wouldn't take painkillers. He needed a clear head.

"Let's go over everything again, starting with what we've learned about Leif Morrisey. We need a list of all his connections and associates."

"Owen Connors." Nathan grabbed a marker and wrote his name on the board.

Jack blew out a long breath. "Tell me again what happened when Sarnes questioned Owen."

"They stopped by the ranch and found him home. It looked like he'd been asleep. He didn't want to wake Robert, so he spoke to them on the porch. We have no reason to believe he's involved at this point. Owen was recovering in a hospital in Germany and has been back, what, two months now? He hasn't had dealings with Morrisey in a year."

"So, the guy just shows up this week. A plane crashes. Jim and

Neva are murdered. We need to find out when Leif got into town." Nathan drew circles on the empty space of the whiteboard.

"The very first event that we strongly believe is connected, and perhaps even the catalyst—the plane crash. We need to find the pilot," Jack said. "Last night, he met with Leif at Bar Wars. Did he say something to set the guy off? And if so, what? Did Leif have PTSD? And have we found Blevins yet?"

"Yes on Blevins," Nathan said. "He took a road trip out of town. His vehicle showed up in Louisville, Kentucky. Cops there caught up with him. We'll question him, so maybe his answers will shed some light. I get the feeling he was skipping town because he was afraid for his life."

Jack nodded. "Smart man, considering what went down last night. I can't wait to learn more about his dealings with Neva. But the pilot . . ." Jack pointed at the whiteboard. "Our identity thief, Chance Carter, he stuck around to meet with a dangerous man. And we need to know why."

"Where do you think Leif was heading after he left the bar?" Nathan asked. "Just throwing you off his tail?"

"Maybe he was going to meet someone, and then because he was tailed and made a mess of things, he was murdered." Jack pressed the heels of his palms into his eyes.

"And that murderer had to have been close and somehow took out Morrisey while cops were combing the area." Nathan frowned. "You want me to search again?"

"Did you talk to the people who live in the farmhouse?"

"Sure did. A widow claimed to have been asleep."

"Then let's go question her," Jack said.

"You're on desk duty, remember?" Nathan capped the marker and put it aside.

"Like the sheriff said, he needs all his resources on this. I'll stand idly by while you do the questioning."

"Why do you want to question her again?" Nathan asked.

"She's lying."

"Maybe you should have stayed home to rest today. You can't be serious."

Jack scratched his jaw. "Dead serious. Nobody could have slept through that."

FIFTY-NINE

SAC Dan Murphy, Terra's superior, called early this morning and wanted her in for a debriefing of last night's events when he returned from a conference in three days. Unlike Jack, Terra never actually fired her weapon in the incident with Leif. Still, she was much too close to the investigation given Owen's relationship with Leif. She almost laughed at that. But until her superior said otherwise, she was still investigating the archaeological crimes/murder case. In the meantime, she took the morning off to get her bearings.

She fixed brunch for Gramps.

His favorite—a BLT sandwich. The sandwich waited on the table while she waited for Gramps. He had a conference call with Marcus Briggs. Gramps was really going to do this.

Terra rubbed her shoulders to ease the tension. Every sound made her jump.

Her precious family—those in her inner circle whom she trusted most—was near being torn apart. She hoped that Owen was off the hook, but she couldn't be sure. Then add to that, Gramps had hired someone to break into his safe? She hoped Owen had misunderstood.

All these thoughts fought for her attention, while her heart still ached at the way she'd walked out on Jack. She didn't recognize herself—how could she ever be that cold?

His words echoed constantly through her mind. *"You don't understand. Terra, wait—"*

She blinked back tears and focused on the current crisis.

Owen had agreed to stay out and work with the horses, giving Terra time to speak with Gramps. Her brother probably also needed to work off the pain he felt at losing Leif and learning what his friend had done.

Staring at her own sandwich, she knew she couldn't stomach it today.

The office door opened, signaling that Gramps was on his way. Terra's hands shook as she poured coffee, grateful when the mug rested securely on the table next to his sandwich. She eased into the chair across from his place setting and waited.

He emerged from the hallway and took in the food and Terra.

"How'd it go?" she asked.

"Marcus says I have a good track record. I understand the industry in the state, and my daughter's heroism will play well into the campaign." Gramps eyed the table as if he had to think about whether or not to eat.

"I hope you're hungry. I made your favorite."

He offered a tenuous smile and sat at the table. "Thanks. It's good you're here. I'm only just learning a few things about last night. I'm glad you're okay."

"Well, it's over. I'm here and I'm okay. Now, eat up. You need your strength for the campaign trail."

He took a few bites. "Owen's connection to Leif could be an issue, and don't tell me different."

"I think you could easily overcome it. Owen isn't linked to Leif other than that he served with him." Terra took a breath. She should dive in before she lost her nerve. "But there is some other business I need to ask you about."

Gramps drank from his mug, his eyes boring into her from over the brim. That same displeased look he'd given her when she was a kid and he meant to scold. How ridiculous it was that she felt like a young teenager again, fearing admonishment from him. Fearing she would be the cause of his displeasure. He'd taken her father's place, after all. She looked up to him and loved him.

He set down his mug. "Why don't you tell me what this is about, then. I had a feeling you were buttering me up."

"I don't like the way you're using Mom's heroism to propel you into the political arena." Those weren't the words she'd meant to say.

He crossed his arms and eyed her. Gramps could be formidable—another reason he made a great politician. "Are you saying you haven't used your mother's death to propel your own career? That her job with the forest service played no role in your current job as a special agent? Or your quick transfer from the National Park Service?"

Terra couldn't do this. She lowered her gaze.

"Terra, honey, I'm sorry. That was uncalled for. If anything, you've used her heroism, her legacy, to drive you. You long to live up to her. And there's no need."

Tears gathered in the corners of her eyes. "You're trying to change the subject."

"Maybe I am. I love you, and I don't think this is a conversation we need to have. It only hurts."

"Last night, a man tried to kill me. Owen's friend Leif."

"I know all this."

"Leif was in your office. What did you talk about? You told me that conversation was about Owen. But I want the truth."

Gramps didn't speak for a few moments, then he stood and Terra feared he would walk away without answering. She had no idea what she would do if he did. But he grabbed his mug and went to the counter. Poured more coffee and stared out the kitchen window. No doubt buying himself time.

"I'm sorry that someone tried to hurt you, Terra. That's why I didn't want you in law enforcement." Gramps took a sip of coffee. "I'm not involved in whatever is going on here. But I think you need to recuse yourself and stay out of it. Your life could still be in danger."

"What was in the safe? Tell me what was stolen."

"I've already told you. Now it's time for you to stop this nonsense. I think you need some time off. This investigation is getting to you."

Terra wouldn't put it past him to call her supervisor and get that for her. Gramps knew the man. There wasn't anyone in this county he didn't know. Plenty of people were on his payroll, whether at the trucking company, the granary, or the airport.

Gramps . . .

That was it, then. He wouldn't tell her the truth.

One thing she knew, her grandfather was hiding something.

Terra couldn't go into the office today and face the questions or the paperwork. Instead, she should just head home to see her cat and thank her neighbor. Crash on her own sofa and get some perspective. Terra texted Jack her plans and that she wouldn't be meeting him at the sheriff's offices today.

An email came through on her cell—Nells, the forest service archaeologist assigned to the artifacts. Nells had identified the pieces, and as Terra suspected, they had been trafficked from the Southwest—except for the headdress. Terra and Dan would work to return the headdress to the local Crow tribes and dispatch the rest through the appropriate channels, but they also still needed to learn the names of the intended buyers.

As soon as she closed her email, her cell buzzed. She glanced at the number. The museum? "Special Agent Connors speaking."

"Agent Connors, this is Valerie Harris. You left a message on our answering machine that you had stopped by yesterday and asked for anyone with information to contact you. I'm the one who checks the messages. I think I'm finally ready to talk. I'll be at the museum this afternoon."

"I'm on my way."

Terra pulled on a jacket and grabbed her bag.

Half an hour later, she parked on the street in front of the museum. When she entered, she flashed her credentials to a silver-haired woman behind a counter. "I'm here to speak with Valerie Harris."

A twentysomething woman approached.

"I'm Valerie." She glanced nervously at the woman behind the counter. "Maggie, I'm going to take a few minutes, okay?"

Maggie nodded. "Sure, dear. I'll cover for you."

"Is there a private room where we could chat?" Terra asked.

Valerie found them a room in the back of the museum.

"Are you a volunteer, or do you get paid?" Terra asked.

"I'm interning and get college credit. I admit that's why I took some time to think about calling the police. Then you left that message, and I knew I should contact you."

Terra was eager to hear what the young woman had to share. "I'm glad you decided to make that call. I'm here to listen."

"I'm sorry I didn't call sooner, but I had a lot going on that day."

"What day are we talking about?" Terra asked.

"The day the police came to take the knife—the murder weapon. I found that knife the day before. It was in the alley behind the museum. Seeing it there freaked me out. I thought that somehow someone had gotten into those artifacts—they're my responsibility—without me knowing and then dropped it in the alley. Maybe they had wanted to return it but were embarrassed so they left it there. Whatever the reason, I thought

316

that I'd messed up, so I put the knife in with the other similar knives and said nothing."

Terra had suspected that the murderer had taken it from the museum and returned it in order to hide it or to mislead them.

"Why didn't you come forward before now?"

She shrugged. "No one asked me about the knife. The police had it, and I figured it didn't make any difference and—"

"You were scared." Terra patted her hand. "I believe you. But do you have any idea who could have taken the knife and then dropped it in the alley?"

She frowned. "No. All I know is that night I heard the back door shut as I was entering the room. The thing is, I put the knife in with the others. I panicked. But I've been thinking about the mistake I made, and it's important."

Terra shifted, trying to hide her impatience.

"I'm trying to tell you that the knife didn't belong here to begin with."

"What do you mean?"

"I catalogue each item. When I had the chance, I went back through the data and that knife is an artifact, yes, but it isn't ours."

Terra hid her surprise. "We need to find out who dropped the knife in the alley. It could be someone who never even came into the museum. But the proximity makes me wonder . . ."

"We had a couple of tour groups that day."

Maybe someone wanted to mislead the investigation, like she suspected. Make them look closely at the museum. Or dropping the knife could have been a mistake. Criminals inadvertently leaving evidence behind was how law enforcement found them. Terra pulled up a picture on her cell of Leif Morrisey at Owen's and showed it to Valerie. "Have you seen this man before?"

Valerie's eyes widened. "Yes. In fact, I answered some of his questions on the Native American displays. He asked if we had other artifacts—from the Middle East—but we don't have those."

Terra's cell rang, and she let it go to voice mail.

Could the knife have come from Jim's collection at the cabin? She could imagine Leif following Jim to the cabin or meeting him there and killing Jim. Leif must have intended to slip the knife into the collection at the museum but dropped it.

"We'll look at the security videos again." They had been focusing on the volunteers and employees.

An elderly man with white wisps of hair and spectacles cleared his throat. Terra hadn't realized he'd entered the room. "The sheriff's offices . . . well, Detective Tanner has a copy of the security footage. Oh, excuse me, I'm Dr. Bellinger. Curator and manager." He thrust out his hand.

"USFS Special Agent Terra Connors." Terra smiled. "Okay, then, I'll check with the detective. I appreciate the information. Please contact me if you think of something else that could help."

Terra exited through the back door and found herself in the alley. Sure enough, the back of Bar Wars was conveniently located across from the museum. Star Wars collectors, clandestine meetings between possible artifact traffickers? The murder weapon dropped in the alley between the two?

What had Leif been up to? Planting a murder weapon? Searching for the package? Looking for a connection between the bar's collectors and the museum and the artifact? Whatever the reason, his search had killed him.

And too many others.

Her cell buzzed. She glanced down and read the text from Jeremy. He'd learned something more and wanted her to call when she was free. She listened to the voice mail that had come in earlier. Marcus Briggs wanted to meet with her to talk strategy? He must be as good as Gramps made him out to be. He could want to get a better read on her support of her grandfather so he could know what he could count on, or what he was up against.

Terra rubbed her scalp as she headed to her vehicle. She was much too popular today. She still felt shaken from last night's experience. Early in the conversation with Valerie, a distant drum had started beating in Terra's head, and now the pounding had closed in and decided to stay. She'd contact Jeremy later and instead stick to her original plan to stop by her apartment. She needed her own space. Before heading out, she called Jack but got his voice mail, so she detailed her meeting with Valerie, including that the security videos should be reviewed again. She also let him know she needed space today and would reach out to him tomorrow.

With no more news from her superior, Terra headed home. On the drive, she thought about her conversations with Owen and Gramps. It was probably best if she were removed from the case. She suspected the additional agencies—the FBI Art Crime Division in particular—could possibly take over soon. And she wouldn't have to work with Jack anymore.

She wouldn't have to see him again.

At her apartment, the place felt strange and empty—and also lonely without Sudoku. She texted her neighbor Allie to see if she was home. If so, Terra would be over soon to see if Su remembered her. When she didn't receive an immediate text back, she showered and changed into jeans and a fresh T-shirt.

Adrenaline rushed out of her, and she sank onto the sofa and let the tears fall.

All the recent events charged at her.

The images, the emotions that took front and center related to Jack collapsing. All the blood. Then the tender and yet passionate kiss—years of pent-up emotions finally liberated—and Terra's subsequent statement, declaring an end to any hope of a future for the two of them.

Who was she kidding? She still totally cared about the guy. Okay, well, she would admit to herself in this moment . . . she still *loved* him.

Loved?

Had she ever truly stopped?

In his letter, Jack had told her, *"I love you enough to let you go."* At the time, she'd thought he'd simply chosen his career over her. He'd hurt her, but she got it now. Jack had believed she deserved better than him or what he could give her. He believed he wasn't good enough. And look, he'd come full circle. He'd proven himself . . . well, to himself. He'd moved beyond the lack of self-worth and profound pain his father had left him with.

"You did it, Jack," she whispered.

Then why couldn't Terra knock down that wall in her heart to risk loving and losing again?

Mom's words to her, mere hours before she was killed, came back to her.

"The direction your life takes can often come down to one decision, one moment in time."

Terra had begged her to stay home that day. Mom had chosen to go. She couldn't have known her decision would cost her life.

Considering the life decisions Terra had made so far, that one moment, that one decision that would change her life, had not happened yet as far as she could tell. Unless her walking out on Jack in his hospital room counted. It felt pivotal. It felt life-changing. It should be freeing. Instead, it was anything but. And like Mom, how could Terra know when that all-important pivotal moment was on her? Maybe one never really knew, and it wasn't so cut-and-dried as Mom had suggested.

A knock came at the door.

She'd told Allie to text when she was home and Terra would come over. She wasn't quite prepared to see Allie. She wiped her face on her sleeves and opened the door. Surprise and confusion filled her. "Oh, hi. What are you doing here?"

"I need your help."

She opened the door wider. The sooner she got it over with, the sooner she could be done.

"Would you like tea or coffee?"

"Coffee would be nice."

Terra turned to head for the kitchen and a prick stung her arm. Dizziness swept through her, then darkness took her.

SIXTY

Jack stood with Nathan at the farmhouse. They believed Leif's murder had taken place around the grain silo and away from the home.

The door opened and an older woman—maybe late seventies, even early eighties—stared back, surprised. Nathan flashed his credentials. "I'm Detective Nathan Campbell, and this is Detective Jack Tanner."

"I already told the others everything I know, which is nothing, but come on in." She opened the door wide, and Jack followed Nathan into a small but comfy living room with decades-old furniture. Doilies and all.

"Have a seat, detectives. Can I get you anything to drink?" she asked.

"No thank you." Nathan sat. "We won't be here too long. Just have a few more questions."

Jack remained standing. The plan was for Nathan to ask the questions. Jack perused the photographs on the walls. The fireplace mantel. The side table. Then he turned his attention back to the conversation.

He approached and eased into the chair nearest the woman

while Nathan engaged in small talk. Jack was anxious to get down to business and leaned forward.

She smiled at Jack. "Detective."

"Just call me Jack."

"And you can call me Ruby, please."

"All right, Ruby." Jack shared a look with Nathan, letting him know he would take it from here. "I was involved in the shooting last night." Then again, might as well get right to the point.

Her eyes widened, and her gaze dropped to his arm. "You're wearing a sling. Is that because of last night?"

"Yes, ma'am. I was almost killed, along with another law enforcement officer, who also happens to be a dear friend." Jack didn't miss that I-told-you-so expression on Nathan's face. Terra would be a "dear friend" to Jack even if he had no romantic feelings for her. He cleared his throat. Focused on the topic. "When I heard that you insisted you hadn't heard the gunshots last night, I had to hear that from you myself, Ruby."

Ruby's demeanor shifted to one of shame. Her shoulders sagged, and she stared at the floor. "My Will died this last spring. My son Butch comes from the next town over to check on me now and then. He manages the crops. Drives the combine. Hires help as needed. But at night, I'm alone. I still can't get used to this old house. Every creak, every noise wakes me. I stopped watching those murder mysteries. That did help me some, but then . . ."

"It's all right, Ruby. Take your time, dear," Jack said.

She gave him a shy smile. "When I heard the guns go off, at first I thought it was firecrackers. I went to stand on the porch, and I realized someone had machine guns. I . . . I was scared. I did like Will always instructed me to do. I ran down into the basement. He kept a loaded shotgun for me down there. It's our safe room. I bolted the door and grabbed the shotgun. Down there, I couldn't hear the gunfire. I'd planned to call the police, but I'd left my cell upstairs." Ruby glanced at Jack. "I waited for what I thought was a good long while, then I started back upstairs. But that's when I heard someone come inside the house. I thought I would have a heart attack. I froze in the shadows down under the stairwell, holding that shotgun I never had need to use in over six decades."

Tears slipped from Ruby's eyes, but she straightened, sitting tall in the chair. "That's when I heard Will's voice in my head. To be the strong person I had always been. I stomped right up those stairs and pointed the shotgun at a man standing in the hallway. I told him to get out of my house or I'd blast a hole through him."

Jack shared a look with Nathan.

"What happened next?" Nathan asked.

"He lifted his hands as if he meant no harm. Didn't say nothing, but he marched out the front door. I ran to the door and bolted it. I guess I hadn't locked it earlier, so I only have myself to blame for him coming inside. I tell you, my heart was pounding so hard. The sirens came then. The police. So I knew I was safe."

"Ruby," Jack said. "Why didn't you tell the other officers this story?" Jack tried to keep his incredulity concealed.

Ruby hung her head again, then just as quickly lifted it. "I'm ashamed, son. I truly am. But it was always my Will's mantra that we mind our own business. We don't borrow trouble. We stay out of it. I thought I was doing what Will would want. After all, what does it matter that the guy came in the house and left of his own accord? He's dead, I hear."

"Yes, and he was found inside your silo."

"I didn't kill him." Determination carved deeper into the lines on her face.

Jack could almost smile at that. She was a feisty woman, ready to defend her home and herself. He couldn't blame her for that. "We know you didn't, Ruby."

He couldn't see her climbing up the silo ladders or steps, much less carting Leif's body up and dumping it, though he wasn't clear on the events of the murder. Then again, Leif could have made his last stand up on the catwalk at the top of the silo, battling it out before being shot and killed. Even then, Ruby wasn't a suspect. He glanced at Nathan. "Just how did we learn Leif was in the silo?"

Nathan cleared his throat. "Tracks through the cornfield. More bullet holes in the tower." He looked at Ruby. "Sorry, ma'am."

"I already know this. No need to be sorry. Anything else I can answer for you?"

"Did you get a good look at the man in the house?" Jack asked.

"It was dark, but I got some of him. He was like a ghost."

On his cell, Jack showed her an image of Leif. "Was this the man in your home?"

Ruby shook her head. "No, that's not him. Who is he?"

Her reply surprised him. Then again, he knew there was another shooter out there—Leif's killer. Jack sent Nathan a warning look. He didn't want to scare Ruby by sharing that the man who had entered her home was not the man who had died in her silo.

"I appreciate your help, Ruby," Jack said. "Here's my card. Please call me if you think of anything else."

Nathan thanked her too, and they headed for the door. As Ruby opened the door for Nathan, Jack lingered at the mantel and looked at the family photographs again. Ruby came rushing over and was only too happy to tell him the names of her children. Three sons and a daughter. Twelve grandchildren. Quite a few pictures of the kids and their activities. Soccer. Football. Twirling. Running around in the backyard with dogs. The usual.

A photograph of a soldier standing next to a helicopter drew his attention, and Ruby was quick to notice.

"Oh, that's my son. He died years ago when his helicopter crashed overseas."

"I'm sorry to hear that." He waited a few moments in case she would share more, but she seemed lost in thought.

"Well, thanks again, Ruby." Jack joined Nathan, who'd been waiting on the porch.

Following Nathan down the steps, Jack stumbled on the last one but caught himself. Pain ignited in his arm.

"You okay?" Nathan asked.

"No." Jack continued toward the vehicle and climbed into the passenger side.

Nathan hopped in the driver's seat and started the vehicle. "You want to tell me what's wrong?"

"I recognized her son who supposedly died."

"What? No way."

"Yes way. He looks much different now than he did years ago when that picture was taken, but there's some resemblance. Ruby believes her son is dead, so she would never think that the man she saw standing in her house was him. Instead, she said he was like a ghost."

"Well, come on, man, who is he?"

"Robert Vandine's campaign manager. Marcus Briggs."

SIXTY-ONE

The darkness slowly edged away.

Terra's head pounded. She couldn't remember a thing beyond . . .

Oh no.

A familiar laugh sent dread through her. Nausea roiled in her stomach. Terra opened her eyes. Gramps sat across from her on the other side of his desk. His desk. In his office.

She'd been transported from her apartment to the ranch.

Gramps tried to appear calm, collected, and in control. He was failing miserably.

"She's awake now. I didn't need her awake for this, but the more the merrier." His back against the wall, Marcus Briggs held a gun and pointed it at her grandfather.

"What's . . . what's going on?" Terra asked.

"Bringing her here, using her against me like this doesn't change anything," Gramps said. "I don't know where it is."

"Where what is?" Her words, the rising emotions, were too much, too loud against the constant throbbing in her head. Even as she asked the question, she suspected she knew exactly what Marcus wanted.

"The artifact. I have a buyer, and he's growing impatient."

"Why does he think you know where it is?" Terra stared at her grandfather through blurred vision.

The fear in Gramps's eyes rocked through her.

"He's a desperate man." Gramps ground out the words. "I don't have anything to do with this business."

If this man was behind the murders, then he would have no problem killing her and her grandfather. But where was Owen? Her heart pounded as fear for her brother, for Gramps, mounted.

Terra found the strength to push from the chair and stand, only to realize her wrists were bound. "You killed Jim and Neva? Or did you make Leif do it? He must have worked for you."

Marcus pointed his gun at her. "Sit if you want to live. Morrisey didn't work for me."

"I don't understand." Terra needed to buy time. Get him talking so she could figure a way out of this.

"He was trying to find me so he could kill me, but I found him first." Marcus aimed the gun at her head. He still stood too far for her to take the gun from him, if she even could with bound wrists. "Now, I need my property."

The Janus has many connections, political and social, and probably travels a lot. Jeremy's words came back to her.

"You're . . . you're the . . . the Janus."

He laughed. "If that's what you want to call me. I've developed the connections and the reputation. And that reputation is going to receive a big blow if you don't tell me what you did with it. This is the deal of my life. I've waited a long time to get my hands on it."

"Gramps, please, if you have it, just give it to him."

"But I don't have it," Gramps said. "That's what was stolen from my safe."

She gasped. What?

Frown lines grew deeper in his forehead. "Jim came to me. He brought me the package. He was to get the package at the airstrip, but the plane crashed. He retrieved it when he saved the pilot but realized he couldn't store it at his cabin. He needed to put it somewhere for safekeeping until his meeting to hand it off. But he was scared after he realized what the object was. He'd gotten in too deep and wanted out. He needed time to think about what to do with it."

"Why did you agree to keep it? You were going to be running for office. Something like this could ruin it all." And *would* destroy his chances of election.

"I wanted to give him a chance to do the right thing. I owed him for getting me out of a financially sticky situation. Besides, I could claim that I didn't realize the item's provenance. And honestly, I still don't."

"I agree. I'd like to know what all the fuss is about." Keep this guy talking. Find a way out.

She wished that Jack would come looking for her, except why would he? She'd walked out on him, and then put him off again. Jack could very well be giving her the space that she'd asked for.

"There's something you don't know," Gramps said.

Terra was getting the picture that there was a lot she didn't know.

"We don't have time for the family reunion." Marcus kept his distance from Terra as he held the weapon aimed at her head. "Jim brought it to you, Robert. You must still have it. If it was stolen, then that's all part of your plan and you know where it's going."

Terra thought through possible ways to remove the gun from him.

"Step away from her." A man spoke from behind, his voice menacing.

Marcus's entire demeanor shifted. Fear crawled over his face as he stared at the new arrival behind Terra. "You can't shoot me before I kill her."

"I don't want to shoot you," the man said. "I want to negotiate."

"You're in no position—"

Terra turned to see who the newcomer was.

The man from the bar? The pilot? She'd never gotten a good look at him. Chance Carter held up a box in one hand—an offering—and pointed a gun at Marcus with the other.

"My deal was to deliver this package—my last delivery. Then my plane went down, and all bets were off when I woke up in the hospital and the package was gone. I knew I had to find it and find you and deliver it to you in person so I could make sure I would never be blackmailed again. Only I didn't know who was behind the blackmail. But I figured it out."

Chance lowered the box to the floor while continuing to aim the weapon. Then he held the gun with both hands. "My first clue was when I saw what was inside the box." His face twisted. "I had to ask myself, what is that golden jeweled crown, a Nimrud artifact looted from the Iraq Museum, doing in Montana? What was I doing delivering the item I had walked away from years ago?"

"Your actions cost me everything," Marcus said.

"Imagine my surprise when I discovered that this whole time, it was you blackmailing me, Tony. I thought you died in that helicopter crash in Iraq. Instead, you took on a new identity and obviously kept building your trafficking business. You forced me to leave my family to keep them safe. But now I have it in my hands, and I found you. I'm done for good. I just have one question—why me? Why did you send me to deliver this?"

"The artifact that cost me everything? I lost my family because of you," Marcus said. "Even if I hadn't survived the crash and disappeared, I would have been court-martialed and lost them anyway. You deserved to pay. I thought the crown was apropos for your last delivery, since that was the very item that was lost to me when you wanted out. I was able to get my hands on it again, diverting it from being returned back to Iraq." Marcus shrugged. "So you would deliver it for me, completing what you wouldn't complete years ago, and I would finally get my millions."

"It doesn't belong to you. It didn't then. It doesn't now."

Marcus sighed. "We're all a little older and a little wiser. We all made mistakes. Give me the box, and I'll let them go. With the money, I can reinvent myself all over again."

The pilot looked intently at Terra. Emotion welled in his eyes. A pang shot through Terra's heart. She hadn't seen beyond the pilot. Behind his scruffy beard, older broken features. Behind the baseball cap and a thicker body . . . she hadn't seen who he really was.

Her vision blurred. She wasn't thinking clearly. No . . . "Who *are* you? You're not . . . you can't be—" But she knew in her heart that he was. Recognition slammed into her, knocking the breath from her. She gasped for oxygen, and then words. "Dad?"

"Yes, baby. It's me."

"What? Why? I . . . I don't understand. What are you doing here now? Why did you leave in the first place?" The questions overwhelmed her, and the precarious situation shook her to her core.

"As for what I'm doing here now, as soon as I realized who was behind everything, I knew I had to warn Robert. I knew Robert, you, and Owen were in danger, but I got here too late." He growled those last words out, glaring at Marcus. "But it's okay because I have the leverage needed. As for the past"—his tone softened as he turned his gaze back to her—"I had no choice. Because of my mistake in Iraq, staying here would have put you in danger. Even though leaving hurt us both, it was better for you. Safer. After your mom died, I couldn't lose you too. Briggs forced me to leave my family, to leave you to keep you safe. But I see now that my efforts made no difference. You're here now because of my mistakes."

Tears erupted. "You did lose me, Dad. You lost me and Owen. You left us. How could you think that leaving would ever be better?"

"Terra, I—"

"Don't beat yourself up, honey." Marcus/Tony, whoever he was, interrupted her father so he could be kind now? "I required that of him. I didn't need anyone catching up to Chris Connors to ask more questions about the looting. I could have nothing lead back to me. I had to create a new identity, and Chris had to as well. He had to lose his family, like I lost mine. I helped him create his new identity—Chance Carter, courier for an airfreight company in which I'm the majority shareholder."

"And Leif Morrisey?" she asked. "He wanted revenge for his sister's death. He was looking for you. What did you do to his sister?"

"She was fencing for me in Morocco and got into a bad situation. That's on her, not me. I had to focus on collectors in the United States for the last couple of years."

Terra was done with the man pointing a gun at her. Except her hands were in plastic ties, and he held the gun. There were no defensive moves she could use that wouldn't risk either her grandfather or now . . . her father.

"You." Marcus directed his words to her father. "You put your gun down and back away from the package. Come over behind the desk and join Robert."

"I'm not losing my gun. I don't trust you."

"You won't get a shot off before I kill her. Do you want to risk it?"

"Don't do it, Dad," she said. "He's bluffing."

But she saw in her father's eyes how precious she was to

him, and he would do anything to save her. He'd given her up in order to save her. He hesitated before finally acquiescing to Marcus's request, putting the gun down and stepping away from the package. Terra hoped that wasn't a mistake.

Once Dad stood next to Gramps, he said, "Okay. Take the package and get out of here."

"I'm taking the package, but she's coming with me," Marcus said. "Terra, pick up the package and let's go."

"I'm not going anywhere with you. Why would you want to take me?"

"I'll let you go when I'm safely away."

"Are you crazy?" Gramps asked. "You'll never escape your crimes!"

Marcus exploded with anger. "You're wrong, Robert. I've escaped my crimes for nearly two decades. Now, pick up the package!"

The sound of too many bullets flying, pinging Jack's car, accosted her. Marcus was about to lose it. Like Leif? She couldn't let him kill her family.

"My wrists are bound. How can I pick it up?"

"Reach down and grab the corner with your hands."

Suit yourself. She stood from the chair and then bent over for the package, using the opportunity to kick out her leg and clip his gun. But he maneuvered quickly like a trained soldier. Terra tried again.

Marcus fired the gun toward the desk.

"No!" she shouted. She scrambled toward the desk, but Marcus snatched her back.

Gramps pressed his hands over Dad's midsection as blood seeped through his fingers.

"Come with me now or I'll shoot your grandfather too."

She'd just got her father back. She couldn't lose him again. She tried to be so strong through it all, but the strength drained out of her. "No . . ."

"Pick up the package, and let's go."

Terra picked it up, her hands straining against the plastic ties. It seemed too light to be of any value.

"Leave her!" her father shouted.

He sounded strong, but for how much longer? She'd watched Jack nearly bleed out.

"We had a deal! I brought you the package, now let her go. Leave us alone."

Marcus dragged her along with him through the house.

"What are you doing?" She had to convince him to leave her. "You can't get away with this."

"I have a plane waiting at the airport. I'll be gone, out of this country, before the police even arrive at the ranch. I'll just have to find a different way to deliver the artifact now that Neva is gone. I had been planning to move my operations back to Morocco anyway."

Uh-oh. Marcus telling her his plans didn't leave any doubt as to his intentions. He would kill her when he was done using her.

He dragged her toward the meadow between the ranch house and the base of Stone Wolf Mountain, where a running helicopter waited.

Marcus pointed the gun at her. "Get in."

"What? You can get away now. You don't need me anymore. Let me make sure my father's okay since you already stole him from me for half my life!"

"If you prefer, I can shoot you in the leg and you can suffer in agony, but you'll still be with me. I'll keep you alive until I no longer need you."

Grimacing, she climbed into the helicopter, which was no easy task with bound wrists.

Marcus piloted the helicopter, which lifted straight up, then started west toward Stone Wolf Mountain's silhouette, dark against a moonlit sky. Terra could only bide her time. When he landed at the airport, she would refuse to get on that plane.

Others would be nearby. Even if he shot her for resisting, she could get help there. But her father was far from emergency services.

But please, God, oh, God, save my dad.

A warning signal blared, joining a blinking red light. The engine sputtered.

"What's that?" Terra asked, a new fear winding around her heart.

Expletives poured from the man's mouth. "We're losing altitude."

The rotors slowed. "What's going on?"

"Shut up!"

"Engine failure? We're going to crash?"

"Not if I can help it. Now shut up!" He pointed the nose of the helicopter downward.

Terra yelped.

They sped toward the ground, rotating as they went. At the last minute, would he pull the helicopter upward to land it?

Except there was no flat ground on which to land.

Only trees below them.

Terra glanced out the side window and looked at the starry night. Were these the last moments of her life? She took in the view below, barely illuminated by the helicopter's lights. The trees, the ground, were much too close.

She twisted until she was able to open the door with her still-bound hands.

"What are you doing?" Marcus grabbed her. "You have a better chance of surviving inside."

"But the trees. There's no place to land."

"Whatever happens, a crash is survivable. You hear me? I know from experience. I've survived both a helicopter crash and a plane crash, so don't worry. This helicopter was designed to absorb the impact and protect you. That said, you need to brace yourself for a hard landing."

This man who'd forced her here at gunpoint, who'd shot her father, who thought himself invincible suddenly had a heart?

The helicopter dipped until the rotors chopped trees and a path through them to the ground, screaming and twisting all the way down. Terra squeezed her eyes shut, gritted her teeth, and prayed under her breath, her heart pounding like it would escape her chest.

The impact jarred her. Then she felt nothing. Saw nothing.

///////////////////////

"Wake up. Get up."

Terra fought off the words, the pain. Someone shook her.

She groaned, then opened her eyes. Marcus stood over her. She'd hoped that it had all been a bad dream.

"I told you it was survivable. Now get up."

"Why do you care if I survive?"

"I need you more than ever now." He took a step back.

A sound drew her attention. He kicked the box Terra's father had given him and shined a flashlight into it.

A plastic Darth Vader mask.

Marcus growled.

"It doesn't look like—"

"It's not. Your father never had the artifact. I'm an idiot! I should have looked inside. But . . . Argh. I didn't want the others to see too." Marcus let loose a string of foul words, shouting them into the night. He gasped for breath, then seemed to calm down. But his eyes narrowed and slid back to Terra. "I'll keep you with me until I get it back. Get up. We have to leave the crash site."

Should she fake a twisted ankle or broken leg? No. He'd just kill her. She climbed from the seat. "I'm going to need my hands free. I might need to climb."

As Marcus shined the flashlight around, Terra recognized this part of the mountain.

"It's fitting, don't you think? This is near where my plane crashed fifteen years ago. Where the SAR team rescued me and an avalanche took them out."

Terra fought to comprehend his words. "What? Are you saying—"

"Yes. It was my plane that crashed. Your mother and her team saved me, and died in the rescue."

Stumbling, Terra dropped to her knees. Her father's sudden appearance in her life, his business in all this, and now Marcus/Tony's connection . . . it was all too much to grasp. And yet, it was starting to make sense. All these secrets buried in the past had been unearthed and were coming to light.

Marcus approached and stared down at her, a twisted smile on his face. "I'd been on my way here to face off with your father for bailing on me back in Iraq. I thought I might even kill him. But I never got to see him. He didn't even know I was still alive. Nobody did. They all thought Anthony Gray had died in the helicopter crash in Iraq on the way to the court-martial hearing. That reporting mistake was fortuitous for me—and I created a whole new identity in Marcus Briggs."

Marcus took an audible breath and continued staring at her.

"After the plane crash here and my rescue, I learned Chris had lost his beautiful Sheridan when she'd saved me. Telling him that news would have been sweet revenge before I took his life, but then I realized he was worth more to me alive. He would suffer even more if I put him to work for me. I knew one day I would let him know the truth about who had cost him everything. Revealing that truth to him didn't unfold like I had planned, what with *his* plane crash, but Chris knows I was the one behind all his misery. Behind forcing him away from his family. And I shot him, in the end. I got him."

Tears surged. *Oh, God, please let Dad live. Please don't let him die.* How she hated the man who stood over her now, who had disrupted her life from afar all these years. But she couldn't hold on to hate. Somehow, she had to let it go.

"It was you, wasn't it? You're the one who destroyed the memorial. You targeted Mom's plaque." As if at this juncture, any of that even mattered, but she had to know the truth—all of it.

"Sorry to disappoint you, but that wasn't me. Now get up. We have to go."

"You're a sick, sick man." If held on to long enough, bitterness, grudges, and regrets created monsters.

She'd already lost too much on this mountain, and now she was here with a monster.

SIXTY-TWO

Discarding his sling, Jack ignored the pain and climbed onto Lilly, one of Owen's horses.

When he'd heard the crash on the mountain, his heart felt as though it had been ripped from his chest. But he'd learned how to push past the debilitating pain of loss, and he would again in order to find Terra.

She couldn't die like this. She had to be alive. He would hang on to that hope. It was the only thing that kept him going.

The pain he felt over Sarah's death and his inability to get to her in time clawed at him but also drove him forward. Compelled him to find Terra, the woman he . . . loved.

Owen groaned. "I had no idea he was going to take her, or I never would have rigged a slow oil leak to cause engine failure in his helo. I returned early from a meeting in Bozeman, so he wasn't expecting me. I simply wanted to stop a madman from destroying more lives. I didn't think I could get into the house to get my gun without drawing Marcus's—"

Jack held up his hand, signaling for Owen to stop. "You didn't know. It's okay."

"I only meant to prevent him from flying away and escaping."

"There's no time for regret. We can hope they survived. Let's go find her. Let's get our Terra back."

After he and Nathan had left Ruby's, they headed straight for Robert Vandine's ranch while Jack tried to reach both Terra and Robert. Neither of them responded. Jack and Nathan were already on their way when they got the message from dispatch—Owen had called to report trouble.

Now Owen urged his horse forward, and Jack followed. At some point they'd have to get off the animals. The area was stony and treacherous, and the horses could slip on the rocks. He'd left Nathan behind at the ranch to wait with Robert and Terra's father for an ambulance and backup. Jack had grabbed some climbing gear from Nathan's vehicle, just in case the helicopter dropped in a precarious place on the mountain.

He urged Lilly up and forward, behind Owen's horse on the trail. "How much farther?"

"I'd say a mile," Owen said. "I can't be sure about the location of the crash."

"I heard it go down."

Anguish filled Owen's voice. "I was in the barn looking for a potential weapon when I saw him drawing her out to the helicopter and forcing her on. I shouted and ran after them, but I don't think Marcus heard me over the rotor wash." Owen slowed his horse to a stop, then got off. "I think we're headed the right way. Let's go in on foot now. The horses could twist an ankle."

Jack got off Lilly and handed the reins to Owen, who simply dropped the lead ropes to the ground. "I'm leaving them ground tied in case we need them. They're trained to wait unless otherwise directed, and they'll come to me on command. Now, let's go get my sister."

Jack appreciated that Owen spoke about her as if she was still alive.

Just hang in there, Terra . . . We're coming.

Jack and Owen hurried through the trees, their flashlights set to wide angles. Despite his prosthetic, Owen appeared to keep up with Jack just fine, though Jack was moving slower because of his injury. The bright eyes of wild animals reflected back to him now and then. Jack's panicked gasps for breath echoed around him, along with his own footfalls.

The pain in his arm stabbed through him, and he stumbled as Owen moved ahead of him. The pain didn't matter. Only Terra mattered—and getting to that dirtbag Marcus Briggs, or rather, Tony Gray.

Owen slowed. "I see the helo up ahead. Looks like the rotors separated from the fuselage. One's stuck in a tree. The good news is, the fuselage appears relatively intact. I'm betting the trees slowed the descent, but then he wasn't able to pull up at the last moment to land using the autorotation maneuver."

Jack huffed. "English, please."

"It was still a hard landing, and they could be injured or dead. I suggest a slow approach because he could still be dangerous. Oh, right, you wanted me to speak English. I'm saying he could put a bullet in both of us."

Jack readied his gun, and Owen did the same. They spread out, each approaching the helicopter from opposite sides, Jack sending prayers up for Terra's safety.

He crept forward, his heart pounding and breath quickening. He shined his flashlight on the cockpit.

Empty.

Terra could have been thrown from the helicopter. *No, no, no, no . . .*

He flashed the light around. "Terra!"

She could be hurt and dying. He rushed around the crash site, taking in the helicopter parts sprawled throughout this part of the forest.

"Terra!" Jack called as he searched.

In his heart, he would still keep hoping, still keep believing Terra was alive.

A box lay opened next to the body of the helicopter. Robert had explained that Terra's father had brought the artifact to negotiate. Was this it? But the only thing Jack saw in the box was a plastic Darth Vader mask.

"Looks like dear old dad didn't have the artifact, after all," Owen said.

"So that means, if they both survived, Tony has her. He'll keep her as ransom for it."

Owen rubbed his whole face, as if wiping away the anguish twisting his features. "Which way do you think Briggs would go?" Owen asked. "What do you think would be his best escape?"

"I vote for heading east. He could make his way down. Maybe steal a vehicle. Search and rescue would take a different path, but we should split up, just in case. We can't lose her."

"Agreed. And Jack?" Owen hesitated.

"Yeah."

"Watch your back. Stay alive."

"You do the same. We'll find her."

Jack relied on the flashlight to light his path but remained cautious that he didn't head off a cliff. A gust of wind foretold of the arctic winter to come, blasting a strong hint of bitter cold he could feel to his bones.

Outside the ring of light from the flashlight, darkness felt like it closed in around him.

Where are you, Terra?

Be alive. Just be alive.

The hair on the back of his neck rose. He stiffened, bracing for danger. Wind rushed over him milliseconds before a form slammed into him, knocking him into a granite boulder and bumping the flashlight from his grip. His gun flew from his hand as the breath whooshed from his lungs.

The beam of light flickered and went out, leaving him in

darkness. Sensing movement again, he rolled out of the way. A fist caught the side of his jaw. Jack landed on his bum arm, and he swallowed a cry of pain.

His pulse roared in his ears. He refused to let panic get the best of him, but where was the gun?

"Briggs. Give it up. I know who you are." Slowly standing, Jack calmed his breaths. Evened his tone. "The cops know you're Tony Gray. Your mother saw you in her house last night. She thought she was seeing a ghost. My guess is you were worried that Leif had gotten to her."

Jack listened and waited. Where was Briggs?

A crack sounded behind him. Jack ducked as he whirled and rushed forward. He caught Briggs in the waist and shoved forward with all his strength, tackling until the man stumbled backward. Jack forced Briggs to the ground as they neared a cliff, mere feet away from the ledge.

Jack knew where he was. He'd scaled that granite wall before.

Then Jack straddled Briggs, resisting the desire to pound his face. "Where is she?"

Briggs gasped for breath. Jack could make out blood spilling from his nose in the moonlight that broke through the clouds. He had been injured in the crash but still fought like he had no pain.

"What did you do with her?"

"I don't know where she is."

"You're lying." Jack raised his fist. "You know I can kill you with one move."

The man coughed up blood and laughed. "She got away."

If Jack got up, Briggs could attack him or run into the woods and Jack would lose him. To subdue him, he needed his gun.

"You looking for this?" Terra hobbled forward and pointed the gun at Briggs.

Jack got up and took the weapon from her. He wanted to

wrap his arms around her, to look her over, but he couldn't take his eyes off the man behind it all. Though, if he understood correctly, Leif was the one who killed Jim and Neva on his mission to find the man behind his sister's murder, gutting Briggs's trafficking network in the process.

"Are you okay?" Jack asked.

"More or less."

"What happened?"

"He had to untie me so I could make it down the boulders. Before we even tried, I fought him. Got the gun, but it misfired. So I ran. I heard you shouting. I knew you'd run into Briggs, so I came back to help you."

He handed his cell over.

"See if you can get a signal and call for backup."

"You didn't already?"

"Yes. But they need to know where we are. Top of Stone Wolf Canyon. Call your brother. He's out there somewhere looking for you."

"I'm here." Owen emerged from the trees and pointed his gun at Briggs too.

"It's okay, Owen," Terra said. "You can put your gun down. Detective Tanner has it under control."

Owen's eyes blazed with anger as he continued forward.

"Owen? What are you doing?" Jack feared he would shoot Briggs. "Owen, stand down."

"Leif's sister is dead because of you. That's why he was searching for the man behind moving the artifacts. The man his sister had worked for."

"Well, he found me." Briggs spat.

"And you killed Leif." Owen edged closer. "You deserve to die."

"Don't let him take you from me, Owen." Terra rushed forward. "You've come back to me. I can't lose you again. You kill him, you'll go to prison."

The tension rolling off Owen was palpable. Jack edged closer too, hoping to take the gun from him before he did something crazy and Terra got caught in the crossfire.

"Owen, please." Terra pressed Owen's arm until he lowered the gun.

Rotors thrummed in the distance, the sound growing louder. Terra snatched the flashlight and waved it toward the sky to signal their location.

Briggs kicked out his leg, knocking Owen over.

"Terra, shine the light on them," Jack said. "I can't see."

She flashed the light on the fighting men. Marcus had Owen pinned.

"Owen!" Terra rushed forward.

"Terra, watch out!" Jack called.

Marcus pushed her away, and she teetered on the edge of the cliff.

"Briggs," Jack said, "you have two seconds to get away from Owen before I shoot you."

Briggs tore the gun from Owen and rolled, then aimed at Terra, knowing he would inflict the most pain on both Jack and Owen by killing her.

"Noooooo!" Jack pulled the trigger at the same moment Briggs fired at Terra.

Briggs went limp and dropped the gun, just as Terra disappeared over the cliff.

SIXTY-THREE

Heart pounding, eyes squeezed shut, Terra clung to the tree root bursting from the bedrock. Her breaths quickened as fear snaked around her throat and tightened.

She forced back the screams that threatened to erupt. The whimpers from her anguished soul.

Just hang on. You can do this.

Breathe in. Breathe out.

Briggs's aim had been off, and she hadn't taken a bullet. She was still alive. But she could very well die anyway. The root she clung to for dear life hung precariously over a drop of hundreds of feet.

Terra tried again to calm her breaths—she needed to think clearly.

When I am weak, you are strong, God. I couldn't be any weaker than I am at this moment. Be strong for me.

Terra worked to stave off the panic. She waited and listened. The only sound other than her pounding heart was the river's roar from below as it echoed against the granite-faced cliff. But the sound failed to soothe her nerves.

Her arms started cramping. She didn't know how much longer she could hold on to the root. Had Jack been shot? Owen hurt?

Terra would have to get herself out of this. She attempted to climb up the root, but it shifted as if it would break away from the bedrock. Dirt and pebbles poured over her. Squeezing her eyes shut again, she pressed her forehead against the root.

A few minutes had passed already, though it seemed like hours, and she knew she couldn't stay like this forever—the root wasn't going to last much longer, even if she could.

God, where are you?

"It's okay, Terra. I'm here." Jack's calm voice washed over her from a few feet above.

She opened her eyes, and he shined a light down on her. "Jack!" she gasped, relief flooding her. *Thank you, God.* "Jack . . . this root isn't going to hold. I don't know what to do."

And it wasn't like Jack could help her. He had a bum arm. Owen wasn't a climber. She was going to die.

"Take deep breaths. Just remain calm and still," he said.

Jack shouted over his shoulder to someone behind him, but she couldn't make out the words. Her pulse ticked up, roaring in her ears, and her palms started sweating, making her grip on the root slippery.

She repositioned her hold and was rewarded with more dirt. One more shift on her part, and the root might give way completely.

Oh, God, I don't want to die on this mountain. I don't want to die like my mother. If I die here, it wouldn't even be to give my life for someone else like she did.

A gust whipped over and around her. She was exposed out here. Even as sweat beaded on her temples and back, the bitter wind made her shiver. Her hands trembled.

She was slipping.

Terra squeezed her eyes shut again, hoping to keep the tears from sliding down her cheeks. She was stronger than this, wasn't she?

A noise from above drew her attention.

A form slipped from the edge. "I'm coming for you, Terra."

"You can't, Jack. Your arm! Just lower the rope to me."

He was next to her before she finished the sentence. "I'll do better than that. Grab on to me and hold on. I brought a rescue tether, but you can't get it on without risking a fall. With my bum arm, I risk losing us both. But hold on tight, okay?"

Using his legs, he pushed closer to her. She reached over and climbed onto his back. She held on with her life, for her life. She felt the strength of his toned physique, the muscles ridged in his back. "Are you sure I'm not hurting you?"

"Seriously?"

"Your arm, Jack. You were shot yesterday. You're still weak."

"I'm not too weak to save you, Terra. Although, I didn't have time to set up my gear, so this could be a bumpy ride up." He lifted his face. "Okay, Owen!"

The rope lifted them higher, and Jack used his legs to practically walk up the cliff so they weren't slamming against it. They reached the ledge. Jack continued forward from vertical to horizontal without even stumbling. He stopped and Terra climbed from his back. She bent over her thighs to catch her breath and slow her racing heart.

Owen sat on a horse where the rope had been tied to the saddle horn, using the horse as an anchor. Owen grinned as he hopped off. "Basic cow horse training."

Jack laughed. "Owen came up with the idea to use the horses. He called them, and they followed his voice and brought the gear I packed."

"See? I told you he was like a horse whisperer," she said.

"Not like. He *is*." Jack's gaze turned dark as though he only now contemplated their near-death experience.

"You came for me." She swallowed the tears building in her throat. "Thank you."

"Did you have any doubt that I would?"

"I wasn't sure you would even know . . ."

Terra's knees shook. She assisted Jack in freeing himself from the ropes, though maybe he didn't need her help, but it was the least she could do.

"Terra."

The way he said her name, she lifted her gaze to meet his. The wind whipped around them, but his strong, steady form was unyielding, and it shielded her. In the moonlight she could make out his chiseled features and the longing in his eyes.

"I never stopped thinking about you," he said.

Though barely detectable, she didn't miss his sudden wince.

"You're in pain." She finished disentangling him from the gear.

No one ever would have known the guy's agony or just how significant it had been for him to scale the cliff to Terra, even with Lilly lowering him slowly down the ridge. He kept in such good shape that the strength of his entire body made up for his injured arm.

She looked up into his eyes again, her breathing ridiculously fast. The strength in Jack's heart and mind had to make up for his past mistakes.

She saw that now.

Would it make up for her mistake of telling him she couldn't go there with him?

Jack stepped back and moved to Briggs, leaving a cold vacuum in the space where he'd been. She feared that he wouldn't be willing to risk pursuing a relationship with her, after all. And this time, that was all on her.

Owen took Jack's place and stood near Terra. "Are you all right?"

Terra hugged her brother, holding back sobs of relief.

"I'm glad you're okay, Terra," Owen whispered in her ear. "You should go to Jack. He needs you."

She eased from Owen, surprised to hear that from him. He released her. Terra had to make the first move. Jack was leaving that to her. She turned and strode to Jack, who knelt next to Briggs.

Rising to his feet, Jack sighed. Terra rushed to him and wrapped her arms around him. Without hesitation, he held her good and tight the way she liked as she pressed her face into his chest and breathed in his masculine scent of mountain and pine and sweat. She shuddered as adrenaline rushed out of her.

Terra started to pull away, but he wouldn't let go. She could handle that. Finally, he relaxed enough that she eased away, though she could have stayed in his arms forever. She needed to talk.

"I'm sorry for what I said to you in the hospital."

"I understand being afraid of losing someone. I almost lost you on this mountain, Terra." He held her at arm's length. "I lost you before, too, because I was stupid, and I walked away from the best thing in my life."

I love you enough to let you go. Because he'd loved her enough to sacrifice. But how did he feel about her now?

She pressed her hand against his cheek. "Stop. You were wounded. Trying to prove yourself. Trying to prove something you didn't need to prove. Besides, I forgive you."

He smiled for her—that smile boasting warmth and dimples, edged with the pain and exhaustion of the last few days. Longing filled his gaze, emanated from his presence, and maybe he didn't have the strength to hide from her something she knew had been there just under the surface the whole time since he'd returned to Montana.

Terra stood on her toes and leaned in to kiss Jack. He reeled her in much closer and kissed her. Gently—Owen stood there, after all—but she sensed the love Jack held back, the passion he reined in.

She ended the kiss. "Where do we go from here?"

Flashlights shone in the forest. A helicopter suddenly

swooped in close and shined a line directly on them. Terra and Jack stepped apart.

Nathan rushed forward from the forest and shouted over the noisy chopper. "Oh, thank goodness, you guys are safe. I thought we were going to be too late to save the day." He directed the beam of light to the ground. "I see you got Briggs."

"I shot him in self-defense," Jack said. "He shot at Terra. So, yeah, self-defense."

Nathan holstered his weapon. "Terra, your dad is in the hospital. He's going to be okay. Except he could be charged because of his involvement in the trafficking. I don't know what will happen, exactly. The FBI is involved now."

"As I figured they eventually would be. The artifact. Does anyone know where it is?"

"I think I might," Owen said.

SIXTY-FOUR

Hours later, Terra stood with Jack and Nathan in the barn. Owen was holding a pitchfork and moving hay around. "I startled Gramps one day. I guess he thought I was still in town. He was out here shoveling hay. I thought it was strange then. Now I think I might know what he was up to."

Jack scratched his chin. "Why don't we just ask him?"

"Not to alarm anyone, but he's in the hospital too," Nathan said, "getting checked out. The EMTs thought he looked pale and sweaty. With the trauma he experienced, they feared he might be having a heart attack, but it's just a precaution."

"What?" Terra asked. "Why didn't you tell us?"

"I'm telling you now. There's been a lot going on, okay?" Nathan lifted his hand, a half apology.

"There. I feel something." Owen dropped to his knees.

"Wait." Nathan pulled on gloves. "I'll take it from here, Owen. This is one convoluted mess, and I wouldn't want someone to have a reason to point at you."

Owen nodded. "Right. That makes sense. Already easy to do if this is it and it's in my barn."

Nathan slid the box out. Jack and Terra crouched closer and shined their flashlights as Nathan gently opened it.

A thick gold mesh crown filled with colorful jewels reflected the light. Terra gasped. "So, the murders, all of it, was over this." Terra noticed a stone tablet in the box behind the crown. "Looks like the rest of the corner that I found. An ancient cuneiform-inscribed tablet. It must go with the crown for some reason. Some information about whoever wore it."

Maybe Jim had taken this to his cabin, but had he dropped it? Broken the piece off? Then he decided he wasn't the one to keep it? She hoped they could eventually put all the pieces together.

"Gramps did know where it was all this time. He lied to Marcus." Terra crossed her arms. "Why would he do that? He risked our lives. He could have turned it over to him."

"Your grandfather probably believed his only bargaining chip was the artifact, and likely feared that Briggs would kill you all once he got his hands on it," Jack said. "Robert is shrewd, Terra. I have no doubt he made the right call here. He was simply buying time until someone else came to save the day."

Owen stood and leaned against a post. "That makes sense. I think after Jim was killed, Gramps hired someone to break into the safe so he could say the item was stolen if ever asked about it. He could claim he didn't know what it was. He'd just taken it for a friend. And then it was stolen. No harm, no foul—at least in his mind."

"And what was he planning to do with it then?" Terra shook her head.

"You know, we could just ask Gramps," Owen said, "but if he's in danger of having a heart attack, I agree that all this can wait. We know the main player now."

"Briggs mentioned to me that with Neva taken out, he would have to deliver the artifact himself." Terra sighed. All this murder. Leif had definitely been tightening the screws around Briggs's operation.

"We learned that Neva and Jocelyn Porcella, daughter of the Bar Wars owners, had been close friends in high school," Nathan said. "We are looking into that relationship, and the private auction house activities. Neva might have traveled back from Algiers with items or to Algiers with items. Back and forth to the auction house, or to secure items for collectors."

"So that could be why Leif wanted to plant the murder weapon—another part of Briggs's network he wanted to take down. But who was this crown heading to?" Terra asked. "Who had Marcus sold it to—some wealthy rancher collector here in Montana?"

"That part of the investigation is still ongoing."

"The artifact isn't worth the cost of so many lives," Jack said.

"Which brings me to this," Terra said. "I'd like to know exactly what it is worth. Can I borrow your cell?"

Nathan handed it over, and Terra used it to call Jeremy.

"You know his number?" Jack asked.

She shrugged. "Come on, I've called him plenty of times."

Jeremy answered, despite the late hour.

"Hey, it's Terra," she said. "You texted that you had more information. What can you tell me?"

"I can tell you the FBI Art Crime Division is closing in on buyers and sellers in a big trafficking ring. They were already here today because I'd been asking questions. I happened to overhear something about an auction house operating out of a bar there in Big Rapids."

Terra shared a look with Nathan and Jack. "Anything else?"

"Yes. I tracked the piece you showed me to one of fifteen thousand that have gone missing in Iraq since the 2003 invasion."

"I'm looking at a golden crown and a tablet right now. I heard the word *Nimrud*. What would that be worth?"

Jeremy released a breath. "Nimrud was an ancient Assyrian Mesopotamia city, a thriving metropolis from 1350 BC to

610 BC. Much of the Nimrud collection was thought lost but then discovered in a vault. That's probably the only reason it wasn't looted and lost forever during the Iraq Museum looting in 2003. Still, some of the collection was smuggled out of the country. Something like fifteen thousand items are still missing today. If this is one of those pieces from the Nimrud collection, I would say it could be worth millions. But maybe . . . now . . . it can now be returned to Iraq."

Millions? She steadied her voice. "Okay. I appreciate your work on this, Jeremy." She started to end the call—

"Terra?"

"Yes."

"Are you okay?"

"I'm fine. It's over. The bad guys are dead."

"Congratulations, I think."

"Thanks, Jeremy."

"Don't end the call yet. I'm not done."

Aware that three sets of eyes were watching her, she said, "Listen, Jeremy, I really can't talk right now."

"Are you and that detective together?"

Seriously? She locked eyes with Jack. Warmth flooded her. "I hope so."

SIXTY-FIVE

Jack wanted to rush down the sterile hallways to Aunt Nadine's hospital room, but he took it slow and easy. He might need to get his wound looked at—and soon. No telling what he'd done to his arm last night while fighting with Briggs/ Gray and then getting Terra up that cliff to safety.

He'd do it all again, of course. Whatever was necessary.

But right now, he gritted his teeth because fire burned through his arm. He'd give the NSAIDs some time to take effect. Now that he had answers about the murders, he could take a few days to recover.

Jack entered Aunt Nadine's room and found her sitting up and smiling. She was her old self again. Jack had learned from his neighbor that Aunt Nadine had woken up on the sidewalk outside her house disoriented and confused. She could have gotten lost. Succumbed to the elements.

He exhaled his relief. She sat safe and secure in that hospital bed. A bump on her head, but that was all.

"I'm sorry I couldn't be here sooner." He grabbed her hand, hoping she understood just how much she meant to him.

"Did you get him? Did you get that murderer, Jack?"

"In a manner of speaking."

"I'm glad to hear it. I know how hard this has been on you." Aunt Nadine sighed as if she carried the weight of the world on her shoulders. "There's something I've been wanting to tell you."

Jack released her hand and crossed his arms. Was this about his dad? He didn't think he could go through this again.

"Growing up, you were so driven to prove yourself. You said you wanted to be a hero. You had to do something to prove you weren't like your father."

Jack covered his eyes, released a pent-up sigh, then dropped his hand. "Aunt Nadine, I—"

"Don't interrupt me. I have to get this out. I should have told you this long ago."

"Okay. I'm listening."

"You're just like your father."

Jack wanted to turn his back. Not this. Not now.

"You don't understand. He was a hero, Jack. Your father was a good guy. He . . . he took down some bad guys in a drug cartel."

Okay. Aunt Nadine . . . His heart cracked. He didn't think there was anything left to break.

"Before you were born," she said. "He worked undercover for the DEA. He was a hero. The story was that, unfortunately, he had played his role so well that he'd also become addicted to drugs. He quit the job. Got into rehab. He got a desk job at the county. Met your mother and got married. Had a baby— you, Jack. But the truth is that he was never addicted to drugs. The brother of the cartel gang leader your father took down found him. Your father's death was actually a murder, as was your mom's car accident."

What? Jack found the chair next to the wall and eased into it. He rested his head in his hands. "How do you know this?"

"Before I took you in, I demanded answers from his superiors and was silenced with the truth. I could never speak a word of it, or else I could bring danger to myself and to you. The story for the news was that he had struggled with addiction and that he committed suicide. I know it's not fair for a hero to go down with such a dark story, a lie. I see now how that affected you, but that was for our safety, Jack. Please don't jeopardize your safety by digging up that past. I simply thought you should know that you are a hero like your father was a hero."

The news stunned Jack. More than anything, he wanted to believe her words, but his aunt struggled with dementia and could be confused. He wasn't sure he trusted her story. If he did any digging of his own, he could bring danger to Aunt Nadine's door. He would give it some time and speak with her about it again, but right now Jack chose to believe this new truth about his father.

A fiftyish woman wearing a white coat and stethoscope entered. "I'm Dr. Presser." She flashed a smile. "Just call me Carol."

"Hi, Carol," both Jack and Aunt Nadine said simultaneously.

"I spoke briefly with your primary doctor, who filled me in on the dementia you've been experiencing."

"I don't have dementia. He keeps telling me that. Just a few memory problems."

Jack kept his face straight.

Carol hesitated as though considering her next words. "I think you could be experiencing a reaction to your anxiety medication. That, combined with the fact you have very low levels of vitamin B. Either or the combination of both can cause symptoms of dementia. We're switching up your medication, and I'm prescribing vitamins. You could see significant improvement in your memory."

Jack shared a stunned look with his aunt. Confusion lined her features, then her face relaxed. Acceptance.

Aunt Nadine nodded. "I hadn't wanted to admit I had a problem. I was too scared. Admitting there was something wrong with me . . ." Her eyes teared up. "Well, now I don't have to be scared. You've made my day, doctor, I mean, Carol."

Carol nodded and smiled.

Aunt Nadine returned the smile, unshed tears shimmering in her eyes. "I'm feeling better already."

Carol patted Aunt Nadine's hand. "As you should. Now, if you'll excuse me, I have other patients. We'll keep you one more day, dear, to make sure you tolerate this new medication."

Carol said her goodbyes and exited. Jack followed her out. "You mean to tell me that her medication has been causing her memory issues?"

"I'm sorry, I can't discuss a patient's private health information. HIPAA and all that."

"She raised me, I'm family, and she's signed the appropriate documents, so you could speak to me."

Carol skimmed through the paperwork and appeared to make a decision.

"Well, I'm not telling you more than I said in the room. Yes, in some patients—especially older patients—we've seen a strong correlation between symptoms of dementia and this particular medication. It's true of low vitamin B levels as well. We'll do what we can and hope for a positive outcome."

Jack swiped a hand down his face. He couldn't believe what he was hearing. "This whole time . . . Doctor, I gave up my job to come be with her. I wanted to make sure she's all right."

Carol studied him. "You sound like a nice young gentleman who cares deeply about her. I hope you'll consider sticking around, even if her memory improves."

He nodded as he watched Dr. Carol Presser head down the hallway and enter a room four doors away.

Jack stood alone in the hallway, soaking in the news. Aunt Nadine was going to be all right. Part of him wanted to be angry at the medication for wreaking such havoc on their lives. Jack realized that even if he hadn't been shot, even if he hadn't failed Sarah, he would be back in Montana and, yes, probably working for the Grayback County Sheriff's offices.

And he realized that if he weren't Detective Tanner, then he wouldn't have run into Terra again. Was Providence throwing them together? Were they meant to be? Was this their second chance? He didn't know.

"A penny for your thoughts." Terra spoke from behind.

He turned and tried to absorb her lovely smile and the look in her eyes that reflected her compassionate heart. Jack didn't mind her gorgeous hair, striking eyes, and rosy cheeks either. But who was looking? He grinned to himself. He thought he might actually measure up this time, at least in his own mind, but would she feel the same way? Was he the man for her?

"How is everyone?" he asked.

"Gramps is getting released this morning. Dad is recovering. He'll be here a couple more days. He could have died. I still can't believe any of it. Part of me wants to be angry at him. I was so hurt that he left. I carried around with me the memory of that conversation I overheard—Gramps telling Dad not to leave. I rushed to him and begged him not to go. I understand now that he thought it was the only way to keep me safe. But as a kid, how could I have understood any of it? People, those I loved, left me. Dad chose to leave me. But I can't waste time being hurt and angry now that I have him back."

Jack had experienced a similar situation when he let Robert's conversation he'd overheard get to him. Those words had changed his future, had torn him away from her when he made the decision to love Terra by leaving her. What he'd done was not too different from what her father had pulled—and both men had crushed her more with their actions than either of them could ever have known.

Jack wanted to tell her about overhearing Robert's claim that Jack didn't come from good stock, but he kept it to himself. Sharing that would only hurt her more. No need to open old wounds. There was enough pain to go around at the moment.

And the way she looked at him now, Jack had no doubt he had nothing to be ashamed of—even if he hadn't learned his father was a hero and he did, in fact, come from good stock. What Terra alone thought of him meant more than anything else.

"They don't think your dad's a flight risk, do they?" he asked. "I mean, he fled the hospital before."

"He's cooperating fully. Sharing everything he knows about Tony Gray, who became Marcus Briggs."

Poor Ruby. When would the news of her son's activities and ultimate demise be shared with the family?

"You okay?" he asked.

She nodded. "Dad could be in trouble for the crimes he committed back then. I'm not condoning his actions, but he's already paid a high price for his mistake. Are you going to charge him for punching Sarnes?"

"That's out of my hands. But, Terra, in the end he was a hero. He saved the day. And I made sure to emphasize that in my statement."

"You weren't there."

"Doesn't matter. He came to save you and to negotiate."

"He's not perfect. He messed up, but at least he's home." She sniffled and wiped her nose, staring at the floor as if disturbed all over again. "I haven't told him that someone vandalized the Rocky Mountain Courage Memorial. Oh, wait, he left before that was even built."

Coming to grips with all that had happened would take time. In the meantime, Jack needed to redirect Terra's focus to something else she could take joy in.

"Hey." He lifted her chin.

"I want you to see something." Jack took her hand and led her in to see Aunt Nadine. He shared what the doctor had said.

"Oh, that's wonderful, Nadine." Terra moved closer to the bed, leaned in, and hugged his aunt. She released her and stood back. "I couldn't be happier." Terra ran a finger under both eyes.

"Tomorrow," Jack said to his aunt, "when I come to pick you up, I have a big surprise for you."

////////////////////

The next day, Jack and Terra sat at Aunt Nadine's kitchen table. Aunt Nadine hummed in the kitchen, insisting on making them sandwiches. She appeared to be feeling better than she had in a long time.

Jack winked at Terra.

Freckles was in the backyard with Dusty and Tux and started barking at the sliding glass door.

"Shush, Freckles," Aunt Nadine said.

The doorbell rang. Right on time. "I'll get it," Jack said.

He opened the door, and Ruby stood on the porch with her grandson, Ferris. Jack couldn't help the smile that split his face. He opened the door wide and let the two in.

Aunt Nadine glanced up at the visitors, a smile and a confused expression sharing space on her face. Freckles barked and jumped at the sliding glass door in the back.

"What on earth, Freckles?" Aunt Nadine opened the door, and the dog raced through the house and into Ferris's arms.

Freckles wiggled and barked and licked. Ferris laughed. "I'm here, boy. That's a good boy. It's okay, Max. I'm here."

"What?" Terra's smile was beautiful. Aunt Nadine and Ruby smiled and laughed at Freckles's reunion with his boy.

"I'm just trying to tie up all the loose ends. Solve all the mysteries, as it were. I spotted Freckles in a picture at Ruby's home when Nathan and I questioned her."

Aunt Nadine and Ruby followed Ferris and Freckles/Max into the backyard.

Terra smiled up at him. "You're really amazing, you know that? Got any more loose ends to tie up?"

"I thought you'd never ask." He pulled her close and pressed his nose against hers. "I've been trying to solve the mystery of you and me for as long as I've known you."

She sucked in a breath. "You once told me that you loved me enough to let me go, so I think solving that will depend on your answer to my question."

Jack's heart beat erratically. "What's that?"

"Do you love me enough this time to stay, Jack?"

That was easy. "I love you, Terra. I always have, and I'm sorry I walked away before. I can't lose you again, and I hope you feel the same way."

Jack kissed her, just in case she was having any doubts about how she felt about him. He kissed her until she was breathless.

Her hands pressed gently against his chest, and she eased away from him. "Jack, your aunt. This isn't the place."

"There's no better place. No better time. I want you with me forever. I need to know how you feel."

Terra seemed taken aback by his words. A measure of fear spiked through him.

"I love you." Terra's voice shook. "And . . . even though loving can be risky, I'm willing to risk that with you."

"And the forever part? How do you feel about that?"

"Is that a proposal?"

He tugged a small box from his pocket and popped it open. "I had a different plan in mind, but I'm done wasting time. I . . . I bought this before."

"And you've kept it all this time?" Her bright blue eyes shimmered as she stared at the diamond.

"I could never let go of hope, even though it seemed like a distant dream for so long."

She let him slip the ring on her finger.

"Mystery solved," he whispered against her lips.

ONE

PUGET SOUND

For a few hours every Saturday morning, Erin Larson could forget that evil existed.

And usually, only on the water.

She dipped the double-bladed paddle into the sea, then again on the other side—*left, right, left, right, left, right*—alternating strokes in a fluid motion to propel her kayak across the blue depths of Possession Sound. Her friend Carissa Edwards paddled close behind.

Left, right. Left, right. Left, right.

On the water she was close to nature and far from the chaos and noise of the city even though she and Carissa paddled along the shoreline and could see the cityscape in the distance. The quiet calmed her mind and heart. The rhythmic paddling mesmerized her. The exertion exhilarated her. Cleansed her of the stress and anxiety acquired after a week of forced labor.

Okay, that wasn't fair. Her suffering certainly wasn't physical in nature.

Water. Mountains. Sky. She took in the sights and once again . . . forgot.

Beautiful snowcapped Mount Baker—the Great White Watcher—loomed large in the distance to the east.

Left, right. Left, right. Left, right.

The slosh of paddles along with the small waves lapping against her boat soothed her and were the only sounds except for seagulls laughing above her—*ha, ha, ha.*

To the west, the impressive Olympic Mountains begged for attention. Erin couldn't wait for Mom to join her out here, when she finally convinced her mother to move.

A salty ocean breeze wafted over her as peace and beauty surrounded her.

She couldn't ask for more.

She *shouldn't* ask for more.

But God . . . I need answers.

Carissa caught up with Erin and paddled next to her kayak. "Thanks for coming with me today. I needed this."

"The exercise or the scenery?" Erin had just broken a sweat despite the early morning cool.

"How about a little of both. And the company makes all the difference, I'm not going to lie."

"Yeah," Erin answered with reluctance. She and Carissa had an understanding between them. On their kayaking excursions, peace and quiet would reign.

"By the way, I listened to your podcast last night," Carissa said.

Maybe she'd forgotten their unspoken pact.

"Oh?"

Erin wanted to know Carissa's thoughts, but at the same time, she didn't want to hear the criticism. Nor would she trust any praise.

"Why keep it anonymous?"

"It could get complicated."

Carissa's laugh echoed across the water. "In my case, I'd probably want the dean of the college and my students to know, but then again, I wouldn't be talking about crime or missing people. I'd be talking about history. So, what took you so long to tell me?"

Erin lifted a shoulder, opting for silence. Maybe it would be contagious.

Now she wished she hadn't told Carissa, but letting her friend in on her secret was a step toward opening up. She kept too much hidden inside. Erin had never been good at letting others in, though as a psychologist her job was all about learning what made people tick on the inside.

Erin breathed in fresh air, listened to the mesmerizing ripple of water, felt the warm sun against her cheeks, and chased away thoughts of crime and work.

"Cold cases . . . do they ever get solved?" Carissa asked.

Left, right. Left, right. Left, right. "Some do." Few.

"Why do *you* do it?"

"I need a hobby, I guess." Erin couldn't begin to explain the complex events that drove her to talk about missing person cold cases in hopes that answers could still be found.

"I've been thinking." Carissa's kayak inched ahead.

Erin remained silent.

"We do this every Saturday," Carissa continued.

Left, right. Left, right. Left, right.

"It's been a lifesaver," Erin said. "Thanks for inviting me along." After a week of working for the State of Washington, the endless hours spent researching and writing reports for forensic evaluations, she needed the break. The job wasn't what she had dreamed about when she'd become a criminal psychologist. Still, she hoped it was a means to an end. In the meantime, she'd started the cold case crime podcast.

"How about we switch it up? Go hiking. Mountain trails and lush forests all around us."

"This is close. We don't have to drive far. Plus, I really love the water." And have an aversion to dense forests. Carissa didn't need to know that as a psychologist, Erin was a walking oxymoron.

"I thought you might enjoy a change."

"No, I'm good with this." Erin's shoulders and biceps started burning. She was relieved they would soon turn around and head back.

"I hope you'll think about it. I'd love for you to join me next weekend. I'm hiking in Mount Baker National Forest, and I'm inviting you to join the group."

"What? You're ditching me to go hiking?"

"Um . . . Is it just me, or is that boat heading directly for us?" Panic edged Carissa's voice.

Erin glanced over her shoulder in the direction of Carissa's wide-eyed stare. A thirty-foot cruiser sped toward them. She and Carissa had strayed a bit from the shoreline. Regardless, that boat shouldn't be approaching them in this area or at that speed.

"Hurry." Erin quickened her pace. "We can get out of its path."

"We won't make it." Carissa stopped and raised her paddle, waving to get the boater's attention. "Hey, watch where you're going! Kayakers on the water!"

Arms straining, Erin paddled faster and propelled the kayak forward. Her friend hadn't kept up. "Carissa, let's go! Just angle out of the path."

Carissa renewed her efforts and joined Erin. Together they paddled toward the shoreline that had seemed so much closer moments before.

Carissa screamed. Heart pounding, Erin glanced over her shoulder. The boat had changed course and was once again headed straight for them.

Fear stole her breath. "Jump! Get out of the boat and dive!" It was all she could think to do.

"Now, now, now!" She sucked in a breath and leaned forward to flip the kayak until she was upside down in the water for a wet exit. Holding her breath, she found the grab loop and peeled off the skirt. Then she gripped the sides and pushed the kayak away from her body as she slid out. Instead of heading for the surface, she kicked and dove deeper. She was grateful she wore a manually inflatable life vest or it would drag her back to the surface, which was normally a good thing.

But today that could get her killed.

She pushed deeper, deeper, deeper . . . away from the surface.

We're going to make it.

Erin twisted around to glance upward. The water was murky and visibility was only about ten feet, but she could still see that her friend struggled to get free of her kayak. Terror stabbed through her. Erin swam back to Carissa to help her, even as the boat raced toward the kayaks and was almost on them.

Her eyes wide, Carissa pushed forward, freeing herself.

The hull of the boat sped right over the top of the kayaks, breaking Carissa's in half—the stern of her broken kayak propelled toward Carissa. Her head jerked forward.

All the bubbles of air burst from her lungs, then her form floated—unmoving. Unconscious? Or was she lifeless?

Her pulse thundering in her ears, Erin swam toward Carissa, grabbed her, and inflated their life vests. Erin gasped for breath as she held Carissa. The water remained disturbed from the speeding boat's wake and crashed over them.

Erin confirmed what she already feared. Carissa wasn't breathing. Adrenaline surged through her. She had to keep moving. Holding on to Carissa, Erin started swimming them back to shore.

She spotted the errant boat making a big circle.

Coming back? Had someone lost control? She had to make it to shore to give Carissa CPR. And maybe even to save them both.

Stay calm. Panic wouldn't help either of them. The water was cold, but not so cold she needed to worry about hypothermia. At least not yet. The whir of a boat from her left drew her attention around, kicking up her already rapid heartbeat. Taking in the slowly approaching trawler—a far different boat than the speeding cruiser—relief eased the tension in her shoulders. Three men and a couple of women waved.

The silver-haired man in a Seahawks cap shouted. "Do you need help?"

"Yes! Hurry!"

The boat edged slowly toward her, and she swam to meet it. The men reached down and pulled Carissa up into the boat.

Erin used the ladder on the side. "She needs CPR. She's not breathing!"

When she hopped onto the deck, one of the men had started administering CPR.

A redheaded woman wrapped a blanket around Erin. "Oh, honey, are you okay?"

Hot tears burned down her cold wet cheeks. "No . . . no, I'm not okay." She dropped to her knees next to her friend.

Carissa coughed up water and rolled onto her side. When she'd finished expelling the seawater, she sat up and looked around.

Erin hugged her and spoke against her short, wet hair. "I thought you were done for."

Carissa held on to Erin tightly, then released her to cough more. Erin took in the group standing around them, their watchful eyes filled with concern.

"I'm Vince. And this is my wife, Jessie." The man with the Seahawks cap gestured to the redhead, then made introductions. John, his son, and Terry, John's friend, and Mavis, John's girlfriend. A family affair.

"I'm Erin, and this is Carissa."

Jessie placed a blanket around Carissa. "Why don't you have a seat? I'll get you something warm to drink."

"Thank you." Erin sat with Carissa on the cushioned bench and took in her friend. She looked shell-shocked, and why shouldn't she? Was she going to be okay?

Carissa closed her eyes. Was she in pain or thinking back

to what happened? Jessie had disappeared below deck to grab warm drinks. Mavis, Terry, and John were trying to recover Erin's and Carissa's kayaks and bring them onto the trawler.

Vince remained standing there, his arms crossed as if he were a sentinel to protect them. And at this moment Erin needed that reassurance.

"If you hadn't come when you did," she said, "I don't know what would have happened. I can't thank you enough." She searched the waters around them. "Is that boat . . . Is it gone?"

"What boat?" Mavis approached and glanced at Vince.

"You didn't see that?" Erin got to her feet and pulled Carissa with her. She searched the waters. "A boat came right for us. Ran over our kayaks and almost killed us. They must have lost control. Maybe they were drunk or something."

"I saw a boat heading west," Vince said, "but I didn't connect that to seeing you in the water swimming to shore. Kayaks and canoes are hard to spot sometimes. I'm sorry that happened. But I'll contact the Seattle Police Harbor Patrol and let them know. In the meantime, is there somewhere we can take you?"

"Back to the marina at Port of Edmonds. We could talk to the police there and tell them what happened."

"I'll let SPHP know we're on the way and to meet us there. Should we get you to the hospital?" Vince eyed Carissa.

Erin shared a look with her friend. "She sustained a hit to the head. Maybe an ambulance could be waiting for us when we get to the harbor."

Carissa nodded but said nothing. Erin ached inside. She'd almost lost Carissa. She was grateful that her friend had survived. They had both survived.

Erin replayed the events in her mind. Had the boat deliberately veered toward them or had she imagined it? These boaters who'd helped them had simply been out enjoying the day when they spotted Erin and Carissa in the water, their kayaks floating, Carissa's in two pieces.

I can't believe this happened.

The water had been her place of peace and tranquility.

But no more.

Erin pulled her ringing cell from the protective plastic. She didn't recognize the number, but it was a Montana prefix. Her heart jackhammered as she answered. "Erin."

"Dr. Larson . . . Erin." The familiar male voice hesitated. "This is Detective Nathan Campbell."

Dread crawled up her spine. Nathan would never call her without a good reason. "Nathan . . . what's going on?"

"It's . . . your mom. She's okay. But she tried to commit suicide. I'm so sorry."

A few heartbeats passed before she could answer. "Wha . . . what?"

Nathan apologized again and repeated the words.

The air rushed from Erin. She couldn't breathe. She headed for the rail and hung her head over the water, gasping for breath.

"Erin! Erin, are you there?" Nathan's concerned voice shouted over the cell loud enough she could hear it over the boat's engine and rushing water.

Carissa joined her at the rail. "Erin, what's happened?"

The darkness closed in on her all over again, but this was different than before. Why hadn't she seen the warning signs? She had to fix this.

Squeezing her eyes shut, she lifted the cell to her ear again. "I need details."

Nathan relayed that her mother was in the hospital but in stable condition.

Ending the call, Erin stared at the cell. Mom was in trouble. The fact that the awful news had come from the man she'd left behind compounded the pain in her chest. This, after she and Carissa had barely survived a boating accident.

Evil wouldn't let her forget that it existed, even for a few hours.

Author's Note

As with all my novels, I take truth—some interesting story that snagged my attention—and create a fictional tale based in reality. I've always been fascinated with artifacts trafficking and have read several books on the topic over the years. Like all my stories, I begin with a premise, then develop and grow the idea as I write. My USFS special agent would investigate archaeological crimes, and in this scenario that would mean crimes against Native American cultural items. Within this context, I realized I wanted the story to reflect a global issue, one of many that happens behind the scenes and in the cover of darkness—places like the dark web or even online and right "in our face," as it were. The artifacts-trafficking world requires many players, starting with those who dig and loot from recorded archaeological sites or previously unknown sites, to museums, private collectors, and even antique road shows. Most of us go about our lives unaware of such happenings.

Still, we can relate on some level. We all grew up watching and loving Indiana Jones, but in truth (ask any archaeologist), he is a tomb raider. Hey—I still watch those movies over and over. I love them!

As I continued to research for my story, I again came across the Iraq Museum looting that happened during the US military invasion in 2003. In fact, I've always wanted to write a story that would somehow convey to a bigger audience the historical and cultural pilfering that happened to the museum. In the region as a whole, it continues to happen, even though governments have joined together to crack down on those who would steal cultural items. Museums and countries have since been required to return items to the countries of origin (and yes, the United States is included in countries returning illegally acquired artifacts). And as you might assume, some countries are more cooperative than others.

But back to my story and the Iraq Museum—the facility held and displayed tens of thousands of relics from Mesopotamian, Babylonian, and Persian cultures. As of this writing, according to the FBI government site, up to ten thousand items remain missing, though elsewhere I read that nearly fifteen thousand are still missing, but obviously items continue to be found and returned. The FBI still lists the "Iraqi Looted and Stolen Artifacts" under the FBI Top Ten Art Crimes.

In my research, I learned how the Iraq invasion opened the doors for opportunists around the globe, including some within our armed forces, to take these items and sell them to the highest bidders, private collectors, and willing museums. My character, Chance Carter, was born to carry the burdens of these crimes from the past during his service in the Army to the present in modern-day Montana—and the deeper, sinister layers of my fictional story based in truth were born.

Acknowledgments

Special thanks to John Byas, US Forest Service Special Agent in Charge, for numerous phone calls and emails to answer my many questions and provide opportunities for my character to proceed as planned within the novel I had plotted! That said, mistakes are all on me along with taking a little artistic license.

Big thanks to Roxanne Henke and her small-plane pilot husband who prefers flying to acknowledgment. I appreciate learning everything that could go wrong in a small plane and also how to crash-land on a forest road! My deepest gratitude to my writing buddies who persevered with me through those years before we were published and now through the even more grueling years of keeping up with writing deadlines! You encourage and support me, and you're there every day via our virtual world as if sitting in the cubicle right next to me—Shannon McNear, Lisa Harris, Susan Sleeman, Sharon Hinck, and so many more. You know who you are.

A very special thank-you to Janet Langell for taking in the strays and sharing your story about the dog who lost his boy. I loved that precious tale, and I'm so glad you allowed me to share it here (though Aunt Nadine was a complete figment of my imagination, and you are quite different and amazing!). And thank you, too, for watching out for my "lost boy" who stayed behind in Michigan to finish his degree when we moved to Washington.

I'm so grateful for the most amazing publishing team at Revell! Lonnie Hull DuPont, you ushered me into the trade publishing world. You will always be near and dear to my heart. Rachel McRae, I'm so grateful that God brought you to this place and that you chose me and this Rocky Mountain Courage story as your first acquisition. Amy Ballor, you keep my stories and facts straight! Karen Steele and Michele Misiak, you always have my back, and for that I'm eternally grateful.

Steve Laube, you took me in and guided me through—what, this is going on over ten years now? I can hardly believe it. But you helped me to make my dreams come true.

Most of all, I appreciate you, Dan, for rooting for me all these years before I was even published, and your support when I was lost in my writing world for hours at a time. All my love to my amazing, creative, and dedicated children, Rachel, Christopher, Jonathan, and Andrew.

Jesus, you really are the Way Maker.

Elizabeth Goddard has sold over one million books and is the award-winning author of more than forty romance novels and counting, including the romantic mystery *The Camera Never Lies*—a 2011 Carol Award winner. She is a Daphne du Maurier Award for Excellence in Mystery and Suspense finalist for her Mountain Cove series—*Buried*, *Backfire*, and *Deception*—and a Carol Award finalist for *Submerged*. When she's not writing, she loves spending time with her family, traveling to find inspiration for her next book, and serving with her husband in ministry. For more information about her books, visit her website at www.ElizabethGoddard.com.

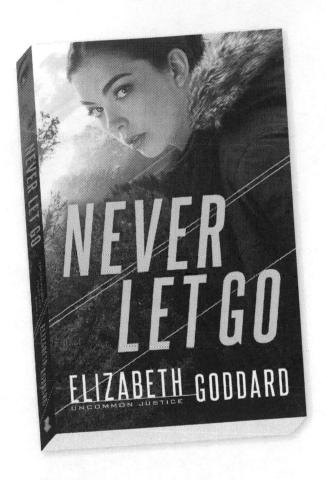

CONNECT WITH ELIZABETH

at **ElizabethGoddard.com**